>> *A Live Coal in the Sea*

E COAL

IN THE SEA

>>

MADELEINE

L'ENGLE

HarperOne
An Imprint of HarperCollins*Publishers*

HarperOne

This work was originally published in 1996 by Farrar, Straus & Giroux. It is hereby reprinted by arrangement with Farrar, Straus & Giroux.

Excerpts from Tell the Truth but Tell It Slant reprinted by permission of the publishers and Trustees of Amherst College from *The Poems of Emily Dickinson,* edited by Thomas H. Johnson, The Belknap Press of Harvard University Press, Cambridge, Massachusetts, copyright © 1951, 1955, 1979, 1983 by the President and Fellows of Harvard College.

HarperCollins books may be purchased for educational, business, or sales promotional use. For information please write: Special Markets Department, HarperCollins Publishers, 10 East 53rd Street, New York, NY 10022.

HarperCollins Web site: http://www.harpercollins.com

HarperCollins®, 🔥®, and HarperOne™ are trademarks of HarperCollins Publishers.

FIRST HARPERCOLLINS PAPERBACK EDITION PUBLISHED IN 1997

Library of Congress Cataloging-in-Publication Data

L'Engle, Madeleine.
A live coal in the sea / Madeleine L'Engle
ISBN: 978-0-06-065286-9
1. Family—United States—Fiction.   I. Title.
PS3523.E55L58   1996
813'.54—dc20   96-4909

11 RRD(H) 20 19 18 17 16 15 14

>> *To my daughter Maria*

with thanks for her help

>> *A Live Coal in the Sea*

ONE

THE RECEPTION was held in the president's house. Camilla was seated in a large wing chair by the windows which looked out to a lake, around three sides of which the college buildings were scattered, red brick, white clapboard, grey stone, a casual architectural mix which had an unexpectedly pleasing effect.

Champagne was uncorked. Fruit punch and ginger ale were offered. White-aproned college students served hors d'oeuvres. The large room was filled with Camilla's colleagues, friends, students. Her family. One of the young girls, offering her a tray of smoked salmon, whispered, "We're really proud of you, Dr. Dickinson."

The award ceremony had been held in Hiram B. Hingham Hall, Camilla standing on the stage to receive the Maria Mitchell Medal for distinguished work in astronomy. For a modest little medal, she thought, the college was treating it like the Nobel Prize. She was, nevertheless, pleased.

Her children were there. Taxi had driven up from New York, warning her that he would have to leave early. He was the star of a soap opera and would be taping at seven in the morning. He stood beside the president of the college, shorter, but equally distinguished in his tux, and certainly arresting with his black hair and fair skin and always an aura of excitement in the way he carried his body, looked around him, as though expecting something to happen, either marvelous or terrible, one could not be sure. Thessaly, his wife, was obviously happy and excited, arm in arm with Frankie—Frances—Camilla's daughter, who had flown in from Seattle for the occasion. Light from the crystal chandeliers highlighted Thessaly's sleek chestnut hair, pulled back from her face and into a neat roll as she had worn it when she was a dancer. Frankie's hair, dark like Taxi's, was beginning to be streaked with white, but she was a handsome woman, Camilla thought, taller than Taxi or Thessaly, but carrying herself well.

Raffi, Camilla's beloved granddaughter, Taxi and Thessaly's daughter, was a freshman in the college, delighted at all the attention being paid to her grandmother.

Camilla looked around the crowded room. It was time to stop sitting like an elderly dowager duchess in the chair the president had led her to. She stood up, champagne glass in hand, so that she could talk more easily with the guests.

Taxi, moving with as much grace as his wife, though he had never done any professional dancing, came over to his mother, along with a white-bearded man who was chairman of the physics department. Camilla introduced them, and the physics professor shook Taxi's hand, saying, "It seems that a number of the students are quite excited by your presence." He sounded interested, but puzzled.

"Taxi is an actor," Camilla said.

Taxi shrugged gracefully. "I'm presently in a soap."

"A what?"

Taxi smiled. "A soap opera—daytime television. College students manage to watch it, though I doubt if the eminent professors do."

The professor laughed. "No, I'm afraid we don't. My wife and I occasionally get in to New York to the theatre."

Camilla said, "Taxi often does plays, too. There was one that opened early in the season—"

"And immediately flopped," Taxi said. "It was a terrific show, really, but the critics simply didn't get it."

"Well, better luck next time." The professor moved off to join a group of colleagues.

Taxi said in a low voice, "Mom, you really didn't need to mention that disaster."

"Sorry, Tax. You were wonderful in it."

"The critics didn't give me much credit. I haven't had a hit in two years." He glanced around to where his daughter was standing with a group of girls. "How's my Raffi getting along?"

"She's doing beautifully. Several of her professors have told me how bright she is."

"Of course she's bright." He sounded impatient.

Camilla, too, looked at the girl, easily identified in her group of friends by her brilliant red hair. She wore a bulky orange sweater which both clashed with and showed it off. One of her teachers had told Camilla, 'Raffi's fragile. She's popular, and she does well, but sometimes I think some key word might break her in two.'

Taxi continued, "Thessaly and I have been doing considerable quarreling and it upsets the child. It's not important. We're nowhere near separation or divorce. I've had enough divorce. Raffi simply doesn't understand that parents are human, too."

Camilla asked, "When you were Raffi's age, did you?"

"Believe me, Mom, I did. I hope Raffi will never have to go through what I went through."

She felt cold. The windows onto the terrace were open and a breeze was blowing into the room. "Taxi, darling—"

"Oh, I survived it, Mom, I'm a survivor. I just hope Raffi is, too. Thessaly and I are very grateful she has you to fall back on."

"I'll do whatever I can."

"I know you will, Mom. You always do."

Even when it's abysmally not enough.

Taxi looked around the room again. Laughed. "It seems most of your professor pals don't watch the soaps."

"Most of them teach during the day."

"I doubt if that's what deters them. Well, their loss."

"The students, however," Camilla said, "are ardent admirers of yours. How many autographs have you already signed tonight?"

"On your program," Taxi said. "They'll just lose them."

"Not necessarily. You mean a lot to them." She smiled as two more girls came up to him, one with an autograph book, one with the evening's program. He turned away, lavishing them with his presence.

But he had made her feel in the wrong, something he managed to do whether she had done or said anything wrong or not. As though she deserved to be punished. She shook her head. Most parents probably deserve to be punished for one reason or another. Mostly their children don't act on it.

Frankie came over, put an arm about her mother. "Mom, what a terrific evening. Your medal is impressive, but who is that guy on the other side of it?"

"The King of Denmark."

"What on earth is the King of Denmark doing on a medal for astronomy?"

Thessaly, just behind her, said, "Maria Mitchell discovered a new comet, and the King of Denmark gave her a medal."

"Oh. How do you know so much?" Frankie smiled at her sister-in-law.

"Your mother told me, of course. Maria Mitchell's big thing was studying sunspots, and moons—satellites of planets. And she was the first woman to be admitted to the American Academy of Arts and Sciences."

"All I remember is that Mom admired her, and wasn't she born in Nantucket?"

"She was."

"Mom, I'm driving back to New York with Thessaly and Taxi so I can fly out first thing in the morning. This has been a terrific occasion."

"Frankie, thank you for coming all this way. That means more to me than I can ever tell you."

Frankie gave her mother a hug. "I wouldn't have missed it for anything."

Raffi joined them, taking Camilla's hand and holding it. "Grandmother, this is marvelous. All my friends are wildly excited. I'm so glad Dad could get away for it. And you, Aunt Frankie."

"I couldn't be happier," Camilla said. "Not so much about the medal, though it's an unexpected honor, but about having my family here."

"I bet you miss Grandfather."

"Yes. He'd have been pleased."

"I wish I'd known him."

"I wish so, too. You're both such important parts of my life it's hard for me to realize he died before you were born."

"Hey, Grandmother, Dr. Rowan's here, did you know?"

Camilla's face lit with pleasure. "Luisa? Wonderful! Where?"

Raffi indicated a woman detaching herself from a small group. She wore a beautifully cut silk suit, but her hair, red with streaks of white and grey, was untidy and needed trimming. She hurried over to Camilla, arms wide in greeting.

"Hi, Raffi, Frankie, Thessaly. Especial hi, Cam. I got in halfway through the ceremony. The traffic was terrible, I should have taken the train. Congratulations, I'm not sure what this medal is all about, but whatever it is, I'm sure you deserve it."

"Lu, what a wonderful surprise! I thought you were off to Zurich."

"I am. Tomorrow. I couldn't miss this."

Taxi, followed by a small retinue of adoring students, came over to them and put his hand on Raffi's shoulder. "Mom, I have to get on the road. Raffi, you're coming home for the weekend?"

"Sure, Dad. I'll drive Aunt Frankie to the airport in the morning. Grandmother, I'm taking the early train back on Sunday. Can I come have supper with you?"

"Of course. I'll look forward to it."

Camilla said goodbye to her family, went to the door to watch them leave. None of the other guests seemed ready to depart. She sighed, and went back to the crowded room.

Camilla walked rather wearily along the path from the president's house to her own. It was only two houses away, for which she was grateful. She had stood overlong in dressy shoes, and her feet hurt. Her house was one of the white clapboard ones that dotted the campus in pleasant contrast to the more institutional brick or stone buildings. She carried the medal in its leather and velvet case. Minor honor or not, it still gave her a feeling of being appreciated and recognized. The evening had been as rewarding as the award, except for that one brief conversation with Taxi.

Guilt. He could always make her feel full of guilt. Had he been jealous that all the attention was on her? Taxi was used to being the center of things, the sun, with the planets and the moons circling about his brilliance.

She shrugged it off. Frankie had come, all the way from Seattle. Raffi had been like a bright flame amid her cluster of friends. Colleagues, especially in Camilla's own department, had been genuinely delighted for her. Most of them. But her department was amazingly free of politics.

She unlocked her door and went into her house, one of the most desirable faculty houses on campus. It had originally been lived in and added on to by the college's one Nobel Prize-winning physicist. She entered the front hall with its wide floorboards, then turned into the long living room, which was part of the addition, a gracious room full of books along one side, French windows along the other, and fireplaces at each end. She had left on a couple of lamps, which she now turned off, then went to the kitchen to warm some milk. A mug of milk with nutmeg was a comfortable way to relax when she had been overstimulated. She heated the milk in the microwave in an old blue-and-white mug with cracked glaze. The mug was an icon for her, an icon of love and possibility. Mac, her husband, had given her bitter and muddy coffee in that mug the first evening they met. Yes, she still missed him, he who had shared so much joy and so much anguish and then—as happens—betrayed her by dying.

She took the heated milk upstairs to her bedroom and put it on the round table beside her bed, a great old brass bed given them as a wedding present by her parents-in-law. She kept it brightly polished, with the help of an occasional student. Like the mug, it was continuity, the bed, the old mahogany highboy that had belonged to her mother, the chaise longue with its comfortable cushions. The room was full of old friends. She lived fully in the present, but her past was still part of that present. This evening just over was the first time in several years that Taxi and Frankie had been together. And it had been all right. Nearly all right.

Above the bed was a large photograph of such fine quality that many people thought it a painting. It was of Taxi and Frankie in front of Mac's parents' cottage on the beach in North Florida. The children were sitting together on a high dune laced with dark vines of beach morning-glory. Sea oats seemed to be moving in the wind. Frankie had her hands clasped about her knees. Her hair, straight and dark, fell to her shoulders. Taxi's hair was also dark, but softly curly. The two children were often taken for twins. Taxi had a handful of sand and was letting it dribble between his fingers. The picture was full of light and movement, the best, the artist said, absolutely the best picture he had ever taken.

A time long gone. A time of innocence, if innocence had ever been possible in this sorry century, or in her own lifetime. A time of loveliness caught fleetingly by the eye of the camera.

'Mommy,' Taxi had asked her, 'why does the camera see upside down?'

'Because our eyes see upside down,' she had answered.

Taxi frowned, thinking. 'Daddy?'

When had they had this conversation? Before or after? Taxi was only four when—

She shook her head, trying to recall what had been said.

'Sorry, Taxi,' Mac had said, 'I'm no scientist.'

Frankie held up her hand, as she usually did when she wanted attention. 'Remember, in the olden days, when photographers took pictures, they got under a black cloth cape thing, and what they saw was upside down, and they had to turn it around in their minds.'

'Well, it seems very peculiar,' Taxi had said, 'that God or evolution should make creatures that see upside down and then have to reverse everything. Is there a reason?'

'It's just the way it is,' Mac had answered, smiling.

'Like life,' Taxi had said. 'Upside down.'

Yes, she remembered.

On Sunday afternoon Camilla puttered around in her kitchen, preparing a simple meal for herself and Raffi, mushroom Stroganoff and a salad of green beans and tomatoes, which still, in October, were red and full of taste. She snipped some basil off a plant in the window. Raffi was as dear to her as her own children, although since Camilla had left New York to teach in this college, from which she had graduated so many years ago, she had seen less of her than when they were just a few blocks apart.

She set the table in her breakfast room, which was a glassed-in half-moon off the end of the kitchen and was bright and seemed sunny even in the winter when the skies were grey and dull. Her table was round, with a marble top which Mac had given her for her fortieth birthday. When she saw Raffi coming up the path, she went into the living room and lit the fire at the far end. In the winter both fireplaces were used regularly, but on this autumn evening she lit the fire more for pleasure than necessity.

Raffi rang the bell and pushed open the door, which Camilla locked only at night. She gave her grandmother a hug, then shucked off her navy pea jacket and sat on the low bench in front of the fire. "Grandmother—" Her voice was tight.

"What's the matter?" Camilla asked, coming over to her and sitting beside her on the bench.

"What I want to know is—" She gasped, as though out of breath.

"Raffi, what is it?"

"What I want to know is, are you my grandmother? Or not?"

For a few moments Camilla stared into the fire, as motionless as though she had been petrified, like stone that was once living wood. Slowly, she turned to look at the girl. Raffi, as usual, wore blue jeans, and a heavy sweater which was several sizes too large for her and completely concealed her young body. When Camilla felt that her voice was under control, she said, "That is a very strange question, Raffi. What caused you to ask it?"

Raffi pushed her fingers through her hair, which she had had cut over the weekend. Always short, it was now shorter than that of the most conservative males, as though she wanted it to show as little as possible. She said, "I'm the only redhead in the family. Is it some recessive gene? Did either of your parents have red hair?"

Camilla shook her head. Neither Rose nor Rafferty Dickinson had had red hair.

"There's none in Mom's family, either. A mutation, perhaps?" Raffi's voice was harsh.

Camilla placed her hand gently on the girl's knee. "What's brought all this up, Raffi? Tell me."

"Something my dad said. Your son. Is he your son, Grandmother? I know he has black hair, like yours before it went white, and he even sort of looks like you."

"More than sort of," Camilla said.

"Okay. He looks like you. But—"

"Isn't that enough for you, Raffi?"

"No." The girl lurched to her feet and began putting more wood onto the fire, jabbing at the logs with the poker.

Camilla looked around the familiar room as though she was a stranger, letting her gaze travel along the white bookshelves, the comfortable couches and chairs covered in chintz, the soft green of the Chinese rugs on the floor.

Raffi finished her attack on the fire and sat down. "Grandmother."

"Yes?" Camilla turned from her inspection of the room, from the wall of windows which overlooked the lake, softly silver in the dwindling light. Leaves were drifting down from maples and beeches, occasionally clinging to the window screens before dropping to the ground.

"Who's Red Grange?"

Camilla stiffened.

"Grandmother?"

Carefully Camilla said, "He was a well-known football player a great many years ago. I didn't know you were interested in football."

"I'm not. My father, the soap-opera star—" There was undisguised bitterness in her voice. She shifted. "You know Dad's collection of those weird old records—78s, he calls them. From 1978?"

"78 r.p.m.s."

"What?"

"Revolutions per minute. I'll explain later if you're interested. Raffi, what's going on? What about your father's collection?"

"This weekend while I was home, after I drove Aunt Frankie to the airport, Dad kept playing one old record about a ghost.

> *With her head tucked underneath her arm*
> *She walked the bloody tower,*
> *With her head tucked underneath her arm*
> *At the midnight hour.*

Dad sang along with it. He has a pretty good voice, actually."

"Go on," Camilla said. Instinctively she pressed her hand against her chest.

"He kept repeating—"

"What?"

> *"The sentries think that it's*
> *A football that she carries in ..."*

"Yes ..."

> *"They think that it's Red Grange*
> *Instead of poor old Anne Boleyn ..."*

Camilla closed her eyes.

> *"... with her head tucked underneath her arm."*

Raffi's eyes were demanding. "Grandmother?"

"Yes, Raffi." Yes, Raffi. What else was there to say? Why does the camera see upside down? Why do we?

Raffi continued, "I asked Dad who Red Grange was, and he said, 'A football player,' and Mom told him to stop playing that idiotic song, and I could tell she was furious. And upset. And nobody would explain why. I mean, actually, I thought the song was kind of funny, but it obviously had a hidden meaning for them, and I want to know what it's all about."

Camilla folded her hands together, whitening the knuckles. "This still doesn't explain your first question."

The green of Raffi's eyes (who else had green eyes?) was suddenly brightened with tears. "I said something about you, Grandmother, and how glad I was about being accepted here at your college, not so much because it's such a good one as that you're here, and Dad said"—her voice broke for a moment—"he said, 'Keep your illusions that she's your grandmother,' and Mom slapped him. I've never seen her hit him before, but I think their marriage is lousy, and I want to know what it's all about." Now the sobs came and she put her head in Camilla's lap and wept.

When Raffi's sobs had dwindled to an occasional hiccup, Camilla patted her gently. "Let me get supper on the table. I have a small group of seniors coming over at eight for a seminar."

Raffi sat huddled on the bench, staring into the fire, while Camilla put food on the table, poured water into silver goblets (wedding presents), lit candles. Raffi stood up, a little stiffly. "I'm sorry. I haven't been any help."

"There'll be other times."

"Grandmother, are you going to tell me?"

Slowly, carefully, Camilla heaped Raffi's plate. "Yes. Under the circumstances, I think . . . But it goes back a long way. To when I was in college." She looked at her watch. "It's nearly seven."

Raffi paused with her fork halfway to her mouth. "We have an hour."

"It's a long story, Raffi. It'll take more than an hour."

"You can at least start."

"You'll have to be patient with me."

How much to tell? How much of the truth was truth? Whose truth? Upside down? Surely Taxi's truth would be radically different from Camilla's. But the beginning of the story went much further back, to long before Taxi was born.

•

Camilla was a senior in college. It was winter, and the bare branches of the trees were stark against a snow-heavy sky. Camilla, walking across campus, blinded by tears, crossed Elm Street and almost ran into a young man who was coming out of a grey stone building with a blue door.

'Hey!'

'Oops! Sorry!' They spoke simultaneously.

He held out a hand to steady her. 'What's up? Can I help?' He took her firmly by the elbows and steered her along the path.

'Nothing,' she replied automatically. 'I'm sorry—' She choked on a sob.

He gave her a quick, appraising glance. 'You look half frozen, if nothing else. There's coffee within. Come along and I'll warm you up before you go on to wherever you're going.'

Where was she going? Almost as though she were sleep-walking she followed him in through the blue door, along a long hall lined with doors to offices on either side, many of them with half doors opened at the top. He spoke casually to several people, said to an older man in a turned-around collar, 'I'll be down in the kids' room for a few minutes if you want me for anything.' Then he led Camilla down a flight of stairs, and into a big room made comfortable by a rug, a chintz-covered sofa, some shabby but comfortable chairs. There was one picture on the wall, a silk screen of a Rouault clown. It was a picture she knew and liked. Through another open door she saw half a dozen cribs, and some small round tables with low children's chairs.

Not caring who the young man was or where she was, she struggled for control. He went through a door, calling out to someone, and returned with a mug of coffee which steamed in the chilly room but smelled strong and stale. He put it in her automatically outstretched hand, then sat cross-legged in a sagging armchair, a slight, dark-haired young man with bright eyes partly veiled by long lashes.

'If you don't want to say anything it's fine,' he said. 'But you're obviously terribly upset. Do you want to talk about it?'

She was outraged to the point of bursting: 'My mother, at this moment, is fucking my once favorite astronomy professor.' There was no word she could use which would be vulgar enough for what she felt. They were certainly not making love. Rose, Camilla's mother, did not, she thought, know what it was to love. To be loved, yes; not to love.

She hugged her arms about herself, holding in a deep shudder. The young man did not reply. She looked at him as he sat quietly in the overstuffed chair with sagging springs and rips in the red slipcover. His expression was alert and interested, and she did not feel that she was being judged, or found wanting. After a while he broke the silence. 'I'm really sorry. That's got to hurt a lot.'

She got up and walked aimlessly about the shabby room, trying to pull herself together. He waited until she returned to her chair. She said, 'Sorry. Sorry.'

'Hey, you've got plenty to be upset about. Puts my own problems into proportion. Where do you live? Where's home?'

'I grew up in New York.' Her voice steadied. 'Then Italy. Now we live in Chicago.'

'But your mother's here?'

'She always comes East to buy clothes, and she likes to hop up here and be taken for my sister.' She added, 'She's very beautiful.'

He nodded, as though absorbing. 'I'm Mac. You?'

'Camilla.'

Suddenly the name sounded strange to her. Camilla. Camilla Dickinson. Where was her mother, who was making her so incoherently angry? In some motel, she supposed, like someone in a bad novel. Tears welled up again, streamed down her cheeks. She knew what would happen in the morning. There would be promises, promises that it would never happen again. It was her father who was the only man in Rose Dickinson's life. Why did her father put up with it?

She closed her eyes, suddenly overwhelmed with exhaustion and sleep. Her mother couldn't manage without Rafferty Dickinson. It's an illness, that's what the shrink had said.

She opened her eyes. This was no place to fall asleep. 'Well. I've taken enough of your time, almost knocked you down, drowned you with my tears and my talk—' She stood, putting the untouched mug of coffee on the table.

He stood up, too. Shorter than she, but nicely built. 'I'll walk you back to your dorm.'

'I'm okay.'

'It's still sub-zero out there, and I have a feeling that if I let you go now I'll never see you again.' He helped her into her coat, pushed into his jacket.

When they got outside, she shivered, looked around. 'Where are we?'

'Just outside the Church House.'

She hadn't taken it in. Now she saw that the grey stone building was next to a church, which was across the street from the campus. She had hardly noticed it. Her dorm, her classrooms, were mostly at the other end of the campus. 'Oh.' Her voice was still brittle as ice; it could crack at any moment. Then she said, 'Thanks for rescuing me.'

'You're a very nice person to rescue,' he said. 'I'm sorry you needed rescuing, but I'm glad I was there.' They walked the rest of the way across the campus in silence. The night was brutal. Occasionally a branch would snap in the cold with a loud crack. Ice crunched under their feet. The old buildings seemed to reflect cold. The sky was white.

At the entrance to her dorm building he said, 'I don't

mean to pry, but what are you going to do about your mother and your professor? Not that it's any of my business.'

She stopped. 'I don't know what I'm going to do. This is the first time she—she's crossed my orbit.'

He pulled her into the vestibule, which was steamy hot, smelling of snow and wet wool. 'Will she come back to the dorm?'

'Not tonight.' Her face hardened. 'I'll send her back to Chicago.'

'Will she go?'

'Yes.'

'Camilla, this is a lousy situation. What about your professor?'

'I have a three o'clock class with him tomorrow afternoon.'

'And?'

'And nothing. Nothing. I'm certainly not going to refer to it.'

'Will that make it go away?'

'No. But it may make him give me an A.'

'Cynicism doesn't become you.' His voice was gentle.

She shrugged. Laughed. 'I'd get an A anyhow.'

'Will you have a cup of coffee or something with me tomorrow?'

A group of girls shoved into the vestibule, laughing, brushing past them. 'I'd like that.' She glanced at the girls, grateful that none of them was one of her particular friends. No one who would say, 'Oh, wow, who's your boyfriend, Camilla?'

She walked slowly into the hall, still feeling caught in pain, said hello to four girls at the card table in the smoker, playing their interminable game of bridge and piling up cigarette butts in the ashtray. If they ever studied, they kept it a secret. And yet they were seniors, ready to graduate in the spring.

She climbed the stairs. She had to pass Luisa Rowan's

room to get to her own, and she shook her head, willing Luisa's door to be closed. Luisa was her oldest friend, her only school friend from New York, sharp of eye, quick of mind, insatiably curious and, where Camilla was concerned, possessive.

The door was open. Luisa was on the floor, breathing into an open notebook filled with diagrams of the various parts of the equine brain. Luisa was on full scholarship and studied wherever she was, a cigarette in the corner of her mouth, long slugs of ashes dropping onto the pages. When Camilla commented on her nicotine-stained fingers Luisa replied that she had to have one vice, and when she got to medical school she probably wouldn't be able to afford more than one pack a month. Smoking was still more a matter of morals than health, and Luisa liked to make her statements as clear as possible.

Of course Luisa looked up to see who was passing. 'So where've you been?'

'I went for a walk. Where's Nan?'

Nan was Luisa's roommate. At least Luisa had the sense not to want to room with Camilla.

'Can't you hear her?'

She had not been listening, automatically isolating herself from sound. She let her ears open and heard the clear notes of the piano in the living room downstairs. Nan would be at the upright piano, her left leg stretched out to the side in her typical position (Luisa nagged her about it, saying that it would never do in a concert hall), her right foot hovering over but not touching the damper pedal. She was playing a fugue. As far as Nan was concerned, she and Scarlatti were alone in the living room.

'Well?' Luisa demanded.

'Well what?'

'She gone? The Rose of Sharon?'

'Tomorrow morning.' Thank God, she thought, Luisa did not know about Rose Dickinson and the astronomy professor. Luisa's concerned curiosity burned like flame on an open wound. 'I'm going to take a bath.' Camilla fled. She could get away from Luisa. She could not get away from her mother.

•

And that, it seemed, was true for all her life, Rose's shadow thrown darkly across it, even after her death. Even now, Camilla thought as she sat in the pleasant living room of her campus house with Raffi, even now Rose's presence was there. Genetically she was visible in neither Camilla nor Raffi. Camilla's hair had been black, her skin clear and very fair; Rafferty Dickinson had had some Welsh forebears. Raffi looked like Raffi. Perhaps her triangular face with high cheekbones came from her mother, Thessaly, but her bright hair and eyes were uniquely her own. Her eyes were hidden now as she took her fork and ran it idly around her empty plate.

Camilla said, "My mother was so beautiful artists kept wanting to paint her."

"Some did, didn't they?" Raffi asked. "Isn't there one by Carroll at MoMA?"

Camilla nodded.

"She was—what's that word I just came across in a novel? She was—ravishing."

"Yes. And, as far as she knew, that's all she was. That was her only sense of herself."

Raffi scowled. "At least I don't have that problem."

"Most of us don't," Camilla said. "And believe me, it is a problem. She believed that when her beauty went she would be nothing. She needed constant affirmation."

"That could be a bore," Raffi said.

"For my mother, ordinary affirmation wasn't enough. She needed the affirmation of many men. She had an affair with one of my favorite professors when I was in college."

"Ugly." Raffi looked sharply at her grandmother.

"Very ugly. But it's also how I met your grandfather."

Camilla took their plates out to the kitchen, gently removing the fork from Raffi's fingers. She did not need to tell her, not yet, that the professor was Grantley Grange, nicknamed Red after the football player.

•

Someone had had to explain to Camilla who the original Red Grange was. Football, basketball, baseball, meant nothing to her. She had been in an Italian convent school during high school. When she came to college her friends laughed at her and told her to keep her head in the stars.

She had been confused. 'So there was another Red Grange?' she asked one day after astronomy class.

One of her friends had answered patiently, 'Yes, Camilla. There was the real one, a famous football player.'

'So what about Professor—'

'Professor Grange has red hair, and he just borrowed the nickname. Wanted to be named after somebody famous, maybe? though I can't imagine Professor Grange with a football.'

'I don't know anything about football.'

'Relax. It's okay. Our Red Grange, the professor, is a top-notch teacher, and if he wants to call himself Red I don't suppose it does any harm.'

—Naïve, she thought. —I was unpardonably naïve.

She left Luisa's room, and climbed the final flight of stairs to her own room and closed the door, leaning against it with a sigh of relief. She loved her room, a cubbyhole under the eaves, one of the few singles in the house, with dormer windows, and the bed pushed against the slant of the roof. Luisa had called it an Emily Brontë room.

She undressed, took towel and robe, and went to the washroom with its long rows of basins and showers and, thank heavens, one ancient tub. She lay back in the water, relaxing until she was pink except where her knees rose above the surface, suddenly surprised because the face of the young man who had taken her in out of the cold and given her coffee (undrinkable but hot) had for a moment superimposed itself over her mother and Professor Grantley Grange. She shivered, determined to keep her mother's present infidelity from Luisa. She was so angry that she was completely caught up in her own head and could not get outside it, as had happened once when she'd had a bad case of flu and was nothing but a mass of aching bones and burning fever. That was similar to the present psychic pain in which she was trapped.

If this was not her mother's first affair, it was the first one in which Rose had encroached on Camilla's own territory. Camilla was, or had been, Professor Grantley Grange's favorite student. Now she never wanted to see him again, even while she knew she would be in her place when he taught his next afternoon's class.

The door to the bath cubicle was pushed open and Luisa stuck her head in. 'Oh, good, it's you.' Of course she hadn't knocked.

'Go away, Lu, I'm relaxing.'

'You won't relax until you wave your mother off. She been making waves again?'

'She's always making waves.'

'Thank God my mother never comes to visit, and if she did, she wouldn't be taken for my sister. The school of hard knocks shows in her face. Something's up. I haven't seen you this tense in a long time.'

'I'm always tense when my mother's here.'

'Not this tense.'

'Get off my back, Luisa.'

Luisa perched on an old stool, once white but now with much of the surface paint chipped off, revealing layers of blue and green underneath. 'Listen, old pal, I care about you, that's all.'

'I know. Thanks, Lu.' She lay back in the tub and closed her eyes.

Luisa was not central to the story Raffi wanted Camilla to tell. Neither was she peripheral. Luisa had been part of Camilla's life it seemed forever, an irritant, like that grain of sand in the oyster shell. Camilla pulled herself back from the past of her own college days to the present, to her comfortable house, to Raffi sitting opposite her at the marble-topped table, to Raffi's unexpected and disturbing questions. "You know my friend Luisa Rowan?"

"Dr. Rowan, the shrink. Sure, I like her a lot. Does she have something to do with all this?"

Camilla sighed, then stood up as the doorbell rang. "Here comes my gang."

"You can't stop now."

"I can't go on, with a room full of students."

"When, then?"

Camilla sighed again. "Tomorrow. I don't have anything on tomorrow evening. Come and we'll eat together." Why did it seem that opening old wounds, old but never completely healed, would be easier over food?

"I'll go out the back door," Raffi said. "I still look like hell."

Raffi let herself out the kitchen door and went across the campus to her dorm. She was in one of the old Victorian brick buildings, six storeys high.

In the lobby she paused at the mailboxes, though she was not expecting any messages. But there was something in her box. She pulled it out, a copy of the new *TV Guide*. On the cover was a picture of her father. Taxi. He did not use his last name, not too surprising with a name like Xanthakos. Her grandmother, too, used her maiden name, Dickinson, professionally. Someone had put a note in the magazine, with the scrawled message, 'Thought you might like to see this super picture of your dad. Stick it in my box when you're through. Dorry.'

Raffi looked for Dorry's box and shoved the magazine in. Dorry meant well, she knew that. But Raffi did not like being known as a TV star's daughter, rather than as Raffi Xanthakos, with her own personality, and her own gifts, whatever they were.

"Raffi! Taxi is your father!"

"God, he's gorgeous!"

"What's it like having Taxi for your dad?"

"I absolutely adore him!"

"Why doesn't he have a last name?"

To that, she would reply, "With a name like Xanthakos?"

"I think it's chic, being known as Taxi. Is that his real name?"

"Artaxias," she would explain, not amused at their laughter.

"Weirdo."

"Cute."

"Some Greek god or something?"

Raffi would tell them, "Artaxias was one of the generals of Antiochus the Great. He revolted and became an independent sovereign."

More delighted laughter.

"Sovereign! That's Taxi!"

"And you, Raffi? Are you named after an archangel? Rafael?"

Raffi would smile. "I'm named Rose Rafferty after my dad's grandparents."

"Cute!"

"What a super family, Raf."

"And your mother's a dancer?"

She lifted her shoulders slightly. "Till after I was born. A dancer's life is pretty short" —but not that short. Mom could have gone on dancing. Dad wanted her to quit.

She turned back to her friends, found herself overexplaining, "The New York ballet season's pretty short, and my dad didn't want her away on those long tours."

"If I was married to Taxi I wouldn't mind staying home."

What Raffi thought about her father was not coherent. She loved him passionately, and she was afraid of him. She was never sure what his reactions would be, and when he spoke to her with scorn, something inside her withered.

—I'm like a dog, she thought, —never knowing whether my master is going to stroke me or kick me. How does Mom manage to be so calm, so casual about it all?

Raffi's mother was Taxi's third wife. He had married at eighteen, divorced at nineteen, married again, quickly divorced. Somehow Raffi's mother hung in, disregarding his volatile temper. "I'm like a duck," she told Raffi. "I let it slide off me. It's just Taxi's way. It doesn't mean anything."

Didn't it? Raffi didn't like unpredictability, didn't like irrational anger directed at her mother, or herself.

She climbed the stairs, calling out greetings as she passed her friends. If Taxi could act, so could Raffi, always making everybody think everything was all right. Nothing ever bothers Raffi. Raffi's always okay.

Yay.

She could act in real life; she could act in all the school plays, and loved doing it, until, as always happened, her father managed to put her down. Why? She would put her tail between her legs, as it were, and swear she'd never try out for a play again, but when the time came she was always there, happy and excited, tail wagging hopefully.

She went into her room and shut the door. What had she expected her grandmother to tell her? Not a long-winded story about how she had met Raffi's grandfather. What did that have to do with it?

Something. Raffi trusted her grandmother.

On her bookcase were several framed photographs, one of

Camilla and Mac standing under a large pine tree, with two small children beside them, Raffi's father, Taxi, and her Aunt Frankie. Beautiful little kids, not scrawny and freckled and skinny as Raffi had been at their age.

Another frame held a wedding picture of Raffi's parents. Her mother was, Raffi thought, serenely beautiful. A small gold tiara held a flutter of veil. She could have danced Cinderella at the ball, and Taxi was spectacular as the prince, even though the ballet prince's costume would not have been a tuxedo. If it had been hard for Camilla's mother to be beautiful, were his amazing looks hard on Raffi's father?

"Thank God I'm ugly," she said aloud, and knew she was lying to herself. If she was not beautiful, she was far from ugly. She had filled out. Her eyes were like chinks of emerald in a gamine's face. She was attractive in her own rather unconventional way, and she had as many dates as she wanted, though she didn't take them seriously. Time for seriousness later. Time now to ask why she lied to herself so often.

Did her grandmother know that Raffi went regularly to Luisa, Dr. Rowan, the shrink, and was helped? Even now in college she still went to her, taking the train down to New York and back again the same day. But Dr. Rowan had left for Switzerland for a conference right after the Maria Mitchell ceremony, so had not been in New York when Taxi played that silly song and made his odd remarks. If Dr. Rowan had been available, Raffi might not have questioned her grandmother.

She looked out the window. Many of the trees were already bare. Lights were on all across the campus, shedding comfortable warmth.

What had her father been hinting at? What was the hidden message behind that silly song? He had been brooding, simmering, all the way down to the city from the college after her grandmother's reception, barely listening as Frankie talked about Seattle, and how popular Taxi's show was with all

her friends. He was not satisfied with being 'merely' a successful television personality, Raffi thought; it was not enough. He
was the star of his soap opera, was a frequent guest on the
nighttime shows, did an occasional Broadway play, an occasional movie. But enough was not enough. He was not happy
with himself.

When had she begun to realize that?

Who was Red Grange that her mother had slapped her
father, struck him across the face, because of him?

Red Grange, a football star in the twenties, because of the
borrowing of his nickname, had affected Camilla in college,
blasted her again after her marriage, and now, all these years
later, was rising to upset Raffi.

Surely the old football hero did not know how widely his
influence extended.

—I don't give a hoot about football.

Raffi scowled, and plunked herself down at her desk and
opened her notebook. Who was Red Grange, anyhow?

—Red Grange was a stupid nickname, Camilla thought,
but maybe not for those who set far more importance on sports
than she did.

After her group of seniors left, she banked the fire, turned
out the lights, went upstairs. She had left on the reading light
by her bed and it reflected brightly against the brass, picked
out the delicate colors in the flowered wallpaper, the cushions
on the chaise longue.

The phone rang, and Camilla leaned across the bed, reaching for it. "Hello?"

"Mom, it's Frankie."

"Darling, hello, it's good to hear from you. Everything
okay?"

"Fine. That was a terrific bash the college gave you. Ben's really sorry he couldn't get away."

"I am, too. But you were there, and that was wonderful."

"We're proud of you, Mom."

Camilla laughed. "Darling Frankie, it really wasn't that big a deal."

"It was, to us. You did enjoy it, didn't you?"

"Of course I did. It warmed the cockles of my heart."

"My niece Raffi's a really nice girl," Frankie said.

"She's a love. Bright and inquiring and brave."

"She'd need to be brave with Taxi for a father. Sorry, Mom, that wasn't nice of me. I guess Taxi has a right to be difficult. Thank God for Thessaly. She not only puts up with him, she loves him. And mostly she can manage him. I really like my sister-in-law."

"I wish you saw more of each other."

"We're all too busy. Even you, Mom, you hardly ever get out to Seattle. When are you going to retire?"

"When the college decides it's time, I suppose. Not for a while yet. I love my work."

"And I love mine. I'm doing more painting now, and less book illustrating. We're lucky to enjoy what we do, aren't we?"

"Very."

"Good night, Mom. I'll call again in a few days."

After she'd said goodbye to Frankie, Camilla drew a hot tub, then pulled the phone on its long cord into the bathroom with her. No matter when she bathed, it seemed that this was always the time for someone to call her, and she hated heaving out of the tub and hastening, dripping, into the bedroom for the phone.

—Why are we so compulsive about phones? Because there have been too many traumas, too many urgent calls. The more people we love, the more vulnerable we are, and the more likely to rush to answer the phone . . .

It rang. Taxi.

"Mom, who am I?" This was not unlike Taxi, cosmic questions out of the blue.

"You're Taxi, darling."

"Am I?"

"Of course you are."

"Mom, I don't know who I am. For the past ten years I've been so bound up with the idiot I play on my show that I'm not sure I have any identity of my own."

"Of course you do."

"When people recognize me wherever I go, and they do—"

"Yes, Taxi, they do."

"They don't recognize me, Taxi. They recognize a character written by somebody else."

"That's how real you've become for them."

"Ironic, isn't it? My life has outsoaped any soap opera, yet here I am, depending for my living on one of these idiot shows."

"It's not an idiot show, Taxi. It's pretty good."

"What would happen to me if, for some reason, I wasn't on the show anymore?"

"That's not likely to happen, is it?" She kept her voice quiet, reasonable. "Your show has high ratings. You're a household name."

"But who am I?"

"Taxi," she repeated. "Artaxias Xanthakos."

"I'm named after someone I called Papa, who was, more or less, my grandfather."

"He was your grandfather, Taxi."

"Oh, God, Mom, I'm glad you're there. I'm lonely."

"So is everybody, love. It's the human predicament. You know that."

"You're not lonely, are you? Always surrounded by adoring students. And your stars. All you have to do is go out at night and look at your stars and you're never alone."

"In a manner of speaking. I'm glad you have Thessaly."

"Do I?"

"Yes, Taxi. Thessaly loves you and is there for you, no matter what. She's proven that."

"She's a fool to put up with me."

"No, Taxi, she's very wise."

"Good night, Mom. Thanks for being there." He hung up before she had a chance to say good night.

Why had he called? Why this sudden questioning of his role? Why hadn't she called him to ask him why he had played that record in front of Raffi, why, after all these years, he had exhumed Red Grange? Why hadn't she asked him now? Why was she afraid?

She drew some more hot water into the tub. When she felt warm enough she got out and wrapped herself in a bath sheet. She dried herself, glancing at the pictures on the wall, photos of her children, her grandchild. Raffi as a baby, a little girl, an adolescent. Taxi as a baby, a handsome three-year-old, and as Hamlet. The production had not been a success, but the picture was of Taxi brilliant as a flame against a dark night. He himself had come off well in the reviews, some critics going so far as to say that the production was worth seeing because of Taxi's performance, which lit up an otherwise inept cast and clumsy interpretation. 'Why don't you take that down?' he would sometimes ask, but the picture was striking enough for his protestations to be fleeting.

She climbed into bed. It was apparent to her that she was too restless to sleep.

Nothing more, now, please. Nothing more. They had moved into a period of moderate peace. She did not want it disturbed, old pains reawakened, old anxieties resurfacing. There had been enough. Enough.

She pulled a book out of the small case by her bed, a battered paperback of Saint-Exupéry's *Wind, Sand, and Stars.* The beauty of his writing would calm her. She read for half an hour, until all the taut muscles in her body had relaxed. Before she turned out the light she looked again at the picture of

Frankie and Taxi, and a wave of homesickness so violent that it shook her swept over Camilla. If Mac's parents had not had that picture taken, there would be no visible memory of that time which was shortly and violently taken away.

By Red Grange.

•

In Professor Grange's class the day after Camilla had met Mac, she looked at the older man as though seeing him for the first time, a reasonably good-looking man, middle-aged, middle height, middle build. Reddish-gold hair. Fleetingly she wondered if the rest of his body hair was that same sunny color. Was his affair with her mother part of that famous midlife crisis? His wife was a handsome woman who taught in the history department. Could Professor Grange just forget about Rose Dickinson when he went to bed with his wife? Could he forget his wife when he went to bed with Rose?

Camilla had had her own daydreams about Grantley Grange. She knew he was married; she'd even taken a survey course with his wife. But his marriage was not a problem in fantasies which were never going to be realized. He was the best teacher she had, and their minds sparked off each other, and she knew that he liked that as much as she did. It was, in fact, a kind of intercourse. She wanted to sit across from him in a small, dark booth and drink coffee, and then have him reach out and hold her hand. That was about as erotic as her fantasies went because, to her, eros spelled nothing but trouble.

Grantley Grange had done more than hold hands with her mother. How could he? After what he and Camilla had together? But they had nothing. Nothing.

My mother, Rose, the seductress. In the old days, didn't seductresses get stoned to death? Or was it only adulteresses? Camilla did not want to have her mother stoned, but she was still angry. Angry with her mother, with her professor. Angry at the loss of her betrayed daydreams. There was no way she could continue to fantasize about a man who had bedded with her mother. It would be, she thought, scowling, incestuous.

Professor Grange's voice broke across her thoughts. 'All right, Camilla. Tell us what the equivalent electromagnetic radiation is to the background radiation which indicates the beginning of the universe?'

Her mind snapped into focus. 'It's equivalent to what's called a black body,' she replied.

'Right. And at what temperature?'

'2.7 K, or minus 270° Centigrade.'

'Feeble, wouldn't you say, as a manifestation of the wonders of the beginning of the universe? Nonetheless, fascinating. But even for radiation with energy corresponding, as Camilla pointed out, to a black body with a temperature of only 2 K, the marvelous thing is that there is as much energy in this feeble hiss of radio noise as—hear this, class—the mass energy of all the bright stars in all, all, mind you, all the galaxies put together. So, in cosmic terms, what we have picked up with our radio telescopes is extraordinarily significant.'

Was it only her imagination that he kept glancing at her during the hour of the class? He taught well, with energy and verve. He was popular. Many of the students raved over how cute he was, how dreamy his hazel eyes, his light red curls. Luisa had asked if the curls were real, or if he'd had a perm and a touch-up. Camilla had paid more attention to his mind than to his looks.

He asked her another question, which she answered. The bell rang. With the other students she gathered up her books, headed for the door.

Mac was waiting for her. She jumped. She had not really expected him to be there. She felt herself flush with delight.

'I thought you might like a cup of coffee.'

'Thanks. I would.' —Even coffee as bad as the cup he had given her the night before.

'He's a good lecturer, your astronomer prof. What's his name?'

'Grange. Grantley Grange. Yes, he's good.'

'I sat in the back of the room for most of the class. What's this K you kept referring to?'

'K stands for Kelvin, after Lord Kelvin, who was important in our understanding of heat.'

'You really know your stuff, don't you? I couldn't make head or tail of it all, but you answered his questions as though he'd asked you two times two.'

'Well, it's what I'm majoring in. Today was just memory work, but it's interesting. Funny, when he came into class it was as though he'd hit me and I thought I'd forget everything I'd ever known, but then when he asked me anything the answer just floated up to my conscious mind. Thank heaven. He asks me because he knows I won't let him down.'

'You care about letting him down? After—'

She shook her head, her dark hair for a moment covering her face. 'I did. Now more likely I don't want to let myself down. I certainly didn't want anybody in class to know I was upset.'

'You succeeded. If I hadn't already known, I'd have thought you had nothing on your mind except astronomy. Come on. Let's go down the back stairs and out the side exit.' He opened the door. 'It's frigid out there. Let's run.' Ducking their heads against the biting wind, they ran down the path, brushing against other hurrying students. Slipping her hand out of his, she panted. 'I want to apologize.'

He turned toward her, surprised. 'For what?'

'Dumping myself all over you last night.'

He reached for her hand again, holding it firmly. 'You didn't dump. You were legitimately upset. I could have smacked your professor this afternoon, with half the female population swooning over him.'

—I came close to swooning myself, she thought, —until last night.

He led her past the church, the Church House, down a side street to a coffeehouse which catered to faculty and towns-people, rather than students. He opened the door and as she stepped in she saw several groups of older women, and a table with faculty, including Dr. Grange's wife. Instinctively she pulled back.

'What's the matter?'

'Mac, I'd rather not go in here—'

'Okay.' He led her out, looked at her, raising his eyebrows.

She tried to laugh, gesturing back toward the table. 'Professor Grange's wife was there—'

'And you'd rather not see her?'

She nodded. 'I know it has nothing to do with her—'

'Sure, it's understandable. Let's go back to the Church House, then. There'll be coffee and maybe some cookies. People may come barging in, but it shouldn't be overly busy at this time of day.'

They went into the room where they had been the night before. He settled her in a sagging chair. All the chairs sagged. The room smelled of basement mustiness, overlaid by steam heat. 'I'll be right back with coffee. What do you have in yours?'

'Milk, if possible.'

'Is possible. We have an ancient fridge for milk and Cokes and stuff.' He left the room, walking with an easy lope, and returned with two blue-and-white mugs. 'I hope you like it strong.'

Strong? It tasted as though it had been boiling all night. 'Sure. Thanks.'

'Camilla.'

'Yes?'

'Camilla what?'

'Dickinson.'

'I'm Macarios Xanthakos.' He laughed. 'We didn't introduce ourselves properly last night. My grandfather was a Greek immigrant, a peddler who ended up doing moderately well for himself.' He stopped, and something dark clouded his face. 'My mother's from Charleston, South Carolina, one of those rare birds. There's nothing like a Charlestonian. How about your parents?'

'Oh, they're Easterners. Nothing special. My father's an architect. When we came back from Italy when it was time for me to start college, he joined a firm in Chicago. It still gives me a thrill when a building is going up to see a sign reading RAFFERTY DICKINSON, ARCHITECT.'

'What's he like?'

'Tall.' Mac winced slightly, but her eyes were half closed and she did not see. 'Strong. I used to think he was like Atlas, holding up the world. You know that statue in Rockefeller Center?'

Mac grinned. 'With one foot slipping.'

'I used to worry that Father's foot would slip and the world would fall. Every time I went past that statue I'd beg him not to slip, not to let it go.'

Mac said, 'He's still holding on.'

'Um. My father's a good man. Thoughtful. Whenever I was home from school he'd take me to museums, talk to me as though I could understand all about art and architecture. He's—rather Anglo-Saxon, I suppose, not overtly affectionate. Not cuddly.'

'Passionate?'

'I suspect so. But with one's parents one doesn't tend to think about that part of their lives—unless one's mother's proclivities force one to do so—'

'Have you talked to anyone about this?' His voice was tentative. 'I mean a therapist, or—'

'Her psychiatrist. I think he wanted to see things from my point of view. My point of view is that my mother is a tramp, a high-class tramp, but a tramp. I could forget about it when I was away at school and remember the good things about her, about both my parents—'

'And?'

'I loved—love—them both, and I get angry with them both. My father somehow couldn't give my mother the—the little pettings that she needed. He couldn't fill some vast hole in her that needed to be stuffed with reassurance.' She was surprised at her words. She had never talked to anybody about her parents in this blatant way. Not to Luisa, who never stopped probing. Not to anybody.

'And you?'

'What about me?'

'Do you have a vast, unfilled hole, too?'

She paused. Then, 'I don't think so, not more than the normal holes we all have.'

'Yeah, you're right.' His voice suddenly went bleak. 'We all do, don't we?'

Before she could wonder what his hole was, she heard the clicking of high heels and two young women came in, dangling empty mugs. 'Any more famous Greek coffee left? Or did you finish it?'

'Half a pot at least,' Mac said. 'Help yourselves.'

Camilla rose. 'I've got a paper to write. I'd better get back.'

Mac glanced at the two women as they went on through to the kitchen. Then he turned back to Camilla. 'Do you have a class with Grange tomorrow?'

'Friday.'

'Okay, I'll pick you up afterwards—unless you have something else on.'

'No. Friday would be fine. Thanks for the coffee.'

He walked her back to the dorm. 'Is college being good for you?'

'Very good. Much better than that Italian boarding school. I like my classes, and being challenged academically, and I have friends, good friends.'

'People you can talk to?'

'About ideas. Politics. Art.'

'About Grange?'

She shook her head, tried to smile. 'Most of my friends think my mother's terrific, and I'd just as soon not tarnish that image. She's truly beautiful, all blond and blue and golden and sunny. A lot of artists have painted her, trying to catch the light.'

'You're beautiful yourself. I'm partial to people who are moonlit and starlit.'

'Thanks. That's nice, really nice. I don't have an ugly-duckling complex. But compared to my mother . . . But you know, I don't think I want to be that kind of beautiful, so that you're terrified of losing it. Her dressing table's crowded with all kinds of lotions and creams, and little ivory rollers for wrinkles, and whatever's the latest to keep people looking young.'

'Does it matter to your father?' he asked. 'That she keep looking young and beautiful?'

'He loves her beauty. I think she still dazzles him. She was a child bride, nineteen, my age, when she married Father, twenty when she had me, so she's only thirty-eight . . .'

'And your father?'

'Oh, older. He's forty-seven. I don't know why he keeps on loving her, except that she's so beautiful and so insecure. Why is she so insecure? I know my father loves me, but he's always trying to put the marriage back together, and he tried to protect me from Mother's—from her infidelities. I love him, but I'm hardly ever home. Listen, I've been blabbering on and on about me, which is something I don't do.'

'I like your blabbering,' he said. 'Next time I'll blabber, too. See you Friday.'

They had reached her dorm. For once the vestibule was empty. He kissed her.

She went to her room. Luisa's door was closed. No one stopped her. She sat at her desk but did not reach for her

books. She felt suddenly happy. A strange, unfamiliar feeling.
Wonderful.

Wonderful, and not to be defined.

What is happy?

How often had Taxi said, 'I just want to be happy, Mom.'

—I am moderately content, Camilla thought, —but I'm no
longer sure what being happy means. Did I really know, all
those decades ago when I first met Mac? Is happiness only for
the very young? Maybe being content is enough.

She looked out her bedroom window, away from the lake,
at the familiar campus. It was still early enough for lights
to be on in most of the buildings, for students to be crossing and crisscrossing the ice-dark paths, still looking very
much as they had looked when Camilla was an under-
graduate.

Plus ça change, plus c'est la même chose.

Maybe.

The phone rang, and she turned back to the bed table,
heard her daughter-in-law's voice. "Thessaly!"

"Mom, I hope this isn't too late."

"Of course not. I've just come upstairs. How are you?"

"Oh, fine. There was a movie I thought I might like to see
tonight, and I missed being able to call and suggest that we go
together."

"I miss that, too. Is something wrong?"

"Oh, no, not really. Taxi isn't happy, I mean more so than
his usual state of not being happy. He upset Raffi. Did she tell
you?"

"About Red Grange? Yes."

"I don't understand what got into him. I just wanted to
say—well—Raffi—"

Camilla sat on the edge of the bed, holding the phone
between ear and shoulder. "I'm going to tell her."

"Oh, good." There was a long-drawn-out sigh on the other end of the line. "We should have, long ago, shouldn't we? But Taxi—"

Camilla's voice was tired. "We're doing the best we can, under the circumstances."

Thessaly sighed again. "That's all we can do, isn't it? Mom, I miss you."

"I miss you, too, Thessaly. Maybe during spring break, when the weather's more clement, I can come in for a few days and we'll see some shows."

"Like old days. Let's."

"And Thessaly—if there's anything—call me, will you?"

"I will. Of course. I always do. Thanks, Mom."

She said good night to Thessaly and got ready for bed. So Taxi wasn't happy. Why now?

•

Happy. Camilla's heart lurched with happiness when she saw Mac sitting in the back row of Professor Grange's class on Friday.

'I turned up the heat in the kids' room,' he said, taking her books from her, 'so let's just go over to the Church House, okay?'

'Sure.' As they walked along the path to the blue door she asked, 'Tell me about you. Are you a student?'

'No, I was ordained last spring. I'm assistant minister here at the church.'

'Oh.' She knew nothing about ministers from personal experience. When they were in the 'kids' room' she regarded him suspiciously, sitting there benignly, looking, with his legs in lotus position, vaguely Oriental, like a Greek Buddha, if there could be such a thing.

'You're paid to listen to college students pouring their hearts out?' She felt indignant, betrayed.

'No, Camilla, I am not. I've had no training in therapy, or

pastoral counseling. My job is to take care of the Sunday school and run an evening program for the teenagers.'

Torn between anger and curiosity she asked, 'Do you know the Grange kid?'

'The younger one, Noelle. Is she related to your professor?'

'His daughter. Is there another?'

'An older brother, Andrew. He's in college, so he's about your age. A gentle stutterer with flaming red hair. When he's around he comes to the youth group with Noelle. What are you, by the way, a sophomore?'

'A senior. I suppose I'll go on for an advanced degree.'

'In what?'

'I have a double major, astronomy and physics. In that area.'

'How often does your mother come up here?'

'It seems like all the time. Maybe it's two or three times a year. I'm like Father. I keep forgiving her. I suppose you'll tell me that's what I'm supposed to do, forgive?'

'I don't know what you're supposed to do, Camilla. I don't think you're supposed to let it destroy your own life.'

'It won't. You're just seeing me when she's been here and been—been destructive—encroaching—and I'm feeling vulnerable. Damn. I don't want to cry.' She reached for a box of tissues on the table by her chair and blew her nose. A lot of students probably came into this room to weep on Mac's shoulder. 'It's nice of you to keep Kleenex handy. Do you get lots of people coming in here and unburdening themselves?'

'I told you. I work with the kids. Some of them have problems, sure. But the tissues are there because I had a cold last week, and half the kids have perpetual sniffles. What's come over you, Camilla, suddenly going all hard like this?'

'I don't talk this way, throwing myself all over someone. I'm sorry. I don't know what got into me.'

'Don't be sorry. You've been being real, being who you are, with no brittle sophistication.'

'You're being very kind. I'm not accustomed to— Thank you.'

'Do you know that you have sea-colored eyes? Not Homer's "wine-dark sea" eyes, but after all, Homer was blind. Not blue, not grey, not green, but like the sea, deep, changing. You're someone I'd like to get to know. Most of the time I'm surrounded by little kids and early adolescents.'

She blew her nose. 'Is that all you do? Kids?'

'I also, when my boss is away, baptize, marry, bury, and most important of all to me, I celebrate what my tutor in Oxford called the Holy Mysteries. I hold the bread and wine in these ordinary hands, and I offer you the Creator of the Universe.'

'So what do you think about the creation of the universe?'

'I don't think it was made in seven earth-days, if that's what you're worried about. From what we know now, it would seem that long before time started, or anything else, a tiny, sub-atomic particle opened up to become all the galaxies in the universe, so we're all made of the same substance as stars.'

She looked at him wonderingly. 'You're not at all my idea of a minister.'

'Or priest?'

'You're Catholic?'

'Episcopalian, and I most certainly do not plan to be celibate.'

She smiled. 'I don't think the nuns in my Italian convent had even heard of Episcopalians. It was made clear to me that since I wasn't Catholic I was an outsider. I sat in a classroom and studied math while the others went to Mass.'

'Why on earth did your parents send you there?'

'The school was famous for languages. My parents were so preoccupied with their own problems they just wanted to dump me somewhere safe so they wouldn't have to worry about me. It was okay. I did learn languages.'

'Are you bitter?'

She looked at him. 'What's the point?'

Mac's eyes met hers. 'I don't think any of us escape bitterness entirely.' He looked away. His mouth was closed in a very straight line.

They saw each other at least two or three times a week, sometimes going to a movie, or a concert, discovering that they loved the same kind of music, music which had an affirmative structure in a world becoming daily more structureless. They loved Dvořák's Trios, Fauré's Requiem, Vaughan Williams's *Hodie*. She began helping him out on Sunday evenings with his group of kids, learning to cook vast quantities of spaghetti, setting out bowls of salad and platters heaped with cookies which various parents had provided. She did not go to church, feeling that that would be totally hypocritical, nor did he ever suggest it.

In early March the temperature suddenly soared.

'It's much too early for spring,' Mac said, 'but let's take advantage of it. If you don't mind a bit of a tramp, I know a place across the river where they won't mind if we just sit and drink a cup of coffee. Or tea, if you'd rather.'

'For a change,' she murmured, her arm in his.

The trees were delicately laced against the sky, no sign yet of the softening of buds. But the breeze was not cold, and they walked along in companionable rhythm.

'You make me happy,' Mac said.

She leaned into him. He was half a head shorter than she was, yet their bodies seemed to meld together.

The road led through a young woods. 'This would be a great day for a tree house,' Mac said. 'Did you ever have a tree house when you were a kid?'

'I grew up in New York,' she reminded him.

'Poor, underprivileged kid. I had a tree house in the woods behind the rectory in Nashville. It was the place I could go to when I was upset, or confused, or angry. Did you have an escape route?'

'When I grew older, I mean when I didn't have to go out with a nurse or governess, I used to go to the Metropolitan Museum, because it was close to home.'

He laughed. 'Oh, Camilla, how different we were! And yet in many ways we've come out into the same place in our thinking, our concern for the kids, for peace. Someday I want to show you my tree house. My friend T.J. and I built it. We met in first grade and were real best friends until he died.' He was silent then, so silent that it seemed the woods around them were quieter. Then a truck roared by, breaking the stillness.

'I'm sorry. What happened?' She spoke in almost a whisper.

'Leukemia. T.J.'s family lived in a sort of shack across the railroad tracks—wrong side, of course. They didn't know what to do, and basically there wasn't much to do. There are more treatments now. Then—they just let him die, inch by inch. In the summer when it got too hot they put his cot out on the sagging porch. I stayed with him, read to him, talked. My parents were wonderful, understanding that T.J. needed me, to get his medications, to see that he took them. Mama brought us food, quietly, never intruding on T.J.'s family. But they just took it all for granted, her help, my being there. They didn't know what to do, so they just didn't do anything. His parents stood there and endured. Cissie, his sister, was sorry, but she didn't know what to do and she was off on a succession of dates, getting away from it.' He shuddered. 'It went on for a little over a year. Then, one summer night when the mercury never got below body temperature, he died.' Mac turned off the road, toward a white clapboarded green-shuttered inn. 'Here we are.'

She followed him into the building, into an empty dining room, where they were seated at a small table with a freshly ironed pink tablecloth. Mac ordered tea, his voice distant, controlled.

'Mac. I'm sorry. How awful for you.'

'That's life,' he said. 'Death. It's the result of life, isn't it? You can't have death where there hasn't been life. There was a funeral. People pitched together and paid for the stone: THOMAS JAMES JENSEN, and his dates. I went back to school in the autumn. But I was out of step with everybody. I'd spent all my time with T.J. I did all right academically, but I couldn't relate to the other kids. I suppose I was grieving, and grief is embarrassing.'

She nodded, watching him pour milk into his tea. Suddenly he smiled. 'You know, that first night we met, you were doing some real grieving about your mother and your professor, and I wasn't a bit embarrassed.'

'I was,' she said.

'You needn't be embarrassed with me. Not ever.'

•

And she wasn't. That was the amazing wonder of it. She wasn't even embarrassed that she'd told him about her mother and Grange. She felt freer with Mac than she had in a long time, and she was passionate about keeping their friendship strictly private, which largely meant keeping it from Luisa. Luisa sometimes clumsily tried to find dates for Camilla. 'You know, you don't have to compete with your mother.'

Camilla shrugged. 'Good. Since I obviously can't.'

'Are you jealous?'

'Of Mother? Of course not.'

'Are you sure?'

'Yes!' But was she? She answered, slowly, 'If my mother was happy, I might be wildly jealous. But she's not happy. And a lot of the time I am.'

'You can't be happy all alone.'

'I have lots of friends.'

'But you haven't had a boyfriend since my parents split and Dad took Frank off to Cleveland. You're not still carrying the torch for my brother, are you?'

'No.' Camilla shook her head. 'After all, I haven't seen or heard from him in years.'

'But you were pretty close, back when we were fifteen.'

'That was a long time ago, Luisa.'

'Camilla, you have hormones just like the rest of us, and sooner or later they're going to erupt and play havoc.'

Were they erupting in her growing friendship with Mac? When she was not actively studying she was thinking about Mac, waiting for the next time she would be with him, waiting for the touch of his fingers, his cheek pressed against hers, his lips . . .

Telling no one. When he picked her up after class to go out for coffee and conversation, she made sure that she was back in the dorm in plenty of time to do her job of setting the tables or serving.

She lied, which was contrary to her nature, about spending Sunday evenings with Mac and his kids at the Church House. She told Luisa that she was doing some studying in the library for a paper on electron waves. Since she often worked in the library in order to avoid the noise of the dorm, this was acceptable. And she was careful to return to the dorm at exactly five minutes past library closing time.

She didn't notice that she was no longer even tempted to fantasize about Professor Grange. It was not just that her mother had smirched it, but that Mac was everything in her life that Grange had not been. She was in love with Mac, and she believed that it was reciprocal, and she wanted to keep it for the two of them alone. She was amazed at how sweet it was.

Mac bought her an album of Dvořák's "Dumky" Trio. 'It's our music,' he said. 'An unbirthday present. Whenever you play it, wherever I am, we'll be together.'

She did not think of her parents, even though she made a duty call to them once a week, during which they hardly touched each other in any way. She did not want them or anybody else to know what she was feeling. There was nobody she could talk to, though sometimes she wanted to shout out loud her love of Mac.

But the thought of Luisa's response kept her mouth closed. Luisa would hoot at the idea that Camilla was helping an Episcopal priest with a batch of adolescent kids in a church youth group. She would laugh even louder at the idea that Camilla enjoyed it, that she was coming to care for the kids. Some of them sought her out to talk to her, to ask advice, or to air grievances, knowing that Camilla would listen, fully focused on whatever the problem was, and that she would care, but not condemn.

She was joyful, actively joyful for the first time in several years.

Nan Neville remarked that Camilla seemed extraordinarily happy. She smiled at Camilla and did not ask why. Then she said, 'Hey, I love that Dvořák Trio you keep playing. I'd like to work on it someday myself.'

'I love it. I'd love to hear you play it.'

'Where'd you discover it?'

Camilla equivocated. 'Oh, you know, I just came across it.' Nan, bless her, did not push.

Camilla knew she could not keep Mac to herself forever. But she would, for as long as she could.

One Sunday evening she and Mac were doing the final clearing up. They were comfortably, companionably tired, ready to sit down and relax over a cup of coffee (Camilla was almost beginning to like Mac's coffee). He finished swabbing down the wooden top of one of the tables, put the sponge in the sink, then turned, as had become their pattern, and took Camilla in his arms. Her arms went around him. They stood, holding each other, closer, closer, Mac's mouth searching hers ...

A bang on the door startled them. Still holding each other, they turned. Luisa burst in.

TWO

CAMILLA SHOULD HAVE known there was no way she could keep Mac a secret. She should have known that ultimately Luisa would track her down.

'Cam, you in here?' Then, 'My God, Macarios Xanthakos, what are you doing here?'

'I might ask the same, Luisa Rowan.'

'I go to college here, for cripes' sakes.'

Camilla, separated from Mac, her back pressed against the wall, feeling like a moth pinned to blotting paper, asked in a thin voice, 'You two know each other?'

'In a manner of speaking.' Luisa hitched herself up onto the table Mac had just wiped down, which was still damp. 'He's not one of my many ex-boyfriends, in case you're worried. Or, to be more accurate, I'm not one of his many ex-girlfriends.'

Mac put a bottle of catsup in a cupboard and slammed the door.

'Well, well, Camilla Dickinson,' Luisa ran on. 'Still waters run deep. I went to the library looking for you, and someone said they thought you were here. I couldn't believe it, but I thought I'd better check it out. So you've been cuddling up with Macarios Xanthakos.' She slid the Greek names easily off her tongue. 'Why didn't you tell me?'

Mac wrung out a wet towel as though he were wringing Luisa's neck. 'You are not in charge of the universe, Luisa. What makes you think you have the right to check on everyone Camilla sees?'

'Camilla's my oldest friend.' Luisa was defensive. 'Why haven't I seen you around campus?'

'This is my first year here. This is a large campus and your interests don't take you to church. If they did, you could have seen me any Sunday.' Tension crackled between them.

Camilla tried to break it. She felt as though a cold wind had blown through the room. 'How on earth do you two know each other?'

'Frank and Mac—' Luisa started.

Mac said in a dull voice, 'Frank is Luisa's brother.'

'I know,' Camilla whispered.

'Camilla knows who Frank is. Frank and Mac—' Luisa started again.

Mac cut across her words. 'Frank and I were classmates in seminary.' His voice had a flattened-out timbre, as though Luisa had steamrolled over him.

Frank in seminary? Camilla asked, 'Frank's ordained?'

'Yes.' Mac's voice was sharp.

'I don't know why I'm surprised,' Camilla said.

Luisa swung her legs. She had on long green stockings and brown-and-white saddle shoes. "Frank was Camilla's first real boyfriend. Did they ever have a hot thing going!'

Camilla said, 'I don't know why I was surprised at Frank's being ordained. He was the first person who ever talked to me about God in a way that made sense.'

Luisa bent down and scratched one ankle. 'Frank and Mac met in Korea.'

Mac took plates from the drying rack and slammed them into a cupboard. 'In case you weren't noticing, Luisa, Camilla and I were having a private conversation.'

'Sure, sure, I'm leaving. Frank and Camilla had a real storybook romance.' She made a face. 'Like most romances, it got smashed. Our parents split, and Frank went to Cleveland with our dad, and I stayed in New York with our mom.'

'It was a very long time ago,' Camilla said. Not so long chronologically, perhaps, but long in her understanding of her life.

'Frank's changed. Gone from reason to religion.'

'Luisa.' Mac's voice was stony.

'See you in the dorm, Cam. If you can tear yourself away from Xanthakos, come have a cup of cocoa with Nan and me.' And Luisa breezed out. Or hurricaned out.

Mac, still in that flattened voice, said, 'I knew perfectly well Luisa was on this campus. Frank told me. I just managed to block it out.'

'Well,' Camilla's voice, too, was flat. 'Small world.'

'Too small for Luisa and me.'

'You rub each other the wrong way?' There was something dead about Mac's voice beyond a normal reaction to Luisa.

Mac rewashed some glasses Camilla had already put in the dish drainer. 'I just thought we were unlikely to bump into each other. There are several thousand students around, and Luisa's a pretty belligerent atheist.'

'At least she cares.' Camilla tried not to look at Mac too closely, tried to understand the vehemence of his reaction.

'Are you roommates?' Mac demanded.

Camilla laughed. 'We have too much sense for that. We'd kill each other in a week. But—as she said—we've been friends for a long time.' She paused. 'So Frank's ordained.'

'I suppose Luisa keeps that a deep dark secret. You and Frank haven't kept up?'

No. No, they hadn't. Luisa had been jealous of Camilla's friendship with her older brother, and seldom mentioned him. 'Frank came into my life just when I had to accept that my mother . . .' She paused. Swallowed. 'It was very wonderful, the timing, when I had to let my parents go, be themselves, and

Frank helped me see that I was myself, too. His and Luisa's parents used to have screaming fights, and I realized mine weren't the only ones with problems. And then—geography split us far apart. Frank was in Cleveland and I was in Italy and we might as well have been on different planets.' Her voice was low, her head down; she looked at a worn place on the old rug.

'When did you last see Frank?'

She looked up, surprised by the intensity of the question. 'I haven't seen him since that winter when I was fifteen. Luisa kept in touch. She always wrote at Christmas.'

Mac nodded. 'She does odd things, for an atheist.'

'I saw her on our occasional trips to New York. Luisa's a tenacious friend; that's one of her nicest qualities. All I know about Frank is that he's off somewhere, in Turkey, I think.'

'That's right.' He opened and closed his fists, as though trying to ease tension.

Silence hung between them like a heavy cloud. Breaking across it, Camilla said, 'Luisa says his big thing is literacy, bringing literature and literacy to underdeveloped countries. That's something she understands.'

'It's something that means a lot to me, too.'

'But here you are, running a youth program, across from a college known for its academic excellence.'

'You can't take academic excellence to Turkey, or El Salvador, if you haven't experienced it. Anyhow, you've helped me with the kids enough to know they're illiterate in their own way.'

Camilla tried to lighten the atmosphere. 'Sure, charity begins at home.'

'True. But I also spent a year in Kenya, and I've worked several summers in Egypt, and one in Ecuador.'

'And you and Frank met in Korea?'

He slammed more dishes onto the shelf. 'Yes.'

The Korean War had more or less passed Camilla by. She

had been aware of it, a little frightened that it might escalate and lead to nuclear warfare. But nobody she knew had been involved in it, and her mind had been on her studies. She lived, she thought ruefully, in a very small world.

Mac's face was turned away, but she could see the twitching of a small muscle in his cheek. Tentatively she asked, 'Was it bad?'

'Bad. If it hadn't been for Frank—' He dropped a glass, and it shattered. He swore.

'I'll clean it up.' She went to the corner for broom and dustpan. Mac had already picked up most of the larger pieces, and Camilla swept up the smaller shards, not understanding, frightened by what seemed a violent overreaction to Luisa. Yes, Luisa was abrasive, but she was intensely loyal and she had a brilliant mind. Mac must have known that.

'Well.' There was a studied casualness in Mac's tone. 'The next time Frank's back in the States, you two will have to get together. Or would that bug Luisa?'

He certainly knew Luisa's weak points. 'She can be possessive.'

'God, how different siblings can be,' Mac said. 'Frank is good for the world, actively good, and the best most of us can say is that we don't do it any harm.' He shut the cupboard doors. 'I'll walk you back to the dorm.'

He held her hand while they walked, but his hand was cold, and he did not talk. And he did not kiss her good night.

Luisa's precipitous arrival had been like a smashed plate, leaving broken shards.

•

Luisa, Dr. Rowan.

She had helped, Raffi thought. The Luisa that Raffi knew had changed, grown, was very different from the college student who had so irritated the grandfather Raffi had never met.

Dr. Rowan. As old as her grandmother, with skin much

more wrinkled and weathered, but with tousled hair still holding touches of red. Dr. Rowan was a redhead, too. That was part of what had drawn Raffi to her.

Dr. Rowan had been loath to take her on as a patient. 'I know your parents, Raffi. Your grandmother has been my friend for years. I'm too close.'

Raffi had been persistent. 'That'll make it easier for both of us. Please, please, Dr. Rowan, I need somebody and I don't want to go to anybody else.'

'Do your parents know about this?'

'God no! I've saved money, I can pay for you myself.'

'I'm rather expensive for a high school student.'

'I know that. I've talked to your secretary. I've figured it all out. I've saved all my baby-sitting money. I've done computer stuff for some of the kids at school. I'm not coping with my parents, and because you know them you'll be able to tell where I'm seeing things on a slant.'

'What kinds of things?'

'Are you going to take me on?'

'We'll give it a try. We won't start today. Next week at the same time. How are you going to get home?'

'From here? I'll take the subway and then walk. You're only a few blocks from my school. It's easy.'

She left Dr. Rowan's office and headed west to the subway. As she neared the entrance a young man came out of the shadows and grabbed at her backpack. She jerked away. Screamed. She thought she saw a knife. A policeman came running up the subway steps and the young man turned and ran.

It all happened quickly. The policeman explained that the thief had probably been going to cut her backpack straps. He was not an expert. Clumsy.

She told the policeman that she could not identify her assailant. He looked like any young man out to get money for drugs. But she was shuddering with terror. She felt violated. The policeman used his walkie-talkie and a squad car pulled up and she was driven home, the siren shrieking at her request.

Her parents had come out at the sound, thanked the cops. Her mother sobbed with relief. 'Oh, thank God, thank God. You're safe. You're all right.' They led her up the brown stone steps.

Taxi gave her a quick hug as they went into the living room. 'Interesting. We're doing a mugging scene on my show tomorrow. I, of course, stop the mugger.' He grinned wryly. 'I'm the soap-opera version of Superman. I don't know why people fall for it.'

'Daddy, this wasn't TV. It happened to me.'

'But nothing happened, did it?' Taxi asked her. 'New York's Finest actually came through with a rescue act.'

'But, Daddy—'

'He didn't touch you, did he?'

'No, not exactly, but—'

'But me no buts. You're a street-wise kid, Raffi. You've grown up in New York. Don't go all soft.'

'Do you have homework?' her mother asked.

'Some.'

Her father said, 'Then go do it.'

They were dismissing her and what had happened, and it hurt, even though she knew they were involved with themselves and their own problems.

She needed Dr. Rowan.

•

Luisa was there when Camilla climbed the dorm stairs. There were things she wanted to find out from Luisa. She walked down the hall and knocked on Luisa and Nan's door. The sounds of a Brahms Intermezzo floated up the stairs. Nan was down at the piano, so Camilla would be able to speak to Luisa alone.

'Well, Camilla Dickinson.'

'Well, what? I've come for that cocoa you offered.'

'All right, all right already, you'll get it. Why didn't you tell me about Mac Xanthakos?'

'Why should I?'

'He's Frank's best friend.'

'So I discovered tonight.' Camilla sat on Nan's bed, pulled a stuffed lion onto her lap.

'So what did you and Mac do?'

'We work with the kids, feed them and talk with them.'

'Talk is not what I'm talking about. How much did you two make out? How far did you go?'

Camilla's cheeks burned. 'It is none of your business.' Her words were sharp and separate.

'I know you've been brought up to believe that nice girls don't—though how, with your mother's example—'

'Luisa, shut up!'

'Oh, Christ, sorry, I went too far, but I'm worried about you, I love you, and I don't want you hurt.'

'I can take care of myself.'

'Can you? I suppose those nuns taught you all about virginity, but this is not the nineteenth century.'

'I know what century it is'—Camilla was fierce—'and I can promise you that my standards are my own, and not my mother's or the nuns'. Don't you have any faith in my intelligence?'

'Your intelligence, sure, but intelligence is not what I'm talking about. Did you have to lie about being in the library?'

'Self-defense.'

'Gee, thanks for your confidence. Listen, Camilla, take my advice. Don't get in too deep with Mac. Don't let him get in.'

'Does that have a double meaning?'

'If you want it to. Gawd, this is worse than I thought. Mac Xanthakos is likable, I grant you that, and bright, but he's Greek, and he's unreliable.'

'I didn't know that was a Greek characteristic.'

'Will you stop for a minute and listen? I know Mac, and I know he has a weak—'

Camilla cut her off. 'You and Mac are really abrasive, aren't you?'

'It's stupid, plain stupid, to get involved with a priest or anybody who's got religion. They're intolerant and hypocritical and—'

'Hey, wait a minute. Frank's not like that, is he?'

'No, but—'

'And neither is Mac.'

Luisa reached for two mugs on the shelf above her desk. Plugged in a hot plate on which a pan of water waited. 'Why couldn't you have fallen for a Taoist and done yoga?'

'Taoism and yoga are not the same thing. Here.' Camilla handed Luisa a box of instant cocoa.

Luisa changed her tack. 'I never thought I'd see you teaching Sunday school.'

'It's hardly Sunday school. We feed the kids and let them talk about whatever's on their minds.'

'And you and Mac put it in a Christian context?'

Sharp Luisa. Those were Mac's words. 'If you like.'

'And you buy it, because you've fallen for Mac.'

No. Mac had in no way proselytized, tried to convert Camilla, get her to go to church or even ask her what, if anything, she believed. When they were together on Sunday evenings he answered the kids' questions forthrightly, including Camilla in his responses, but not singling her out. Mostly she liked what he said, though it was less in the forefront of her mind than her visceral response to the dark-haired young man and his loving enthusiasm.

'Mac, what about power?' Noelle Grange had asked him. Noelle Grange: Professor Grange's daughter.

'What about it?' Mac was twirling spaghetti around his fork.

'Was Lord Acton right? Does it corrupt?'

'Sure,' Mac had said. 'Look at any history book.'

'Is sex power?'

Camilla looked at the girl, her pale face intense, her rather stringy brown hair pulled back with a barrette. Did she suspect something about her father and Rose Dickinson? No. No.

Mac answered her question. 'It can be. It shouldn't, but it can be.'

The students had finished eating. Some of them were scraping leftover spaghetti into the garbage can, throwing out paper plates.

'What about Jesus?' someone else asked. 'Was he hooked on power?'

'No. He turned power upside down,' Mac said. 'He was powerful because he rejected power.'

'Sex,' Noelle persisted. 'It has a lot of power, doesn't it?'

'Like a river,' Mac said. 'If there are no banks, there is no river.'

'You sound like my brother, Andrew,' Noelle said. 'Except he's doing pre-med at Princeton, not theology. But he'd agree with you.'

So did Camilla; she liked what Mac said. She did not think Luisa would agree with it, but Luisa loved to disagree.

Luisa disagreed.

Luisa smashed.

Luisa handed Camilla a mug of hot cocoa. She took it, murmuring, 'Thanks.'

'What love can do! If he was a Taoist or a Mormon or a Buddhist you'd take that on with equal devotion.'

Camilla sipped the cocoa, almost burning her tongue. There was truth in Luisa's gibe. As long as what Mac believed did not conflict with Camilla's understanding of the universe— and nothing had—she was willing to accept it because she accepted Mac. All of him. The slightly smoky smell of his tweed jacket, not cigarette smoke, but a woodsy aroma; the way his silky dark eyebrows almost met in the middle; his long, strong fingers, the nails clean and tidy. His lips, warm, searching—

'Want a marshmallow?' Luisa asked.

Her interior description of Mac had been right out of a romance novel. Her lips twitched. 'No, thanks.'

'Mac certainly got uptight when I said he and Frank met in Korea. The Korean War was shit, and people did shitty things.'

Turning her mind from Mac's body, she asked, 'Isn't that a rather broad statement?'

'Sure, I'm famous for broad statements, broad that I am. You still have your head in the stars. Korea's down in hell, and that's where Frank and Mac met.'

Camilla took a long drink from the hot mug. 'Cocoa's good on a cold spring night. I like that thing Nan's playing.'

'She'd better quit.' Luisa looked at her watch. 'Nearly eleven.'

'She always stops at eleven. I wouldn't mind if she didn't. She'd play me to sleep.'

'Not with some of the modern stuff. It'd give you nightmares.'

Camilla put her mug down. 'Say good night to Nan for me. I have to study.'

Back in her room, she could not concentrate. The conversation with Luisa had told her nothing about Mac that she had wanted to know.

But something had happened, something had been broken, and she did not know what, or why.

•

Mac was waiting for her Monday afternoon after Professor Grange's class. He smiled at her, reached for her hand. Said, 'The weather's lousy. Let's go right to the Church House. I've made coffee.' It was all as usual, and yet it wasn't.

When she was seated in her regular chair, a mug of coffee in her hands, he said, 'I have something to tell you.'

She looked at him. Waiting.

He reached in his jacket pocket and pulled out a letter on official-looking paper. 'This is an invitation for me to go back to Kenya, something I've really wanted to do.'

She waited.

'Camilla, this may seem strange to you, and maybe abrupt, but I'm going tomorrow.'

She gasped. 'To Kenya?'

'No, home to Nashville. I need to be with my parents for a while before I leave, and I have to have some shots, typhoid, malaria, and so forth. This is a really terrific opportunity, one I can't afford to skip. My boss says, Go for it. I'll write you. Send you postcards of some of the wild animals.'

'If it's what you need to do—' she said faintly. Then, clearing her throat, getting her voice back, she asked, 'Did I do something wrong?'

'You? Of course not. You're the best thing that's happened to me since—'

'But—'

He was urgent. 'Camilla, a chance like this comes once in a lifetime. I have to take it.'

'Yes. Sure. Thanks for the coffee.' She rose.

'Will you come see me off?' Mac asked. 'I'm taking the ten-forty train to New York. Do you have a class then?'

A survey of French literature. With Luisa. She did not want to see Luisa. 'It's okay. I can cut it.'

Why why why?

Why was he leaving so unexpectedly? What had she done? Had she thrown herself at him too obviously? Had she come on too heavy? Had he felt smothered? Then why did he want her to see him off? It didn't add up.

'Is something wrong, Cam?' Luisa asked at dinner. 'You look pale as a ghost.'

'I think maybe I'm getting that flu bug that's around. If you'll all excuse me, I'm going up to bed.' She put her hand over her mouth and left the dining room. A few minutes later, when she felt a presence in her room, she kept her eyes closed and the covers over her head and feigned sleep. As she heard the foot-steps leaving, she opened one eye. It was Nan, not Luisa. But she did not want anybody's sympathy, anybody's concern.

She skipped breakfast, but left the house in plenty of time to be at the train station at ten. He was standing there with two battered-looking cases. He reached out for her hands, but not her lips. He did not pull her close to him. Their bodies were separated by all the miles between the college and Kenya.

When the train came he swung up the steep step to the car and stood, looking down at her. She waved him off, as she had so often waved her mother off.

And then he was gone.

•

She could not avoid Luisa forever. Luisa caught up with her after dinner as she was on her way to the library.

'Cam, you okay?'

'Sure. Maybe I still have a little fever from that bug . . .'

'Where's Mac?'

'He had this terrific opportunity to go back to Kenya.'

'God, Cam, I'm sorry, but you had to know, sooner or later, it's a pattern. Whenever anything gets heavy he splits. I told you he had a weak—'

Camilla's voice was cold as ice. 'That's enough. Leave me alone.' She shoved past Luisa and went down the path to the library. It was frigid. She slipped on a frozen puddle and nearly fell.

•

It was six weeks before she heard from him, a long, informative letter. She read it quickly, gulping it, then going over it slowly. It was not a love letter, even though he did sign it Love, Mac.

At least he wrote. And she answered. And played the "Dumky" Trio and wept.

•

One day when she was walking to the music building to listen to Nan play, she heard footsteps thudding behind her and there was Noelle Grange, panting, her hair covered by a woolen cap, a matching woolen scarf wound about her neck.

'Hey, Camilla, wait up!'

She stopped.

'Where're you and Mac? Why aren't you at the Church House on Sunday? Did he have to go back to seminary or something?'

'Or something.'

Noelle wailed. 'He could at least have said goodbye!'

Camilla said, 'It all happened sort of suddenly.'

'We don't like that creep who's taken his place. Why aren't you coming anymore?'

Camilla looked into Noelle's troubled hazel eyes, dropped her gaze. 'I was there to help Mac.'

'Well, it's lousy. Half the kids don't come anymore on Sunday nights. I only go because Andrew says I should.'

'Andrew?' Her mind was on Mac, not Noelle.

'My older brother. I s'pose he's right. He usually is. But I miss you. I wish you'd come back.'

'Thanks, Noelle. I miss all of you, too, but my course load is extra-heavy . . .' It wasn't a good excuse but it was the best she could offer. She didn't know why she hadn't told Noelle that Mac was in Kenya. Maybe it sounded too final.

•

The letter to Mac inviting him to Kenya had been real. She had seen it. Why had it come when it came? Why did it seem tied in with Luisa's barging into the Church House? Why did it all seem to have something to do with Korea?

Finally she went to the library to look up books and articles about the Korean War. She took a stack of papers and magazines to her carrel to go over in moderate privacy. What she read did not comfort her. She could not relate it to the young man who had taken her into the Church House, given her his full concern as she poured out her anger and anguish, helped pull her back into perspective. Nor to the young man with whom she drank coffee and talked about books, about stars, about music, about the kids and their problems. Who kissed her with a wonderful totalness. Who had her love.

The Korean War was the first war in which Americans had fought where there was a complete collapse of morale among prisoners. One of every three American prisoners of war, she read, actually was guilty of some kind of collaboration with the Communists.

No.

There is no objectivity in history. This was one writer's point of view. It had nothing to do with Mac.

She shoved the article away, knocking it to the floor. Picked it up. Leafed through another journal. Almost worse than the collaboration was the lack of loyalty among the men, the lack of any esprit de corps. P.O.W.s scrambled over each other for privilege. For food. Informed on each other.

On the next page of the magazine was an article attacking Pope Pius XII for proclaiming the dogma of the bodily assumption of the Virgin Mary. It made about as much sense as what she was reading about the lack of morale in Korea.

A shadow fell across the page and she turned to see Nan, the pianist.

'Cam? Are you okay?'

'Sure. I'm fine.'

Nan glanced at the magazine. 'This doesn't look like physics.'

'Nan, do you know much about the Korean War?'

Nan shook her head. 'I'm a music major. Why?'

'Luisa's brother Frank was over there.'

'And?'

'It seems to be a total hole in my education. If I spend the summer with Luisa I'll probably see Frank, so I thought I'd better . . .' Her voice trailed off. Her words sounded lame. 'Nan, do you know if Frank was a prisoner of war?'

Nan shook her head. 'I'm not sure. I think maybe Luisa did mention it.'

'Thanks. And, Nan, if you don't mind, don't tell Luisa I asked.'

Nan laughed. 'Luisa's my roommate and I love her, despite myself. But remember, I live with her. Give me some credit.'

'Thanks.'

'And take care of yourself, Cam. Stop skipping meals. I'm giving an all-Bach recital in Page Hall Saturday afternoon. Will you come?'

'Sure. Of course.'

'And then we'll go out somewhere afterwards and eat.'

'Good. That'll be fun.'

Nan left, with an anxious glance over her shoulder at Camilla, who turned to another article. She felt vaguely queasy, and wondered what she had eaten that had upset her. It seemed that the young Americans were not prepared for any kind of deprivation, for unfamiliar food, for ideological indoctrination. Affluence had made them soft.

No. Not Mac. And certainly a lot of the men who fought in that war did not come from affluent backgrounds. Some of them went to escape grinding poverty. The writer was making stupid generalizations. She shoved the magazine aside, opened another.

Read. Frowned. Pushed her hair out of her face. Read. It

was the first time an enemy had tried to convert prisoners of war to their way of thinking. The writer of the article was convinced that some of the prisoners believed what they were told, that the Americans were warmongers, and it was the Communists who were working for peace. These men were willing to make broadcasts praising Communism and downgrading democracy.

The articles explained nothing, certainly not Kenya. It was not so much that Mac had gone to Kenya as the way he had gone, abruptly, without warning, as though she didn't matter, as though the love growing between them didn't matter.

She returned the magazines and papers and went back to her dorm for supper. Nan gestured to an empty chair at one of the round tables. Luisa was not there.

'So?' Nan leaned toward Camilla, speaking softly. 'Learn anything?'

'It seems I know more about Copernicus et al. than I do about the twentieth century. I was trying to fill in the gaps.'

Nan cut open her potato and poured catsup over it. 'You know what? When my mother was a child there was no Pentagon. Can you believe it? As long as there's a Pentagon, things like Korea are inevitable. Stick to the stars. They won't betray you.'

Another girl nodded. 'My father's an actor. Listen, I'm going in to New York this weekend to see the Agatha Christie play. My dad's understudying. I can probably get a break on tickets if anybody's interested.'

'Hey, Cam,' another girl asked, 'what do you think about Britain exploding a thermonuclear bomb in the Pacific?'

Camilla shook her head. 'Worse than playing with matches.'

'Pandora's Box,' her questioner said. 'We've opened it, and now we don't know what to do. What *I* think—'

Camilla stopped listening. The conversation continued around her, fairly typical for her particular group of friends.

She had friends who cared about her. Not just Luisa and Nan; half a dozen others. But no one she could speak to about Mac. She could not talk about Mac any more than she could talk about her mother.

It was her week to clear the tables. She did her job, then headed for the library. As she was walking along the path she saw a young man heading toward her, tall, bespectacled, slightly stooped. A cap was pulled over his red hair. He looked at her, paused. Stopped. Finally smiled. 'Hi. You're Camilla Dickinson, aren't you?'

'Yes.'

'I'm Andrew Grange. Noelle's b-brother.'

Interesting. He identified himself as Noelle's brother, rather than as Red Grange's son.

'Hi,' she greeted him. 'I thought you were off at school. Harvard?'

'Princeton. Har-harvard might have b-better pre-med courses, but Princeton came up with a b-better scholarship. Are you okay?'

She looked at him questioningly. 'Sure. Fine.' She didn't know him. He didn't know her. There was no way he could know of her pain at Mac's departure.

'L-listen. Thanks for helping my s-sister. She misses you.'

'I miss her, too.'

'When Mac gets back—'

'Sure. We'll get together again.'

'That's g-good. 'Bye. Be s-seeing you.' He ambled past her, his long legs covering the ground with amazing speed. What an odd young man.

Then it occurred to her: maybe he wasn't just thinking about Noelle; maybe he knew about their father and her mother. No wonder he stuttered.

The year drew to a close. Mac's letters came regularly, but the only personal part of them was the closing, the Love, Mac. Who was he?

•

"What about my grandfather?" Raffi asked Dr. Rowan. "Who was he? What was he like?"

Dr. Rowan twirled her pencil between her palms, then put it down. Smiled. "He was someone who helps remind me that people can and do change. When I was your age, an arrogant little know-it-all, I didn't believe that people could change in any major way. But Mac Xanthakos did."

"How?" Raffi demanded. "I know my grandmother loved him a whole lot."

"She loved him totally. And he loved her, enough to make some radical changes in his behavior. It took a long time but he did it."

"Like what?"

"Raffi, we are here to talk about you, not your grandfather."

"It matters to me," Raffi said. "He's part of my genetic pattern, isn't he?"

For a moment Dr. Rowan was silent. Motionless. She picked up her yellow pencil, put it down. "He fought his demons until they no longer controlled him."

"He had demons?"

"Certainly. We all do."

Raffi leaned toward her intently. "Will my dad be able to conquer his?"

Dr. Rowan returned Raffi's gaze, then leaned back in her chair. "It was primarily your grandfather who taught me that people can always fight their demons. Not everybody wins, but far more than I believed when I was your age."

"What about Grandmother?"

"We all have demons, Raffi. She's fought hers, and well."

•

Camilla would not have described herself as a dragon fighter. She simply did what she felt had to be done. She spent the summer vacation between graduation and her return to college for her master's degree in New York with Luisa. She had already applied for and received a teaching assistantship for the following year, and had found a small apartment in a faculty building which would not be available until the autumn semester started. It was good to be back in New York, staying in the Rowans' old Greenwich Village apartment. Mrs. Rowan was away on a consulting job for July and August, so the two girls had the place to themselves. Camilla took a couple of math courses at NYU. Luisa was dating a medical student, and was worrying about medical school and where she would be accepted with a good scholarship. Occasionally she would arrange a double date, and they would go to a concert, or a play in the park, or ride the Staten Island ferry to cool off. It was moderately pleasant. But Camilla wanted to talk to Luisa about Frank, so that perhaps Luisa would also talk about Mac and inadvertently give Camilla some kind of clue. Luisa was interested only in talking about her own boyfriend.

Camilla was glad when it was time to go back to college, though Luisa hugged her and said she'd never had such a happy summer, and hadn't it been wonderful to be together.

Back in college, Camilla settled into her little apartment, the old routine of classes and the new one of teaching, and waited for Mac's letters. Studying was not an escape; it was something she actively enjoyed. She endured her mother's visits, accepting Rose's need to be considered young, Camilla's sister, Camilla's friend.

THREE

LUISA CAME UP for a weekend. 'Medical school is hell, and I love it. I have two days off because of the Jewish holidays, so I thought I'd better come check on you.'

'I'm fine. I like teaching.'

'How's your social life?'

'Okay.'

'Idiot, you can look at a man without turning into a nympho,' Luisa, being Luisa, continued, 'like your mother.'

'I just haven't met anybody interesting.'

'Because you don't want to. Listen, I'm having a generous impulse, take advantage of it. Frank's going to be in New York next weekend. Can you come?'

'Sure. I can take the train down Friday after my last class in the morning. I'll have to be back Sunday evening.'

'Good. I don't want to lose touch with you.'

'You won't,' Camilla said. She was nervous about seeing Frank again, someone she hadn't seen since she was fifteen, someone who was the close friend of the man whose letters she so anxiously awaited.

Luisa had moved uptown and lived in the maid's room of what had once been a grand apartment on upper Riverside

Drive, within easy walking distance of her medical school and hospital. She shared it with six other medical students 'of assorted sexes,' she told Camilla. 'I'm glad I was able to get this hole back here behind the kitchen. I'm not a nester, and I'd drive the others bats with my sloppy ways. At least this room is so small I have it to myself. The rich people who used to live here didn't treat their maids too well.'

A desk, cluttered with books and papers, had been designed to go under a high bunk bed, making the best possible use of the limited space. The desk drawers were partway pulled out, with bits of clothing hanging out. Large tomes were lying open on the desk, on the floor. Anatomical charts decorated what wall space there was.

'Even if I end up a shrink,' Luisa said, 'I've got to know my patients' bodies, check out and see if physical problems are aggravating psychological ones. How are you?' She peered at Camilla. 'What's on your mind?'

'Astronomy. My math background simply isn't adequate. The nuns in my school in Italy were not fond of math. I'm trying to take enough courses so that I'll be able to fill in the empty chinks.'

'Your math is fine, or you wouldn't have got your teaching assistantship. You know that's not what I'm asking. How's your ma? How's your love life?'

'Question one. My mother is my mother. Question two. No comment.'

'No love life, hunh?'

'Wrong.' Yes, she had a love life, even if it had been put on hold. She did not fantasize about Mac, because her feelings about Mac were beyond fantasy.

'In other words, you're not talking.'

'Correct.'

Luisa was not deflated. 'Just don't fall in love with Frank again. He's got a nice girlfriend. He met her in Cleveland, but her parents are in England for a few years. I think her father's an international banker or something like that.'

'So where's the girlfriend?'

'In Turkey, working at the same press as Frank. Am I jealous of my brother? Not nice of me, is it? Regressive. Juvenile. I should have grown up, instead of unloading all my insecurities over my parents' divorce on you.' She pushed her fingers through her short red hair. 'Thank God for drip-dry hair. I don't have time to put my hair around rollers like some of my female classmates. How they sleep with their heads done up that way I don't know. I'm glad you're here, Cam. I'm feeling very low. My guy ditched me a couple of nights ago, and I thought we had a real thing going. Why did he ditch me? I come on too strong. And I didn't like the way he looked at other women. Is jealousy genetic? It's ugly, I know that. Am I stuck with it, or can I train myself out of it?'

She paused for breath.

Camilla asked, 'When's Frank coming?'

'Any minute now. I'll take you into the living room. We've got a pull-out bed we use for guests.'

The communal living room was comfortably but shabbily furnished with secondhand furniture acquired from generations of medical students. The windows faced east, onto a courtyard, so had no view of the river, and the room was rather dark. A girl, her hair up in those rollers Luisa scorned, was just putting away a vacuum cleaner, and hurried off as she heard the doorbell.

And there was Frank. It had been hard for her to visualize him as an adult, and not the teenager she had known. He was taller than she remembered, and solid, with great strong shoulders like a football player's. He came to her, his hands out.

She took them, looking at him. She did not know what she had expected to feel, but she had expected something, some fluttering in her stomach, some prickling of her skin. But what she was looking for in him was word about Mac. He was Mac's best friend. Maybe he could tell her . . .

'Okay,' Luisa said, 'if we're going out to dinner, let's go. I had a hard time clearing my schedule for this.'

Frank grinned. 'If it's too much for you, I'm quite capable of taking Camilla out on my own.'

'Nuts to you, Frank Rowan, let's go.'

They went to a neighborhood pizzeria, at Frank's request, since he said he hadn't had pizza since he left New York. He smiled across the small table at Camilla. 'You've changed.'

'It happens.'

'We were kids, and now life has caught up with us. So you're still living with the stars.'

She smiled. 'It's a little less vague than that.'

'Sure. Sorry. And Lu's in medical school.'

'That isn't vague, either,' Luisa said. 'I have to admit I was relieved when my cadaver turned out to be an old man in his eighties. One of my friends got somebody our own age. That was tough.'

Camilla leaned back, listening to Luisa's tales of medical school, but looking at Frank. She liked him, liked the man he had become, but he awakened none of the old ecstasy. Nor, she felt, did he respond to her with anything beyond friendship.

'As soon as we finish eating,' he said, 'I've got to go downtown to see Mona.' His and Luisa's mother. 'Life hasn't been easy for her.'

'She's doing okay,' Luisa said. 'She can pay the rent and go to the theatre and she dates occasionally.'

'She's still not happy.'

'Why does everybody expect to be happy?' Luisa demanded. 'Most people aren't. What is it that guy said? Most people lead lives of—of—'

'Quiet desperation,' Camilla said. 'Was it Thoreau? Or Emerson?'

'Thoreau,' Frank said. '*Walden*.'

Luisa made a face. 'Mona's desperation is seldom quiet. More power to her. God, what our mothers put us through!'

'What we do with what they put us through is up to us,' Frank said.

'Don't be pompous.'

'If we have kids ourselves, we'll probably put them through a lot, too. It's the nature of the beast.'

Camilla enjoyed the evening. Before he left for the subway Frank invited her out to dinner the next night, to Luisa's displeasure, since she had classes she couldn't cut and wouldn't be able to join them.

'Then I'm off to Cleveland to see Dad, and then back to the Middle East.'

•

He took Camilla to an Italian restaurant in the Village. 'Remember?'

'Sure. I haven't been here since—'

'Since?'

'Since we were here together. It's exactly the same.'

'But we're not.'

'It would be pretty regressive if we were. So what do you do in Turkey?'

'I run a small Christian press.'

'Christian?'

He replied mildly, 'In my own modest way I'm a sort of a missionary.'

'What does that mean?' She had learned enough from Mac not to jump to uninformed conclusions.

'That I believe people have a right to literacy, to learn how to read and write.'

'Oh.'

'Do you share my sister's prejudices?'

'Not necessarily. I just don't know much about it. What I do know comes from Mac.'

He looked at her across the table, raising his brows slightly. 'Luisa tells me you and Mac saw something of each other for a while.'

'Yes. Mac does good work, and he says you do, too.' She spoke too quickly, trying to keep emotion out of her voice.

'We try. "Christian" is a trampled-on word. What it means to me, and to Mac, too, is that everybody should have a chance for enough to eat, reasonable medical care, and an opportunity to get off the treadmill and have a chance to pray or worship without fear. My part in the process is presses, so that pamphlets and papers and ultimately books can be taken from village to village, to reach as many people as possible.'

'Not just Christians?'

He laughed. 'You've been listening to Luisa, haven't you? If I understand the Gospel, the Good News is for everybody, and is to be shared by concern and example, not coercion or propaganda. If people matter, I have to care about the fact that they're poor and hungry and illiterate, whether they're Moslem, Hindu, Buddhist, or whatever.'

Lifting ravioli to her mouth, she paused and smiled at him with delight. 'Oh, Frank, you haven't changed. You're just more the same person you were when we were kids, and I'm glad.' The same, and yet her reaction was not the same. She liked him, but that wild and tremulous beating of love was no longer there. Not with Frank. 'Mac,' she said. 'You're friends . . .'

He nodded. 'Lifetime friends.' He looked directly at her. 'Are things good with the two of you?'

She took her hands from the table and placed them carefully in her lap. 'We're friends,' she said slowly.

'Mac's written to me about you.' Frank continued to look at her steadily.

Startled, she asked, 'What did he say?'

Frank smiled. 'He likes you. As you've probably noticed, Mac's a very private person. He's been hurt, betrayed, so he's cautious. I'm glad the two of you've come together.'

They had. And then Mac had left, taken them apart. She looked down at her plate. 'He told me you met in Korea.'

He looked at her in surprise. 'He usually tells people about our being classmates in seminary.'

'Oh. Yeah.' Was it Luisa, rather than Mac, who had talked about Korea?

'We were raw kids,' Frank said, and added a few drops to her barely touched glass of wine.

She looked at the garnet liquid, but saw the desk in her library carrel with papers and magazines spread out on it. 'Did guys really rat on each other? Accuse each other of collaboration even if it wasn't true?'

Frank said, 'This is good, crusty bread. Have some. You may remember that I grew up on the streets of New York. If I was ever innocent, I've forgotten.'

'You were idealistic—'

'Idealistic, but not innocent. And not good. And I didn't expect other people to be good. But Mac did. Maybe it was growing up in the South, being a preacher's kid—I don't know. He'd seen a lot of bad stuff in his life, but he still expected other people to be good. So he told you about Korea.' He pulled off a chunk of bread and put it in his mouth.

'No. It was Luisa. Mac didn't tell me anything.' Now she remembered clearly. Luisa had brought Korea up and Mac had closed down.

'As I said, Mac had seen some really bad stuff in his life, but nothing to prepare him for Korea. I suppose Luisa told you we were both prisoners of war?' She shook her head. Frank continued, asking, 'You've heard of brainwashing?'

She shuddered. 'Yes.' Brainwashing. It was a new phrase, come into the language with this war.

'Mac and I were tried for being collaborators. Ultimately we were exonerated and given honorable discharges.' His voice was level, controlled. Then for a moment it shook. 'We were in hell together, Mac and I, and that will make people either hate each other or love each other forever.'

'You love each other.'

'Yes. One thing about having been in hell is that it gives one a keen appreciation for all the little lovely things in life.

Like food. This is good ravioli. Like being allowed to sleep through a whole night without interruption. No sleep deprivation, my God, it's good. Like—oh, I even enjoy having spats with Luisa.'

The candle on their table had burned out. They sat in the shadows of their booth.

'You're good to be with, Camilla. Mostly, like Mac, I don't talk about Korea. You've always known how to listen. Not many people do. And now both you and I have someone we've given our hearts to.'

Again she did not respond.

'You'd like Bethann. She reminds me of you, not just because her parents have money, unlike mine, but because of a certain quality, a realness. Is it that way with you and Mac?'

'I haven't seen Mac since he went to Kenya.'

'But he writes.'

'Yes.' Not love letters. But he did write.

'He's a good guy, one of the best.' Frank stood up, helped her into her coat, took her elbow as they went up the steps to the sidewalk. 'How about a friendly kiss?'

She laughed. 'I'm not sure what a friendly kiss is, anymore. My mother has muddied the waters.'

'I gather she can't keep out of your life?' He pressed his cheek against hers. It was slightly rough; comforting.

Camilla leaned against him. 'She loves being taken for a student. Not for a mother.'

'Sorry, Cam.' He touched his lips lightly to hers, then tucked her hand under his arm. 'We're stuck with our parents' messed-up lives, aren't we? But we don't have to let their messes be part of our own lives.'

Without thinking she asked, 'What about Mac's parents?'

'They are amazing and terrific people. I love them. But they've had their own messes.'

'As bad as—'

'Don't try to make comparisons. By whose standards do

we compare? Yes, at least as bad as. That doesn't make them any less wonderful. You haven't met them?'

'No.'

'You'll love them when you do.'

Why did he think she would ever meet Mac's parents? They walked along toward the subway, Frank holding her close to his side as they moved through the crowded streets.

They rode the subway uptown, Frank finding a seat for her and standing in front of her, holding on to a strap. At the entrance to Luisa's apartment he kissed her good night. A fraternal kiss. They did not mention Mac again.

•

What did all this have to do with Raffi's questions? Questions to which Raffi was owed an answer. All the memories which were flooding Camilla were part of the story, but only marginally. Frank barely touched on the central events. Mac, even Mac, was not the central character in what Camilla had to tell Raffi. No, it was not her husband but her mother, Rose, on whom the story hinged.

•

Rose was in the forefront of her mind as little as possible. Camilla was liked by her colleagues, by the students. She was a good teacher. She enjoyed working with the undergraduates, teaching basic astronomy to them, not quite the equivalent of Freshman English, because they had to have a good math background; still, elementary astronomy. Her own enthusiasm was contagious.

Her life and the lives of her parents were both geographically and physically far apart. Her mother, she suspected, continued to have affairs. Why should that change? Camilla went home, dutifully, for the Thanksgiving weekend and, at her father's request, went to the psychiatrist her parents were seeing.

'I can't do much for your mother,' he said. 'She is emotionally retarded. It's not going to change. I can help your father. He's quite right when he tells you he is necessary to your mother. He's the only emotional ballast she's got. She would kill herself if he left her, not a fake suicide, a cry-for-help suicide, but a real one. It's not an easy situation. Do you love your mother?'

She smiled sadly. 'She's very lovable.' Then she asked, 'Am I in any way a threat to her?'

•

Raffi asked, "Am I in any way a threat to him, Dr. Rowan?"

"Should that be your concern, Raffi?"

"If I'm a threat to him, then he'll take it out on me."

"In what way?"

"He'll put me down."

"How?"

"Not physically."

"How, then?"

"I never know if what he's saying is true."

"Does he?" Dr. Rowan asked.

"Does he know if what he's saying is true?"

Dr. Rowan nodded.

Raffi laughed harshly. "He's a good actor."

"Why do you wonder whether or not it's true?"

"He told me my grandmother was viciously selfish. That's what he said. Viciously selfish."

"Do you think she is?"

"No! I don't think she's selfish at all. At any rate, not any more than the ordinary selfishness we all have. I mean, we're all trapped in our own bodies and our own minds. My grandmother has always been wonderful to me. I've missed her terribly since she left New York. Back when I was little, when Mom was still dancing and went on tour, she used to come stay, and take care of me. I love her, and I know she loves me."

"Why do you think your father would want to spoil that?"

"I don't know. That's why I'm here. I just don't know. Mom loves my grandmother. Admires her. They get on really well. Sometimes Grandmother comes in to New York and they go to the theatre or ballet together. I think my grandmother misses my grandfather and the things they used to do together."

"They were married for a long time," Dr. Rowan said, "and they went through a lot together."

"Well, I just hope my mom will hang in there with my dad. I know she calls Grandmother sometimes, just to talk. She's an easy person to talk to."

•

'You're easy to talk to,' the girl said. 'You don't put me down or make me feel I'm being judged, or anything.' She sat opposite Camilla on one of the old chairs in the Church House.

After Mac left for Kenya, Camilla did not go near the Church House until the young man who took Mac's place begged her to be available once a week for the students who needed to talk. 'They trust you,' he said. 'Please. Just one afternoon a week. I've got more than I can handle and I really need help.'

Finally she gave in, despite her feeling that she was unqualified.

'You know how to listen,' the young man said, 'and mostly that's all that's needed, someone who's willing to listen actively, not passively.'

There was an attempt to protect the anonymity of both student and listener. No name was posted on the door. The student coming in to talk did not need to reveal identity. But Camilla's afternoon was Tuesday, it was easy enough to figure out, and she had a steady stream of regulars, to whom she listened with concern and often with growing affection.

One day a freshman came in, a young girl who lived at home, not in one of the dorms—one of the few "townies." She looked very young, with pale gold hair which she wore straight, falling halfway down her back. She reminded Camilla of Professor Grange's daughter, Noelle, who had been one of Mac's Sunday-night group. But Noelle had rather ordinary brown hair and she would have been too young for college. This girl was more angular in manner and more glamorous in dress. She told Camilla that she frequently stayed overnight with friends in one or another of the dorms, rather than going home.

'You do let your parents know when you do that, don't you?' Camilla asked.

'I let Mom know. Dad's away on sab—away for a few months.' She was obviously angry and rebellious. She had had a fleeting affair and was terrified that she might be pregnant.

So Camilla was relieved when she appeared the next week and said she'd started her period. 'I suppose I was a fool. I was just experimenting. I thought maybe it would help me understand my father better.'

'How?'

'He plays around. You know that.'

'No,' Camilla said. 'I don't know who your father is.'

'Don't you recognize me?' the girl asked. 'I was sure you did.'

Camilla shook her head. 'Sorry.'

'I'm Noelle Grange.'

'Noelle! But your hair—and you were younger—'

'I'm still younger. I'm fifteen. I'm not the only freshman who's fifteen, but there aren't many of us. And I guess I have changed. I mean, I'm very mature-looking for my age. And I've turned into a blonde. After all, Dad touches up his hair, makes it that nice reddish color to go with his nickname. He thought he had us all fooled, but I found the stuff in his office.

My brother, Andrew, is the one with the real red hair. I don't entirely blame Dad for playing around a little. My mom's a bit of a fascist. I love them both, but I try to be realistic.'

Did Noelle realize that her father had played around with Camilla's mother? She thought not. Surely Noelle would not speak with her as openly as she did if she knew. And there was no reason she should know.

Noelle asked, 'You really didn't guess who I was?'

Camilla shook her head. 'Sorry, Noelle. You really do look very different, and quite lovely.'

'Thanks. That makes me feel good. Andrew likes my hair this way, too.'

'Your father's away on sabbatical?' It was hardly a question. She knew that Grange was away.

'Yeah. This semester. He'll be back in January. Don't you know where he is?'

'No.'

'The University of Chicago.'

'Oh.' Camilla turned her face away to hide her surprise. That Grange should be in the same city as her mother seemed too blatant to be believable. She had simply been grateful that he was not on campus when her mother came to visit.

'I'm sorry,' Noelle said. 'Maybe I wanted to hurt you.'

So she did know.

'I don't like myself very much. I don't like the world much, either.'

'It's really better than you think,' Camilla said.

'Is it? I saw your mother once last spring. She and Dad were having a drink at the Taverna, but I saw them. Actually, Andrew and I were looking for them, though neither of us said it. Andrew just suggested, Let's go have a soda. Anyhow, they were there. She is beautiful. And young-looking. Oh, God, she looked so young. If I hadn't known, I'd have thought she was a student. I think she dazzled Andrew. He stuttered like mad the rest of the evening.'

'Noelle.' She ached for the anger in the girl's eyes. 'I'm sorry you had to know about all this.' She had been the same age as Noelle when she first understood that her mother was being unfaithful to her father.

'It's the way of the world,' Noelle said. 'I mean, I'm not shocked or anything. Andrew was shocked. Hurt. Not me. Andrew's worried about Mom, but she's very self-sufficient. She got tenure before Dad did. I don't really blame Dad for trying to assert himself.'

Noelle's time was nearly up. 'Noelle, you don't have to—'

'What?'

'Having an affair is not the best response to your parents' problems. They're their problems, not yours. It was difficult for me to understand that my mother was not just my mother, but that she was also a confused adult with far more problems than I could begin to understand.'

'Oh, I'm aware that they're confused adults.' Noelle's voice was brittle. 'Do you know what my mom did? She pulled up all her favorite rosebushes. Quoting *Henry VI*. Plantagenet says, "Hath not thy rose a canker, Somerset?" And Somerset answers, "Hath not thy rose a thorn, Plantagenet?" There'll be no roses in my mother's garden.'

Camilla did not reply.

Noelle said, 'Don't worry, I'm not going to go around having affairs, at least not without being prepared. As a matter of fact, I didn't like it much. I wish I were still young and moderately innocent, like my brother, even if he is lots older than I am. He's in medical school, did you know?' Camilla nodded. 'I love Andrew,' Noelle said, 'more than anybody in the world, I think. He always shows it when he's hurt, by stuttering more than usual. I don't stutter. I either babble like a brook or shut up like a clam. Listen, I think I'm tougher than you are. I didn't really mean to hurt you, and I can see that I have.'

'Don't try to be tough, Noelle. It doesn't help.'

'You bet it does. Realism, that's where it's at.'

'Whose realism, Noelle? It isn't as easy as that. I don't think you're anywhere near as tough as you pretend to be.'

Noelle's voice held a slight quaver. 'I need to be tough. Honestly. And thanks for listening. And for caring. You and Mac are the only people I've trusted, and where is he?'

Camilla looked around the shabby room as though expecting to see Mac sitting cross-legged in his usual chair. 'Kenya.'

'Kenya? In Africa?'

'Yes.'

'What on earth's he doing there?'

'Helping people with literacy, I think.'

'Hell, we're illiterate enough right here. Do you miss him?'

'Of course.'

'You've helped me, truly. I've never shocked you, and I've tried. You're not going to stop me from coming to you, are you?'

'Not if it's a help.'

'It is. And I'm glad you know who I am, now. That helps, too.'

•

At mid-year Noelle told Camilla that she was transferring to another college. 'They've offered me a terrific scholarship, more than I dared hope for. Dad's coming back from Chicago and I'd just as soon not be around. Over to you. You can cope. With the rose and the thorns. Sorry, I know she's your mother, but as far as I'm concerned she's a canker sore up my father's arse. There. I've finally succeeded in shocking you.'

'You've finally shown me how much all this hurts.'

'Sucks. This is the worst one he's had. Mostly they've been one-night stands, or not much more. There was supposed to be some woman at the University of Georgia, but she didn't last.'

So I was wrong again, Camilla thought, wrong about his not playing around.

Noelle asked, 'You do think I'm doing the right thing to go away?'

Camilla nodded affirmatively. Perhaps she, too, should have thought about going somewhere else for her degree. Too late now. If Red Grange was back on campus, would her mother keep finding excuses to come East? Probably.

'I'll be a little nearer to Andrew, and that'll be good,' Noelle said. 'I bet he'll make a terrific doctor. He's way at the top of his class and he has bundles of friends. Maybe I'll marry one of them. I'll miss you, Cam.'

She did not think she would miss Noelle, who was too much a reminder of Grange. But she held out her hand. 'I wish you well. And that when you get away you can shuck off that hard shell.'

'Being vulnerable's for the birds,' Noelle said. 'Merry Christmas to you, too. In case you didn't get it, that's a pun.' She left, slamming the door behind her.

•

Camilla was grateful that Noelle was not around when Rose came East, to buy clothes, to visit Camilla. To see Grange? If so, they were somehow or other managing to be discreet.

Camilla was again taking a course with Grange, a required course nobody else was teaching. She believed that she could be mature enough to separate the challenging professor from the dallying man, and mostly she succeeded. She looked at his reddish-gold hair, showing a little brown at the part, and felt that it was rather pathetic. But he was a good teacher, and she found herself, despite herself, enjoying him again, rather than just learning from him.

'Oh, darling,' Rose said, as they went from shop to shop, 'it's always so much fun to be with you. I don't like that skirt on you, it's loose and shapeless and too long, here, try this, oh, it's so much fun to shop together.'

Had it ever been fun? She was too aware of all the eyes on her mother, male eyes, of her mother's own eye, roving . . .

'Golly, Camilla, is that your mother! She's gorgeous, and so young! I thought she was one of your students.'

How her mother loved that, how she loved the shopping, having the salespeople saying that she couldn't be Camilla's mother, oh, no, she must be her sister . . .

Camilla smiled. And smiled. And longed to get back to her little apartment. Her small stipend for her teaching assistantship gave her just enough to pay for her own way as long as she lived frugally. She was learning to cook for herself, and enjoying it. She had never cooked before. When she was a child her parents' servants did not want her in the kitchen. In boarding school and college she had become used to institutional food. Now she bought cookbooks and pored over them, at first following the recipes with meticulous accuracy, slowly learning to add her own variations. As a popular young teacher she was often asked to one of the dorms for dinner, but she really preferred puttering about her own little kitchen.

Her mother wanted to take her out to dinner.

'No, Mother, I've got everything ready.' She did not want her mother on display any more than necessary. She had prepared a dish of flounder stuffed with crab in a light sauce.

'Darling, you're marvelous. This is delicious. Who are your beaux? Are you dating anyone special?'

Yes. No. He's in Kenya.

Camilla took the dishes out to the kitchen. Her voice was stiff. 'I keep my nose pretty well to the grindstone.'

'But, darling, that's not healthy. I don't want my little girl to be a greasy grind.'

'I'm not your little girl anymore, Mother, and I'm not a greasy grind. I'm an astronomer and good at my work.' She turned on the water in the sink to cover the quaver in her voice.

Rose's laugh was lilting. 'How stuffy you are, just like your father.'

We put up with you, Camilla thought bitterly, and then was ashamed of her anger.

•

Yes, she was angry.

She waited after class to speak to Professor Grange, standing by the low dais with his chair and table, until the other students had left.

'Oh, hello, Camilla. I handed back your paper, didn't I?'

'Yes.'

'Your apt use of quotations from Lewis Carroll for each section was delightful, absolutely delightful. So. What's your problem?'

'My mother and you.'

His eyes went cold. Hazel eyes with no light in them. He ran his fingers through his thinning hair. 'Is it any of your business?'

'On this campus it is, yes.'

'Camilla, just forget about it, please. You aren't going to cause trouble, are you?'

'I want it to stop.'

'She's leaving today, isn't she?'

'Yes.'

'Then it's going to stop, isn't it?'

''Is it?'

'Aren't you being a little naïve? Your mother is charming, refreshing.'

'But she's married, and so are you.' In her mind's eye she saw Grange's wife, the history professor, with a sharp, intelligent face, brown hair pulled back into a bun, dressed in comfortable tweed suits. She and Rose Dickinson could not be more different. Camilla raised her eyes and glanced at Grange. 'You couldn't go on keeping it secret.'

'You wouldn't—'

'I wouldn't, but somebody else would. My mother always makes a splash when she's on campus. She's noticed. Who she is with is noticed. If you think you can be discreet with my mother in a place as small as this, you're more naïve than I am.'

He had been appallingly calm. 'Perhaps you're right. You'll have your master's soon. It's your last year here.'

She did not tell him that she planned to stay on for her Ph.D.; it was not that she had any burning desire for the advanced degree, but while she was marking time she did not know what else to do, and if she was to continue to teach, she would need that piece of paper.

He smiled at her. 'Let's not let it make a difference between you and me. It wasn't anything important, either to your mother or to me.'

'It's always important to Mother,' she said, 'while it lasts.'

With her mother she had been less controlled. 'How dare you! In a place like this, with someone who is—was—my friend.'

'But of course he's your friend, darling. He told me how marvelous you are, how brilliant, and that made me so happy. Red's a dear man.'

'He's married. He has a wife.'

'Oh, darling, how old-fashioned you are. She's a dried-up prune. All intellect and no soul.'

'She's still his wife. She may not be as patient as Father. Mother, don't ever have anything more to do with Professor Grange. Ever again.'

'Oh, darling, you're so . . .'

'Mother.'

Then the inevitable tears came, pleas for forgiveness, promises that it would never, ever happen again.

'Not with him,' Camilla said. 'Not with anybody I know. Or I'll never speak to you again.'

Noelle wrote, less abrasive in her letters than she had been in the Church House. 'I'm not the only one whose parents are a mess. I was overdramatizing myself, Andrew made me see that, and I got angry with the world and slapped you. You told me the world wasn't that bad, and I'm finding it isn't. I've made some good friends here, and I like my professors, or, at least, most of them.'

It was easier to be fond of the Noelle of the letters than of the angry adolescent. But Camilla could never quite separate her from her father.

•

One day during the spring semester Professor Grange asked Camilla to go out for coffee with him after class.

'Sorry. I can't.'

'Why not?'

She smiled faintly. 'The ghost of my mother.'

Standing on the small dais, he looked at her, below him on the classroom floor. 'Camilla, you and your mother are very different people. Whether or not I occasionally see your mother is really none of your business. But let me reassure you that I do want to keep my wife, and that means circumspection, at the very least.'

'Was that why you asked me out for coffee, to tell me that?'

'Actually I wanted to talk to you about astronomy and some implications in the equations in your last paper which bring up interesting questions, particularly your addressing of the paradox between Maxwell's speculations and Newton's absolute space.'

'Oh. Sorry, then. Another time?'

'Why not? Another time.'

She left the classroom, managing to push Grange out of her mind by thinking of the impossibility of catching up with the speed of light, which, in Newton's absolute space, should be within possibility. If one chased a beam of light at the velocity of light, then the caught-up-with light should be at rest. But, as Einstein was to show, velocity is inherent to light.

She went out into the spring evening. Eight o'clock. With daylight saving time, it was not yet dark. The sky was flushed with pale green and lemon yellow. Daffodils and tulips were blooming in the flower beds. The trees were soft against the sky, not fully leafed out. She stopped under a maple. Lilies of the valley were blooming in its shade, sending their fragrance into the evening air. She went close to the tree, pressing her ear against it.

'What on earth are you doing?'

She turned in surprise. 'Mac!'

MAC HELD OUT his hands, grasped hers. His hands were warm. She thought she could feel his pulse, steady and strong. 'I'm back. What were you doing?'

She felt herself flush. 'Listening to the tree sing. It's a little like putting a seashell to your ear. Every tree sounds different.'

He put his arm about her, balancing himself as he leaned in to the tree, listening with a delighted expression. He was thinner, and tanned from the African sun; her heart was thudding so wildly that she felt dizzy.

'I want to listen to an elm,' he said. 'There won't be many more chances.'

'Why?'

'Dutch elm disease is getting them. One by one, they're going.'

'Oh.' She shook her head. 'I should have know that. I'm a city kid. One of my friends who was a music major taught me to listen to the trees. I don't want them to die.'

'Can't stop it, Camilla. It's a lousy disease. Coffee?'

'Sure. Thanks.'

'I've checked out our old haunt. Nobody's there. C'mon.'

They went into the familiar room in the Church House where Camilla still sat and listened on Tuesday afternoons. Mac dug around in the shelves until he found the same mugs they had used before, far in the back. He talked about Kenya, and how much he had learned. 'From the animals. From the people. From what they've endured without losing their joy. They love each other, and they love the planet in a way we've lost in our affluent society. You listen to the trees, and that's wonderful. They listen to the stars. They taught me so much— they even taught me when it was time to come home.'

He had been gone a year.

He asked, 'How's your mother?'

'She's not going to change.'

'What's it doing to you?'

Me?

She thought of Grange, and her inability to go out for coffee with him. 'Not too much. I don't fall apart as badly as I used to. I'll have my master's in June.'

'Then what?'

'I'll probably go on to get my doctorate. I'd like to write something about non-linear time.'

'What about this summer?' He took her empty mug from her hands and put it down on the table. 'More?'

'No, thanks. I can probably get a job at summer school here.'

'I sense a lack of enthusiasm.'

'Oh, I'm moderately enthusiastic. I enjoy teaching, and I'm good with the freshmen, and a lot of them go on to major in astronomy. I'm moderately innovative.'

Mac put his hand over hers. 'But you listen to the singing heart of a tree. Does it tell you anything?'

She shook her head. 'I just listen to it sing. That's enough.'

'The Bushmen listen for guidance in the tapping of the stars. Sometimes I thought I could hear them, too.'

She looked up. Through the dirt-streaked window she

could see Venus, bright against the darkening sky. A single star glimmered above it. 'They probably give better advice than people.'

'If we listen right. Oh, Cam, you remind me of a passage in John's Revelation when he said of the people of Laodicea that they were neither hot nor cold. So then, he said, because they were lukewarm, and neither hot nor cold, he would spew them out of his mouth. You're not lukewarm, Cam. Listen, I'm going to be spending a couple of weeks in Nashville with my parents in June. Why don't you come?'

He had been gone nearly a year and he was talking with her as though their conversations in the Church House had never been interrupted. 'To your parents? Me?'

'Of course you.'

'But would they want me?'

'Of course. It'll be hot in Nashville, but the bedrooms are air-conditioned. Please come.'

'I'd really like to, if you think they wouldn't mind.'

'They'll love you,' Mac said, 'and you'll love them.'

She realized that what Mac was offering her was extraordinary.

•

She received a warm invitation from Mac's mother.

And what else would she do with those two weeks (so carefully checked out and planned by Mac, she learned later)? School would be over, summer school not yet begun. Luisa wanted her to come to New York, but she could not envision spending more than a night or two on that pull-out couch, surrounded by medical students.

Mac met her at the airport and drove her to the rectory, a spacious old house of soft-pink brick, a few blocks away from the church. A large screened porch in the back overlooked a green sweep of lawn at the end of which was a small stream. A ceiling fan moved the air so that there was a feeling of coolness.

All the rooms were high-ceilinged and many-windowed to catch the breeze. There were marble mantelpieces surmounted by portraits in heavy gold frames.

'My wife's relatives,' Mac's father told her, 'mostly long gone. The camera has replaced the paintbrush. The present cousins, aunts, and uncles still aren't used to this second-generation usurping Greek American, but they all think Mac is perfect, and they can pretend that his name is really Mac-Arthur instead of Macarios.'

'Nonsense. Don't listen to Art,' Mac's mother said. 'The sun rises and sets on him, and my family is very aware of it, even if one of my cousins insists on calling him Arthur, knowing perfectly well his name is Artaxias. I'm sorry you couldn't come in the spring when this place is a riot of blossom. Right now we're mostly green.' She noticed Camilla looking at a portrait. 'That's my Great-something-or-other-Aunt Olivia. I'm named after her. Isn't she lovely?'

'Lovely,' Camilla agreed.

'There are some fascinating family stories about her behaving like a little flibbertigibbet but going behind the lines with messages during the—what we still call The War. I'm told that her favorite place in all the world was a rambly old cottage up on the dunes in North Florida. I was left a nice piece of land on the beach between Jacksonville and Saint Augustine, and Art and I have built a little cottage, an escape route. I'd like to retire there, rather than Charleston. Art's father came from Florida.'

'He was an itinerant peddler,' Art said. 'But he read classic Greek, which is not usual, and he believed I could do anything I wanted to do. I love the beach house.'

'You'll have to see it sometime,' Olivia said.

What was Olivia Xanthakos taking for granted?

Camilla had not been prepared—though why not?—to have the Xanthakoses be even shorter than Mac, both delicately-boned, with small hands and feet. But large in love

and welcome. She had never been in a household like this
before. No tension crackled from the walls. There was laughter, and acceptance.

•

How had they managed, Mac's parents, to get to the place
of radiance in which they lived? Was there a secret? Mac was
relaxed, and so was Camilla, far more than she had expected to
be able to be. The second night, she helped Olivia prepare
dinner, set the table with silver, china, crystal, light the candles.

'Quite a lot of the china is chipped,' Olivia said calmly,
'but I've never seen the point of saving it for special occasions.
Every dinner that has us gathered around the table together is
a special occasion and deserves our best. Now I think everything is ready. Let's call our men.'

Our men, Camilla thought. Are they?

Art said grace, then turned to Camilla. 'What do you
know about Thales of Miletus?'

Camilla almost choked on a mouthful of rice and gravy.
'He is believed to have calculated the height of a pyramid by
measuring its shadow at exactly the moment when the length
of his own shadow was the same as his height.'

Art Xanthakos clapped his hands. 'A mathematician's response!'

Camilla smiled at his enthusiasm. 'It's a mistake to under-
estimate the pre-Platonic philosophers. Anaximander, also of
Miletus, thought that our world was only one of an infinite
number of worlds.'

'Not so dumb, eh?' Art said. 'Neither are you, lovey. I'm a
Greek, but the average college education doesn't necessarily
include the early Greek philosophers.'

'And,' Olivia said triumphantly, 'Camilla likes my okra
casserole. Not many Yankees like okra.'

Mac smiled. 'Camilla has an experimental palate. Not

many people of any kind like the coffee I produce in the Church House.'

•

After dinner Art announced that he would do the dishes, and Mac took Camilla behind the house, across the stream, and a little way into the woods. 'My tree house,' he said, 'that I promised to show you a year ago.' There was pride and also a strange shyness in the way he pointed to the wooden platform built into the fork of an oak. 'We won't climb up it tonight. I have to test the rope ladder. Camilla, darling, will you marry me? I'd planned to wait until much later in the visit to ask you, but if I don't do it right now, my parents will beat me to it.'

Her body felt like water. 'Anaximenes, who came a little later than Thales and Anaximander, thought everything came from water. Water is condensed air, and he pushed it even further, so that air was the origin of water, earth, and fire.'

'Camilla! Did you hear what I just asked you?'

'Yes, I heard you. Yes, I will.'

She was still water, but she was also fire as his arms went around her. Finally he pushed himself away from her, reaching into his pocket. 'Years ago Mama told me I could have her mother's rings for my bride. So I raided her jewelry box this afternoon. Is that okay?'

'Raiding your mother's jewel box?'

'My grandmother's rings. Or do you want me to buy you something? Some people like platinum now instead of gold.'

'No platinum, thanks. I'd love your grandmother's rings.'

He held out his hand, revealing a wide gold band, and a smaller band with a diamond in a Tiffany setting. 'It's old,' he said, 'and pretty good. I mean, I probably couldn't buy you that good a diamond today.'

'The size doesn't matter. It's that—that—oh, Mac, you're sure your mother would want me to have these?'

'Of course I'm sure. She's practically proposed to you on

my behalf already. So has Papa. You don't know what you did
for him, knowing all about his favorite old philosophers. Oh,
my darling, are you sure you're sure?'

She had been sure the whole year he was in Kenya, though
she had not believed that this would ever happen. She took his
face between her hands, put her mouth to his.

•

Olivia and Art were, as Mac predicted, ecstatic. Art pro-
duced a bottle of Armagnac. 'I've had this for fifteen or more
years, and pour from it only for the most momentous occasions,
and the bottle is still half full. So, to this most momentous of
momentous occasions, and to our beloved children—' He
poured them all a small amount and raised his glass. 'Praise
God!'

Yes, Camilla thought, she, too, felt like praising God,
though those were words she had never heard in her own household, or even from any of her friends.

•

Camilla watched Olivia and Art Xanthakos with awe,
their gentleness with each other, occasional light touching of
finger to finger, smiles of mutual understanding. Sometimes
they argued, loudly, with great gusto, enjoying every minute
of it. Art waved his arms and threw in Greek words, and
Olivia's Southern accent deepened with the argument.

She found herself laughing at Mac's parents and falling in
love with them and hoping that she and Mac would have the
same radiance in their marriage. But she was not yet ready to
argue with Mac.

On Sunday she went to church with them, sitting between
Mac and Olivia, watching Art in his role as priest, liking his
evident affection for his people, and theirs for him. She liked
the way the service flowed, music and words in easy counter-
point with each other. She did not know what she had ex-

pected, something less gracious, more formidable. Art talked about the Eucharist, which is, he said, the Greek word for 'Thank you.'

She had expected to be embarrassed by church, but she was entranced, sitting there with Mac's arm unembarrassedly around her.

After the service they had a picnic with some parishioners in a screened-in summerhouse, and Camilla was introduced as Mac's fiancée.

•

Camilla helped Olivia in the garden, transplanting, thinning, pulling weeds. A yard man came once a week for the heavy work, but there was still plenty to do. Olivia Xanthakos might be tiny and delicate, but there was amazing strength in those small hands.

'My dear,' Olivia said one afternoon, sitting back on her heels on the grass, 'how well do you know Mac?'

Camilla, too, sat, her lap full of green clippings. 'I'm not sure. He's wonderfully warm and generous, but he's a very private person.'

'What about you?'

'I think I'm basically pretty private, too. But with Mac I haven't been. When I literally bumped into him on the campus I just blurted everything out, about—about my mother's infidelities.'

'Mac told us a little about her problems. I'm sorry, my dear. It's hard. Hard on you all.'

'Does it make any difference?'

'To what?'

'To your feelings about my marrying Mac?'

'Oh, Camilla, dearest, of course not. Mac is marrying you, not your mother.'

'I'm like my father,' Camilla said, 'as my mother keeps reminding me. Square. But I love Mac.'

'He loves you. That is quite apparent.' Then, 'Do you ever wonder about Kenya?'

—All the time. All the time. What could she say to this perceptive woman? 'He left very abruptly. I didn't understand.'

'But he kept in touch?'

'He wrote. Nice letters.'

'Not love letters, you mean?'

She nodded. The short grass prickled against her legs. 'He did sign them Love, Mac.'

Olivia laughed, then sobered, picking up her garden shears, opening and closing them. 'And then he came back.'

Camilla looked at Olivia, at the kindness in the soft blue eyes. 'I was so glad to see him. But it was also strange to me. He picked up as though nothing had happened.'

Olivia gently touched the ring on Camilla's left hand. 'That didn't make you hesitate?'

'I love him.'

'And it is evident to Art and me that he loves you. Camilla, you were upset at his leaving so suddenly?'

'Yes. He got the letter from Kenya and he left the next day.'

Olivia pulled grass from around some sweet alyssum that bordered the path. 'He'd had the letter from Kenya for quite a while.'

'But—'

'There are times when Mac just goes away. Escapes whatever it is that is too much for him.' She looked questioningly at Camilla, her hands full of grass and a few flowers.

Camilla said, slowly, 'When Mac told me he was leaving for Kenya, it seemed to have something to do with Korea.'

Olivia asked, 'Did he talk to you about Korea?'

Camilla shook her head. 'No. Luisa Rowan—'

'Frank Rowan's sister?'

'Yes. We're old school friends. She, well, she discovered I

was seeing Mac, and she said something about Mac and Frank meeting in Korea, and it was much bigger than it seemed.'

'Yes,' Olivia said. 'It would be.' She smiled at Camilla. 'Mac will probably tell you about it.' She got onto her knees, then pushed herself up and stood, looking down at Camilla. 'I need to go take a small rest before I think about dinner. Tomorrow we're going out. I hope you don't mind being shown off. You make us very happy.'

•

'Camilla, Camilla,' Mac said. 'You make me so happy. Let's go to the tree house. I tested the rope ladder this afternoon and it's fine. Last summer I replaced the ropes and some of the wooden slats. It's easy enough to climb up.' She followed him across the little stream and into the woods. Mac held the rope ladder firmly for Camilla, who scrambled up easily enough. He followed her, then pulled up the ladder and grinned.

'Now nobody can get to us. I'm glad I told you about T.J.'

She nodded. 'Your friend who died of leukemia.' She leaned her head against his shoulder. There was hardly any motion of the leaves, and she could just hear the murmuring of the brook.

'I told you about T.J. but I didn't tell you everything,' he said, 'and I think I need to.' Camilla looked through the canopy of leaves, found a star. She waited.

Finally Mac said, 'T.J.'s sister, Cissie, was the girl everybody knew was a cheap lay. Sorry. That's what she was. She got pregnant. Was careless. Said I was the kid's father.'

Camilla opened her eyes wide, as though to see him better. He sat up and put his arms about his knees.

His voice was thin. 'I was a virgin. And I had, oh, God, I had such a reputation for being perfect. People wanted to believe I wasn't as good as all that. And I wasn't—of course I wasn't. Nobody is. But I was a virgin.'

'If a girl's a virgin, it can be proved by a doctor—'

'Not a male. There's no membrane to be broken. I'd had wet dreams, though not even those for a while. I was still healing from T.J.'s death. I don't know why Cissie wanted to pin it on me. But she did. The Methodist minister's daughter said it was a known fact I was always over at T.J. and Cissie's. The fact that I hadn't been there for nearly a year didn't seem to occur to anybody. The only person to say the accusation was absurd was the rabbi's daughter, and it didn't do her any good to try to stand by me. Well. She's still a good friend, married to a cellist, and she plays the oboe.'

'What happened?' Camilla asked.

'I went to the local recruitment center and joined the army and was sent to Korea.'

'Oh, Mac—'

'False accusations.' He spoke with controlled violence. 'I was falsely accused of getting a girl pregnant. And then Frank and I were accused of collaborating with the Communists.'

'But you didn't—'

He rolled onto his back. 'I did, Camilla. I bought the lies. America looked pretty smutty to me when I fled Nashville. And I was a P.K.'

'P.K.?'

'Preacher's kid. Taught to believe what Jesus said, about giving up your coat, and turning the other cheek, and walking a second mile, and all that stuff, which, if taken seriously, is more or less what Communism ought to be and isn't.'

A terrible ache ran down Camilla's back. She eased her position against the tree.

'I bought the lie about the U.S. being the only aggressor, entirely responsible for starting an unjust war. Part of the lie was true, but it was a twisted truth.' He reached up, pulled a leaf off a twig, and shredded it. 'I agreed to do some broadcasting.'

She caught her breath. Did not speak.

There was a long, dark silence. She thought she could hear

Mac's heartbeat, a rapid drumming. Finally he spoke again. 'Anything that was said about Cissie and me was a lie. But there was a worse lie, which was at least partly true.' He groaned. 'Oh, God, Camilla, there was a girl. She was beautiful, straight black hair hanging all the way down her back. That strange flat—to me—Korean face with incredible dark eyes and lashes. I had never seen anything like her. I fell for her, and I believed that she loved me, that she truly loved me. The horror of it was that she believed, totally believed, everything she told me. There wasn't an iota of cynicism in her. She was on fire with love of her country, and with the ideology she had been taught. Her religion. When she kissed me it wasn't part of a plan of seduction.'

Again the silence came between them, so tangible she felt it dampening her palms.

'Oh, God, she was lovely, and she loved me and I loved her. I caught her faith. At first her superiors thought our love could be useful, that she could use me for their purposes. Frank saw what was going on, and at night he would talk to me quietly, not pushing, not getting excited, but gently, and when I began to listen to him, to tell her what Frank was telling me, when she started to ask questions, they were angry. When I backed down from the promises I had made, when I refused to do the broadcasting, they gave her, I guess, a chance to change my mind, to go back to believing what she believed, and when I refused, when I tried to make her understand, they took her away. I never saw her again. I don't know what happened to her. I couldn't find out. I killed her, Camilla.'

'No—no—you don't know—'

'I'd like to kid myself, but I don't think she's still alive. I was wild with anger and grief. She was my first wonderful experience of physical love, and it was blown to bits as though they'd dropped high explosives on us.'

'Mac—Mac—I'm so sorry.'

'Frank held me together, kept me sane enough not to return to the insanity that had gripped me. Camilla, it was a terrible time in my life. I am not ashamed of my love, because it was beautiful and real, but I am ashamed of what I started to believe, and my—my capitulation to the lies I was fed. And Frank suffered for it, too. When I refused to do what I had said I would do, both Frank and I were punished for my refusal.'

Sleep deprivation, she remembered Frank saying. What else was done to them?

'It taught me the meaning of friendship. I would have been given a dishonorable discharge from the army if it hadn't been for Frank's intervention.'

She put the back of her hand against his cheek, rubbing it gently.

'Does this make you'—he paused—'not want to marry me?'

She shook her head. 'Oh, Mac, darling. I'm grateful to you for telling me.'

'That I loved someone else—'

The words did not come easily. 'I'm glad—I'm glad you told me.'

'Darling,' he said, 'if you're going to be my wife, I need to be honest with you about myself. I'm a pretty square guy. After we got home and I was with Mama and Papa for a while, and then when Frank and I went to seminary, I was moderately serious about a couple of girls, but I wasn't the womanizer Luisa accused me of being, and it wasn't until I met you that I knew—not just with my mind and body but with all of me, with my soul, if that doesn't sound too corny, that I love you. Camilla, I love you. You listen to the heart of trees,' he said, pulling her toward him until her head rested on his chest. 'Can you hear my heart, darling Camilla? It's yours.'

•

Camilla offered to cook at least one dinner.

'Let's do it together,' Olivia suggested. 'That will be fun.'

It was. Olivia helped shred and chop while Camilla made a delicate sauce, using some of Olivia's homegrown herbs.

'What a delight you are,' Olivia said. 'Art and I have always wanted a daughter, and you are everything we could have wished for.'

—I've always wanted a mother, Camilla thought, but could not say it and thus betray her mother. 'You and Mr. Xanthakos—'

'Art, lovey.'

'There's a peace in your house, a kind of serenity I've never known. You and Mr. Xan—Art—can be quiet together, and it's good. I hope it will be that way for Mac and me.'

Olivia was busy chopping cilantro. Finally she said, 'My dear, it does not come free, or without leaving scars. When china is broken, no matter how well it's mended you can still see the crack. When bones are broken they have to be skillfully set, and sometimes rebroken and reset. One of my favorite cooking utensils is my rice cooker, which I'll get out for you in a few moments. You'll notice that it has a patch on the bottom from where I let it burn dry. We used to mend our pots and pans. Perhaps today we tend to throw away rather than mend.' She looked at Camilla. 'That's not an answer to what I hope for you and Mac, but it's at least a metaphor. When I think of Art and myself I know that our patches and glued-together cracks are visible, but they've held.'

Camilla asked, 'Perhaps Mac's going to Kenya the way he did was the first of our cracks?'

•

There did not seem to Camilla to be visible cracks in Olivia and Art. She loved the way they looked at each other, touched unobtrusively, a hand laid for a moment against an arm, a shoulder.

Mac, too, touched her inconspicuously whenever they were

not alone, something learned from his parents that she treasured. She needed the reassurance of his hand, his fingers against hers.

Art was affectionate with her, far more overtly than her father had ever been, but never in any way that made her uncomfortable.

One Saturday morning when he was going over his sermon she took him in a midmorning cup of coffee, and he indicated a comfortable leather chair beside his desk. 'Sit down for a moment, can you? I need to take a break.'

Camilla curled up in the big old chair, looking around the study, which was full of books, many, she thought, in Greek. Magazines and papers were falling off tables and extra chairs. There was a smell of leather and old books and the fresh coffee she had brought in, very different from the Church House coffee.

Art asked, 'You and Mac getting enough chance alone to talk? Olivia and I aren't too much around?'

'We have lots of chance to talk,' Camilla said. 'We've gone out to the old tree house. Mac told me about T.J.'

'Thomas James. Tragic. He was a brilliant boy.'

'And Cissie.'

Art leaned back in his chair. 'I'm glad Mac told you. T.J. had the brains. Cissie had the smarts. It was a clever ploy, but it didn't work.'

'It sent Mac to Korea.'

'Yes, and that was hell, but a different kind of hell than he knew here.' He picked up a pencil, looked at it thoughtfully, and sharpened it with a penknife. 'How much did he tell you about Korea?'

'He told me.'

Art was silent for a long time, nodding slowly, affirmatively, as he looked across his desk at Camilla. 'It is terrifying how untruth can be taught. Mac and Frank and the others were put in schoolrooms with the great blue-and-white flag of peace covering one wall. And taught. At first it was mesmerizing. And then there was the girl. He told you?'

'Yes.'

'When the instructor accused the U.S. of starting the war, Frank pointed out that it was odd that the North Koreans were already in Seoul. Mac heard. Dazzled as he was, he heard. Thanks to Frank's steady clear-sightedness, his gentle persistence, the scales fell from Mac's eyes. He tried to speak to the young woman, out of love, out of naïveté. It was a bad time.'

Art put down his coffee cup. 'Enough. It serves no good purpose to dwell on that time. It is fitting that you should know about it, but now you and Mac need your own lives. There are other things as grievous as— No. Not now. Olivia and I are more happy than we can say that Mac has found you. That you have found each other. Now, before you set a wedding date, Mac must find out what he is going to do next.'

» FIVE

CAMILLA WENT BACK to New England to teach summer school. Mac returned to the seminary to take courses and to look for a job.

Every week or so Art or Olivia would call Camilla, and she felt that she was beginning to understand, at last, what it was like to have parents.

•

"Parents," Raffi said, "are a liability. They mess up their lives."

"Not always," Dr. Rowan said. "Some manage to work through their griefs and betrayals into real love."

"Name somebody."

"Your grandparents."

"I never knew my grandfather. He died while Mom was pregnant with me. They were really good together?"

"Yes. They went through the grinder and they came out and put themselves back together."

"They did?"

"Yes, Raffi."

"But I thought they had it pretty easy."

Luisa looked down at her yellow pad. Smiled. "Love is never easy, Raffi."

"Who else?"

"My brother, Frank, and his wife."

"Do you think my mom and dad can make it?"

"From what you've told me, I think your mom is working hard to keep things going."

"Thessaly." Raffi was contemptuous. "My dad made her change her name to Thessaly. Her real name is Esther."

"Maybe Thessaly is a better stage name."

"If two people make it, is it just an endurance test?"

"Sometimes."

"Is it worth it?"

"If it's no more than an endurance test, probably not."

"Is it ever?"

"Oh, yes. It is worth it."

"Why?"

"When two people, lovers, or sometimes friends, have an enduring care for each other, allow each other to be human, faulted, flawed, but real, then being human becomes a glorious thing to be. If the human race ever makes progress, that is how."

"What about you?"

"What about me?"

"Did you make it?"

Again Luisa laughed. "With husbands, no. With friends, yes. I'll see you next week, Raffi."

"But you still think marriage is worth it?"

"Yes. I do."

•

Camilla and Mac were to be married the following spring. It was a year of separation, with Camilla in New England, Mac in New York, Camilla working on her doctorate, Mac getting a master's degree at the seminary, with occasional trips for interviews. In January he accepted a call to be rector of a small church in Georgia, and they were able to make plans.

Camilla was completing her course work for her Ph.D., and her dissertation topic on aspects of non-linear time had been accepted, with Professor Grange enthusiastically behind her. They were not, never could be, quite back to their pre-Rose enjoyment of each other's company, and she was glad that they were both leaving the college at the same time. He had accepted a permanent post at the University of Chicago, and his wife had been offered a position there, too, in the history department. Camilla was beginning to realize that Grange's wife was as respected in the academic world as her husband was.

Chicago. What irony. Rose and Rafferty were not in Chicago, but in Paris, where Rafferty was on some kind of commission that would keep him abroad for at least a year. They came home fairly regularly on brief trips. Rose was having the house redecorated, and needed to check in with the decorators. Still, they were based in Paris, and that was a relief to Camilla, and not only because of Red Grange. Rose seemed to do best when she and Rafferty were traveling.

• • •

In order to get closer to Mac, Camilla audited a couple of courses in the religion department. It was a world of which she knew absolutely nothing. One class she dropped after a few sessions, because the professor found a conflict between religion and science. If that was true, she and Mac would be in trouble, but he seemed excited only when she talked to him about the vastness of the outer universe, and the equal enormity of the universe of sub-atomic particles.

She was fascinated by an old, bearded professor emeritus who taught Hebrew Scripture, a retired rabbi who saw Scriptural time as being non-linear, and compared it to some of the astrophysical theories of non-linear time. 'There are constant chronological difficulties in Scripture,' he said, 'if you are looking for time to work out in a tidy, linear way. It doesn't. There are two Creation stories, which are amazing only in their closeness to what the scientists now tell us. Jump to the famous David story, and he enters in two separate ways. In one, David is playing the harp to soothe mad Saul, and in the other he is still up in the hills, minding his sheep, and no one has ever heard of him. Saul dies two different deaths. It is the story, the myth of the people, that matters.'

He and Camilla went out and drank coffee together and talked, each nurturing the other. If Red Grange had learned that her interest in non-linear time was becoming philosophical as well as scientific, he might not have been as pleased as he was with her dissertation topic.

When Grange left for Chicago he arranged for her to transfer to the University of Georgia in Athens, which was about half an hour's drive from the little town of Corinth, where the church was. He had also talked to a colleague there, Dr. Edith Edison, who would take over as Camilla's dissertation advisor.

She said goodbye to Grange with mixed emotions. She did not know whether or not he would see Rose again when her parents returned to Chicago. It was, she hoped, none of her business. She had her own life to live, and she wanted no part of theirs.

•

Camilla went to Nashville in early April. Rafferty had to be back in the States for a couple of weeks at that time, and the wedding was timed to accommodate his and Rose's schedule, rather than Camilla and Mac's. It was, as a matter of fact, not at all convenient for Camilla. She would have to go back to college right after her marriage, to finish the semester, give exams, hand in grades, before joining Mac in Corinth.

Corinth! Athens! Mac and Art laughed uproariously at what they considered the appropriateness of the Greek names.

Nashville was the glory of flowers Olivia had lamented when Camilla was there in June. Camilla was grateful for her few days alone with the Xanthakoses, time to get to know them better, and to reunite with Mac.

They spent hours sipping iced tea out on the screened porch, surrounded by azaleas, camellias, birdsong. Camilla was often with Olivia alone, because Art was in his office at the church, Mac with him.

'So Mac told you about Cissie.' Olivia was stretched out on a white wicker chaise longue, her tall glass on a table beside her.

'How could anybody do something like that? Accuse Mac, when she knew it wasn't even possible?'

'You're still very innocent, my dear.'

'I don't feel innocent.'

Olivia smiled. 'People wanted to believe the worst of Mac. That was what hurt so, people wanting him to be guilty. And he was young, incredibly young for his age. I don't know what Art and I could have done that we didn't, but surely something. And we had not discouraged a tendency in him to run away whenever things got rough.'

'Kenya,' Camilla said. Olivia nodded, pushed her fingers through her silver hair. Camilla continued, 'When my friend Luisa—Frank's sister—blundered into the room in the Church House where Mac and I were, and said that he and Frank had met in Korea, the next day Mac told me he was leaving for Kenya.'

'Yes. That is Mac. I'm sorry. He still had not come to terms with his experience in Korea. He was still overwhelmed with guilt, far beyond reason, and he was terrified of losing you. So he fled.'

'That doesn't make sense,' Camilla said.

'No. Fear seldom does.' Olivia picked up a paper knife from the table and drew her finger along the blade. 'When Mac finally told you about Korea it was a beginning of his acceptance that he was deeply ashamed, but also that what he had done was not beyond the realm of comprehension and forgiveness, and that he was going to be able to live a good and honorable life. I think he needed the year in Kenya to come to terms with himself before he could offer himself to you.' She put the paper knife back down on the table. 'Parents have a tendency to want to fix everything. To rationalize. To excuse. But we can't fix it. We have to let be. I think Mac will make you happy. And Art and I will try not to interfere.'

'Oh!' Camilla exclaimed. 'I love you and Art so much. I look forward to seeing lots of you, to getting to know you better.'

'Thank you, my dear.'

'My parents—my parents are coming next week and you'll meet them. My father's tall and strong and doesn't talk much. My mother's beautiful and talks all the time. When they sent me to boarding school I left them. Not just physically.'

'That is understandable,' Olivia murmured.

'I know this doesn't need to happen. Some of my friends have stayed close to their parents, I didn't. I feel closer to you than I do to my mother.'

'Oh, my dear—I will love your mother, because she gave you to us.'

•

The love between mother-in-law and daughter-in-law is not as unusual as it may seem. Camilla had deeply loved her mother-in-law. She loved her daughter-in-law. She and Thessaly had a warm, rich friendship.

She looked at Raffi, seeing a glimpse of Thessaly in Raffi's high cheekbones. Not in the red hair. That had not come from Thessaly's family.

"My mom says the best thing about marrying my dad was getting you and Grandfather for parents-in-law," Raffi said. She sat again on the stool in front of the fireplace in the long living room of Camilla's white clapboard house.

"Your mom's a great blessing in our lives."

"I guess Mom's own parents were pretty stuffy."

"They were good people," Camilla said. "You never really got to know them, did you?"

"They were kind of old when they had Mom, and they didn't like to travel. And Dad thinks Iowa's somewhere in the Middle Ages. Mom took me there a couple of times when I was little, to visit my grandparents, but I don't remember much. They died in some kind of flu epidemic. Mom had a much older brother and sister, and they thought dancing was a sin. I remember at the funeral they were stiff and funny."

"Do you remember the house?"

"It was a yellow house with a porch across the front. And I remember inside there was a stone fireplace and on the mantelpiece was a picture of Mom and Dad, a wedding picture. Even then I realized that they were totally glamorous, and the picture was out of place in that house. I think I remember, after the funeral, that the brother took it down."

Yes, that wedding picture had indeed been glamorous. It had been in most of the New York papers, both Taxi and Thessaly having made names for themselves in the world of theatre and dance. They were married at the Little Church Around the Corner, as the Church of the Transfiguration was affectionately known, the church willing to marry actors and dancers and other marginal characters at a time when the more fashionable and traditional churches turned them away. By the time Taxi and Thessaly were married this had changed, although the fact that this was Taxi's third wedding raised questions, so they did not look elsewhere. It was Taxi's choice. The question of the seminary chapel, with Mac officiating, was not brought up, and Camilla and Mac held their peace.

Thessaly's parents flew in from Iowa, calling their daughter by her baptismal name of Esther, looking baffled when Taxi called her Thessaly. She was still Esther in the ballet program, Esther Jennings, but she was to become Thessaly Xanthakos.

The Jenningses had been ambitious for their late-born,

letting her come to New York to study ballet when she was still a teenager, settling her in a small box of a room in a brownstone house which accepted only young Christian girls of good moral character.

'She's a good girl,' Mrs. Jennings said to Camilla. 'I know she lives in a world of sin and temptation, but she's held on to what she believes.' They were in a guest apartment in the seminary which had been made available to the Jenningses. 'She danced before she walked, and the minister's wife had a little dance studio. I know it was our fault—'

Camilla smiled. 'Was it a fault?'

'To be honest, Mrs. Xanthakos—though you're also called Dr. Dickinson, Esther says—?'

'It's easier, professionally. Do call me Camilla.'

'To be honest, it is not the life we would have chosen for her. Her teachers all told us how talented she was, but we still thought the dancing was something she would outgrow.'

'She's a lovely dancer,' Camilla said. 'Do you remember that Moses' sister, Miriam, danced after the crossing of the Red Sea?' This was something that had pleased her when the old professor had talked about it, his face radiant with delight.

Mrs. Jennings clasped her hands tightly. 'We're Presbyterians, Jim and I. We don't know much about the Episcopal Church, but it does make us feel better that your husband is a minister. And he teaches?'

'Spirituality,' Camilla said. 'Prayer, and so forth.'

'I see,' said Mrs. Jennings, who did not see. 'Did it ever worry you, your son being an actor?'

Camilla replied carefully, 'Our children always worry us, one way or another, don't they? But acting seems to be Taxi's métier, and we're grateful he's found it.'

'Esther is not his first wife—'

'No. He was very young when he—' She wondered if Mrs. Jennings knew that there had been two wives before Thessaly—Esther.

'Let me tell you one thing, Mrs., uh, Camilla. Esther is not a quitter. She takes marriage seriously. When she makes her vows she will keep them. Divorce is not an option. I don't mean to imply—I know your son is a good boy. He loves my Esther.'

'Yes. She's a very lovable young woman.'

'Esther left us long ago. We recognize that. She's gone beyond us into another world. My other two resent that. They don't approve. But all her father and I want is for her to be happy.'

—We all want that for our children, Camilla thought, —even though it may not be the best thing we can want for them.

Mrs. Jennings continued, 'Your son is handsome. Almost beautiful, in a masculine way. Girls must fall all over him.'

'Sometimes.'

'I hope he will be good for our Esther.'

Camilla nodded. —I hope so, too.

'She will be a good wife. She will not put her career before her marriage. I know her. But she's far from home, Mrs., uh, Camilla. I'm glad she will have you and Reverend Xanthakos nearby. I worry about her. But I suppose we all do that.'

'Yes, we all do that,' Camilla agreed.

Perhaps the greatest blessing of this wedding for Camilla was that Frankie flew in from Seattle to be there, quiet, sketch-book always in hand, calmly loving with her parents.

'I like Thessaly—Esther, whatever her name is,' she told them. 'She has stability. I think this one will take.'

'I hope so,' Camilla said. 'Your father and I like her, too.'

•

"Mom really loves you, Grandmother," Raffi said. "She says you're a stabilizing influence."

Camilla said, "Your mom is a stable person."

"Most of the time," Raffi said. "She's really missed you since you moved up here."

"I've missed her, too," Camilla said. "Our unplanned 'Let's go out to dinner and the movies,' or just sitting together over a cup of tea and talking."

"It hurt Mom that her brother and sister did't come to the wedding. She said you made all the difference."

•

For the few days before Camilla and Mac's wedding, Rose and Rafferty stayed in a nearby family hotel largely inhabited by widows and widowers who lived there permanently, who wanted their beds made and their rooms cleaned and an available dining room if they did not want to cook. There were always a few rooms for transient guests, and it was only a few minutes from the church and the rectory. Their room contained a large bed, a comfortable sofa and chairs, a tiny kitchenette, and a sizable bath-dressing room. Although Rose protested that it was shabby and not what she was used to, it was comfortable and much more convenient than one of the modern downtown hotels where transportation would have been more of a problem.

Rose quickly got over her miff and plunged into wedding preparations. When she was not following her uncontrolled desires, Rose knew how to behave, and was at her most charming, delightedly appreciative of all the Xanthakoses were doing. She wore pastel-colored dresses and matching cardigans and sandals and went into an orgy of shopping.

Camilla had bought her wedding dress at a shop near the college, knowing that if she did not choose it ahead of time her mother would want something far more elaborate.

'Shoes,' Rose said. 'We have to do something to make up for that dress. I know it's what you want, darling, but it's so plain.'

'Mother,' Camilla protested, 'this is a small and simple wedding. Just you and Father, and Mac's parents, and Frank and Luisa. A ten-foot veil would be completely out of place.'

Rose laughed. 'Don't exaggerate, darling. This is your

wedding, your wedding!' And she was off on a waterfall of reminiscences.

Camilla followed Rose from shop to shop. She would have preferred much less fuss. So, she was certain, would Art and Olivia.

Olivia said, 'Your mother is gracious indeed to allow the wedding to be here.'

'We could hardly go to Paris!'

'Nevertheless, it's generous. Let her have her fun.'

Mac reassured, 'My mother's used to this kind of wedding. It doesn't bother her, and it gives your mother so much pleasure.'

'Mac, it's supposed to be our wedding.'

'It is. I agree with you. I don't like frills, either. But it's the only thing we can give your mother.'

'But—'

His arms went around her. 'Darling, this is our wedding, and you're not like your mother, except that you have the very best parts of her, her enthusiasm, her joie de vivre, plus the stability and intelligence of your father, plus all the little lovelinesses that are yours alone.' Then his mouth was against hers. Finally he stopped long enough to say, 'If your mother hasn't been the best example in the world for you in her marriage, if your parents' problems are still unresolved, then look at my parents. Their problems are resolved, by some strange grace, but what they had to overcome to get to where they are makes Mount Everest look like an anthill.'

Camilla reached for his mouth again, first saying, 'I just hope Luisa will be tactful.'

Luisa and Frank were to arrive the day before the wedding, Frank coming all the way from Turkey and meeting Luisa in New York so they could fly down together. Once it had become apparent to Luisa that Camilla and Mac were indeed going to get married, she had dropped her dire forebodings and had become, instead, loyally supportive.

While they were waiting for Mac to bring Luisa and Frank in from the airport, and Rose and Rafferty were resting before changing for dinner, Camilla and Olivia sat out on the screened porch. The fan droned quietly overhead, stirring the breeze. Camilla loved the porch, which was more room than porch, with white wicker furniture covered in green-and-blue chintz with touches of yellow, so that there was an effect of water and sky and sunshine.

Olivia said, 'Your mother is very lovely, my dear, and your father treasures her.'

Yes, Rose had been at her most charming with Olivia and Mac, with their friends, giving no hint of the willful child. Camilla looked over at Olivia, at her slight smile, tolerant eyes. 'My father has been incredibly patient. My mother—' Her voice choked and she broke off.

Olivia nodded. 'Poor thing. It's a sad affliction when it's uncontrolled.'

'Can it be controlled?'

Olivia's mouth tightened. 'Yes, my dear. It is not easy, but it can.'

Olivia was on the chaise longue, her legs crossed at her slim ankles, her small feet in comfortable sandals. She wore tan khaki shorts and a blue shirt, an outfit Rose would never have been found in. Camilla said, 'There are times when she makes me terribly angry.'

'That's understandable. She's your mother. The biological bond can keep us from seeing clearly. It's easier for me, from my distance, to be objective, to feel compassion for her.'

Camilla leaned forward. 'Mac says that in the very early days of human beings, when the earth was sparsely populated and the tribes truly didn't know whether there would be more births than deaths, whether the human race would make it, people had to have a lot of aggression built into them, and a very strong sex drive, in order to survive.' She laughed. 'I do sound like an academic. Sorry. All I'm trying to say is that my mother didn't get the aggression, but she did get the sex drive, all out of proportion.'

'I'm glad she has your father to take care of her,' Olivia said.

'He does the best he can, without giving up his own work, and the doctor says he shouldn't do that.'

'I'm sure that's wise.'

'Being my mother's husband often seems to me to be the biggest part of his work. I hope I'll never hurt Mac.' As she said it, she laughed at how unrealistic her words were.

'Oh, my dear, of course you will. Human beings hurt each other. That's part of our humanness. But you won't hurt him the way your mother has hurt your father, so don't worry about that.'

'I do. I took a sociology course sophomore year in college. Children who have been abused often end up as abusive parents. Children of alcoholics usually swear they'll never touch a drink and yet, statistically, many of them become alcoholics.'

Olivia remarked dispassionately, 'You show no latent tendency to be like your mother. You have, I think, your father's capacity for fidelity, and also the capacity for enjoyment your mother would have had if she'd been able to grow up.'

'You're so kind to me . . .'

'My dear, I love you, and so does Art. We're grateful beyond words that Mac has you in his life.' Tiny Olivia, like her son, had a way of making people feel enfolded in love. She reached out to put her hand lightly over Camilla's, her fingertip delicately brushing over the ancient ring. 'Do you know how happy it makes me that you want my mother's rings?'

'I'm happy, too.'

'You're a deeply loving young woman, despite all your parents have put you through. It has made you strong.' Olivia paused, looking steadily at Camilla. 'Mac did good work in Kenya, but he went for the wrong reasons. You should know this, my dear, because it may happen again.'

Camilla looked her unasked question at Olivia. She did not want it to happen again. She did not know how to prevent Mac from retreating.

'Enough,' Olivia said. 'We should be concentrating on joy, not sorrow. A good, long-term marriage does not come easily. God knows it didn't for Art and me. But it's worth all the struggle.' Suddenly her blue eyes were bright with tears.

•

Rose wept tears of pleasure, of loss, at the small dinner party at the rectory the night before the wedding. After dinner Luisa, who had barely had time to change clothes because the plane was an hour late, pulled Camilla aside.

'I won't get a chance to talk to you tomorrow. Are you all right?'

'I'm fine.'

'You're really happy about marrying Mac?'

'Yes.'

'Have you—oh, shit, Camilla, are you still a virgin?' Camilla turned away. 'I know, I know, that's how it's supposed to be, but it doesn't necessarily make for a good wedding night.'

'Let me worry about that.'

'At least Mac's not a virgin. That will help. There was one girl while he was in seminary I thought he—but she suddenly married someone else.'

'Luisa,' Camilla started to protest.

'I just want things to be good for you,' Luisa said. 'You're such a nice girl, Camilla, I mean that in the best sense of the word, I don't want you to be shocked or surprised or—'

'Hey, Luisa, I do know the facts of life.'

'Be happy,' Luisa said. 'You're not like your mother; you'll enjoy without going overboard, and you're better wife material than I am.'

Frank came after them then and drew them back into the living room. 'Don't hog Camilla, Lu. People are beginning to ask where she is, and it's nearly time for the party to break up.'

When the guests left, Rose put her arms around Camilla and begged, 'Come back to the hotel with me, baby. Please. If you stay here you'll sit up all night and talk to Luisa. That girl's changed. She was really very nice to me. But I want my baby to be with me.'

It seemed the least Camilla could do. Her father stayed at the rectory, and Camilla went with her mother. While Rose was undressing, smoothing creams onto her face, her body, Camilla washed her hair in the shower, then got into a hot tub. When she went back into the room, Rose was sitting up in bed, wearing a fluffy bed jacket.

'Rafferty and I—' Rose started. 'Things have been good with us since your engagement to Mac. I don't know why it should have made such a difference, but it has.'

'That's good.'

'We've been—we hadn't been sleeping together. But now we are again, and I like that. I don't like being celibate.'

Camilla took her mother's outstretched hands with a flash of understanding. Sleeping with other men did not constitute the breaking of celibacy for Rose. If she was not making love with her husband, she was being celibate.

'It's easier for me to be good,' Rose went on, 'when it's like this, when your father and I—when I feel that he loves me.'

'You know he loves you, Mother,' Camilla said. She could not add, He wouldn't have put up with you otherwise, because that was something Rose would not understand.

'You'll be a good wife for Mac,' Rose said. 'He's a nice lad. It's too bad he's a minister, he'll never make much money. But your father and I'll see to it that you'll never want.'

'We'll manage,' Camilla said. 'We'll be fine. We don't need much.' Then, feeling ungracious, she added, 'Thanks for everything you've given me, all the lovely clothes.'

'I'm sick that you aren't going to have a proper honeymoon, just a couple of nights. Your father and I would have been glad to—'

'I know. Thank you both. But I have to finish the semester. And Mac has to get to his job.'

She lay awake beside her mother for a long time. Wondering. Uncertain. She could not speak to her mother of her doubts. Something else her mother would not understand. To her mother, marriage was still all-important, and in her mind Camilla was almost old enough to be an old maid.

She felt very cold. Understood why Mac might flee when things got too much for him. She was ready to get out of bed, get, somehow, to the airport, back to college, to safety, to certainty.

•

'I'm not certain,' she said to Mac, standing before him in the skimpy lace nightgown her mother had bought.

'Hey,' Mac said, 'don't worry. We won't rush anything.'

He picked her up and put her on the mattress of the canopied four-poster bed in the old inn where they were staying for two nights. The foreplay in which they had often indulged had delighted Camilla but—'Oh, Mac, my mother— I've been so repressed—maybe I'm frigid.'

Mac laughed. 'Not you, my love.'

'Yeah, but what's terrified me most about sex is that I've been so afraid I'd like it, and if I did, I'd become like my mother, in bed with whoever was stroking her ego—'

'Sweetie, shut up,' Mac said, and put his mouth over hers.

When she had her first orgasm she ascended like Elijah in a chariot of fire.

SIX

CORINTH WAS an inferno of heat when she joined Mac in the early summer. She had never felt such steamy humidity, even in New York, but she had seldom been in the city for the hot summer months.

The old rectory had the blessing of high ceilings and a shaded veranda, a Southern house built for shade and breeze in the summer. It had been furnished largely by the parishioners. Camilla had sent down the furniture from her little college apartment, and Mac had a few odd pieces, plus an old leather chair discarded by Art when his congregation gave him a new one. With pictures and flowers Camilla made it into their home.

Sometimes, after Mac was asleep, after their lovemaking when they were slippery with sweat, she would lie awake in bed, looking at her rings, and feeling that she had moved to a distant planet, and only the old gold circlet that had belonged to Olivia's mother was holding her together. A small parish in a Southern town was a jolting transition from a college campus in New England. She loved the beauty of the old white pillared houses, the great magnolia trees with their shiny leaves, for which Corinth was famous. But it was alien. Women still wore white gloves to church. She was expected to help with the Altar Guild, with potluck suppers, but Camilla had gone immediately to Athens, to the university, and introduced herself to Dr. Edith Edison. Had Professor Grange hinted that perhaps he and this woman had had an affair? Dr. Edison was considerably older, a striking-looking woman with snow-white hair with one black streak, and black eyebrows over near-black eyes. She welcomed Camilla with enthusiasm, and quickly arranged a teaching fellowship. Camilla's life was more in Athens than in Corinth, and this was resented by the parishioners.

'Don't fret,' Mac said. 'The idea that the rector's wife should be nothing but an appendage of the rector is long gone. I'm proud of you. Maybe you can help with the youth group. That's mainly Sunday evenings, and we work well together with kids.' Yes, they were good with kids, these Southern kids who asked most of the same questions they had heard in the old Church House. 'If God is good, why is there war?' And some newer ones which she found more disturbing. 'My father says that Negroes have a lower IQ than we do.' She let Southern Mac struggle with the racial questions, did better with the seemingly more impossible questions, such as the balance between human free will and divine omnipotence.

She also found out through those Sunday-evening meetings who the big wheels in the parish were. Freddy Lee's mother was the president of the Altar Guild; his father was a champion golfer and as far as she knew lived on inherited money.

Two of their favorites were Pinky and Wiz Morrison. Their mother was president of the ECW ('The Episcopal Church Women,' Mac explained), and their father was the town's most prominent lawyer.

Gordie Byrd was plump and pimply and always had a candy bar in his hand if not in his mouth. His mother was Mrs. Lee's sidekick in the Altar Guild, and Gordon, his father, was the town banker. It also was soon clear that Mrs. Lee and Mrs. Byrd were sisters.

'Basically,' Mac warned, 'you can't say anything about anybody, because they're all related some way or other.'

Camilla said ruefully, 'I'll try to hold my tongue. I get along better with the kids than I do with the parents.'

Mac smiled at her. 'You've never had to cope with parents before, have you? You'll be fine. They'll love you.'

Mac was unduly optimistic, she thought. One by one the women of the parish came to call, accepting glasses of iced tea, looking around the rectory to see what Camilla had done to it.

Mrs. Lee came on a Monday, with the flowers that had been used in church the day before. 'This is not our best season for flowers, Mrs. Xanthakos,' she apologized, 'but we pride ourselves on using what we have.'

'They're lovely.' Camilla took the offering and put it on the sideboard.

'And if you'll return the container on Sunday.'

'Of course.'

'Now, dear Mrs. Xanthakos, we all know how brilliant you are, getting a Ph.D. and all that, but you do have to be careful what you say to the children.'

'I try to be,' Camilla replied. 'Is there any problem?'

'Something about Mac's theory sounded a little to the left for a man of the cloth, if you know what I mean.'

Camilla didn't. Then it came to her. 'Oh! Mach's theory! It has nothing to do with my husband. It's named after a scientist named Mach, M-a-c-h. Macarios Xanthakos has nothing to do with it.'

'Oh?' Polite disbelief.

'When the youth group was over last night the dryer was going, as it so often is, and I asked them if they knew what it was about the dryer that dries the clothes.'

'Heat, of course.' The older woman sniffed.

Camilla smiled. 'Your son knew Mach's theory. Freddy's a

very bright boy. He told us that the barrel in the dryer rotates, and that produces a centrifugal force which pulls the water out. Of course, Mrs. Lee, the heat does help,' she added, trying to be polite.

'I don't know what you're talking about,' Mrs. Lee said.

'It's really fascinating.' Camilla poured more tea into Mrs. Lee's glass, noticing Mrs. Lee's eyes checking the silver pitcher, which had been a present from Art's parishioners in Nashville. 'Mach's theory is that a centrifugal force is relative to the fixed stars.'

'The what?'

'The fixed stars.' Camilla tried earnestly to explain. 'If the fixed stars weren't there, the centrifugal force wouldn't be there, either, because everything in the universe interacts with everything else. And the dryer wouldn't work and the clothes wouldn't dry.'

'This really sounds very—'

Camilla continued, her face eager, 'So the dryer in the kitchen in this one house in Corinth, Georgia, is interacting not only with the fixed stars but with the universe at large, even with the most distant stars and galaxies.'

'Dear Mrs. Xanthakos!' There was shock in the other woman's voice. 'Perhaps this is science, I gather you're quite scientific, but the young people are supposed to be given religion during their youth group meetings. I was shocked by what my nephew Gordie told me.'

'But don't you see,' Camilla urged, 'this is religion. It's an affirmation of the wonderful interdependence of the universe.'

'Mrs. Xanthakos, we expect the young people to study what is in the Bible.'

When Camilla told Mac of this conversation, he laughed heartily. 'Sweetheart, Mrs. Lee—it was Mrs. Lee, wasn't it?' She nodded. 'Mrs. Lee takes the Bible pretty literally. She doesn't get excited about the universe or Mach's theory, which

I'm sure she thinks is a Communist plot. Had Gordie Byrd been talking to her?'

'I think so.'

'That kid's a troublemaker, as bad as his father. No wonder the other kids don't trust him. They're the most reactionary family in the parish, and I'm going to have to get my Thesaurus and look up another word for integration.'

'Mac, your parents don't feel like this—'

'Of course they don't. But, as I keep telling you, they're special. Just hold off on science with Mrs. Lee and her ilk.'

Camilla was defensive. 'She asked me.'

'Oh, my darling, don't worry about it.'

'I do. The kids are okay, but when I'm with the parents I feel they're speaking a language I've never heard before.'

'You'll learn it.' Mac's smile held a tinge of sadness. 'This is not going to be the easiest parish in the world for me, but I'm convinced that they need help, and that no one is beyond help.' He sighed. 'Hey, it's a lovely evening. Let's go sit under the big pine tree and have a glass of wine before dinner, or better yet—'

'Better yet,' Camilla said.

The pine tree was protected by a thick hedge which gave them both shade from the sun lingering in the west, and privacy. This evening there was a slight breeze to cool them off. She could not get used to the unremitting heat. They bought a ceiling fan for their bedroom, which helped a little, but not enough.

Mac sifted rusty pine needles through his fingers. 'Darling, this heat is getting to you. We should get an air conditioner for the bedroom.'

'We can't afford it. Nor what it would do to our electric bill.' Camilla was determined to live on what she and Mac made.

Mac, used to the South, used to the heat, used to the rhythmic nasal accent, did not wilt, and Camilla tried not to show how difficult it was for her to acclimate.

Mac reached for her, pulled up the skirt of her cotton dress, and she turned toward him, wriggling out of her clothes, just as the phone began to ring in the rectory.

Mac jerked, startled, said reluctantly, 'I'll get it. It might be important, some crisis—'

'You'd better run.' Camilla leaned up on one elbow, sniffing the rich odor of fallen pine needles, hoping Mac wouldn't be long. She closed her eyes, waiting, drifting, letting the breeze waft over her body.

Mac came toward her, calling, 'It's your mother.'

She pulled herself to her feet, rearranged her clothes. It was not unusual for Rose to call, paying no attention to either time zones or expense. She hurried into the house and into Mac's study, where the phone was, plopped down into the brown leather chair. 'Mother?'

'Darling! Are you all right?'

'Yes, of course, Mother. Is everything okay?'

'Oh, darling baby, more than okay. I'm not in Paris, I'm in Chicago. We flew over to see my doctor and we're going back tomorrow. I had to call you.'

Camilla felt a surge of anxiety. 'Why did you need to see your doctor?'

'Oh, baby, you know we come home often. Rafferty needs to consult ... And I need to ... But this time ...' Her mother's voice was conspiratorial. 'Baby, do you have any news?'

'What?' Camilla asked blankly.

'Do you have anything to tell me? Anything special?'

Camilla held the phone away from herself, looking at it as though it were alive. She had not yet told Art and Olivia. Only Mac knew that she was pretty sure she was pregnant. She, who was regular as a clock, was three weeks overdue.

'Darling baby,' came Rose's voice, 'do you know what I mean?'

'Yes. I think so.'

'And?'

'Mother, I don't know yet. It's a possibility. How on earth did you guess?'

Rose sounded smug. 'Mothers know these things. How wonderful, how absolutely wonderful, oh, what fun!'

Camilla interrupted. 'Mother, you haven't told me why you're in Chicago to see the doctor. What's wrong?'

'I wanted to see my very own doctor, darling. You see, oh, what fun! What fun we're going to have!'

'Mother! Please tell me what this is about.'

'Darling baby, I'm pregnant, too.'

Camilla was silent with shock.

Rose said, 'Oh, baby, it's such fun. Here, let me put your father on.'

Rafferty confirmed what Rose had said. 'It's quite definite, Camilla, and the doctor said everything should be all right. Rose is in excellent health, she's still in her early forties, women are having babies later and later—'

'Father. How do you feel?'

'At first I was stunned. Unbelieving. It's been so many years since you were born, and nothing—but perhaps this is just what Rose needs.'

'What about *you*, Father? How do *you* feel about it?'

'Numb. Perplexed. When nothing happened after you were born, when it seemed that for no physical reason we were not going to have another child, I stopped thinking about it.'

'But now? Why now?'

'The doctor says that the psychological processes in a woman's becoming pregnant aren't very well known. Her pregnancy is perhaps an affirmation to Rose that she's still young. People used to talk about menopausal babies. Or it may have some connection with your marriage, with her losing, as it were, her first child.'

'She lost me, as it were, a long time ago.'

'I know that, my dear. But she's happy. I hardly remember when I've seen her this happy. Maybe when you were little.'

Camilla thought, bitterly, —Well, this may make her stay

faithful for nine months, at least. She said, 'It will make a big change in your lives, having another child.'

'I know. I doubt if Rose realizes it yet.'

'Father, is she psychologically capable of—'

He said, 'I've talked with the doctors, her obstetrician, her psychiatrist. They agree that the balance is precarious, but that she should not have an abortion. The obstetrician mentioned it as a remote possibility, and she had hysterics.'

'Father, do you want this child?'

A pause. 'Camilla, after you were born I desperately wanted another baby. I just wonder, now, after all these years, after all that has happened, is it fair to the baby? On the other hand, you've survived what Rose and I have done to you, and perhaps this child will have your resilience.'

'Mother says you're going back to Paris.'

'Yes. I could probably wind up my consulting job in a couple of months, but she has an idea that it would be romantic to have the baby in Paris. The obstetrician has given us the name of someone there she considers excellent. And you, Camilla, you're pregnant?'

'Yes. I'm pretty sure.'

Her father sounded tired. 'I don't want this in any way to take away from your own joy.'

'Oh, Father, I'm like you. I don't know what to think.' When she said goodbye, Camilla put the phone down blindly. 'Mac. Did you hear?'

'She told me,' Mac said flatly. 'I suppose it's true?'

'Father says it is. Mac, let's call Mama and Papa.'

Mama and Papa. The affectionate names slipped out easily. Since Camilla called her own parents Mother and Father, she had slipped into calling Olivia and Art Mama and Papa almost without transition.

•

Olivia and Art came, as they often did, for a midweek 'weekend,' delighted at the news of Camilla's pregnancy, accepting calmly that Rose, too, was pregnant. Art laughed so hard at Camilla's trying to explain Mach's theory to Mrs. Lee that tears streamed down his cheeks.

Olivia assured Camilla that as soon as her pregnancy was known to the parish, she would meet with approval for doing what a good young wife was supposed to do.

'What about my mother?' Camilla asked. 'Her baby will be my baby's aunt or uncle.'

They were sitting in the rectory's living room, which was partly library because one wall was covered with Camilla's books, books on astronomy and physics, the mysteries which were her relaxation, and some general reference books. Mac's theological books were half in his odd, long little office, which had been made out of one side of the garage, and half in his office in the parish house. The living room was comfortable. Olivia had brought bright cushions which hid the shabbiness of the couch. Camilla kept flowers on the coffee table in a pewter bowl Noelle had given her as a wedding present. Frank had given her a lovely antique shawl from Turkey with which she covered a scratched old sideboard too big for the dining room. Over the mantelpiece was a mirror in a gold frame. When Camilla had opened the package and read the card, *'With love from Edward Osler,'* and asked Olivia, standing beside her, who he was, Olivia had answered, 'He was one of Mac's teachers, and important in our lives,' in a tone of voice which forbade further questioning.

When there was not something blooming, she managed to make arrangements from weeds and leaves garnered from her walks.

Olivia looked around the pleasant room. 'My dears, Rose's baby isn't going to make that much difference in your own lives. You are married. You have made the rectory into a charming home. And with a baby of your own on the way, you're going to have plenty to keep you occupied. And you, Mac, have a lot of sheep under your care.'

Camilla added, 'And I'd like to get my course work finished and my thesis at least started before the baby comes.'

'Good, but don't push yourself,' Art said. 'You have time.'

'Camilla, my dear,' Olivia continued, 'there's a tradition in my family that every young mother needs help the first six weeks after a baby is born. I hope perhaps you would prefer me to a nurse.'

'Oh, Mama, yes, that would be marvelous. My own mother, well, even if she weren't pregnant with her own baby, she's used to being waited on, rather than—'

'Good. That's settled, then. Now. Art and I do have news, too. Art has been elected bishop of North Florida.'

They had known he was up for election, so the news was not a surprise.

'I think you ought to be pope,' Camilla said.

'Fortunately we don't have popes.' Art grinned. 'I'm not sure I want to be a bishop, but I've prayed about it, and it seems to be what I'm meant to do next. It's Florida, and that's home for me.'

'Jacksonville,' Olivia said, 'where Art grew up.'

'On the wrong side of the tracks,' Art said. 'I'm not too excited about living in the classy part of town in a mansion which will be a lot for Olivia to manage even with help. But it means we can spend time at the beach house, and you can come with the baby and get away from all the Mrs. Lees in the parish.'

Camilla hugged her father-in-law. 'Oh, Papa, I'm excited for you. I don't know much about what a bishop is supposed to do, but whatever it is, you'll do it superbly.' She turned to Olivia. 'Mama, are you happy?'

Olivia replied slowly, 'We've been in Nashville a long time. It's been our home. But it's time for Art to move on. Yes, I think I'm happy, though I'll miss my friends.'

'You'll make new ones,' Art assured her. 'You have a great capacity for friendship.'

'And you.' Olivia turned again to Camilla. 'Are you making friends?'

'Dr. Edith Edison, my advisor at the university, is a good friend, Mama. And I'm getting to know some really interesting people in Athens.'

'Not in Corinth?'

'I feel out of place. I don't have the right accent. I don't do the correct things, because I don't know what they are.'

Mac laughed. 'Darling, don't sound so tragic. You're doing superbly.'

Art said, 'You go to church on Sundays and sit in the front pew where the rector's wife is supposed to sit. You're learning when to stand or kneel or sit. It's a strange world for you, and you're doing nobly.'

Olivia said, 'Give yourself credit, my dear. When I married Art it was a difficult transition for me, even though I grew up in the Episcopal Church.'

Camilla smiled. 'At least I'm not trying to explain Mach's theory to anybody but the kids.'

'The kids adore her,' Mac said. 'Pinky and Wiz Morrison never used to come to youth group, their mother told me, and now they're two of the most faithful.'

•

Mrs. Lee came to call again, bringing wine jelly, an old Southern remedy for anyone who needed strengthening, and surely Camilla, in her delicate condition—

'It's too bad your parents are so far away, in Paris, did you say?'

'Yes.'

'A young woman needs her mother at a time like this. And your husband is very close to his parents, isn't he?'

'Yes. We both are. Mama—' She caught herself. Mrs. Lee would not understand Camilla's closeness to Mac's parents, her distance from her own. 'Mac's mother is going to come when the baby is born.'

'Not your own mother?'

Camilla was not going to tell Mrs. Lee that her own mother was pregnant, would be having her baby almost at the same time as Camilla's. 'Paris is very far away, and Mac's parents are wonderful.'

'You're very lucky, sugar. Not all young wives get on well with their in-laws.'

'I know I'm lucky. I love them.'

'And I gather Mr. Xanthakos is about to become a bishop?' Mrs. Lee was already basking in reflected glory.

'Yes, he is.'

'That must make you very proud.'

'It does.'

'And you, sugar, how are you feeling?'

'Oh, I'm fine. I keep having tiny contractions, but I've had them all along.'

'I don't like the sound of that. You take care of yourself, hear?'

'Oh, I do, and Mac is taking good care of me.'

'And so he should.' She looked around the room. 'My, this is attractive. I like the way you've moved things around. Those chairs by the fireplace are shabbier than they should be. I'll speak to the ladies.'

'Oh, they're fine.'

'You just leave it to me, sugar. Now watch those contractions, hear?'

'I will,' Camilla promised.

But on Christmas afternoon the contractions became labor. 'At least all the services are over,' Camilla gasped.

Mac barely got her to the hospital before she lost the baby.

•

Olivia came to bring Camilla home from the hospital. The fetus had been developing normally, the obstetrician said;

there was no apparent reason for her to have miscarried. 'But it sometimes happens. Give yourself a couple of months' respite and try again.'

'Your body is going to rebel against this interruption,' Olivia said. 'You need petting and pampering. I know you're bitterly disappointed, we all are. But there'll be more babies for you and Mac.'

A cable came from Paris in response to Camilla's letter: TERRIBLY SHOCKED AND SORRY TRIED TO PHONE ALL WELL HERE.

And then a phone call from Rose, full of murmurs of sympathy combined with exultation about her own pregnancy which left Camilla in tears. Tears of anger as well as grief.

Olivia said, 'Of course you're angry. Your mother is doing what you are supposed to do. The chronology is upside down. It's outrageous. Don't feel badly about your reaction. We all share it.'

Yes, it was upside down, as our eyes see upside down, as the camera sees upside down, and no way to right it. Camilla was ashamed at the intensity of her reaction, but there it was. Luisa helped by calling, angry about the loss of the baby, and outraged at Rose's pregnancy. 'It's absurd,' Luisa sputtered. 'Oh, Cam, if you're as angry as I am, you're raging.'

'Yes,' Camilla agreed. 'That expresses it.'

'Let it out,' Luisa advised. 'And if you can't, I'll do it for you. I'm infuriated for you. I hope you'll have twins next time. Triplets.'

'One at a time will be fine,' Camilla said.

•

On Sunday evening the youth group came, bringing a kitten, carried tenderly by Pinky Morrison. Freddy Lee brought cat food, and Gordie Byrd carried a bag of kitty litter.

A kitten to replace a baby, Camilla thought bitterly, but managed to smile, to thank them. The kitten was put in her

lap, but immediately leapt off, dashed across the room, ascended into the air and onto the sideboard, then leapt onto the
newel post, wobbled there, getting its balance, and catapulted
itself back into Camilla's lap. She could not help laughing with
the rest of them.

'Quantum!' she exclaimed. 'That's what we'll call it. It's
surely making quantum leaps.'

'What's a quantum leap?' Wiz Morrison asked.

Mac said, quickly, 'It's time for Camilla—and Quantum—to go up to bed. The doctor said she shouldn't be up for
more than a few hours.'

The young people stood, in immediate apology.

'No, no,' Camilla protested, 'you were wonderful to come.
You've made me feel much better. I'll take the kitten with me
and hope he won't leap all the way back down the stairs.'

When Mac came up she was in bed, with the kitten
curled up on her shoulder, purring in its sleep. Camilla said,
'I'm glad you stopped me from having to explain a quantum
leap. I'm sure Mrs. Lee would see it as something totally un-
scriptural.'

'Um,' Mac said. 'That's the main reason I barged in.
Freddy Lee's a nice guy, but Gordie Byrd would have found
something nasty to say. It was also time for you to get off to
bed. I've fixed a litter pan in a corner of the kitchen, and some
food and water, so let me take the little creature down and get
him used to his new dwelling.'

A week later Camilla received a call from Noelle, who
determinedly kept in touch, as though Camilla continued to be
some kind of lifeline for her. 'Oh, Cam, I'm visiting Andrew in
Atlanta. He's doing a residency at Grady, and that's a really
tough hospital, but it turns out super doctors. One of his best
pals comes from Athens, he's a favorite nephew of somebody he
calls Aunt Edith at the university, so I heard you lost a baby.
That's lousy. I'm really sorry.'

'Thanks. It happens. I'll try again.'

'Listen, we're driving over to Athens tomorrow to pick up Andrew's friend whose car has kaput'ed. Can we stop by on the way and see you for a few minutes?'

How could she say no?

Mac pointed out, 'You could say you're still getting over losing the baby.'

'I suppose I could. I don't think well when I'm taken by surprise.'

'I wish Mama'd been able to stay longer.'

'It was wonderful of her to stay as long as she did. Don't worry. Noelle and Andrew won't hang around. They're on their way to Athens to pick up this nephew of Dr. Edison's.'

'Will you be okay without me? I've got a meeting with my missions committee, and then another with my finance committee ...'

'I'm fine. I most certainly wouldn't want to see their father, but Noelle and Andrew can't be blamed for the problems he's caused us, and I guess caused them, too.'

'You're right,' Mac said. 'Don't dump a lot of junk on those kids that doesn't belong there.'

•

Noelle and Andrew arrived shortly after lunch in a battered car. Noelle was prettier than Camilla remembered, less angular, with a softer smile. Her hair was now an ash blond which suited her delicate features. Andrew was still a tall string bean of a man, no hat covering his brilliant hair this time. His green eyes were already surrounded by fine wrinkles, as though he smiled a lot.

Noelle hugged Camilla. Andrew shook hands with a good, firm clasp, saying, 'Camilla, I'm afraid this isn't a g-good time for us to come. We're really sorry about your b-baby, and Noelle wanted to come tell you in person.' His stutter was minimal.

'Where's Mac?' Noelle asked.

'He's tied up with all kinds of church meetings. He's sorry to miss you.'

'Me, too. I really loved those Sunday evenings with Mac, and you, too, Camilla, when you joined him.'

Andrew said, 'My friend's Aunt Edith thinks you are t-terrific, Camilla. She says you're the brightest l-light on the campus.'

'I think she's pretty terrific, too. I don't know what I'd do without her.' She led them toward the big pine tree. 'Let's sit outdoors. It's so warm today I really believe spring is coming.'

Andrew said quickly, 'Don't go to any b-bother for us.'

'It's no bother, and anyhow I'd like some tea myself.'

When she brought out the tea tray, Andrew hurried to take it from her, setting it down on the card table that they kept outdoors, so often forgetting to bring it in at night that the top was mottled and pocked.

Quantum, who had been having a nap in a sunny spot in the yard, suddenly appeared, seemingly out of nowhere, and in a great leap sat on Andrew's shoulder.

Startled, Andrew jumped, then put up his hand and stroked the kitten, who had started his loudest purr.

'Sorry, Andrew,' Camilla said. 'Did he scratch you?'

'No, he's fine. What a cute l-little thing.'

'His name, of course, is Quantum.'

'Of course,' Andrew said.

'Why of course?' Noelle asked.

'He j-just made a quantum leap,' Andrew explained.

'What's a quantum leap?' Noelle asked.

Both Camilla and Andrew looked at her in surprise.

Noelle defended herself. 'I majored in English. I'm not into science, like you two.'

Camilla and Andrew looked at each other. Camilla asked Noelle, 'Have you ever heard of indeterminacy?'

'Nope.'

'Heisenberg,' Andrew started. 'In the sub-atomic world we can know, for instance, either the exact position of a p-particle or its exact trajectory, b-but not both.'

'You're crazy.' Noelle poured herself more tea.

Camilla asked, 'Surely you've heard of Planck, who, at the turn of the century, realized that energy comes in tiny units he called quanta, rather than continuously.'

'Planck's h'—Andrew nodded—'is as im-important as Einstein's c.'

'C = the velocity of light,' Camilla explained.

Noelle hooted with laughter. 'You're both crazy, absolutely crazy.'

Camilla shook her head. 'No, Noelle. It's a language both Andrew and I happen to speak. I don't quote Shakespeare, and you do.'

'Shakespeare is a lot simpler.'

'Not to those who don't know it.'

Noelle took a swallow of tea. 'Mind if I change the subject?'

'T-to something important.' Andrew grinned.

'To me. I've been dating a guy from Atlanta, Cam, not one of Andrew's doctor pals, but a budding banker. Ferris Hamilton. Isn't that a Southern-sounding name? Ferris Hamilton. God, he's exciting! He's the brother of one of my college friends, and stable without being stuffy.'

'Good man.' Andrew smiled, then turned to Camilla. 'H-how's your m-mother?'

What an odd question. Then Camilla remembered that Andrew had seen Rose with his father, and perhaps more than once. 'She and my father are in Paris for a year.'

'S-she's b-beautiful,' Andrew said. 'I m-m-met h-h—' His stuttering got the better of him.

'Where?' Noelle demanded. 'Where did you meet her?'

'When I was at a con-con-con—'

'Conference?' Noelle suggested.

Andrew nodded. 'In Chi-chi-ca-g-go. W-walking down b-by the l-lake.'

'When?' Noelle demanded

'She was b-back in Chi-Chi-Chi—'

'Chicago.'

'Y-yes. They'd come b-back for a week and were staying at a ho-ho-ho—'

'Hotel.'

'Wh-while her husband d-did some kind of w-work.' He smiled rather helplessly at Camilla.

Camilla knew that her parents made frequent brief trips home for Rafferty's work, and for Rose to consult with her decorator.

The kitten leapt from Andrew's shoulder, made a wide dash around the pine tree, jumped high in the air, and then landed in Andrew's lap. Laughing, he picked up the little creature, who again snuggled up to him, purring.

Camilla smiled. 'Another quantum leap. He didn't scratch you?'

'No, not at all. Animals and I are fine together.' He smiled at her. His stutter was gone.

'Animals adore Andrew,' Noelle said. 'Animals and kids. He's like the pied piper. Cam, I'm really loving college. But I think that's going to be enough education for me. Sure, I can quote Shakespeare, but where's that going to get me in the real world?'

'More tea?' Camilla suggested.

Andrew held out his cup and she filled it. 'How are you feeling?'

'A little tired. I'm okay.'

'It t-takes the body a while.' He looked at her with real concern in his expression.

'Yes. I know.'

'You'll have another baby.' He seemed deeply anxious to reassure her.

She found that she wanted to reassure him. 'Yes. Of course I will.'

'We'd b-better get on over to Athens and leave you to rest.' He took Camilla's hand in both his strong ones. 'Thank you for being a l-lifeline for my sister.'

Camilla demurred. 'I haven't done anything.'

'You've been there for h-her when she's needed you. It's a great b-blessing.'

'He's right,' Noelle said. 'It means a lot to me to be able to keep in touch, and I do plan to keep on doing that, like it or not.' She laughed, but there was a wistfulness that touched Camilla.

'Of course, Noelle.' She gave her a quick hug, then reached out to shake hands again with Andrew. She liked the feel of his hands. He was a nice man. A good brother for Noelle.

She waved after them as they drove off.

•

When Mac came home he brought in the mail, the usual junk, plus a letter from Rafferty, full of loving concern. He said that he did not want to rub salt in her wounds, but that Rose was happier than she had been in years, full of little whims, most of which were easily satisfied: fresh figs, rather than strawberries; frequent drives in the various parks and gardens; visits to churches at odd hours—Rose had never been interested in churches. 'I suspect she's placating the gods or the saints,' Rafferty wrote. 'It seems to me it does her no harm, though I don't like to encourage superstition. However, it's no more irrational than her insistance that fresh figs are good for the baby's brain.'

The letter was not intended to hurt, but it did.

•

Memories hurt. They are not completely healed while they still hurt. Camilla had thought that she had come to terms with her memories, but it seemed that she had not. Raffi's question had precipitated her into the past, the years in Corinth, her mother's pregnancy, Mac's death, and there was still pain where she had believed there was nothing but healed scar tissue.

She got ready for bed, following her comfortable routine of bath and then some quiet reading. But she was not quiet, and the memories she had called up thus far barely scratched the surface. She could tell Raffi in a few words, "Your grandfather and I started our marriage in a small parish in Georgia, and we were happy, loving each other, making friends. I began to believe that my mother and her problems were out of my life, even when she—to my surprise—became pregnant. I lost a baby, and then I became pregnant with your Aunt Frankie."

Surely that was enough. That was all she need tell Raffi about those early years of marriage. But then—

The phone rang, and it was Frankie, who usually called at least once a week. Her calls were healing, because Frankie had made peace with her memories, was happy with who she was, what she was doing.

"Mom, are you all right?"

"Of course, fine."

"Come on, Mom. Something's wrong. Your voice is tight and hard. What's up. Is it Taxi?"

Camilla sighed. "Does it always have to be Taxi?"

"No, Mom, but it usually is. Isn't it?"

"Usually."

"What now?"

"I'm not sure. When you drove back to New York with Taxi after that medal affair, did you notice anything?"

"I'm not sure, either. He made a lot of nasty remarks about various people, and Thessaly tried to calm him down, but it wasn't all that unusual."

"But you noticed—"

"Mom. Yes. Can you tell me what's going on?"

"I don't know what's going on. He gave hints to Raffi that I'm not her—her biological grandmother. He upset her."

There was a long pause. Camilla looked at the dark windows of the French doors that led out onto a balcony where, in clement weather, she ate breakfast. She waited. Finally Frankie said, "Mom, you and Dad let Taxi live with a lie."

"Was it a lie?"

"Yes, Mom, it was. Maybe it was a lie more of omission than commission, but it was still a lie."

"Taxi was so passionate about it, about not wanting to talk—"

"And you and Dad let the silence go on and on. Until it was too late."

"But why now?" Camilla asked. "Why would he want to hurt Raffi?"

"To hurt you, Mom, even if he has to do it through Raffi."

"Raffi wants to know—"

"Are you going to tell her?"

"Yes. I think I have to."

"Good. Oh, Mom, darling, I don't mean to accuse you, or to judge. But silence isn't always golden."

"No. I know. I know."

"Listen, Mom, I love you. You've been—you are—a terrific Mom, to both Taxi and me. Don't ever forget that."

"But terrific Moms make mistakes—"

"All Moms make mistakes. It's easy for me to judge, because I'm not a mother myself, I haven't had the experience of trying to do my best and having it come back and hit me in the teeth. I love you, Mom, and I'll call you in a few days. This, whatever it is, this, too, shall pass."

•

Winter passed. Spring came to Corinth with the loveliness of flowering trees and bushes. The rectory was surrounded with the brilliance of azaleas. Camilla enjoyed her work with the youth group, many of whom had shed sweaters and jeans for bright cottons. She did her best not to shock Mrs. Lee or the other women of the parish. Her work at the university in Athens was challenging, and Dr. Edison became Edith, or Dr. Edith, as Mac frequently called her.

And then there were the plans for Art's consecration as bishop. Olivia drew Camilla in, not only for the great service at the Cathedral, but into the redecoration of the big house on the St. Johns River, sending her swatches of wallpaper or curtain material, and colors of paint.

Art and Olivia were staying in the beach house while the house on the river was being fixed up, and two days before the consecration Camilla and Mac flew down to Florida to join them. Spring was warming, but not heating the air. Camellias were in bloom. New leaves were pushing off the old ones on the water oaks. Mockingbirds were singing. Camilla was pregnant.

She spent the day in Jacksonville with Olivia, walking through the large old house which was the bishop's residence, approving the wallpaper Olivia had chosen, delighted with the big kitchen, which, like all the rooms at the back, looked across the lawn to the great river.

'Everything I need,' Olivia said happily. 'A big freezer. Two ovens. Let's go upstairs. I love this staircase, the graceful way it curves. We'll put a love seat on the landing.' Olivia showed her a large, light bedroom which faced the river. 'This, dearest daughter, will be for you and Mac. And there will be a room for the baby.'

'Oh, Mama, thank you.'

'You can take a rest here after we've had lunch, before we drive back to the beach. You're sure your doctor said it's all right to drive?'

'I'm fine, Mama. Everything is going beautifully this time.'

'We won't go up to the attic. It's not an easy house. Too

much of it. But the diocese insists that I have more help than
I think I need, so we'll manage.'

'It's a big change for you,' Camilla said.

'When I married Art I knew it would mean periodic uprooting. You'll go through it, too. Mac won't stay in that cozy
little parish in Corinth for too long, and it's not going to go on
being cozy indefinitely. Corinth is a big name for a little town,
and big tempests brew in little teapots.'

'Are you speaking from experience?' Camilla asked.

'Naturally. When I left Charleston and moved to Memphis it was almost as much of an uprooting for me as this move
to Florida. But I began my marriage in Memphis, and Mac
was born there. And then we moved to Nashville, and I was
very happy there for a great many years. I think I'll be happy
here, too, as long as Art is happy. I'm grateful for the river.
Now, my dear, we'll have a quick sandwich, and then you'll lie
down. We want you to keep this baby.'

•

The day of the consecration was sunny, but not yet into
the steamy heat which would settle in by the next month. The
windows in the Cathedral were open, and a soft breeze kept the
great space cool. Camilla sat beside Olivia in eager anticipa-
tion. One of Bach's majestic toccatas and fugues poured out of
the organ. Then came the procession. And finally the presiding
bishop began, his voice solemn, sonorous. Camilla's attention
was focused more on Mac's face as he stood beside his father in
his priest's vestments than on what was going on. What she saw
in both Mac's and Art's faces was a love that was radiant.
Ardent, she thought—in French *ardent* means aflame, as the
burning bush was aflame and yet was not consumed.

She was hardly aware of the words of the consecration
service until Olivia's hand in hers suddenly tightened.

'Brothers and sisters in Christ Jesus, you have heard tes-
timony given that Artaxias Xanthakos has been duly and law-

fully elected to be a bishop in the Church of God to serve in this diocese. You have been assured of his suitability and that the Church has approved him for this sacred responsibility. Nevertheless, if any of you know any reason why we should not proceed, let it now be made known.'

Olivia's grasp tightened, tightened, for the brief moment of silence.

Then the deep voice asked, 'Is it your will that we ordain Artaxias Xanthakos a bishop?'

The congregation shouted out, 'That is our will.'

'Will you uphold Artaxias Xanthakos as bishop?'

'We will!'

Slowly, slowly, Olivia's grip relaxed.

•

There was a reception after the service, enthusiastic congratulations, voices rising. Art and Olivia were gracious, bowing, smiling, letting themselves be surrounded, hugged, kissed. Camilla felt as she felt at most large parties, uncomfortable and out of place. But she stood beside Mac, with her smile frozen on her face. She, too, was being shown off, the new bishop's nearly new daughter-in-law.

It was dusk when they got back to the beach.

Art said, 'I need to lie down for a while. I've stood for too long on these old feet.'

'I'm going for a walk,' Mac said. He did not ask Camilla to go with him.

Olivia said, 'I have chicken salad in the refrigerator, and deviled eggs. We'll eat in about an hour.' She turned to Camilla. 'Let's pour ourselves something cool to drink, and sit on the porch.'

Art went upstairs, his footsteps heavy. Tired.

Camilla and Olivia sat on the high-backed green rockers and watched Mac walking up the beach. He had taken off his shoes and socks, rolled up his trousers, and was splashing along at the water's edge, occasionally bending down to pick up a shell.

'Mama—' Camilla's voice held a question.

'What, my dear.'

'During the service—was anything wrong?'

For a long time Olivia was silent. Then she said, 'I clutched you pretty tightly for a moment, didn't I?' Camilla nodded. 'There is no reason Art should not be consecrated bishop.'

'Of course not.'

'But sometimes the past rears its ugly head, if it is known.' She was silent again.

Camilla waited. Listened. The waves rolled in to shore with regular, peaceful breathing. A small breeze stirred the sea oaks on the dunes. A seagull called. Somewhere behind them a mockingbird sang an achingly sweet melody.

'I grew up in Charleston, as you know,' Olivia said at last. 'Insular. Protected. Loved. My playmates were mostly cousins. We had great imaginations for our games, but as far as the rest of the world was concerned, we were moderately thoughtless. There were skeletons in the closets as there are in most families, but they stayed decently behind closed doors. Reality broke in when my father returned from the First World War. Each war has its phrases that come into the vocabulary. "Shell shock" was the one that war brought in. My father was like a ghost in the house, until he swam out to sea. An accident, the paper said. Everybody said. Even then it was my belief that he knew he was killing my mother and he didn't know how to stop except by killing himself. But I held my peace. There are some things better not talked about.'

Camilla sat quietly, nodding agreement, not sure where this conversation was going.

Olivia said, 'My mother died when I was a freshman in college. I scandalized her and all my kin by going to Duke, but she was, in a way, proud of me. That wasn't what killed her.

Cancer did. So both my parents were dead when I met Art, and that was just as well. If they'd known he was going to end up a bishop they might have been reconciled. What snobs we are. As it was, the great-aunts with whom I was living thought I was marrying into the gutter and were grateful my poor parents hadn't lived to see the day. Nevertheless, they stood by me, and we were married at St. Michael's, and then I went with Art to Memphis.'

Olivia rocked in her green chair, back and forth, back and forth, the old wood squeaking as though in pain. Camilla glanced at her, saw a face drawn with distress, and turned her eyes back to the ocean.

'Art's background was completely different from mine. Grinding poverty, though by the time Art was a teenager his father had done amazingly well financially. But he was a strange and primitive man. Dominant. Determined that Art should have all the educational advantages he had not had or even dreamed of. But he also abused Art, physically. Sexually. His wife knew about it. There was no attempt at secrecy. She was a passive woman, assuming that this was the way men were, using, abusing. It was their right.'

Camilla moaned softly.

'It was not unique,' Olivia said. 'It happens in all cultures. It was primitive, but not unique. Art grew up accustomed to brutality. Determined to get away from it. Thought he had by the time he had graduated from seminary, had his first church. Was certain he had by the time he married me.' She looked up, saw Mac coming toward them, up the ramp that led from the beach, over the dunes, to the house. 'Oh, God.'

'Mama?' Camilla asked softly.

'Dearest daughter,' Olivia whispered. 'Enough for tonight. It's all I can—'

Mac came up onto the porch. 'All hail, you two.'

'All hail, my son,' Olivia said.

Mac sat down beside them. 'I wish we didn't have to go back to Corinth tomorrow. I love the beach. Peace.'

Art came out, letting the screened door slam softly behind him. 'Peace. Yes. Thank God.'

•

Peace? Camilla wondered. Olivia had more to tell her, and she had no idea what. Did Mac know that his father had been abused? She visualized Art, and the quiet wisdom in his face, and could not imagine his childhood. How could a father— She thought of her own father. Surely "reticent" would be a good adjective for him.

She woke up during the night. Mac was breathing peacefully beside her. The waves rolled in to shore in a slightly different rhythm. The wind in the palms sounded like paper rattling. She found herself wondering again about what Olivia had told her. It had nothing to do with the great service in the Cathedral, and yet something there had caused Olivia's anxiety.

She remembered her own words about abused children often becoming abusive parents. Surely that was not true in this case. Mac's love and respect for his father was evident. Olivia would never have stood silently by and let her son be abused. Art would not be the Papa she loved if he had acted with that kind of violence.

If she asked Luisa, speculating on an imaginary case, Luisa would guess that her interest was not academic.

She sighed, pushed closer to Mac. If there was more to tell, ultimately Olivia would tell it.

•

Back in Corinth, she had to continue learning to be a rector's wife. As her first pregnancy had helped, so had the baby's loss. For a while she was "our dear little rector's poor wife." She was not going to talk about her present pregnancy until she began to show enough so that it was obvious.

She was watched carefully by her obstetrician. As the heat progressed, so did her fatigue. She had a hard time sleeping. She felt comfortable only at the university, and in Dr. Edison's office, which was in one of the air-conditioned new buildings. Even the university, with its emphasis on sororities and fraternities, was very different from the New England atmosphere of her own college. At first she had thought the students frivolous, that this was a party school, but she came to recognize a core of students as bright and eager as any at her egghead Ivy League school, and a faculty equally dedicated.

The uprooting from New York, the living in Italy, the traveling during vacations, the move to Chicago, should have prepared her for radical changes in culture. Perhaps it had, to some extent.

She cooked a spaghetti dinner for the youth group. Invited the ladies of the Altar Guild for tea, and suspected that they were looking surreptitiously at her waistline. She began her dissertation, which Dr. Edith told Mac was innovative and was going to be worthy of publication.

'I told you you were brilliant!' Mac crowed. 'That's my Camilla. Your profs appreciate you, even if the parishioners are out to trip you.'

'I used to be very good at skipping rope,' Camilla said modestly. 'I'm not as easily tripped as I was at first.'

Their phone was constantly busy. They had two lines, one for their private use, and when Mac was in his office she could ignore the parish ring.

The home number was used regularly by Art and Olivia. Rose and Rafferty called nearly every week. Occasionally Frank, who was engaged to his girlfriend, gave them a call. One day Camilla picked up the phone and heard Noelle Grange's voice.

'Camilla, I'm in the airport in Atlanta, so I thought we could at least talk for a couple of minutes.'

'Fine. Is everything okay?'

'I'm in love. I mean really in love, and I think it's going to lead to something real. I mean permanent. I mean marriage.'

'That's wonderful. Who is he?'

'The guy I told you about when Andrew and I dropped by. Ferris Hamilton. He's in the Harvard Business School now. He's going to be a banker, here in Atlanta, in the family bank. But he's gentle and understanding and not a bit of a chauv. I wish you could meet him.'

'I wish I could, too.'

'Listen, Camilla, I need your advice. I mean, I adore Ferris. I wish our lives began on the day we met. But they didn't. What I mean is, I always want to be truthful with Ferris. But we can't tell anybody everything, can we? So what I want to know is, how much do I need to tell him to be the kind of truthful I want to be? I haven't done a lot of sleeping around. You know that. But a couple of times— So. How much?'

'That's something you have to figure out for yourself.'

'Were you and Mac—did you tell each other?—like, everything?'

'Yes.'

'Was it okay?'

'I'm not sure what okay means. It was essential.'

'That's what Andrew says. He's engaged to one of his classmates. She's terrific. But—Andrew hasn't lived a wild life, he's good, I mean, Andrew's really good. But human. Like, we all make mistakes. Andrew's no exception, and I guess that's a relief to me. He had one sort of fling when he was taking a course in pediatric cardiology at the University of Chicago, just after he met his Liz, but before they— And I think there was another, when he was in Cleveland for some conference. He told Liz. All about it. And Liz told him—about some guy when she was in college, who turned out to be a real creep. I guess I've answered my own question. I guess Ferris and I need to do some talking. But it scares me.'

'Of course it does. But if you're honest with someone, and he doesn't respect you for it, or if he turns against you, the sooner you know, the better.'

'I think I'd die if Ferris turned against me.'

'No, you wouldn't. And if he's as wonderful as you think he is, he won't.'

'Okay. I guess. It was okay with Andrew and Liz. She's good for him. He hardly ever stutters when he's with her. As for my parents—' Noelle paused. 'Things are definitely not good. I've told Ferris about them, and he was really understanding. I'm glad Andrew and I are at a wide geographical distance from them. When we're around they tend to drag us into their morass.'

'Rough,' Camilla murmured.

'Mom and Dad both miss New England. They're both restless. Dad's gone off on a work leave to put some distance between them. He's more or less going around the world, all through Europe, Asia, Africa. He's a good professor, otherwise he wouldn't get away with it, and Mom's got a lot of clout. I'm just as happy to have all the space possible between Dad and me, too. Well, it's time for my flight to be called. I just thought it would be nice to hear your voice. 'Bye, Cam.'

'Goodbye, Noelle.' Camilla had heard more of Noelle's voice than Noelle had of hers, but that was all right. That had always been their pattern, Noelle talking, Camilla listening. She had no real answer to Noelle's question. She believed that honesty was important, but also privacy. What Mac had told her about Cissie, about Korea, did not have to be spread abroad. There was a fine line between confession and discretion, and she did not know where it lay.

How did Professor Grange justify a trip through Europe, Asia, Africa, to the astronomy department in Chicago? Probably he was dropping in at various universities with good observatories. She did not want to think about Professor Grange. She hoped he was out of her life forever.

She was about to be Dr. Camilla Dickinson, and what was she going to do with her doctorate? Dr. Dickinson in Athens,

Mrs. Xanthakos in Corinth. Right now it was enough to be Mac's wife, to think about their coming baby.

At her next visit the obstetrician said, 'You may not realize it, Camilla, but you're overtired. Stay in bed for a few days, read something relaxing. Forget that such a thing as a vacuum cleaner exists.'

'That's not hard.' Camilla laughed. 'I never remember the vacuum cleaner unless it's absolutely necessary.'

Olivia came up from Jacksonville to help out until the doctor allowed Camilla to resume normal activities. She sat on the foot of the big brass bed and said, 'One thing Art and I can do for you is get someone to come in to do the heavy cleaning. It's more important for you to be able to drive over to the university than to clean house. We're going to do everything we can to make sure this baby arrives safely, and at term. Have you told your parents?'

'Not yet. I thought I'd wait until I get a little further along.'

Olivia looked at her thoughtfully, and Camilla realized that if her mother had been like Olivia she'd have been on the phone immediately.

'You'll have to have an air conditioner here in the bedroom,' Olivia decided. 'Let us do that for you, too. Now. How's your mother?'

They could talk about the air conditioner later. 'Fine. Father says she's quite big, but that doesn't bother her, she still thinks it's all marvelous.'

'I'm glad she's doing well. All right, love, you nap now. I have a few things to do.'

Olivia found a young woman who would come and clean the house. She bought and saw to the installation of a window air conditioner, despite their protestations.

'If your mother knew you were pregnant in the Georgia heat she'd be out buying air conditioners first thing. Meanwhile, let Art and me take care of it. Forget your pride. It's for a good cause. Mac may be used to the heat, but you need to be cool enough to sleep at night.'

Camilla had been using the sheet only to wipe away the sweat. She could not disagree. The air conditioner blocked the view of the pine tree, which Camilla regretted. But she also knew that she would sleep better at night.

Again the parish rallied round, bringing baked custard, flowers, a pretty bed jacket, delighted to have a bishop's wife in Corinth even for a few days, basking in reflected glory, asking Olivia to tea with the Altar Guild, to the Garden Club meeting, hosted by Mrs. Lee's sister, Alberta Byrd, who did not approve of Camilla's work in Athens.

'Don't fret,' Olivia said. 'The rector's wife always gets criticized.'

When Mac left the house in the morning Camilla and Olivia had long talks, lingering over the milky coffee Olivia brought Camilla with her breakfast.

Olivia said, 'I don't want to talk overmuch about this baby until you feel life and we're more secure, but we still have Mac's crib and quite a few other things we've been saving for our grandchildren.'

Camilla stretched luxuriously. 'I think this baby's taken. I haven't had any of the little contractions I had before, and I was a lot more nauseated during the first few weeks, so I think everything's proceeding normally.' She put her hands across her belly, enjoying the roundedness, which was more pronounced each day.

The day before Olivia was to return to Jacksonville, and Camilla would be allowed to resume moderate activity, Camilla and Mac received a letter from Frank. He was being married in England, in Cambridge, and he wanted them to be there, to get to know his bride, and he hoped Mac would be his best man.

'It's too bad,' Mac said, 'but of course we can't go.'

'Of course you can go,' Camilla said.

'But you—'

'I can't. I know that. But you have to go. It's only right and proper that you should be Frank's best man, as he was yours. He came all the way from Turkey to us. I'd feel terrible if you didn't go because of me. I'll be fine. Truly.'

Olivia nodded. 'I'll come stay with Camilla while you're away, Mac, and you don't have to be gone more than a few days.'

'You really think—'

'It's Frank,' Olivia said, as though that settled everything.

Olivia returned to Jacksonville and Camilla went back to Athens to teach two classes. Each afternoon she spent a couple of hours lying down, grateful for the air conditioner. She read mystery stories, theology, physics. Wrote a paper that Dr. Edison told her would be published in the *University Quarterly,* a modest honor, but one which pleased her.

Sometimes she lay with her eyes closed, making patterns with numbers. She started with the Fibonacci series, in which each succeeding number is equal to the total of the preceding two: 1,1,2,3,5,8. Then, onto games of her own: the square of any number is one more than the multiple of the two numbers on either side of it. $5 \times 5 = 25$. $4 \times 6 = 24$. And $7 \times 7 = 49$. $6 \times 8 = 48$.

Take it further. Multiply two numbers separated by one number. The answer will be three numbers more than the multiple of the numbers on either side. $3 \times 5 = 15$. $2 \times 6 = 12$. $4 \times 6 = 24$. $3 \times 7 = 21$.

And one more step. Multiply two numbers separated by two numbers. The answer will be four numbers more than the multiple of the numbers on either side. $3 \times 6 = 18$. $2 \times 7 = 14$. And $7 \times 10 = 70$. $6 \times 11 = 66$.

She visualized the patterns on imaginary graph paper, delighted at their beauty. She told Dr. Edison of her pleasure in these mathematical designs, and Dr. Edison jumped into the game, making it more complex, using fractions as well as whole numbers to add to the intricacy of the flowering patterns.

Finally Camilla wrote her parents that she was pregnant again, and that all was going well this time. The babies would be only a few months apart. She still could not quite visualize that her baby would be able to play with her own baby brother or sister. She could not quite comprehend having a baby brother or sister. When she was a teenager, maybe. But not now.

'What you must think about now,' Mac said, holding his hand to Camilla's belly to feel the soft stirrings of the baby, 'is taking care of yourself.' He looked tired, and she reached up to touch his face. It would be good for him to get away from the parish tensions, even if only for a few days.

Frederic Lee, the senior warden, had come to Mac with the appalling news that the Morrisons and the Byrds were in the process of divorcing. Lydia Morrison was seen with Gordon Byrd at the country club. Alberta Byrd had gone to Herb Morrison for counsel over her divorce. This was the biggest tempest to hit the teapot of Corinth in recent memory, and passionate discussion went on for weeks, with people taking sides, and Mac trying to keep them from doing so.

On Sunday evening at the youth group Gordie Byrd had asked loudly during prayer time for Lydia Morrison to leave his father alone. Pinky and Wiz shouted in anger. Mac finally had to roar, 'Quiet! All of you! Gordie, we do not use prayer time to attack each other or to manipulate God.'

Wiz muttered, 'Do that again, Gordie, and I'll kill you.'

Freddy Lee said, 'This is a lousy situation for all of us, but let's not take it out on each other. Wiz, please.'

'They don't think about us, do they?' Pinky demanded.

Freddy said, 'Hey, the only thing we can do is try not to be like our parents. I mean, we live in a different world.'

Gordie said, 'It certainly isn't any better. At least people used to know their places.'

They were heading into another potentially explosive subject. 'Let's turn to the Psalms,' Mac said. 'Freddy, read Psalm 121 for us.'

Later that night he said to Camilla, 'What a mess. I didn't handle that very well, did I?'

'About as well as it could be handled.'

'And I'm going off to England right in the middle of this. It's terrible timing.'

'It's Frank's wedding,' Camilla reminded him. 'If you're not here, they can't use you as a whipping post. Maybe when you come back it will all have blown over.'

'That's wishful thinking. And the kids will all want to come dump on you. Are you sure you'll be all right?'

'Sure. I love the kids, and I'll try to steer the conversation into some kind of quiet waters.'

'Watch out for Gordie.'

'Will do.'

In the morning, after Mac had left for his office, Pinky Morrison knocked on the kitchen door. She was indeed pinky, her face flushed from much weeping.

'Camilla, can I come in?'

'Of course.'

'I hate Gordie Byrd.' Camilla waited. Pinky sat on the couch, hiccuping her anguish. 'I thought Daddy was perfect. He was like a god to me.'

At least Noelle had not made that mistake, and her brittle anger had been better protection than Pinky's raw grief. Camilla put her arm about the girl's shoulders. 'No one is perfect, Pinky. You can't put that load on anyone, even your father. He's hurting over this, too.'

'Is he? He and Mom talk about it all the time, about finding fulfillment and all that stuff, as though breaking up a marriage didn't matter. As though Wiz and I don't matter. Wiz isn't saying anything but he's a total mess. I hate them! I hate them all!'

'It's okay to be angry.' Camilla spoke calmly, firmly. 'You'll get through it, Pinky.'

'Did you? I mean, did you ever get angry at your parents?'

A slightly hysterical laugh bubbled up in Camilla's throat. 'Oh, yes, Pinky. But I got through it.' Any number of times.

Mac came home for a sandwich and lemonade, and then Camilla walked wearily upstairs and lay down on the bed, falling into a deep sleep.

The phone woke her. She answered groggily, then was shocked into wakefulness as she heard her father's voice, calling from Paris, the line crackling as though echoing his anguish.

'Camilla. Terrible news. Rose was out shopping. Things for the baby. Coming home in a taxi. An accident.' He jerked the sentences out. 'She was killed. They rushed her to the hospital, but she— They did a cesarean section. The baby's alive. He'll be all right—it's a little boy. He needs a transfusion and I'll give blood for that. They're cross-matching the blood right now. But Rose is dead, Camilla, Rose is dead.'

'Oh, Father,' she kept saying. Then, 'Call me right after the transfusion. Please. To see if the baby's all right. To see if you're—'

'I'll call,' he said. 'Rose is dead, is dead.'

•

After her father had hung up, Camilla lay there, unable to accept what he had told her. It had occurred to her that her mother might have problems giving birth. But not this—this irrational wiping out of life, just a few weeks before the baby was due to be born.

All she could think of was Rose's constantly stretching out toward life, greedily, always searching for something she could not reach.

She lay flat on the bed, her hands over her belly as though to protect her baby. The quick and the dead, as the Book of

Common Prayer had it. "Quick" was a good word, a live, living word. She felt it, quickening, the affirmation of life within her.

Rose was dead, dead before she ever saw the baby she awaited so eagerly. Rose is dead, Rafferty had said, is dead, is dead.

But they had saved the baby. Camilla had read newspaper accounts of such modern miracles. Probably this, too, would get into the papers, at least in Paris. BABY DELIVERED FROM MOTHER KILLED IN ACCIDENT.

—My brother, she thought suddenly.

She lay there numbly, holding the quick life within her, until Mac came home.

'Oh, my darling,' he moaned, and in the protection of his arms her tears came.

He lay down beside her, putting his hand on her belly. Feeling. Listening.

She said, 'I was so angry when I lost the baby and Mother kept hers. And now—'

'Hush,' he soothed. 'You didn't hold on to your anger. You let it go.'

Tears came again, more quietly now. 'Ambivalent,' she said. 'The best I felt was ambivalent.'

'Hush. You loved her. Let yourself grieve.'

'I did my grieving years ago. My mother died to me when I discovered she was having an affair and trying to use me as a shield to keep it from my father. I was a naïve adolescent to have clung to the image of Mother as perfect virtue for so long. She was so beautiful she had to be good. And when she wasn't, it was death. As much death as—'

The phone rang. Mac was lying on the side of the bed by it. He had done his best to discourage parishioners from calling in the evening, except in an emergency. This was Pinky's mother and the emergency had been going on for weeks.

'I'm sorry,' he said, 'I can't talk now. We're waiting for an overseas call. Camilla's mother has been killed in an accident.'

The parish would have to know sooner or later. Camilla could hear little shrieks of horror from the other end of the line. Mac replaced the receiver, firmly. Pinky's mother would be busy now, spreading the news.

They lay together quietly until the phone rang again. Mac picked it up. 'Rafferty, we're so terribly sorry—'

Then Camilla could hear her father's voice, but not his words, could see Mac's face become still as stone. Then, 'No, Rafferty, we can't come. Camilla's pregnancy is still precarious . . . No, I'm sorry . . . As soon as the baby is old enough to travel, you come to us . . . You can't leave the baby, Raff . . . No . . . He is, after all, Rose's baby . . . I'll tell Camilla . . . You call us tomorrow when you've had time to—' Then he held the phone out as though it had been slammed down on the other end of the line.

'What?' Camilla demanded. Then, 'Mac, what did Father say?'

'Your father's blood is the wrong type for the baby.'

'But is the baby all right?'

'Yes. He's all right. But it's bad news.'

'What?'

'You see, your father's blood and the baby's—'

'Go on.'

'Your father said the doctor told him quite bluntly.'

'What, Mac?'

'Rafferty isn't the baby's father.'

SEVEN

THEY CALLED FLORIDA, Mac simply stating the facts in a flat, unemotional voice while Camilla listened on the bedroom extension.

For a moment there was silence at the other end of the line, then a low cry from Olivia.

Mac said, 'Mama, you are coming tomorrow as planned, aren't you?'

'Of course I'm coming. You'll need me more than ever now.'

Mac said, 'Thank you, Mama. It makes me feel much better about leaving Camilla.'

'Leaving—'

Mac's voice continued, without timbre. 'Mama, you do remember that I'm going to England.'

Art's voice came on the other line. 'But Frank—'

Mac cut across his father's words. 'Frank needs me.'

Camilla let the phone drop beside her on the bed. Mac was downstairs in the study for the usual four-way conversation.

'Cam!' His voice floated up the stairway. 'Where are you?'

She picked up the phone. She could hardly get the word out. 'Here.'

'Oh, my dear.' Olivia's voice sounded flat. Then, 'I'll see you tomorrow.'

Mac's feet could be heard coming up the stairs slowly, not his usual leaping up two or three steps at a time. When he stood in the doorway she did not look at him. She could not stop the tears from sliding down her cheeks. Rose is dead, is dead. Mac is going to Korea, to Kenya, to—to England, to Frank. Oh. Father, poor father . . .

She felt a fresh surge of anger, whether at her mother once more, even in death, revealing her infidelity, or at Mac for his—

So? she asked herself. Mac already had the tickets to England, a special rate; he would be penalized if he canceled or put his flight off.

He went down to the kitchen and returned with hot milk and nutmeg in one of the mugs they had saved from the Church House, cracked and stained, but treasured. He put the "Dumky" Trio on the turntable. Quantum followed him into the room and jumped onto the bed, peering at Camilla anxiously, then beginning to purr.

Again, tears filled her eyes. But that was all right. If she wept he would think it was for Rose, for Rafferty, for the baby.

She pressed her knuckles against her lips to try to stop. But she did not speak to him about her feeling of abandonment. She could not bring herself to say, 'Mac, please don't leave me now. I need you.'

'Mother,' Frankie had once said, 'the trouble with you is that you will avoid confrontation at any cost.'

But what good, in most cases, would confrontation do? It would only exacerbate what was already pain and anger.

Would Mac have stayed if she had asked him?

•

Olivia arrived the next afternoon. Mac had packed quietly, taking his clothes out of the closet, out of drawers, down to his study, leaving quietly as soon as he had kissed his mother goodbye. Camilla went downstairs and sat in the rocking chair in the kitchen, a chair which had been given them by the ladies of the Altar Guild. She had made chicken salad, sliced some tomatoes and sweet onions with basil. That would be plenty for dinner for herself and Olivia.

Olivia perched on one of the kitchen stools. 'How are you, dearest child?'

'Okay.'

'Baby still kicking away?'

'Yes.'

'Does that help?'

'Yes.'

Olivia hooked her little feet, in grey suede pumps, on one of the rungs of the stool. She opened her mouth to speak, then closed it, finally asked, 'Is the air conditioner helping?'

'Yes, and thank you, Mama. The bedroom would be a steamy jungle without it.'

'When Mac returns—' Olivia started.

Camilla looked directly at Olivia, elegant in a grey skirt and grey silk blouse, a cameo at her neck, elegant and beloved. 'You told me it would happen again, Mac's leaving.'

'The sins of the fathers. I don't know. Mac's a grown man. We can't—'

'No.'

'In the past we have found it best not to do anything. Or perhaps we are afraid to do anything, to say no, Mac, not now, you can't go off and leave your wife now.' Then she looked at Camilla. 'Did you ask Mac to stay?'

Camilla shook her head.

Olivia sighed. 'It's hard for us to overturn our background. I, too, was brought up not to ask. It's almost impossible to unlearn.'

Camilla sat back in the rocking chair, closed her eyes,

then opened them, questioning. 'Mama, will he come back? This is not Kenya. He won't go and then stay away for a year ...'

Olivia slid down from the high stool. 'He's going to Frank. Therefore I know he will come back.' She went to the fridge and opened the door. 'Let's eat upstairs in the bedroom where it's at least ten degrees cooler.'

•

Rafferty called while they were eating in the bedroom, taking advantage of the air conditioner. The atmosphere outside was thick, with a low growling in the background. Somewhere a storm was brewing. With the change of time it must have been midnight or after in Paris.

'I don't know what to do, I don't know what to do,' Rafferty kept saying.

'The baby—is the baby going to be all right?'

'He'll live. They gave him a blood transfusion and he's going to make it. What on earth am I going to do with him? What on earth?'

Olivia had gone downstairs to the phone in the study. 'Right now, Rafferty, you need some sleep.'

'Rose—Rose—the funeral—'

'What about it, Father?' Camilla asked gently.

'There's a little church not far from—one night she said that if anything happened she wanted to be buried there. I thought she was just being morbid. I spoke to the priest—we're not Catholics—he wasn't sure—'

'Father,' Camilla said despairingly, 'I don't want you to have to go through this alone.' She had called her doctor, who had said, 'Do you wish to lose your baby in Paris? I'm sorry, Camilla, I can guess how you're feeling, but I don't want you farther from the hospital than the university.'

Olivia spoke with quiet authority. 'Rafferty, Art, my husband, will be with you. We have discussed this, and he will fly to Paris tomorrow. Camilla can't come, you know that, but you will not be alone.'

'I'll be most grateful,' Camilla heard her father saying. Again, tears rushed to her eyes, this time tears of awe at what Art and Olivia were offering.

•

Art and Olivia.

Mama and Papa.

"They were there for me," Camilla told Raffi. "They made all the difference."

Raffi's boots were kicked under the sofa. She sat cross-legged, as Mac had so often sat. Scratched her foot through her heavy green sock. "It's a crazy story, Grandmother."

"As your father remarked, it out-soap-operas his show." —And I haven't told you all, and won't.

Raffi pulled off her sock and inspected her foot. "I need to cut my toenails. Oh, Grandmother, why didn't I know all this long ago?"

"Perhaps the timing wasn't—" Camilla broke off. "I don't know, Raffi."

"I can't imagine it," Raffi said. "I mean, I can't imagine me being pregnant, and Mom being pregnant, too." She pulled off her other sock. "My poor dad. What a way to get born."

What a way.

Even in the midst of it Camilla balked at the irrationality of the situation.

She wanted Mac.

•

Olivia brought Camilla a cup of tea. Camilla leaned up on one elbow to take the cup. 'It's so wonderful of Papa to do this, to go be with my father.'

'Not wonderful at all,' Olivia said. 'Necessary. Rafferty

should not be alone. He is in no condition to make decisions by himself. He needs someone to be there for him. To listen. To care.'

'He's got to be angry.'

'Anger and grief and confusion all mixed together. Yes. Drink your tea, sweetheart. I don't want you getting dehydrated.'

The air conditioner buzzed steadily, fighting the heat. There was too much to absorb. Rose's death. The baby who was not Rafferty's. Rose, Camilla felt occasionally, was within telephoning distance. Mac was not. Upside down. Everything was once again upside down.

The phone rang. Rafferty and the bishop calling. Rafferty sounded a little more in control. 'Art found another church, not far. The priest was kind. It will all be quiet and dignified. She would have liked more of a splash, but—this is the best we can do.'

The bishop asked, 'How are my girls? Camilla?'

'I'm fine. Mama is being wonderful.'

'We're about to turn in for the night.'

'The baby. What about the baby?'

The bishop said, 'There'll be time to talk about all that later. Now let me say good night to Olivia.'

At bedtime Olivia came into Camilla's room, stood looking around as though seeing for the first time the crisp white curtains at the windows, the pale lemon-yellow walls, the polished hardwood floor, the big brass bed. 'My dear—'

'What is it, Mama?'

'May I sit down?' Without waiting for an answer Olivia sat on the side of the bed. 'The night after Art's consecration—'

Camilla looked at Olivia's drawn face. Olivia had started to tell her something that night, and had stopped.

'My son has hurt you,' Olivia stated.

'You told me he would—would leave—sometimes—' Camilla faltered.

'Even though he is my son, even though I know—'

'Know what, Mama?'

'That night at the beach I left off in the middle, didn't I? And I decided that since Mac had come back from his walk and interrupted us, perhaps I never had to go any further. But now I think I must, for two reasons. One, to help you understand Mac. That alone would not make me break silence. The other—oh, Camilla, there has been gossip raising its ugly head and I do not want you to hear a garbled version from some troublemaker. Better you hear it from me.'

Camilla waited. Afraid.

'I told you about Art, what his father did to him. It was not a secret between us. All I wanted was to protect Art, to keep him from suffering that way ever again. We can't do that, you know, can't keep those we love from suffering, doing wrong, terrible wrong.' Olivia's breathing was shallow. She wore a pale lavender dressing gown and the lace at her throat quivered with her breaths. But she continued. 'Art is a handsome older man, but as a young man he was beautiful, like one of those Greek statues. His congregation thought of him as their beautiful young priest, though he was thirty when we were married, and had been assistant at two other churches. But he was beautiful and, in a strange way, innocent. Perhaps I was innocent, too. It was a long time ago. I've forgotten. Almost forgotten that early happiness.' She sighed, a long, tremulous letting-out of breath. 'We moved to Nashville, our first uprooting. But the church was vibrant, and Art inherited a fine music program. We all loved music, Mac, too, even as a little boy, and he often slipped into the back of the church when the organist was practicing, or during choir rehearsal.'

Camilla once more put her hands protectively over her belly, as though to keep the baby within from being hurt by anything Olivia might have to say.

Olivia continued, 'Oh, God, this is hard. Before Art's consecration there was a rumble, quickly squashed, but I had prayed the past would not come up to smear the present. And now, once again—'

Olivia's voice was low, but clear. 'The year that Mac was eight he came home from school one day and went into the church to do his homework in case there might be music. He saw—' She stopped. Put her face in her hands. Dropped her hands to her lap. 'He saw his father and the organist, sodomizing.' She put her hand to her mouth. Put it down. 'Art was bent over, with the organist mounting him. I'm sorry to put it in such an ugly way, but that's what it was. Mac fled. T.J. Jensen was already his best friend. He fled to T.J.'s house. When he was not home for the evening meal we had no idea where he was. He always let us know if he was going to be late. Art did not know what Mac had seen. He had no idea.'

—No, Camilla thought. —No. Not Papa. No.

Olivia continued. 'We were ready to call the police when it occurred to me Mac might be at T.J.'s. They didn't have a phone, so I got in the car and went over. Mac would not speak to me. He lay on T.J.'s bed in fetal position and would not move, and I knew something terrible had happened, but I had no idea what. Finally I went back for Art. When Mac saw his father he screamed. And Art guessed. And told me.

'We couldn't get Mac to come home. The doctor came. Said Mac had suffered some kind of psychic shock and it was best to leave him where he was unless we wanted him straitjacketed and taken to the hospital. So we went home.'

Tears were running down Olivia's cheeks. Camilla was blinded by shock. She looked at Olivia, but she did not see her.

'The organist,' Olivia resumed, 'I do not want to mention his name. We will not be free while he is on this earth, with his resentment, his jealousy of Art. He went to the bishop and accused Art of seducing him. He turned what had happened around, to save his own skin.'

Upside down. Upside down. Not Art.

'I believed Art then and I believe him now that it was a

throwback to his father. He simply did not defend himself. That is a fact, not an excuse. Who the bishop believed I do not know, but he did not believe in airing the Church's dirty linen in public. He went, himself, to the Jensens. I don't know what he said, but Mac came home. We went to a psychiatrist, all of us. But terrible damage was done. It was the beginning of Mac's retreating whenever anything was too much for him. Art and I went to the psychiatrist together, and then I went to another one as well because I was torn apart with anger. He told me that many children who have been sexually abused become homosexual later. He was not helpful to me.' Her small smile was wry.

'Mama—' Camilla breathed.

Olivia nodded slightly. 'Psychiatrists are only people with a little more training than the rest of us. They are not God. The poor man simply added to my confusion. I walked through life like a ghost, reminding myself of my father. One evening Mac's third-grade teacher called me, said, diffidently, that he might be out of line but he would like to talk to me about my son. I had not closed myself off from help. I agreed to meet him after school the next day. Went to his empty classroom. He was a slight young man with a pleasant smile.

'He had a reputation for being the best third-grade teacher around, Edward Osler, and I was delighted when Mac was placed in his class. He pulled up a chair for me, then sat at his desk and looked at me, a long, thoughtful gaze. I just sat, hard as rock. Finally he said, "I love the kids I teach. Mac is one of the brightest and best." I asked him if something was wrong that he had asked to see me, and he shook his head impatiently, then told me that he was putting himself in a position where he could lose his job if our conversation ever was made public. I was in such a dark place that there was no way I could promise confidentiality until I knew what he was going to say. He would have had every right to terminate the conversation, then and there. He told me that he was homosexual, that he had been living with a friend since they were in college. "What you are angry about," he told me, "is not the fact of homosexuality, but people using other people for their own purposes. What Mac saw was not an act of love but an act of abuse, and abuse stretches across all sexuality." I must have looked as though I were about to faint, because he handed me a glass of water.

'Finally I whispered, "How did you know?"

'We live in a very small world, he said, and Mac's behavior in school had made him wonder. It took a while and some general questioning for him to put two and two together, and I know that he didn't tell me everything. There was compassion in his voice, and no trace of fear for the consequences to himself. I found myself talking, telling him what he had only guessed. Promising silence.

'He reached across his desk to me, and took my hands. He told me that people make mistakes, but are not bound by them. He told me that Art and I would love each other more, not less. I sat there and wept because I thought I had lost Art forever, that he might as well be dead. Young Edward handed me his handkerchief, a clean linen square, and quoted to me something written around fourteen hundred, by William Langland.' Olivia closed her eyes, remembering, reciting. ' *"But all the wickedness in the world which man may do or think is no more to the mercy of God than a live coal dropped in the sea."* '

Camilla shuddered. Mercy? If she accepted mercy for Olivia and Art, for Mac, she had to accept it for herself, for Rose, for whoever had fathered the baby.

'Finally'—Olivia's voice was so low it was barely audible—'we all began to heal. I continued to see Edward, the young teacher. We trusted each other. I fed him back the psychiatrist's words. He was a chilly man, and he held a chilly future out to me. Edward laughed heartily, and said that he did not believe in a deterministic universe. "I listen to your husband preach every Sunday," he said. "I take from his hands the body and blood of the Lord. Artaxias Xanthakos is a man of love, not self-indulgence or abuse. You are the one he loves, as Matthew is the one I love. It takes love to recognize love." I asked him, "Have you ever thought of becoming a priest?" He laughed, and said no, he was a teacher, that was his vocation. He and the love he gave me were so great that they thawed the ice in which I had encased myself. I turned, at last, to Art for love. At first I could barely endure it. Then, at last, it became once again a joy. I was able to be a wife. A mother.'

Olivia smiled, a small uplift of the lips. 'When Mac knew once more that I loved Art, that Art loved me, he, too, healed. Slowly. We invited Edward and his Matthew to dinner, and they began to come a couple of times a month. Edward told Mac about the tree house he had built, and the next week Mac and T.J. began building theirs. Edward taught him to pitch a baseball with an almost unhittable curve. Mac very seldom came into the church and we made no issue of it. All that mattered was that we became a family again, through God's inestimable mercy.'

'Oh, Mama—' Camilla reached out to Olivia and the two women held each other.

'You talk about anger, dearest. I know all about anger. I know that it cannot be avoided, that it has to be moved through. You will move through yours because you have a loving heart. You may not understand, because there are things we never understand completely, but you will not stay in anger.'

For the moment Camilla was beyond anger.

Olivia said, 'I have prayed and prayed about whether or not I should tell you this. But the gossip, the ugly hint which came from the organist, who is far, far away in another state, at a large cathedral . . . He left shortly after he and Art—I do not think I could have stood it if he had stayed. But while he is alive there is no peace. The slander was squashed, but then

Mac's leaving you, abandoning you at such a time—I felt you had a right to know. For mercy's sake.'

·

The next evening Olivia and Camilla sat at the battered table under the pine tree to eat supper. For a while, neither of them spoke. Finally, Olivia said, 'You've seen Art and me together. You know that we love each other.'

'Yes.'

'Young Edward Osler was right. Our love became deeper and richer than it had been before. Art forgave me, as I forgave him. It took Mac longer to forgive us, and I knew that I did not deserve forgiveness.'

'Oh, Mama,' Camilla said, 'if we had to deserve it—'

'I know. Forgiveness is a mercy. My only part in it was to accept it. That came fully when Art had pneumonia and nearly died. Mac and I held each other all night long. I held Mac and the child held me, while Art was gasping away his life. The doctors, the nurses, had given him up. But suddenly his breathing eased. And that incredible, anguished, glorious mercy filled our hearts.'

·

When Camilla was undressed and ready for bed she turned to Olivia to say good night. 'Mama,' she said, 'I need to know about mercy, too.'

'Mac—'

'Not Mac. My mother. Her—whoever the baby's father is. They were so happy, my parents, and now—'

'Now we must all love each other more than ever.'

'Yes,' Camilla said, 'I know. But I need mercy, first.'

She slept fitfully, waking with the word "mercy" on her lips. Art. Would she ever feel the same calm comfort from Art? But had not that calm comfort come through fearsome effort?

For no reason, she thought of Luisa, wanted to reach for

the phone and call, even if it was two o'clock in the morning. But she could hear Luisa's slightly abrasive voice, 'Hell, Camilla, you're growing up at last. This is what it's all about.'

Mercy. It didn't mean that everything was okay, could or should be condoned. But we can't move out of ourselves and our own self-justifications until we look in the mirror and know, yes, I, too, could have done this. Or worse. My anger at my mother. At Mama for telling me things I don't want to know. At Mac, for being in England when I need him here.

The baby kicked her. Grow up, Camilla. If you're going to be a mother, you'd better grow up.

•

The rectory was quiet. Olivia saw to it that Camilla ate. Smiled occasionally. Sometimes they reached out and clasped hands. Waited for the phone to ring.

The first time Camilla heard Olivia's merry peal was when Dr. Edison came to visit, bringing a recording of Bach's *Musical Offering*. 'Here's something to make number patterns with. No, no tea, hot or cold, thank you, Mrs. Xanthakos. We drink enough tea in this town to deplete the water level of the planet. Let's just talk. I'm terribly sorry I haven't been in touch before, Camilla, but I've been out of town and just heard the news. How well do you know Latin?'

'Modestly,' Camilla said.

'I'm an old-fashioned Southerner and I don't swear in English.' She burst into a streak of Latin syllables which Camilla more or less understood and which set them all to laughing so hard that the laughter was more than half tears.

'There,' Dr. Edison said. 'I feel better. I can't say I'm sorry, Camilla, because it's beyond that. The poor little baby. How is your father going to manage all alone?'

Camilla and Olivia exchanged glances. Dr. Edison knew only the smallest part of the story, and that was bad enough. 'I don't know,' Camilla said. 'We're still so shocked by my mother's death we haven't got much beyond that. I suppose Father could get a nurse.' That had not occurred to her before, but she had to say something. Dr. Edison knew only what everybody else in Corinth and Athens knew, the bare, tragic bones of Rose's death and the baby's dramatic delivery.

Dr. Edison opened her mouth to speak but was stopped by a loud knocking at the kitchen door. There was a doorbell at the rectory's front door, but it had not functioned for many years, and the door stuck from the damp and was seldom used. 'I'll go see what it is.' Dr. Edison hurried out through the dining room into the kitchen.

'She's marvelous.' Olivia turned to Camilla with her old smile.

'I didn't think I wanted to see anybody, but she's an exception.'

Dr. Edison returned. 'It was a troop of young people, bearing a baked ham and obviously heartloads of love.'

'The youth group.' Camilla opened her arms as though to embrace them. 'People have been bringing in funeral baked meats ever since—ever since it happened.'

'They're thoughtful kids,' Dr. Edison said. 'They handed over their gifts and left. I'll tend to getting the ham in the ice box as soon as—'

She was stopped by the ringing of the phone. Olivia reached for it. 'Hello ... Yes, this is Olivia Xanthakos ... Where? ... What? ... Yes, of course, as soon as possible.' She hung up, as though to forestall further conversation. 'Camilla, that was your father. He's in the airport in Atlanta. I told him I'd drive over and bring him here.'

'No.' Dr. Edison was brusque. 'I'll go. Much more sensible.' She stood up.

'Father—but why—'

'Perhaps he needs to be near his daughter,' Olivia said. 'Perhaps he needs to do some grieving with you.'

Dr. Edison headed again for the kitchen. 'I'll be back as soon as I can.' She picked up the white kid gloves which she carried as a concession to propriety but never wore.

'How will you—' Camilla was too bruised even to demur. 'How will you recognize each other?'

'I'll have him paged if necessary.'

As she left, Camilla said, 'Mama, I don't understand.'

'Neither do I,' Olivia said. 'We'll just have to wait and see.'

'What about Papa?'

Olivia shook her head. 'Art will phone and tell us what's going on as soon as he can. Now, love, it will be a while before Dr. Edison can get to Atlanta and back. Go upstairs and rest. With the afternoon sun swinging around, it's stifling in here. I'll be up in a few minutes.'

Camilla took the record Dr. Edison had brought and put it on the turntable in the bedroom; she often listened to records while she was resting. The pure notes of the *Musical Offering* moved calmly across her turbulence.

Downstairs she heard water running. Heard the refrigerator door open and close. Heard the tumbling of the dryer.

—If the centrifugal force of the dryer is dependent on the fixed stars, so is the life of that baby born of my dead mother and God knows what father (someone in Paris? someone French?). So is the life of my own infant swimming so gently inside me in the amniotic fluid. So is Mac. And Frank. And Mama and Papa. So am I. We cannot do anything in isolation. It is all interconnection. Why is my father in the Atlanta airport?

The fugue wound its pattern about her. She closed her eyes. Did not wake until her father came into the room, casting his shadow across the white coverlet on the bed.

•

She lay flat, her hands as usual over her belly, feeling the affirming movements of the baby, the strongest affirmation in the chaos of all that was happening. Her father sat upright in a straight chair he had pulled up beside her.

'I can't do it, Camilla. I can't raise that child, knowing he's not mine.'

Camilla, wishing Olivia had not tactfully gone downstairs, said nothing.

'I've thought and thought. If I were a praying man you might say I've prayed. The doctor suggested adoption. There are plenty of childless parents looking for children. But I can't do that, either. He is, after all, Rose's child. He's all I have left of Rose. But I can't do it. I'm too old. I'm away too often. I might grow to love the child, but then there would be times when I'd hate him for not being mine. I've weighed various factors and I've come to only one conclusion.'

Camilla waited.

'You and Mac take him. You'll have one of your own soon, and they'll be company for each other. Raise him as your own.'

'But, Father.' Camilla shook her head in confusion. 'Where's Papa? Didn't he come home with you?'

'He's in Jacksonville. He needed to get back to his cathedral. And I wanted to speak to you alone. This is between us. Name the baby after Art. That man saved my life. I was ready to jump in the Seine.'

Camilla made herself breathe slowly, regularly. This suggestion—command—of her father's was almost as much of a shock as her mother's death.

'It's a small way I can thank Art,' Rafferty said. 'Naming the baby after him.'

'But—' Months ago she had written her parents that if she and Mac had a boy they would call him Artaxias Rafferty. If they had a girl she would be Frances, after Frank. Camilla had been happier about that before Mac left for England, but that was not reasonable, was not Frank's fault.

'It would give the child security. And I'll provide for him. You and Mac won't ever want—'

'Father, we don't want money.'

'If you and Mac don't take him I'll have to make some kind of foster-care arrangement until he's old enough for school at least. Camilla, do this for me. I'm devastated. We were so happy. Rose was so much mine these past months, carrying my baby. I'm sure she thought it was mine.'

'Father, who—'

'God knows. There was a small fling with a French diplomat, but it didn't last. However, I suppose—' Dry, heaving sobs began to rack him. Finally he looked at her. 'Camilla, take the baby. Promise.'

'I can't make any such promise without consulting Mac.'

'And where the hell is Mac?' Rafferty demanded. 'Why isn't he with you when you need him?'

Her voice was steady. 'He's in England. Frank is being married, and Mac is his best man. After all, Frank came all the way from Turkey to be with Mac when we were married.'

'Frank doesn't have a pregnant wife whose mother has just been killed.'

'Please, Father.'

'Your father-in-law, the bishop, didn't say much. But a long life with Rose has taught me to read between the lines.'

'Father, it was wonderful of Papa—of Art—to fly to Paris to be with you.' *Papa. Papa. Are you still Papa after what Mama told me? Is anything the same?*

Rafferty rubbed his hands across his cheeks, where stubble was beginning to show. 'He helped me cry. I did cry, but now I can't. No tears left. He's a good man, your bishop, I grant you that. Trustworthy. Camilla, please take the baby. He'll have to be in the hospital a while longer until he's gained enough weight, but then—'

Camilla moved her head in negation back and forth on the pillow. 'How can I? I'm not due till November. I can't—'

Olivia came in with a cup of warm milk and nutmeg for Camilla. 'Can't what?'

'Father wants Mac and me to take the baby.'

•

'You are not even to think about it,' Olivia said. 'He's asking the impossible.'

Camilla smiled wanly. 'You've done a few impossible things in your life, haven't you?'

'Not like this. Lovey, I've got to go over to the store to pick up some more milk. Just rest till I get back. Don't think. This is too much. Put everything out of your mind except your own baby.'

How could she?

While Olivia was gone, the phone rang. Noelle Grange. 'Camilla, I just spoke to Andrew and he told me about your mother. Oh, my God, I'm sorry.'

Andrew's friend was Dr. Edison's nephew. There was no need to keep Rose's death secret. But that was enough. The baby's parentage need not be known. Ever. For at least a while. Until, perhaps, the father appeared to claim his child. 'Thanks for calling, Noelle. Yes, it was a terrible shock.'

'I called Mom and Dad. Dad's really shook up. Camilla, I think he and Mom are going to split. They do nothing but yell at each other. About anything. Your mom. Whatever. I hate going home. Thank God I don't have to, much. I did talk to Ferris and he was wonderful, so I hope Mac is being wonderful for you. I mean, this is really lousy for you. Andrew wants me to tell you how terribly sorry he is about your mother. It's weird. There's so much bad stuff going on all around us, and Andrew and I are both happier than we've been in I don't know how long. When Andrew and Liz are through at Grady they're going to New York to join her father's practice. He's a pediatrician, and that's what they're going to specialize in.

Her father has a huge practice and he needs them, so it's a terrific situation.'

'Good,' Camilla agreed automatically. It was all right for Noelle to talk about herself. To some extent it stopped Camilla from thinking.

Noelle ended with, 'I'm terribly sorry about your mother. It must be awful for you.'

She could not tell Noelle, she could not tell anybody, how awful it was.

RAFFERTY RETURNED to Paris. 'I'll find someone to care for the—for Rose's child until you—'

They left it there. Until. Until Camilla had her baby. Until—what?

Mac and Art came to Corinth together, meeting in Atlanta and driving from there. Camilla did not know who Mac was, who Art was. She looked at Mac's eyes, clouded like dark amber, at his curly dark hair, his slight, tense body. It felt taut, resisting, as he kissed her.

She drew back, looked at Art, at the serenity in his face as he leaned toward her to kiss her, then put his arms around her in a loving embrace. She had thought she might recoil. Instead, she relaxed in his reassurance.

It was late, but they had all waited for dinner. Olivia lit the candles.

The heat bore down on them. The ceiling fan stirred the air and made it almost bearable. Art pulled a large handkerchief out of his pocket and wiped his face. 'Paris was cool. Even Jacksonville is cooler than this, with the breeze from the river.'

'England was cold,' Mac said. 'Frank and Bethann's wedding was lovely, but we shivered.'

Camilla felt her own skin prickle.

Mac continued in a level voice. 'I liked Frank's wife. Too bad Luisa couldn't come but she was in the middle of her residency and couldn't get away. So it was just me and Beth-ann's parents and sister and one aged aunt.'

'Mac.' Camilla interrupted. 'There's more.'

'No.' Olivia's voice was shrill. 'No. It can't be done.'

Art and Mac looked at Olivia, at Camilla.

'My father wants Mac and me to take the baby—my baby brother.'

'No,' Olivia said again.

Art leaned back in his chair. 'Rafferty told me of this request. It is not to be considered lightly, and it is not to be considered at all, daughter, until you have had your baby.'

.

Mac had dropped his bags by the door. When they left the table he went to them, picked them up, turned toward the door, then back, taking his cases to the foot of the stairs and setting them down. A statement. A statement that he had come home.

.

Gravely, adding no advice, Art and Olivia left after break-fast.

Mac said, 'Camilla, I have to go into the church. I have to pray. Do you want to come with me?'

'Of course.' Mac never pushed her. He let her move in her own direction, at her own pace.

She did not know how to pray. She was not sure she even knew how to be with Mac. They had made love the night be-fore, wonderful love, during which time had no meaning and they were free of its tragedies. But night was over. She walked beside Mac to the church into the dim interior of the old build-ing. The stained-glass windows were dull and needed cleaning. The woodwork, the pews, were brown. The walls had once been cream-colored but had darkened so that they blended into the brownness of the wood. It was comforting, rather than depressing. The church's interior seemed to enfold them maternally. Mac was trying to raise money for fresh paint, and while Camilla knew that it was long overdue, she liked the warmth and coziness which seemed to hold all the prayers that had been lifted to God over the centuries. The ceiling was high, with fans stirring the air, and the heat was tolerable. She sat beside Mac in the front row, looking at the simple, unadorned cross above the altar.

Mac looked at the cross as he asked, 'Is naming the baby after Papa a way to pressure us into taking him?'

'Father's grateful to Papa. It was amazingly wonderful of him to drop everything and go to Paris to be there with Father.'

Mac buried his face in his hands, then looked up at the cross again. 'I wonder what Papa thinks of the baby being named Artaxias?'

'He hasn't said no.'

'It's asking more than should be asked.'

'I know. But haven't I heard you say that this is what God does?'

'It's your father who's asking this. What is he thinking of?'

'Himself. He's not thinking of us. He's hardly thinking of the baby. He's like a wounded bear, striking out. He did say that it would be easier for him, for the baby, if people thought he was ours.'

'In Corinth, Georgia?'

'Mac, I'm very confused. But we're not going to be here forever.'

'People aren't exactly beating a path to my door. I don't have any better mousetraps.'

'You're making this place work. I don't know much about church, but I know that much. In spite of everything, people are kinder to each other than they used to be.'

'And we have to be kind, too?'

Mercy. 'Oh. Mac, I'm so confused. I don't know anything.'

'Oh, God.' He groaned. 'Let's pray.' He turned to her, put his arms around her, holding her close, quietly, wordlessly.

Finally he shouted at the cross, 'God, what do you want?'

For a moment it seemed that the fans stopped moving. The branches of an azalea bush that had been scratching at one of the windows were stilled.

Then Mac said, 'I don't see what else we can do. Your father can't handle it. The poor little thing's an orphan, no mother to love and hold, none of the early touching and cuddling that's so important. I swear I remember Mama holding me and rubbing me between my shoulders to make me burp.'

'Mac, are you sure?'

'About Mama burping me?'

'No, no, about the baby—'

'Of course I'm not sure. It's just that the alternatives seem intolerable.'

Camilla's voice was tentative. 'If we're going to take him—'

'Aren't we?'

'He'll have to be our child. As much as our own baby. Mac, is that possible?'

'I don't know.'

Camilla looked at the plain wood of the cross, then at the round, dusty stained-glass window above it. 'The whole thing— Mother's death. I don't want to blame a stupid accident on God.'

'No,' Mac said. 'I don't, either.'

'We've left the Newtonian world of a predetermined universe, everything being acted out according to an ordained, predestined plan.'

'Okay,' Mac said, 'I agree about that. I don't want a predetermined universe, either. You've taught me that much about particle physics, and it makes total theological sense to me. God doesn't plan the horrors. They happen. But God can come into them.'

'When Mrs. Lee arrived, bearing lilies, and talked about its being God's will, I nearly stuffed the lilies down her throat.'

'At least she didn't say it was God's punishment.'

'If she'd known my mother, she would have.'

'I thought you said people were more loving?'

'They are. Truly. But I'm not sure what people like Mrs. Lee think about God.'

'All I know,' Mac said slowly, 'is that I believe God can come into the terrible things and redeem them.'

'Do you think it's God's will that we take Mother's baby?'

'I'm not sure about will. I think that it's what God is asking, and if that's a contradiction, I can't help it. It's a way of bringing some reason into what otherwise seems incomprehensible and irrational.'

'Like Mach's theory—remember when I shocked Mrs. Lee, who still thinks it's your theory? Everything connected. It's as though there are a lot of loose strands around us, and we have, somehow, to bring them together.'

'Cam, if we don't take the baby, what will happen to him?'

'Father won't consider adoption—except by us. He'd get nurses and governesses, and he'd never be able to be a father to the child because he knows he isn't the father, because—because once again Mother—'

'It's a hell of a situation.'

'Hell is right.'

'But, my love, you listen to the singing of the trees. You go out at night and lie under the stars.'

'Okay. All right. When I listen to the trees' song, when I listen to the stars, then I can say God. I'm not sure what I mean by it, but I can say it.' She looked around the small, comfortable brownness of the church.

'Can you say it about taking this child?'

'I'm not sure. I can try. Oh, Mac, do all parents give their children terrible wounds?' She was thinking of Art and Olivia as much as her own parents.

Art and Olivia called that night. Listened, as Mac outlined their conversation.

Art's voice was low. 'I agree with you. I do not think you have a choice.'

'They do!' Olivia cried. 'Why should they be drawn into this situation in which they have no part?'

'I do,' Camilla said. Her fingers tightened around Quantum, who stopped purring and jumped off her lap, then leapt onto the sideboard.

Olivia's voice quavered. 'Art feels drawn in.'

'I was there,' Art said, 'in Paris with Rafferty. Like it or not, I am drawn in.'

'Please,' Camilla begged, 'please don't let it make trouble between you, between us.'

'We shouldn't quarrel over the phone.' Olivia sounded ashamed.

The bishop said, 'What we must look for is God's mercy. God's mercy shown through our own.'

Olivia murmured, 'At the moment I'm not feeling that much mercy.'

'Olivia.' The bishop's voice was stern. 'Of all people, you know about mercy.'

'Yes.'

'You know that we are never outside God's mercy.' His voice choked.

'Never outside it, my darling,' Olivia said. 'I know that. I'm sorry. I just don't want to see our children walking into something that's going to bring them grief.'

•

In his grief, Rafferty called frequently, too frequently. 'But what can we expect?' Olivia said. 'Poor bereaved man— bereaved of his wife, of his son.'

Rafferty said, 'The baby's name is officially Artaxias Xanthakos Dickinson. I have to do that much for him, give him my name, legitimize him.'

When the baby left the hospital, Rafferty wanted to come directly to Corinth, have them find him a hotel, an apartment, a nurse. To Camilla's relief, Olivia was with her when her father called, and vetoed this. 'Give me the phone, please. Now, Rafferty, this is quite impossible. Corinth doesn't have a hotel. The apartments for rent are rooms in people's homes and you wouldn't find them satisfactory at all, nor would anyone want to take in a middle-aged man with an infant. You have a place to live in Paris. Keep the baby in your apartment there ... You have a nurse to take care of the baby. If you need more help it's available ... No, Rafferty, not yet. You must wait until Camilla's baby is born.'

•

"Grandmother"—Raffi rolled her green wool socks into a ball—"you were wonderful, you and Grandfather, to take my dad like that."

"Not wonderful," Camilla said. "We just did what had to be done. We never thought it would be easy. But he gave us great joy. We believed that he was God's wondrous gift to us. He had that same ability to delight that he does today in his acting, that quality that makes him so loved."

"So what's he up to now?" Raffi threw the sock ball up into the air, caught it. "Why did he suddenly tell me you might not be my grandmother?"

"I don't know. I don't know why he raised questions now that he was determined to keep unasked. It isn't like him. It contradicts everything he ..." She went out to the kitchen to stir the sauce she was making over a low flame. Raffi, barefoot, followed her. "I'm sorry, Raffi. This is being a lot harder than I thought it was going to be. I've been going over the past in my mind, trying to make sense of it. It involves a lot of people who died before you were born."

"People I never had a chance to know," Raffi said, scowling, "but who still seem to be very much around. One night when Dad was angry with Mom he compared her to your mother. He called her a whore."

The blood drained from Camilla's face. "That was a terrible thing for him to say."

"But was it true?"

"Of your mother? Of course not."

"But yours—"

"My mother was not faithful to my father. It was a terrible word for Taxi to use, but it wasn't far from the truth. But your mother—"

"She sticks by Dad and sometimes I don't know why. She'd gone out to lunch with an old dancer friend. There wasn't anything to it. Dad wanted to hurt her, and he did."

She thought of Frankie's words. Could the lie with which they had all lived ever be redeemed?

.

Why was Taxi suddenly and deviously opening doors he had been adamant about keeping locked? Didn't he know Raffi would come to Camilla? What did he expect or want her to tell her? "Raffi, your father was born after my mother—his mother—was killed in an accident, and the blood tests showed that my father was not his father." It was the truth, but a truth which explained little.

.

'I'm sorry,' Camilla said. 'Oh, Mac, I'm sorry. Sorry for Father. Sorry for the baby.'

'For your mother?'

She shook her head. 'I don't know. I don't know. All I want to think about is our baby.'

'Yes,' Mac said. 'Our baby.' He pressed the palm of his hand gently against her. 'Any day, now. Can you let everything else go?'

Perhaps not then, but definitely yes, when labor started. Corinth, Georgia, was ahead of some of the United States in one area. Camilla's obstetrician believed in having the father participate in the birth of his baby. Edith Edison provided a small but good tape recorder, assorted Bach fugues to help Camilla along during labor, and a blank tape to record the baby's first cry, and anything else they might want to put on it.

'I'm not horning in,' she said, 'but I do care. Please call me as soon as you start labor, and I'll stay quietly in the waiting room.'

Camilla's labor was long and exhausting, but then came the incredible moment of push and rush and the doctor said, 'It's a little girl, a beautiful little girl.'

Frances. Frances, who shouted lustily at the indignity of being born, and who weighed eight pounds and was nineteen inches long.

How much had Artaxias Xanthakos Dickinson weighed? Certainly less than Frances.

Dr. Edith reported to Camilla that when Mac came out to the waiting room and told her that Camilla had given birth to a little girl, he had looked disappointed. 'But only for a moment. He pulled himself together, and beamed.'

Camilla laughed. 'Thanks for the Bach. He was a big help. I don't think any other mother has timed her labor pains with fugues in this hospital before.' She looked and felt drained, but Frances was in her arms, little lips making tasting noises.

'*O taste and see how lovely the Lord is,*' Dr. Edith said, looking down at her. 'I gather Mrs. Bishop—as your youth group calls her—is coming to help out?'

'Yes.'

'She's a delightful woman. I enjoy her.'

'She's terrific,' Camilla said. 'I love her.' —She and Papa love each other. They are truly lovers. They are in love. Do I really understand that?

'And she loves you.' Dr. Edison nodded. 'There are some

lines of Blake's I've always liked and I think I have them memorized properly. Listen:

He who would do good to another must do it in minute particulars. General good is the plea of the scoundrel, hypocrite, and flatterer, for Art and Science cannot exist but in minutely organized particulars.'

—Particulars, Camilla thought. —Mac talks about "the scandal of particularity." Frances is our particular baby. 'Yes, I think Blake's right.'

Dr. Edison said, 'I saw it as applied to physics when I first read it, but it does apply to people, too. I think your mother-in-law understands particulars. She's not a do-gooder, because most do-gooders deal in generalities. She never loses sight of the particular person, the unique human need.' She laughed. 'I'm moving into my lecturing mode, aren't I?'

'It's okay,' Camilla said. 'I do it, too. It's an occupational hazard.'

'I'm glad you're nursing Frances. She's a lovely baby. When she is six weeks old I will come and show her the stars. It's not too young.'

•

Years later Camilla still remembered Dr. Edison carrying Frances out to the yard and pointing out the constellations, holding the baby up as though she could see and understand.

Raffi was six months old rather than six weeks when Camilla carried her out onto the beach in front of a rented summer cottage. 'And here,' she pointed, remembering Dr. Edison, 'are the Pleiades.'

Thessaly stood by her. 'Where?'

'There.'

'That little sort of blob of stars?'

'Familiarly known as the Seven Sisters, although—' She

stopped as Thessaly started to dance, leaping from the softer sand near the cottage to the firm sand by the water, dancing to Camilla and the baby and the stars, twirling, leaping, her white cotton nightgown fluttering delicately with her movements.

It was a time of peace and joy, as the first weeks with Frances were times of peace and a kind of precarious joy.

Dr. Edison, arriving one afternoon with some new records, asked, 'Do you know what you are doing, Camilla, agreeing to take another baby?'

Camilla, holding Frances against her shoulder, patting her to help her burp, shook her head. 'No, dear Dr. Edith, of course I don't know what I'm doing. One baby has already changed our lives considerably. But what else can we, do?'

'I suppose I think you could say no,' Dr. Edison said. 'I know he's your brother, but it distresses me to see your father abdicating all sense of responsibility for his son.'

Camilla was silent. She did not know how to defend Rafferty. Had Taxi been his own child, surely he would not have wanted to hand him over to Camilla and Mac.

'He has asked it of you,' Dr. Edison said, 'and I applaud your willingness to accept this burden, but I am also fearful for you.'

'Oh, I'm fearful, too,' Camilla agreed. 'And I do count on your friendship and support.'

'That you have, and will have. But please do have second thoughts.'

—Second thoughts, third thoughts, fourth thoughts . . .

•

Frances was a healthy, contented baby. She woke once during the early hours to nurse, and that was a happy time, the baby in bed with Camilla and Mac. 'A trinity of joy,' Mac murmured.

•

One evening after dinner, Olivia asked if she could put Frances to bed. 'Go for a walk. Get some fresh air. You're being smothered with all that's happening. And I would rejoice in some time with my precious grandbaby.'

They accepted her offer gratefully, and after a brief walk went to their favorite spot under the pine tree. Mac took off his coat and spread it out for them to lie on. Camilla put her hands under her head and looked up at the stars, which seemed to twinkle directly onto the branches.

Mac's gaze followed hers. 'The stars make me grateful that Corinth is a small town without many streetlights.'

'Perspective,' Camilla said. 'They give us perspective.'

'Are all astronomers star lovers?'

'In a mathematical sense, certainly. Maybe it's more than that for me because I was a city girl. No tree houses. No gardens. Only one or two of the brightest stars—or planets—at night. Ptolemy said, "Mortal though I be, yea, ephemeral, if but a moment I gaze up at night's starry domain of heaven, then no longer on earth I stand: I touch the Creator and my lively spirit drinketh immortality." '

'Who said that?'

'Ptolemy. Second century. You remember, with earth-centered orbits of sun, moon, and stars—'

Mac ran his finger over her lips, then drew her eyebrows, her nose. 'I'm glad I married such a well-educated wife.'

'Mm.'

'You know a lot more theology than you think you do.'

She was too relaxed to protest, murmuring, 'Ptolemy wasn't a Christian, was he?'

'Don't worry, my darling. He isn't left out.'

'Is anybody?'

'No.'

'Not anybody, no matter what?'

'Darling,' he said, 'you're feeling guilty, aren't you? About your father?'

The November evening was warm, and Camilla wore only a cardigan over her dress, but she shivered. 'I don't know.' She lay with her head on Mac's lap. 'I don't think it's guilt. I didn't do anything to cause this situation. I just resent this intrusion on our first weeks with Frances. I want to focus on the baby, and on us, and when Father calls I'm all torn apart with what he's having to go through. It was one thing for Mother to be unfaithful, but for her to have a baby that wasn't his— I think he's terribly angry, and why wouldn't he be?'

'But he's also grieving for her,' Mac pointed out. He pushed his fingers through her dark hair, gently, soothingly. Quantum came leaping toward them, sprang onto Camilla's lap, and purred contentedly.

'Mother's baby—what is it going to do to our lives?'

•

Raffi sat in Dr. Rowan's office. "Our lives get so messed up. How do we escape from each other?"

"Do we need to escape?"

"From being hurt? Don't we?"

"What kind of hurt, Raffi?"

"You know."

"No. You have to tell me."

Raffi tossed her head impatiently. "Listen, I'm not into this abuse thing. It's the *in* thing now. You're nobody if you haven't been abused."

"Oh?"

"I think my father abuses my mother, but she doesn't see it that way. There's something in him that likes to hurt."

"You?"

"Is laughing at me whenever I talk about working in the theatre abuse?"

"Is it?"

"Mom says he's only trying to protect me, that the theatre is such a tough world. But last year at school in the senior play when I was Viola in *Twelfth Night* he made fun of my performance, and I was good, Dr. Rowan, I was good."

"Yes, your grandmother told me how splendid you were."

"She's my grandmother, and she's on my side. But Dad's the one who knows about theatre, and all he did was criticize. Said I didn't know how to use my body. Said my love scenes were laughable. Said he was only trying to help. Is Mom right? Is he trying to protect me? Or is he afraid maybe I might be good enough to be competition?"

"You're a lovely young girl, Raffi. Can you be competition to a mature actor at the height of his powers?"

"In the theatre, anyone who gets attention is competition. Oh, Dr. Rowan, right now I don't think my father knows who he is, and so I don't know who I am, either."

•

Camilla, nursing Frances, felt wholly and supremely herself, as she often did when she plunged into the world of astronomy, where the movement of the galaxies was beyond ordinary mathematics.

Rafferty had left Paris and brought the baby back to Chicago, where he found an English nurse. It would be easier to care for Taxi, as the nurse called the child, in Chicago than in Paris, 'where I'm known as a cuckold,' he said, his voice on the phone sounding thick with anger.

'Father, people don't think in terms of cuckolds nowadays.'

'Oh, don't they? Even if they don't use the word, they still think it. The baby's fretful and cries at night. But he's a pretty little thing, looks very much the way you did at his age. Black hair and great, shining eyes. Your eyes, that strange mix of green and silver and sometimes blue. I look at him and he could almost be you. That hurts, Camilla, that hurts.'

'Father, I'm sorry.'

'I'll send you some pictures,' he said. 'The nurse insists that I'll want them later. You'll see what I'm talking about.'

When the pictures arrived, Camilla and Mac looked at them, bemused. Although Taxi was four months older than Frances, the picture might almost have been of the little girl.

'They surely look like siblings,' Mac said.

'He's smaller than Frances. He isn't any bigger than she is right now.'

'I don't think I mind calling him Taxi,' Camilla said. 'I'm glad the nurse thought of it.'

They sent pictures of both babies to the bishop. Camilla's favorite was one of Frances asleep on Mac's shoulder, with Quantum perched on his knee.

In the same mail with the snapshots was a cream-colored envelope, the kind used for wedding invitations. The return address was Wickoff, on East 81st Street in New York. 'Who on earth?' Camilla asked.

'Open it,' Mac suggested.

It was, in fact, a wedding invitation. Camilla read it aloud, frowning in puzzlement: '*Dr. and Mrs. James Ansley Wickoff request the pleasure of your presence at the wedding of their daughter, Elizabeth March Wickoff, to Andrew Murphy Grange*—oh! It's Noelle's brother, Andrew.'

Mac raised his eyebrows. 'I didn't know you knew him that well.'

'I don't. Remember—Noelle brought him by while he was doing a residency at Grady. Quantum loved him. I thought he was nice.'

'So did I,' Mac said, 'when he came to the Church House with Noelle. Decent and kind. Does he still stutter?'

'It seems to come and go. Do you think we ought to send them a wedding present?'

'A token, maybe. I'm glad he's found himself a nice girl. At least, I hope she's nice.'

They heard Frances upstairs, calling from her crib, not crying, but making her own special chirrupy noises.

'I'll get her,' Mac said.

'She'll probably need changing.'

'I'm a master diaper-changer,' Mac called as he hurried upstairs.

•

As soon as Frances was six weeks old, Rafferty was on the phone, wanting to send Taxi, with the nurse, to Corinth.

Olivia, getting ready to go back to Florida, took the phone from Camilla. 'Not yet, Rafferty. I'm leaving tomorrow. Camilla will be back in the kitchen again, and taking full care of the baby and the house. Wait until Frances is three months old. By then Camilla will be back in the swing of things.' She came downstairs, carrying Frances. 'I'll get Art to call Rafferty. He'll listen to Art. Oh, my dear, that poor man doesn't realize what he's asking of you. He's so eager to stop being reminded by Taxi of everything that's happened that he's forgotten that Frances is his grandchild.'

'Taking on another baby is a very big thing. Will Mac—?' Camilla could not finish.

Olivia said, 'Mac won't walk out on this. He did his walking out when he went to England for Frank's wedding.'

'Are you sure?'

'No one can ever be sure of anything. But I'm his mother, and that's my hunch. I can't promise you he'll never walk out again when things get rough. But I don't think he'll walk out on this.'

•

And what was Rafferty doing, if not walking out? Who was giving Taxi love during his first months? The nurse? Thinking of this, Camilla nearly picked up the phone to tell her father to bring them the baby, but Mac stopped her, and so did Art and Olivia.

She knew they were right. And wrong.

How many rights add up to a wrong? And vice versa?

$7 \times 7 = 49$. $8 \times 6 = 48$. Numbers are not ambiguous. But what about Mach's theory? Do the fixed stars play a part in this story?

·

She received an invitation to Noelle's wedding, with a handwritten letter: 'I know you can't come all the way North. I wanted to ask Mac to come back to campus and marry me, but then I thought that was terrifically selfish when Andrew's friend says you have a brand-new baby, and anyhow, Mom really likes the new rector here, and I'd like Ferris's and my wedding to be a good time for her.

'By the way, I asked Andrew's Liz to send you an invitation to their wedding. Andrew wasn't sure it was appropriate, but I assured him it was fine. He's deliriously happy. Liz is a brilliant doctor and also a love, and her father seems to think that Andrew was a gift sent him directly from heaven. I'm happy for him. I hope I won't give Ferris the hell Dad and Mom are giving each other. Andrew's not a bit like Dad. Sometimes I wonder if I am, and it worries me. But I can't imagine being unfaithful to Ferris.'

Camilla folded the letter. 'Thank God she didn't ask you to do the wedding. Would you have felt that you had to?' she asked Mac.

'I'm not sure. Fortunately it's a question I don't have to ask myself, so I can forget it. We have the most beautiful baby in the world; she's gloriously healthy; she thrives on her mother's marvelous milk. A year ago Christmas you lost a baby. This year we're baptizing one, and that's all we should think about. It's Christmas Eve, my darling, and we're celebrating birth.'

·

Dr. Edison said, 'Since Mr. and Mrs. Bishop are otherwise gainfully employed at the Cathedral in Jacksonville, I will be the member of the older generation for Frances.'

Camilla put the baby in Dr. Edison's outstretched arms.

'We're so glad you can be with us tonight. And we'll all drive together to Florida for the baptism.'

'We'll take my car,' Dr. Edison pronounced. 'It's heavier, and the tires are better.'

'Frances says thank you to her godmother.'

'I'm a little old to do my proper duty by that blessed child.'

'Mac says a girl baby is allowed two godmothers; I've asked my old friend Luisa, and she can't get away, so you'll have to stand in for both of you.'

Dr. Edison kissed the top of Frances's dark head. 'It will be my joy.'

'Hey, Camilla,' Luisa had said, 'you know I don't believe in all this religion stuff, but I'm honored to be Frances's godmother. I may not be able to do much for her soul, but I'll do my best for the rest of her. Thanks. Thanks for asking me.'

The church was beautiful, decorated with holly and pine branches, with poinsettias banked about, both scarlet and white. Everyone in the congregation had a candle, and the light glowed against the dark wood, against the walls, which were to be painted early in the new year.

The youth group moved about the nave of the church, lighting candles, until the loveliness of light brought tears to Camilla's eyes.

'Behold the light of the world,' Dr. Edison whispered.

Freddy Lee read from Isaiah, the great rolling verses of "Comfort ye, my people," and then Pinky stood and sang, "For He Shall Feed His Flock," her singing voice pure and sweet and in startling contrast to her daily speech. Frances slept through the entire service, despite Dr. Edison's occasional anxious cluckings, which Camilla was sure would disturb the baby. But Frances slept on, unperturbed.

It was after midnight when they got home and opened the bottle of champagne Dr. Edison had brought.

'To peace at Christmas, and in our hearts,' Mac toasted.

They drank. 'Can we say peace in the world?' Dr. Edison asked. 'Do we ever learn? There is still war and prophesies of war, and what would the Prince of Peace think of that?'

'Peace in our hearts,' Camilla said. 'No matter what.'

'It's a big no matter what,' Dr. Edison said, 'just in your own little household.' She held up her glass. 'To peace, then, peace for ourselves, peace for the world.'

•

Dr. Edison drove them to Jacksonville.

At dinner that first evening Art said to Mac, 'It would have been appropriate for you to have baptized your daughter in your own church.'

Mac replied, 'It is even more appropriate for her grandfather to baptize her and give her a start in the new life.'

Camilla looked at her husband, at her father-in-law, at the love in their faces. Olivia, too, looked at them, then at Dr. Edison. 'We are happy to have Frances's godmother with us, dear Edith.'

Frances hiccupped and Dr. Edison asked, 'Is she hungry?'

Camilla smiled. 'I just fed her.'

'Blessed, blessed babe.' The bishop took Frances from Camilla.

'Papa,' Mac warned.

'Oh, the time for constant attention is very brief. There's nothing worse than a spoiled child. Don't worry. We didn't spoil you, did we?'

'There's some difference of opinion on that subject. Were you spoiled, Camilla?' Then Mac answered his own question: 'No, you weren't. You had nurses and all that, but you were still a poor little rich girl.'

'I got over it.' Camilla laughed. 'I really love to cook. But I wish there was a magic wand I could wave so the bathroom would clean itself. Do you think there'll ever be self-cleaning bathrooms, like self-cleaning ovens?'

'It's a long way down the road,' Mac said, 'and I don't trust those self-cleaning ovens.'

'Since we don't have one, it's not a problem,' Camilla said. 'Right now I'm quite happy with my old oven, where I can't even adjust the temperature properly.'

'Don't rush things.' Olivia took the baby from the bishop. 'Be like Frances and take all the spoiling you can get for right now.'

WHEN FRANCES was three months old, and Taxi was seven months, Rafferty sent the child to them. They left Frances with Dr. Edison and drove to Atlanta to the airport. Rafferty himself was not coming. He was sending the baby with the nurse.

Two days earlier a van had backed up to the rectory and unloaded a crib, two high chairs, a double stroller, a large playpen, and several boxes of educational toys and stuffed animals. Rafferty had wanted to send matching cribs, but Camilla had said firmly that Frances was sleeping in Mac's old crib.

As they approached the gate at the airport, they saw the nurse, dressed in a white uniform, with white stockings and shoes, and marceled iron-grey hair, coming down the ramp of the jetway, carrying the baby. They approached her, and she came toward them, not hurrying. 'Mr. and Mrs. Xanthakos?'

'Yes.'

'This is Taxi.' She handed the child, wrapped in a yellow blanket, to Camilla. He was barely larger than Frances. He did not look seven months. The nurse gave Mac a large canvas bag. 'More nappies, and his formula. I have typed out complete instructions for you.' She looked them both up and down in assessment. 'Taxi needs a great deal of love. And discipline. I hope you aren't going to show favoritism. I'll leave you now. I'm taking the next plane back to Chicago.' She turned, said 'Goodbye' over her shoulder, whether to the baby or to them Camilla could not tell, and walked away.

The baby began to cry.

'Oh, God,' Camilla said, patting him. 'He's lighter than Frances. His bones are like a little bird's.'

'Come on. Let's go find a place to sit down.'

They walked to a gate where no plane was listed and the seats were empty. A uniformed woman was apathetically emptying the ashtrays. Camilla sat, put the baby on her knee, jigging him gently, something Frances was beginning to love, and the crying stopped. He looked at her with great tear-filled eyes. Camilla's eyes. Frances's eyes were the rich brown of her father's.

Frances, robust and healthy, with dark hair still short, was often taken for a boy. Taxi, with smaller bones and dark hair curling softly about his face, looked like a beautiful little girl. He reached up one small hand and caught hold of Camilla's hair, stuck the other fist in his mouth, and sucked.

Mac, rummaging in the canvas bag, brought forth a single-spaced typed sheet of paper. He started to read: 'He gets fed every four hours. The nurse does not approve of feeding him sooner. Or later. The bottle is supplemented by baby foods, except at night. She's sent several jars, and two boxes of cereal. Good heavens, Camilla, Frances is already sleeping through the night, and this child is fed at midnight and again at four.'

'He's certainly not overfed.' Camilla's hand went over the baby's back, feeling the little knobs of the spinal column. 'His diaper needs changing.'

Mac reached into the bag for a clean diaper, while Camilla placed the baby across her knees. His stool did not smell sweet like Frances's, but then, all Frances had ever had to eat was her mother's milk. The nurse had provided a bottle of lotion, and Camilla cleaned a red and hot little bottom. 'This is awful,' she said.

Mac stood, holding the soiled diaper in a plastic bag, also provided by the nurse. 'I'll have to dispose of this somewhere, and then we'd better head back to Corinth.'

The baby screamed when they got into the car, until Camilla took him out of the car seat and held him, her seat belt around them both. As soon as they left the traffic of the airport he fell asleep in Camilla's arms. She glanced at Mac's hands on the steering wheel, wondering if the problem of two babies was going to be too much for him. Because of Olivia's assurances, and because Mac was the one who had seemed most certain that it was the right thing—the only thing—for them to do, to take Taxi, she had not dwelt on her fears about Mac. There was too much else to be afraid of.

If God, as Mac seemed to believe, was asking them to take Taxi, what did that God have to do with Rose's death, or with Taxi's conception?

She turned from those thoughts, which, for her, led nowhere but to confusion, and cuddled the sleeping baby. Taxi did not feel like Frances. He did not smell like Frances. She felt an aching pity for this child whose entrance into life had been so extravagantly traumatic.

•

When they got home Dr. Edison was playing solitaire on the kitchen table, and Frances was asleep in her basket, which she was close to outgrowing. Dr. Edison held out her arms for Taxi, and Camilla handed her the little boy.

Dr. Edison, who had learned how to hold a baby from practicing with Frances, put Taxi over her shoulder and patted his back. 'I'm pleased you're going to continue to teach your classes, Camilla. That shows good sense.'

'Not so much sense as that Mac and my doctor insist. We'll have to see how it goes.'

'Your youth group will help. Several of them popped in this afternoon, full of curiosity, and assurance that they could baby-sit two as easily as one. I understand that Mrs. Bishop didn't feel it was right for her to come at this time, and I applaud her sentiment. I'm not going to stay. The kids all think you're wonderful to take this child.'

Camilla took Taxi from her and sat with him in the rocker. 'He's my brother.'

'Yes, and he looks like you. And certainly he looks enough like Frances to be her sibling.'

Frances woke up, gurgling with pleasure.

'Here, let me have Taxi,' Mac said. 'Frances is hungry.'

Camilla held Taxi out to him, then took Frances from her basket. As soon as Mac sat down with Taxi in one of the kitchen chairs, he opened his eyes, then squeezed them tight shut and started to howl.

Dr. Edison was drawing her kid gloves through her hands. Now she put them back in her bag. 'Do you have a bottle for him?'

'In this bag. Frances has never had a bottle. I'm not—'

Dr. Edison drew a bottle out of the bag. 'I'd better warm it.'

'Oh, God,' Mac said, 'this is not going to be easy.'

•

It was an hour before Dr. Edison was on her way, again holding her white kid gloves. They watched her drive off. The babies were up in the nursery. Asleep. For the moment.

It was strange to go upstairs and see two cribs instead of one, plus all the other trappings Rafferty had sent. There was no place in this medium-size room for their comfortable sofa bed, which had been moved down to Mac's study. It opened to queen-size, which meant there wouldn't be much but wall-to-wall bed when Olivia and Art or any other guest slept there. It also meant that Mac would use the chill little box of an office in the parish house more than his study at home. What was a chill little box in the winter, and tolerable for a few weeks in the spring, was a fiery furnace in the summer.

Camilla glanced at the second crib, bigger than Mac's old cherry one, enameled white, with Beatrix Potter animals. Taxi was sitting up, looking at her. Not making any sound, not moving, just staring at her with those great deep eyes. Yes. He was seven months old. Where Frances was trying to roll over, Taxi was sitting. She bent over the crib and he held out his arms to her to be picked up. Holding him, she looked at Frances, who was sleeping peacefully, not disturbed by the light from the hall.

Taxi snuggled against her, his thin arms tight about her neck. She carried him into the bedroom, where Mac was already in bed, reading.

'He was wide awake,' she explained, 'sitting up in the crib, not complaining, just sitting there.' The little boy nuzzled into the curve of neck and shoulder. 'The nurse said he needs lots of love.'

'And discipline,' Mac added.

'But love first. Discipline doesn't work unless it's founded on the kind of security that comes from knowing you're loved.'

'Did you ever have that?' Mac demanded.

She sat on the side of the bed, rocking Taxi to and fro. 'When I was little. And I've always known Father loves me.'

Mac held his forefinger toward Taxi, who grasped it. 'Even with his sending us—'

'Isn't that a sign of love?' Camilla asked. 'But Taxi—I think the nurse loved him, as much as you dare let yourself love someone you know you're going to lose. But here he is, seven months old, and he's never had the kind of spontaneous love most babies—well, maybe not most, but the kind of love your parents gave you.'

'Until I blew it.'

'What?' She had no idea what he was referring to.

'Camilla—Mama told me you know.' He looked at her fiercely.

She held Taxi so tight that he cried out. Quickly she relaxed her grasp, stroking the thin little back gently until he quieted.

'When I left,' Mac said. 'When I went to England instead of staying with you when you needed me. She said she tried to explain by telling you about—about Papa. About what—'

'Yes.' Her throat felt constricted.

'And you still love Papa.'

'Yes.'

'And you still love me.'

'Yes.'

'But we haven't talked about it. About my walking out.'

'No. I'm not good about—'

'We have to learn.' He turned slightly so that she saw his profile, thin, fierce as an eagle's. 'If we're going to take this strange little creature— Darling, we're going to have to talk, not hold back. Otherwise, he may come between us.'

'No.'

'We have to keep open. To possibilities.'

She knew he was right.

'Back when I was a kid and walked into that church and saw—'

'No, Mac, please.'

'Eight-year-olds can be rigidly judgmental. Even when Mama explained what had been done to Papa—I hated him. I hated Mama for not hating him.'

'Mac, you were eight years old. You'd had a terrible trauma. You didn't know how to handle it.'

'Is ignorance ever an excuse?'

'Maybe not, but you were a child, it was completely outside your comprehension.'

'I've known kids who were more understanding than their parents. I wasn't. I felt that I had been vomited over, and I couldn't get clean.'

She wanted to put Taxi down, to go to Mac, to hold him, but the baby began to whimper.

He continued, 'When Papa got pneumonia and nearly died—I think he thought God was punishing him, and justly. I thought God was punishing me. Mama, who doesn't believe in that kind of punishment, was trying to hold us both together. The night that everybody—the doctors, the nurses—thought he was dying, I knew that I loved him, that I couldn't bear it if he died. I sat by Mama in the waiting room of the I.C.U. and we held each other. And love came back.'

'Oh, Mac, darling, darling . . .'

'I love my father, Camilla. I love and respect him. I'm not a psychiatrist and I don't understand what childhood abuse does to people. If Papa has wanted—has wanted other men—he has never acted on it. He's come to a place of fearsome, imperturbable integrity.'

Camilla put Taxi down on the bed. Reached for Mac. 'I would trust him with my life. I want our love to be like—'

'No two things can be exactly alike. But as strong. As secure. As—as full of understanding. And, darling, you've got to learn to be honest with me, not to hold back.'

'Oh, Mac— I'm not good about letting anybody in on what troubles me.'

'You were, that first night when we met, when your mother was on campus and—'

'That was so atypical I can hardly believe it ever happened. I was wild with anger. It was unlike me, totally unlike me. Cool Camilla, that's how I'm known.'

'You were real. I felt your realness. That's why I wanted to see you again. I thought I could be real with you. And you've let me. About Korea. About—'

Taxi began to whimper. Camilla put her thumb against his mouth, and he began to suck. Then he pushed her thumb away and began to yell. 'I'd better go warm his bottle.'

Mac looked at his watch. 'It isn't four hours.'

'I'm not an English nurse.' But she did not want to leave.

She felt as though they had just crossed a fearful, alien landscape and suddenly the sun had come out.

•

An hour later Mac came down to the kitchen to find her sitting in the rocker, nursing Taxi. 'What are you doing!'

'He drank his bottle, and he was still hungry. And I have plenty of milk. Mothers nurse twins. I thought it would give him security.'

'You don't need to be defensive,' Mac said. 'I was just surprised.'

An unexpected sob rose in her throat and she tried to turn it into a laugh. 'Does it seem, in a way, incestuous for me to nurse my brother?'

'If I look at it rationally, I don't have any problem.'

'Darling, it's not going to work if he's only my brother. He has to be my baby, too. Our son.'

•

The next day, Luisa phoned. Camilla was in the kitchen. Both babies, miraculously, were napping. Camilla grabbed the phone at the first ring.

Luisa said, 'I'm drowning in classes, papers, patients, exams, and I ought to be with you right now when you need me.'

'We're okay,' Camilla said. 'Three of the youth-group kids are coming over this afternoon after school. I have lots of help. But thanks, Lu, for wanting to be here.'

'I think you're crazy,' Luisa said. 'You know that. I suppose you've got to keep him for a couple of months till your father pulls himself together.'

There was no argument. Luisa did not know that Rafferty was not Taxi's father.

'You and Mac are naïve if you think you can do this and not have it ruin your marriage.'

'Give us some credit.'

'I do. Huge amounts of credit. But you're human beings, not saints.'

Camilla's voice sharpened. 'We don't have to be saints. Lots of couples have taken in unwanted children. Sometimes it's made their marriages.'

'If it takes that to make yours, things must be pretty disastrous. Oh, hell, Camilla, I'm sorry, I wanted to call and be a comfort and all I'm doing is making things worse. You've done what you've done, and if there's ever anything I can do to help, I'll be here. You do know that.'

'Yes, Luisa, I do. Thank you.'

'Maybe you'll come to love the kid. Maybe it'll be all right.'

•

Would it? Taxi was a demanding child, and he quickly learned to make his demands known, by howling, by flinging himself about. He would quieten whenever Camilla held him, and he would be at his most difficult whenever it was time for her to nurse Frances. She learned to sit in the rocker with a child in each arm, with Frances contentedly suckling, and Taxi drinking his bottle, knowing that later he would be given her breast.

Mac stayed away during the daytime, no longer coming home for lunch. The congregation was growing. There was more and more work for him to do. If it had not been for the eager help of the youth group, Camilla would have had no rest. Even so, she often felt like a sleepwalker, going through the movements of the day, but with no emotion, detached from reality.

After the first two weeks (it seemed two months, two years) Taxi woke only once during the night, anywhere between two and four in the morning. Camilla would rouse to his call and hurry into the nursery to pick him up before he disturbed Frances. Then she would carry him down to the kitchen, holding him on one hip while she heated his bottle.

This was their time alone together, the time when Taxi became her baby, when he became her son, not a strange little half brother.

—Yes, Luisa, I'm learning to love him.

While he drank his bottle she rocked him and sang to him, giving him the physical reassurance he had not known before. After the bottle he would suck at her breast, taking great draughts of milk, as though trying to drink love.

•

Dr. Edison, dropping her white gloves on the kitchen table, said, 'He's beginning to fill out.' Both children were asleep in the playpen, side by side. Frances's hand was flung across Taxi. 'He no longer looks like a starved little bird. He looks like you, not like his mother.'

For a moment Camilla was startled. His mother?

Rose.

Suddenly a sob of sorrow and guilt choked her. She was not grieving for her mother. Her focus was on the baby.

Dr. Edison said, 'Camilla, you look exhausted.'

The potential sob turned into a laugh. 'I wonder how mothers survive twins? Pinky and Wiz Morrison are coming over after school and I can have a nap. I get one nearly every day, and it's what keeps me going.'

'I worry about you.'

'It's getting easier,' Camilla said. 'Truly. I love my kids, Dr. Edith.'

'How about your work? Is teaching two classes too much for you at this time?'

'No, no. It saves me.'

'How's your father?'

'Doing better, I think. He has arthritis, and the damp off Lake Michigan is no good for that.'

Rafferty called once a week, dutifully asking after Taxi. Asking how they were doing.

Mac had said, 'Let him pull away from us for a while. He needs to heal his soul.'

Dr. Edison bent over the playpen. 'I'm not going to wake them.'

'Thanks.'

'If they wake up before I go I want to hold my adorable godchild. Is she as beautiful and good as ever?'

'She is undoubtedly the best little girl in the entire world.'

•

'Don't neglect Frances,' Mac said one day when he came home and found her rocking Taxi while Frances was in the playpen.

'I'm not,' she retorted. 'She's perfectly happy playing with the cradle gym.'

'Darling, don't bristle. I know you wouldn't ever neglect her knowingly. But Taxi does demand attention.'

'He needs it. Frances has always had it. She knows she's loved. Taxi needs to know he's loved, too.' She was a lioness with her cubs. It did not occur to her that Taxi's inexhaustible need for love was not unlike Rose's.

Now he held out his arms to Mac, who took him from Camilla. Taxi reached up and patted his face, then poked inquiring fingers toward his eyes. Mac caught the little fingers. 'Hey, Tax, I need those.' He looked at Camilla. 'Considering everything, I suppose we're doing really well.'

Considering everything. She seemed to live two lives, the life of the mother with her little ones, totally responsive to their needs, sleeping always with one ear open for them. It was an intuitive rather than a thinking nurturing. Luisa had sent her several books on child raising, but they lay on her bed table, barely glanced at. She usually fell asleep before reading more than a few sentences. She loved the children with a great deal of physical contact, holding, rocking, protecting. Often she walked around the house with one baby on each hip. Did all mothers smell the threat of danger in the air, or was her concern caused solely by the strange circumstances?

There was the other Camilla, who drove into Athens to teach, who discussed new discoveries of astrophysics with her students, with Dr. Edison, the Camilla who delighted in the unfolding worlds of both macrocosm and microcosm. Who relaxed by offering her students mathematical games.

'This story came from Persia, I think,' Camilla said. 'It's an ancient one about an emperor and one of his courtiers, who invented the game of chess. The emperor was so pleased with it that he promised he'd give the courtier any reward he asked for.'

'Is this a fairy tale?' one young man asked suspiciously.

'Wait and see. So. The courtier who invented chess put the chessboard in front of the emperor and asked if he would put one grain of barley for him in the first square, two in the second, four in the third, eight in the fourth, sixteen in the fifth, and so forth.'

'Geometrical progression, eh?' someone asked.

Camilla smiled. 'What do you think the emperor would make of this request?'

'Not much.' The young man who had asked if Camilla was telling a fairy tale shrugged.

'It's a trick, I bet it's a trick,' one of the girls said.

'It's not a trick.' Camilla smiled. 'It's arithmetic. Surely you all have a good background in math.'

One of the students had pulled out a small pad and was scribbling away. 'You keep on going up, squaring each number,' she said, 'and you've got sixty-four squares on the board—I can't give the exact number without my calculator, but the emperor would have to give the courtier more grains of barley than could be grown in a year. Wow!'

Camilla laughed. 'That's right. There's no way the king could satisfy that request. The end of the story, I'm afraid, is that the emperor had the courtier's head cut off.'

'I don't get it,' someone said.

'It's simple,' the girl with the pad said. 'What's 16 times 16? Square that, and keep on squaring.'

'Oh. I'm a dolt. Of course.'

Everybody laughed. It would be a long time before Camilla could play this kind of game with her little ones. It was good to be free of babies for a few hours, to be herself, rather than an extension of their needs.

When she was in Athens she could forget the demands of the household, of the parish. Only a few miles, and she was in a different world.

On Sunday evenings she usually helped Mac with the youth group. 'My mother wants to know what Taxi is going to call you,' Pinky said. 'I mean, it's really weird that he's your brother, isn't it? Frances is certainly not going to call him Uncle Taxi. Sometimes we forget he's not your own baby, he looks so much like you.'

Pinky and Wiz's mother, bitter over her divorce, not yet remarried, was venting her frustration on the rest of the world. She came with Mrs. Lee to call on Camilla.

'Are you feeling better, dear Mrs. Xanthakos?' Mrs. Lee dripped solicitude.

'Fine, thanks, never felt better.' That was the appropriate answer for the rector's wife.

Mrs. Morrison asked, 'Do you think it was wise for you to go back to teaching so soon? Are you strong enough?'

'My doctor urged me to return to the university.' Camilla tried not to sound stiff. 'Pinky is my very best baby-sitter.'

'Well, my dear, I suppose you know what's best. Pinky tells me that when she has given Taxi his bottle he immediately goes for her breast.'

Camilla felt herself flush. She had never nursed Taxi in front of anyone except Mac. 'He's just a baby,' she defended. 'It's quite natural.'

Mrs. Lee looked sharply at Camilla. 'You're very brave, Mrs. Xanthakos.'

'Not at all. And Pinky is so good with both children—I don't know what I'd do without her.'

'That girl adores you, Mrs. Xanthakos, just adores you,' Mrs. Morrison said.

Mrs. Lee added, 'You do have enormous influence on the young people.'

'They're terrific kids,' Camilla said. 'And I don't think Pinky adores me. We're all good friends.'

'But you are aware of your influence?' Mrs. Lee demanded.

'Mac and I both feel the responsibility. We try never to abuse it.'

'Oh, Mrs. Xanthakos, that was not our intention—'

Camilla stood up. 'It's time for me to nurse Frances. Thank you, both of you. I love the rocking chair.' She smiled at Mrs. Lee. 'I'm sure that was your idea, and I'm very grateful for it.' She was not certain what the two women were going to make of this visit. Something, that was sure.

That night she reported the conversation to Mac. He was sitting propped up in the big brass bed, reading. She said, 'When the children begin to talk, it's going to be difficult. What is Taxi to call us? Except when somebody reminds me he's my brother, I feel like his mother. I certainly don't want him to call me Sis.'

Mac put down his book. 'Taxi's not quite a year old. It'll be a while before he talks. We'll deal with the problem when it arises.'

'I wish we could move. Corinth is too small, too gossipy—'

The book fell on the floor as Mac put his arms around her. 'If I'm not called to another parish in a year or so, I'm going back to seminary, get my doctorate. After all, I have to keep up with my wife. I think I could get into a program at General Seminary. Would New York be big enough for you if they accept me?'

'New York's home for me. I was born there. But I love our rectory, our first home. I love the youth group, and most of the congregation. But I let people like Mrs. Lee throw me off balance. Oh, Mac, I don't want my foolish little mother's tragedy blown all out of proportion.'

'At least they don't know all of it.'

'God help us if they did.'

•

"God, your mother started a real mess, didn't she?" Raffi continued throwing the ball of socks up in the air and catching it.

"Yes." Camilla wanted to add, 'Please stop playing with your socks,' but held her peace.

"And no one had any idea who she'd been fuc—who she'd been having sex with? I mean, who was my dad's father?"

"Not then."

"Didn't you try to find out?"

"We had enough to do, taking care of two babies. Mostly we didn't even wonder, we were so exhausted. When Mama and Papa asked us to come to the beach for a week right after Easter, we jumped at the chance."

•

'It will do you good to get away from Corinth for a few days,' Olivia said. 'And now that we've added a little wing to the cottage, there's plenty of room for the grandchildren.' Once Rafferty had sent Taxi to them, Olivia had not voiced aloud any further reservations she had about him. She had come to Corinth for several visits, and Taxi, toddling around on shaky small legs, followed her everywhere, holding on to her for support, climbing into her lap. The eager search for love which had been inappropriate in the grown Rose was delightful in the little boy. He was growing, filling out, until he was almost as sturdy as Frances. By Easter he was sleeping through the night, and while Camilla missed her hour with him in the kitchen, she was grateful for the extra sleep.

Taxi wailed in the car on the way down to Florida until Camilla had to unbuckle him from his seat and hold him in her lap. Frances was slumped over in her car seat, sleeping. Camilla said, 'Taxi may be afraid we're going to abandon him.'

'Possible.'

'This is the first long trip he's had since Father sent him to us.'

'I wish he'd stop howling.'

'He'll be asleep in a few minutes.'

At last his stiff little body drooped in Camilla's arms.

When they arrived at the beach and he saw the familiar figures of Art and Olivia hurrying out to greet them, he was eager to get out of the car, to be picked up and hugged. Mac unbuckled Frances, still fast asleep, and carried her.

Art and Olivia had added two more bedrooms and another bathroom to the cottage, and had continued the porch, so that it wrapped all the way around the house. Like many beach places it was up on stilts. Part of the underside was used as a garage. Art had rigged up a shower, so they could rinse off salt water and sand when they came in from the ocean. The weather was warm enough for wading, but would not be comfortable for swimming for another couple of months.

Olivia said, 'If you want a wet suit like those surfers down toward Saint Augustine, it's all right with me.'

Camilla shook her head. 'I must be getting old. I'm quite willing to wait until it's warm enough for a bathing suit.'

After the children were fed, Olivia served the grownups sandwiches and iced tea out on the ocean side of the veranda. The children were in the playpen, too excited to nap. Taxi was standing, holding on to the side of the playpen and bouncing. Frances, trying to imitate him, fell backwards, landing on a pile of stuffed animals. Sometimes she bellowed with frustration, sometimes she sent out merry peals of laughter. Her bellows never lasted long. If Taxi continued to thwart her by standing, she would crawl to him, put her arms around him, and pull him down, and the two of them would roll about like puppies.

'What a delight to watch,' the bishop said.

Camilla said, 'Frances is doing much of the work of freeing Taxi to be a happy little boy.'

Olivia commented, 'What a radical change.'

Mac said, 'We still have a way to go.'

Camilla explained, 'Taxi was frightened on the way here. I think he was afraid we were going to take him somewhere and abandon him. Not consciously, but somewhere deep inside.' She helped herself to a small sandwich. 'It's really exciting, what you've done to the house.'

'You approve?' the bishop asked. 'Eventually we'll insulate the old part, and put in some kind of heat for winter. North Florida can be mighty cold, particularly in February.'

'Thank God this house is high up on the dunes,' Olivia said. 'Some of the new places down on the beach with only a flimsy sea wall are going to have a hard time of it when there's a hurricane.'

'It's a wonderful house,' Camilla said, 'and the new rooms are perfect, on the other side of the living room from your bedroom, so you won't be disturbed by the children.'

'Do you have enough bookcases?' Mac asked.

'Of course not,' the bishop said. 'There's no such thing as enough bookcases. I hope you noticed the one in your bathroom, full of English murder mysteries and other stimulating reading.'

Mac grinned. 'What's in yours?'

'More of the same. Plus a few books on astrophysics, so we can talk with Camilla.'

It was the beginning of a happy week. The first morning, when Camilla and Mac went into the children's room, Frances was asleep in her crib, but Taxi was not there. For a moment Camilla's heart lurched with terror. Where—

She hurried into the living room and saw Art coming toward her, carrying Taxi. He explained, 'Sometime in the middle of the night I felt breathing on my face, and there was this little one. So he got into bed with Olivia and me and spent the rest of the night.'

'Papa, I'm sorry.'

'Don't be. He was a charming bedfellow, no trouble at all, and didn't wake up till just a few minutes ago.'

Mac laughed. 'His crib at home has much higher sides than the one you have for him. He couldn't have climbed out of that. Tonight we'll try to keep him where he belongs.'

The bishop set the little boy down, who kept his balance by clinging to his grandfather's leg. His grandfather? —Yes, Camilla thought. Please, yes.

'Don't worry about it,' Art said. 'Let be whatever will be.'

And what was, was that somehow or other Taxi managed to get out of his crib, cross the living room on his wobbly legs, and get into bed with Art and Olivia. Into their bed and into their hearts.

One evening as they sat out on the veranda after dinner, watching the pale rose of the afterglow fade from the sky, the bishop rocked gently back and forth in his green rocker, murmuring, *'Tell me, brother, What are we? / Spirits bathing in the sea / Of Deity.'*

Mac raised his arms over his head luxuriously, looking out over the ocean gently rolling in to shore. 'That's beautiful, Papa. One of your favorite unknown poets?'

'Christopher Cranch. Apt, isn't it, for this place, this peace.'

Olivia gave a small shiver. 'This peace. Yes. May it last. Do you ever wonder who Taxi's father might be?'

The bishop turned toward his wife, shaking his head. 'My dear—'

'No,' Camilla said firmly. 'I don't wonder. Very carefully I don't wonder. The four of us and my father are the only people who know that Taxi's father isn't— Maybe whoever it is doesn't know. To the rest of the world, my father is Taxi's father. He's getting old, he travels too much to care for an infant. He's getting arthritis. Taking Taxi's the natural thing for us to do.'

The children were asleep. Mac glanced up as though he could see into their room. 'Camilla and I don't think of Taxi as her brother. Not now, if we ever did. He's our son.'

'He's a love of a child,' Olivia said. 'He certainly doesn't look like Rose, or whoever—'

The bishop said, 'Rafferty talked bitterly of some Frenchman they met at a party. Who knows? Taxi looks enough like Camilla to be her natural son.'

Olivia said, 'Darling Frances has considerable Rafferty in her.'

'Father?' Camilla asked in surprise. 'I think she looks like Mac.'

'She does, but Frances is not going to be small like the Xanthakoses. Height is what she has from Rafferty.'

Art said, 'Let them be who they are.'

'Precious lambs.' Camilla nodded.

The bishop reached for his wife's hand. 'They're our grandchildren. We are very blessed.'

•

But the blessing, it seemed to Camilla, was precarious.

Frank came to the United States for three months' home leave. Bethann was pregnant and had gone to stay with her parents. Frank flew down to Georgia to spend a long weekend with Mac and Camilla.

'Your timing is marvelous,' Mac said. They were sitting at the table under the pine tree, a wooden picnic table Rafferty had sent them to replace the old card table. The children were in an enclosure Mac had made, about the size of half a dozen playpens, where they kept their outdoor toys. 'Camilla and I have a big decision to make.'

'We've made it, haven't we?' Camilla asked.

'Yes. I wish I felt surer that we're doing the right thing.'

Frank put down his tea glass and stretched. 'Dear Mac, if you think you can be absolutely sure about anything, you're in the wrong business. What's this about?'

'I've been offered a parish in Jacksonville. We need to leave Corinth. Everybody who sees Taxi knows that his mother was killed in an accident, and that she was Camilla's mother. They see a tragic story, not a happy little boy.' He looked toward the pen, where the two children were pummeling each other. Peals of laughter rang like bells against the evening air.

'You'd be a priest in your father's diocese,' Frank pointed out.

'I don't think that would be the problem. If we want a new and fresh life for Frances and Taxi, even Jacksonville's too close to everything that's happened. Too many people know.'

Frances's laughter was joyous as she scuttled away from Taxi and sat on a large stuffed polar bear.

'Fankie!' Taxi shouted. 'Fankie.'

Frank laughed delightedly. 'He calls her Frankie! My little namesake. I think you're right, Mac. Frankie and Taxi are sister and brother. They need to be somewhere where they can live out of the spotlight.'

'Meanwhile,' Mac said, 'we're in Corinth. Taxi's beginning to talk. Frances tries to imitate him but she is, after all, considerably younger than he is, in baby terms.'

'What does Taxi call you?' Frank asked.

Was that everybody's question? Camilla asked, 'What do you think?'

Mac said, 'Taxi says Dadada, and Mamama, and Frances comes close.'

Frank nodded. 'You're letting them do what comes naturally.'

Taxi's laughter turned to a whine, and Camilla stood up. 'When they stop having fun, it's time for bed.' She picked the two children up, tucking one under each arm, and headed for the house.

'Good for you,' she heard Frank say. 'You're not spoiling them.'

'It's easier not to spoil two than one. It's simply self-preservation.' The slamming of the screened door cut off their voices.

When she returned to the pine tree, Mac was alone. 'Where's Frank?'

'He went in to take a shower. I told him.'

She sat down beside him on the bench. 'Told him what?'

'That Rafferty's not Taxi's father.'

'Oh, Mac, no,' she protested.

'It's Frank, Cam. I'd trust Frank with my life. I do. You know that.'

'I trust him, too. But the fewer people who know, the better.'

'Frank will never say anything.'

'I know that, but—it's Father—it's so hard on him—humiliating—'

'I needed to have Frank know. Taxi has become as dear to us as Frances. But he is, in fact, not our child. He has no blood tie to me.'

'He does, to me.'

'Frank won't tell anyone, not even his wife. I just have this weird feeling we're on the edge of a precipice.'

'A premonition?' she asked anxiously.

'No. Just—the secrecy. I know we have to protect your father. But one secret leads to another. Sooner or later Taxi will have to know the truth.'

'Not sooner. He's just a baby.'

'He won't be a baby forever.'

'But not yet, Mac, and not ever, about Father—'

'Not now. I know. But—' He shook his head. Changed the subject. 'I'm glad Frank agrees that Jacksonville is too close to home. That's another reason I had to tell him, so I could talk to him honestly about the whole thing.'

She nodded, still wishing he had said nothing about Taxi's paternity. 'We need to leave Corinth. Taxi's bright, almost too bright. I don't want some troublemaker like Mrs. Lee hurting him.'

'Or Frances.'

'Or Frances. But Taxi's in the vulnerable position.'

'We can't protect them forever.'

'Maybe not from the normal things, the ordinary, growing-up things. But vicious gossip?'

Mac bent down and picked up a handful of pine needles, letting their rust-colored stickiness slip through his fingers. 'It needn't even be vicious to hurt them. Cam, darling, I think I do want to go for my doctorate.'

'If you're sure it's what you want.'

'As much as I want anything right now. I've done a pretty good job here. Mama and Papa will understand about Jacksonville. I think they'll agree. But maybe we could go to the beach to be with them for a couple of days, talk it all over, get their advice.'

'In the end,' she said slowly, 'we have to make the decision ourselves.' She had made her major decisions on her own, not even considering consulting Rose and Rafferty. But then, Rose and Rafferty were nothing like Olivia and Art.

Frank came back out, wearing a fresh shirt and clean shorts. 'I'd forgotten this kind of heat. Your little ones are sound asleep, glistening with sweat. I guess they're used to it. Acclimated.'

'I'm not,' Camilla said. 'I wanted to get another air conditioner, but Taxi tends to croup, and the air conditioner isn't good for him. Thank heaven Frances seems to thrive, no matter what. We tried having her sleep away from Taxi, but it didn't work. They both howled till we put them back together.'

'*What a good and pleasant a thing it is,*' Frank quoted, '*for brethren to dwell together in unity.* Not much of it in the rest of the world. Or all around you, with racial unrest increasing. How's Corinth?'

Mac shrugged. 'Still living in the dark ages. Sooner or later the world will catch up with us, but for now we're quiet. Segregated, but quiet.'

Frank sat across from them, stretching his legs along the bench. 'Enjoy it while you can.'

'I'm not exactly enjoying it.' Mac scratched his head. 'The thing is, how much can I say without creating so much antagonism that nothing is accomplished?'

Camilla said, 'The kids talk a little, on Sunday evenings. Gordie is such a reactionary he tends to make the others more open than they might be. Freddy Lee is applying to Harvard, and he'll probably get in.'

'Harvard's not exactly a hotbed of integration,' Frank said.

'It would be a start, and I think Freddy's open to it.'

Camilla wrapped her arms about herself as though a cold breeze had blown across the table. The violence that was spreading in the South had not touched Corinth, and she had isolated herself to some extent through her preoccupation with her little family. With half her mind she listened to Mac and Frank, while still keeping an ear alert to the house and the children's open bedroom window.

When she was in Athens she usually dropped into the library's reading room to catch up on *The New York Times*. If they went to New York for Mac to get his Ph.D. she would return to the world, the wider world, where she could forget that Mrs. Lee did not think she was quite what a rector's wife ought to be, and could remember to be a member of the larger universe.

The children were not an excuse but they were the reason for her isolation. Although Taxi looked sturdy, he was not as strong as Frankie—as they were now calling her. When Frankie had a mild case of chicken pox, Taxi had a bad one, and Camilla and Mac took turns sitting up all night with him until his fever abated and his running sores had dried up.

Frankie was growing into an independent little girl, wanting to do things on her own, to feed herself as soon as Taxi did, to drink from a cup, to imitate everything. Taxi was willing to be dependent, to need cuddling, to count on the unvarying nighttime routine, the same songs, the same prayers, in the same order.

The cribs were replaced by two youth beds, sent by Rafferty. Taxi was usually the first one to waken in the morning, calling softly, 'Ma-ma.' Camilla was his mother, there was no question about that; he was her child as much as Frankie, the little tomboy.

When Mac came home, Taxi would rush at him, 'Daddy, Daddy, Daddy!' followed by Frankie, equally loud, both of them waiting for Mac to pick them up and swing them. Quantum, unwilling to be left out, would make one of his leaps onto Mac's shoulder, and then purr loudly enough to be heard over the children, while Camilla laughed with pleasure.

When the children were in bed, Camilla, often joined by Mac, read to them.

One night Taxi looked at them, asking, 'Who bought Frankie and me?'

Mac said, 'No one could possibly buy either you or Frankie. You're both much too precious to buy.'

'Extweemly pwecious,' Frankie announced.

'But who bought us?' Taxi persisted.

Camilla tried to help. 'You couldn't be bought, Taxi. God gave you and Frankie to us.'

'For Cwistmas,' Frankie said.

'But we was tiny babies. How did we get to be tiny babies?'

Mac said, 'You know how we put seeds in the garden, and they turn into flowers and vegetables? You might say you and Frankie were grown from seeds.'

Camilla looked at him. He was right. Ultimately Taxi would want more accurate stories of his birth.

'But how did you get the right seeds?' Taxi asked.

Mac answered seriously, 'We do have to have the right seeds, son. If we got the wrong seeds, you could have been a tomato instead of a Taxi.'

He and Frankie broke into delighted giggles at this fancy.

'Bedtime, bedtime,' Mac said. 'No more questions tonight.'

He and Camilla kissed the children. Then Camilla went outside and stood looking up at the night sky, at the familiar patterns of the stars, until she felt relaxed enough to go to bed.

'Star-gazing?' Mac asked as she came into their room.

She laughed. 'Yes. Most astronomers don't actually go out and look at the stars, but it's something I've always liked to do, maybe because there weren't many stars visible in the New York night sky. The stars at night were one of the things that got me through my years in boarding school. They're especially beautiful, here, in Corinth.'

Mac rubbed his hand gently against the back of her neck. 'I go into the church and pray, and you go out and look at the stars.' He stretched his arms high. 'God, it's good.' Then he turned to her and pulled her to him.

Later that night, waking from a dream, Camilla went downstairs to write her weekly letter to Rafferty, whose arthritis was worsening, and who had moved from Chicago to New Mexico. New Mexico was far enough away so that Mrs.

Lee no longer asked Camilla why Taxi's father did not come to visit. He sent expensive presents regularly, and Camilla wrote him long, chatty letters about the children.

This chore was the sad point of the week. She had lost Rafferty as her father when he sent Taxi to them.

TEN

EARLY IN THE SPRING, when Taxi and Frankie were four, Mac finally received his seminary appointment. His job would begin in February with the Lenten term. He would be tutoring a group of junior seminarians, and teaching a seminar in ascetical theology, as well as doing his own work for his degree.

'What's ascetical theology?' Camilla asked.

'Oh, prayer, mediation, contemplation. Things like that. I'm glad I haven't been asked to lecture in church history or Anglican polity. Are you ready for the big city?'

'I'll miss a lot of people, especially Dr. Edith, but in many ways I can't wait to go home.'

'Has Corinth been so awful?' he asked again.

'No. Corinth has been wonderful. Frankie was born here. Taxi came to us here. It will always be special. But I'm ready to leave. The children are still young enough to be able to put down new roots. I was brought up in New York, so I don't see it as a bad place for children.'

Mac said, 'There's a playground for them at the seminary, and it's safe enough so they can go about the grounds on their own.'

'What about Quantum? We can take him with us, can't we?'

'Of course. There are lots of pets there. When the kids are old enough, maybe we can get a dog.'

'Quantum's enough for now.'

Mac pulled on a light sweater. 'We'll be here for Christmas with the parish, and I'm glad of that. I'll miss our little brown church.'

'We'll ask Dr. Edith to come to us for Christmas as usual.'

'Of course. And we should have a Christmas party for the youth group.' But his mind went quickly back to the seminary. 'The dean suggests that we come to New York the last week in January, and have a few days to settle in before term starts. We're being given an apartment in one of the buildings on the seminary grounds, and he says it's plenty big enough for the four of us.'

'January,' Camilla said.

'Moving day will be on us before we know it. The dean's going to send us a floor plan of the apartment. It sounds bigger than the rectory. There are three bedrooms and two and a half bathrooms.'

'More than one bath! Bliss!'

'All right, love. I've got to get back to the office. I'm still uncertain about my sermon. Palm Sunday's almost here, and we have all those extra services in Holy Week. You all right?'

She looked out the kitchen windows to the back yard, where the children were on the swings which Mac had made, hung from a frame near the big pine. Frankie was standing up. 'For heaven's sake, get Frankie to sit down!' Camilla exclaimed. 'She's much too young to be swinging that way. Where did she get that from?'

'Not from Taxi,' Mac said. 'He's a cautious little kid. I'll stop the little hellion.' The screened door slammed behind him. She watched as he strode to the swings and made the little girl sit down. She heard him whistling as he walked down the path. He was happy about the New York appointment, then.

•

She went into the kitchen, sitting where she could keep an eye on the children, and poured herself a cup of coffee, glancing at an article on some strange radiomagnetic phenomena, when she saw Dr. Edison coming up the path.

The older woman knocked lightly on the door and came into the kitchen. 'Any more coffee in the pot?'

'Plenty.'

'Here's your mail. I passed the postman on the way in.'

Camilla handed Dr. Edison the coffee and a pitcher of milk, then looked through the mail. Begging letters. Catalogues. A package from Rafferty which looked like books for the children. A letter from Noelle, who was still living in Boston. Noelle was happily married and pregnant. Camilla would save her letter to read later.

'What I really came for'—Dr. Edison put down her cup—'was to see if I could take the children for the morning, it's such a superb day. I thought I'd take them for a walk, and maybe we could blow bubbles or something outdoors.'

'That would be marvelous, Dr. Edith. I have a million things to do, and I can't really concentrate when I'm keeping an eye on the children.'

'I enjoy them, and you look tired and as though you need a break. I'll bring them back after lunch.' She waved at Camilla as she went out the kitchen door and headed toward the children. Taxi leapt into her arms. Frankie stood up on the seat of the swing again, and Dr. Edison pulled her down. Quantum dashed across the yard to the house and pushed and pulled at the screened door, which he had learned to open.

Camilla returned to the article, which she planned to incorporate into her next lecture. Quantum sat on her lap, purring. She worked until the sun was high and she realized that it was after noon and that she was hungry. Bless Dr. Edith. And, yes, she was tired. Two extremely active children saw to that.

Her time at the university was her time off, and although teaching was tiring as well as challenging, it was tiring in a completely different way from mothering, and she would drive home after class feeling refreshed.

She fixed herself a bowl of soup and took it outside. The azaleas were a blaze of color. She had deep red camellias in a glass bowl on the picnic table, shaded by the pine tree. She settled herself at the table. The top needed a good scrubbing. She would do that later.

•

She turned back to the article, then looked up as an open red sports car drew into the driveway and a man and a woman got out. The woman was younger than the man, with short, curly fair hair, and she was wearing jeans and a short-sleeved T-shirt. Camilla focused on her, instinctively not wanting to recognize the man with his receding reddish hair. But he walked toward her.

'Camilla,' he said.

'Profes—' she started reluctantly.

'Grange,' he finished, and held out both hands to her. She took them, wondering what on earth had brought him to Corinth.

'Camilla. You're lovely as ever. Harriet—' He turned to the woman. 'Come and let me introduce you to one of the best students I ever had. Camilla, this is my wife, Harriet.'

The woman's hand was cool, and heavy with rings. She dropped it loosely into Camilla's outstretched hand, and withdrew it, turning away, her eyes filling with tears.

'Won't you sit down?' Camilla asked. 'It's really pleasanter here than in the house.'

Professor Grange sat across from Camilla at the picnic table, gently pulling his wife down beside him, and putting his arm about her waist. To Camilla he said, 'Has everything gone well with you and Edith Edison?'

'She's marvelous,' Camilla said. 'I can't thank you enough.'

'You deserved the best,' Grange said. 'I'm glad I could give you and Edith to each other.'

Harriet pulled a handkerchief out of her small handbag and blew her nose.

Camilla looked at her, at Grange. Why were they here? What underlay this visit? They had not stopped for a casual chat.

Harriet touched her husband on the shoulder. 'Red, darling—'

'Camilla—' His voice was hesitant. 'Something has happened, something totally unexpected, and—perhaps—hopeful.'

She looked at him, fear beginning to tingle along her spine.

'Where are the children?' Harriet asked.

'They're out with a friend.' Why did she not want to tell them that the friend was Dr. Edison? Wouldn't that have been the normal response? But this was not, could not be, a normal visit.

'But you knew we were coming?' Grange asked.

She shook her head numbly. What a strange question. How could she have known?

'Noelle didn't tell you?'

Again she shook her head. Noelle had written bitterly of her father's remarriage. Camilla suddenly remembered the letter which had come from Noelle that morning and which lay unopened on the kitchen table.

'Red, darling,' Harriet said again. 'Don't keep putting it off.'

Quantum came leaping toward them, sprang onto the picnic table, and sat on Camilla's manuscript.

Grange reached into his pocket and pulled out an envelope, which he handed to Camilla. 'Read this.'

She took the letter. There was a faint, familiar smell of tea rose. The envelope was addressed in her mother's round handwriting, with the return address of the apartment in Paris. Inside the envelope was another, blue, marked in capital letters: TO BE OPENED IN THE EVENT OF MY DEATH. Camilla looked at Grange.

He said, 'My wife, my ex-wife, preempted the letter. She gave it to me when she knew she had to go to the hospital for surgery. Cancer. She didn't want to die with this on her conscience.' He looked toward Harriet, then back to Camilla. 'Read it,' he ordered.

> *My darling Red,*
> *I'm five months pregnant and all is going well. I don't expect to have any problems, because I'm incredibly healthy, and my darling doctor says he can't believe I'm over thirty. But it's a chancy world, so I want you to know that I think this baby is yours, and if anything should happen to Rafferty, or to me, you need to know this. After Camilla was born, Rafferty and I never conceived again, so I doubt that this baby is his. Thank God Camilla looks exactly like him.*
> *Dearest Red, I don't want you to do anything with what I am telling you until both Rafferty and I are dead. It would kill him if he thought the baby wasn't his, and I can't do that to him. You know how good Rafferty has always been to me. But after we're both gone, then, if you want to, you can do whatever you think best.*
> *Am I wrong to tell you this and then ask you to do nothing? I don't know. But this morning I felt compelled to let you know. I trust you, dearest love.*
> *Your one, true Rose*

Camilla folded the letter, put it back in the blue envelope, then the white, outer one, and handed it to Grange. She had carefully suppressed any suspicion that Taxi's father might be Red Grange. Taxi had black hair, and he had Camilla's eyes, too. He looked like Camilla's child. There was nothing reminiscent of Grange about him.

'Are you all right?' Harriet asked.

'No. Yes. No.' The color drained out of everything. For a moment she thought she was going to faint. She blinked. Blinked. Slowly color returned to sky, trees, grass. To Red Grange and Harriet.

'Camilla, you really didn't know? You didn't guess?' Grange asked.

'No. No. Father thought—a French diplomat—'

Harriet asked, 'Camilla, can you have any idea what this news means to us?'

No. She could not guess. She had no idea.

Harriet asked again, 'Where are the children?'

'With a friend.'

'When will they be back?'

'I'm not sure. After lunch.'

Grange said, 'Can't you understand? I want to see my baby.'

Her voice shook. 'He's not a baby. He's four years old.'

Harriet said, 'I was thrown from a horse three years ago. It was a bad fall. I can't have children. It's a terrible grief to me. Red and I were actually talking about adoption when—'

Grange put up a warning hand. 'Not so fast, Harriet. All we've come for today is to let you know about—'

'To let you know that we desperately want to see Red's son.'

Camilla said, 'I'm sorry, but I truly don't think that's a good idea, without any preparation at all. Taxi's a happy, contented little boy. All he knows is that Mac, my husband, is his daddy. He's not strong, and I don't want him upset, and he does get upset easily.'

Harriet picked up one of the camellias, dropped it back in the bowl. 'We don't want him upset either, but don't you think his father has some rights? And I—' She broke off as tears came to her eyes again.

'Perhaps,' Grange suggested, 'I could just see him and not say anything.'

'No, Red.' Harriet held up a warning hand. 'He's your son. You have some rights. And he has a right to know, doesn't he? To know who his father is?'

Camilla shook her head as though trying to wake up from a bad dream. 'I'm sorry. I was completely unprepared—'

'Didn't you think,' Grange asked, 'that something like this might happen?'

'No. Not now. At first, perhaps . . . But it was all so horrible, my mother's death.'

'And your father?' Grange asked. 'He knew, didn't he? Did he really fool himself into thinking the baby was his? He must have known . . .'

'Taxi looks like me,' Camilla said. 'Not like my mother or—' She looked at him. The reddish hair. The hazel eyes. There was nothing of him in Taxi, nothing to make her suspicious.

Harriet looked at her watch. 'It's after one. Won't the children be back soon?'

'I need to see my son,' Grange said. 'The little son I didn't know I had.'

They all looked up as they heard children's voices. Laughter. Taxi and Frankie were holding Dr. Edith's hands, pulling her along with them.

'Mommy, Mommy, we blew bubbles!'

'Like rainbows!'

Grange and Harriet jumped up, their eyes on the children, who were both wearing jeans and dirt-streaked T-shirts. Taxi's hair needed cutting, a process he fiercely resisted. Frankie's hair had been cut short for summer. Harriet moved toward her, holding out her arms. 'Taxi?'

Frankie stepped back. Giggled.

Dr. Edison, flushed, slightly out of breath, looked at Grange and Harriet. 'Red!'

'Edith, dear Edith.' He hurried to her, taking her hands, looking at her, saying, 'Gad, you're still a handsome woman!' He drew her to him, kissing her on both cheeks.

She asked, 'What on earth are you doing here?'

Camilla had her arms about the children, nudging them toward the house. 'You may each have two cookies from the cookie jar. I'll be in to pour you some milk in a few minutes.'

'I can do it,' Taxi said.

'All right, Taxi love. Go slowly, and try not to spill.'

Grange watched them scamper toward the house. 'Which one is—'

'They look very much alike, don't they?' Camilla's eyes followed them in, making sure the screened door was shut.

'My boy—'

'The prettier one, with curly hair—' Harriet looked confused.

Dr. Edith asked, 'What on earth—'

Camilla sat once more on the picnic bench. Her legs felt too fluid to hold her up.

Harriet said, 'We haven't been introduced. I am Harriet Grange. We've come to give Red a chance to see the son he's been denied all these years.'

Dr. Edison said flatly, 'I have no idea what all this is about.'

Grange handed her Rose's letter. She read it slowly, then returned it. Then said, 'Now that you've seen this extraordinary document, now that you've seen the child, you are, of course, going to heed the dead woman's wishes?'

Harriet looked at her left hand with its heavy rings, moved the fingers of her right hand across them.

Dr. Edison continued, 'Which are that you do nothing?'

Harriet spoke in a low voice. 'Rafferty Dickinson lives in New Mexico. He has abandoned his child. He might as well be dead.'

'No!' Camilla's voice rose. She tried to control it. 'He is very much alive. Please, please. You've seen Taxi, he's well and happy, you can set your minds at rest. Perhaps, later, we could talk about, what do you call them, visitation rights . . .'

Harriet's voice trembled. 'I don't think you realize how difficult this is for us.'

Dr. Edison said, 'I'm sure it is extremely difficult. But now that you've been reassured that all is well, shouldn't you accede to Rose Dickinson's last wishes and leave well enough alone?'

Harriet reached again for her handkerchief. 'It's not as easy as that. For me—it seems such an answer to prayer.'

'Mommy! Mommy!' The children's voices rose shrilly.

Camilla jumped to her feet. 'They've probably spilled the milk.'

'Let me!' Harriet's voice was eager. 'Let me pour it for them!' She hurried toward the house, her sandals flapping against the stubby grass. Grange followed her.

Dr. Edison asked Camilla, 'Is this true?'

Camilla nodded. 'Mother's letter—I suppose so. We knew that my father was not Taxi's father, but we didn't know—we didn't want to know—Taxi's so dark, and we thought it was the Frenchman when we thought about it at all.'

'Were you, perhaps, deceiving yourselves?'

'I don't know,' Camilla said. 'We weren't thinking. We were trying to protect Taxi—my father—'

She pulled a quivering breath. 'What are they here for? What do they want?'

'Too much,' Dr. Edison said.

She and Camilla went into the kitchen, where Taxi was refusing to take the glass of milk Harriet was offering him. 'I want Mommy.'

Grange touched his wife. 'Relax, darling. This is enough for the first day. Camilla, we'll be back tomorrow to talk further about what's to be arranged.'

Camilla closed her eyes. 'You'll have to give us time. I'll have to talk to my husband about visitation privileges. Please—'

Harriet put the untouched glass of milk on the counter. 'Please, dear Camilla, be realistic. Doesn't Red—'

Before she could finish the sentence the screened door opened and Mrs. Lee came bursting in, 'Camilla, have you had the radio on? Terrible news! President Kennedy has been shot!'

•

The country was in mourning for the violent death of a president. But Camilla's world had shrunk again, to the imperative need to protect her little family.

She walked out to the red convertible with Grange and Harriet, said goodbye in what she hoped was a courteous but final way.

Harriet said, 'You've been so gracious, Camilla. I know how difficult our coming must have been for you, especially if you weren't expecting us. We truly thought you knew.'

Grange said, 'This is no time to talk, with this horrible news of Kennedy's assassination. We'll be by again tomorrow, to talk further.'

'To talk further about what!' Camilla cried as the convertible vanished dustily down the road.

Dr. Edison looked at the children, who were happily kicking a beach ball back and forth. She said, bluntly, 'They didn't come about visitation rights. They want Taxi.'

'No.'

'They're trying to be tactful about it, but Harriet was horridly transparent.'

'No. No, Dr. Edith.' Then she said, as though to herself, 'Harriet can't have children—' She looked at her watch. 'Mac should be through with his meeting. I've got to call him.'

'What an appalling story you've had to live with,' Dr. Edison said. 'It was terrible enough, your mother's death, your father's being left alone with his baby— But this—'

'Oh, Dr. Edith'— Camilla walked slowly toward the rectory—'my mother always left a trail of disaster behind her.'

When Camilla saw Mac walking along the path that led

from the church to the rectory, she ran to him, throwing herself into his arms, blurting out what had happened.

He looked at Dr. Edith, who was walking toward him more slowly. She nodded, then shook her head in sadness.

'You're sure you're not—you're not reading things—'

'No,' Dr. Edison said. 'I'm sorry, Mac. It's possible that I'm overreacting, but I don't think so.'

'They can't mean it.' Mac's voice was harsh.

Dr. Edison said, 'Oh, I think they do. I will certainly testify for you, and so, of course, will Mr. and Mrs. Bishop. I will tell any judge that you are Taxi's parents, and that what Red and Harriet have in mind is criminal.'

'I'll call Jacksonville,' Mac said.

Again the assassination was pushed into the background. Olivia's immediate reaction was incredulity. 'No. You must be mistaken.'

Mac said, 'Mama, listen. The letter from Camilla's mother was real. Grange is Taxi's father.'

'You believe that?'

'It's there, in black and white.'

The bishop's voice was heavy. 'We should have foreseen this.'

'Come to us,' Olivia urged. 'You'll be safer here, if this is true.'

Mac, with one foot still in the world, said, 'I can't leave here, Mama, not with the assassination . . .'

The bishop said, 'I'll speak with some of my lawyer friends, to see if they have a leg to stand on.'

'Do you want me to come?' Olivia suggested. 'Taxi shouldn't be left with baby-sitters, and Edith can't be there all the time.'

'Please come, Mama,' Mac said, 'for a few days, until we get this settled.'

'I'll call you,' the bishop said, 'when I've talked to the lawyers.'

'Dr. Edith,' Mac said, 'thank you for being here.'

Dr. Edison said something incomprehensible and rude-sounding in Latin, then asked, 'Does anybody else know? That Rafferty isn't Taxi's father?'

'My parents know,' Mac said.

'Did you suspect that it might be Grange?'

Camilla shook her head. 'It seemed better not to know.'

Not to know. Is ignorance ever an excuse?

•

"I didn't know." Raffi wrapped her arms about herself to control her shuddering. "I don't think I want to know now." The autumn evening was unusually warm. Hazy clouds hid the stars.

A group of girls came by the open window, singing an old student song Camilla had first heard when she was in college, and it had been old all those years ago, *Gaudeamus igitur, juvenes dum sumus*. They had been immortal then. Camilla looked at Raffi and suspected that Taxi's intimations had been of mortality when he made his vague suggestions to his daughter. Why now? She turned away, body and mind. "The temperature's supposed to drop twenty degrees tonight," she said.

"Grandmother, what you've just told me, about their taking my dad away, it's horrible." She dropped the green socks as though they had suddenly become hot.

Camilla nodded. "Yes, it was horrible. Everybody talked about wanting it to be civilized, but it dragged through the courts."

Swiftly Raffi put her arms around Camilla, holding her tight. "I want you to be my grandmother."

Camilla returned the embrace, assuring, "I am your grandmother. I am Taxi's mother."

"But it's your mother who was my dad's biological mother."

"Yes."

"That makes you my aunt, not my grandmother."

"No. Raffi, that is only a thin and legalistic way of looking at it. Time and experience are the other side of the coin. Mac and I are your grandparents, even if you never knew him. He is Taxi's father."

"Not biologically. And my real grandfather, this Red Grange guy, what a bastard."

"I am beyond judgment," Camilla said. "Surely the real Red Grange, the old football player, would shudder at what has happened in his name. This is enough for tonight, Raffi. I'm sorry. Absorb what I've told you. It's more than enough." Gently she moved away from the girl. The strands of past memories were so closely interwoven that it was impossible to separate them. Why, when in the past Taxi had been so adamant that he was Taxi Xanthakos, did he put questions in Raffi's mind now? Was it the old need to hurt, to punish the universe, out of control again? To punish Red Grange and, failing that, since Red was dead, to punish Camilla, even if he hurt Raffi in so doing? "Raffi, darling, I've hurt you."

"Being surrounded by stuff I can't understand hurts me."

"You may never understand it all. I don't. I wish Mac was here."

"You miss him, don't you?"

"Yes."

"He died before I was born. So I can't miss him the way you do."

"It's fine, Raffi. Missing Mac. I mean. We'd gone through our garbage."

"Was there a lot?"

"Plenty. But we'd reached a place of—of mercy. I don't think I can tell you a great deal more until I have more mercy in my heart than I do at this moment."

"How long is that going to take?"

"Not too long. I don't want to leave you with painful questions any longer than I have to. But some of them don't have any answers."

"Okay, Grandmother. Let's put on some music and relax."

She pulled a disc from the bottom shelf of the bookcase, and the strains of Dvořák's "Dumky" filled the room. Camilla closed her eyes to hide the tears.

•

When Raffi left she did not go straight back to her dormitory. She went instead to one of her favorite hiding places, the great greenhouse which during the day was filled with biology and botany students. Now it was empty, sweet-smelling, warm. There was a dry ground cloth on the floor at the back, and she lay down on it, on her side, curled up, too battered by what she was hearing from her grandmother even to cry. She slid into a place beyond thought, a place of dark, silent emptiness. But the strains of Dvořák's piano trio broke across her mind's ear. She pulled her knees up, her head down.

•

The "Dumky" Trio was one of Taxi's favorite records. Camilla and Mac often played music in the evening to help put the children to sleep, and Taxi would shout out, 'Dumky! Dumky!'

The children, sensing the tension in the air after Mrs. Lee's announcement of President Kennedy's death, were slow to quiet down that evening, after Grange and Harriet left, muted by the news. The phone kept ringing, with people wanting to talk about a service for the President. In between calls, Camilla and Mac talked again to Mama and Papa in Jacksonville, seeking some kind of reason within the irrationality which surrounded them.

Frankie called for *Hansel and Gretel,* and Taxi shouted over her, 'Dumky!' It took both records before the children were at last asleep. Camilla went down to the kitchen and saw Noelle's unopened letter on the table. She opened it and read:

Oh, God, Camilla,
What hell. I'm having twins, and that's not the hell, Fer-
ris and I are delighted. It's Dad. I can't believe what he's
done, leaving Mom when she's having a mastectomy. It's a
terrible thing, psychologically, for a woman. The only
male equivalent would be losing his balls, and Dad's lost
his all right. No matter how much Mom says he has every
right to be angry with her, he doesn't have a right to take
up with this rich bitch. As far as she's concerned, Mom's
no more than a piece of junk dropped on the floor. She
gives Dad horrible presents, like a bright red open Thun-
derbird. We hate her. She's no older than Andrew and
she's superficial and selfish and she can't stand it that
Dad has kids and is about to be a grandfather. Maybe he
deserves deballing . . .

As Camilla finished reading, the phone rang. It was the bishop. He had been talking with his lawyer friends, who said it was a great pity they had not legally adopted Taxi. They were going to put into motion the adoption process, which would make it harder for anyone to take Taxi away. They hoped it was not locking the door of the stable after the horse is gone.

'I'm driving up in the morning,' Olivia said. 'Art and I feel that one of us should be with you.'

'Please, Mama,' Mac said.

'I have no magic wands. I just want to be with you.'

Overnight the weather turned cooler and it was raining, the whole country in mourning. Azaleas dropped their petals.

Grange and Harriet arrived right after breakfast, sub-dued, grave. Harriet asked to see Taxi. Camilla had sent the children out to play with Pinky, and called to the girl to bring them in. This time Camilla did not need Dr. Edison to translate what their intentions were. Harriet looked longingly at Taxi, ignored Frankie.

Pinky, unaware of any problem, offered tea.

Harriet shuddered and said that it was hot, but maybe a glass of sherry ...

'No, my love,' Grange said. 'We must leave. We have an appointment in Atlanta.'

Harriet nodded. 'We will be in touch.'

The children were, in a sense, protected by Pinky's presence, by parishioners coming in and out, wanting to draw together not only by the horror of the assassination, but by the latest scandal to rock Corinth. Herb Morrison and Alberta Byrd were married, but Gordon Byrd had no plans to marry Lydia Morrison after all. He was moving from the bank in Corinth to a much larger one in Atlanta, and he was renting an apartment with another banker, a man. This rocked Corinth far more than the death of the President.

The events of Corinth and of the wider world masked Camilla's and Mac's inner turmoil. Pinky stayed to get away from her own troubles, playing with the children. Wiz and Freddy came to join her, while Camilla, Mac, and Dr. Edison sat at the kitchen table, drinking tea and talking in muted voices. It was a relief when Olivia arrived after lunch.

The children, responding to the multiple tensions, were whiny, and after Pinky had fed them and left with her brother and Freddy, Camilla put Frankie and Taxi to bed.

'The lawyers were appalled at our naïveté,' Olivia said as they sat at the dinner table. She had made her okra-and-tomato casserole, remembered to light the candles, to hold on to some kind of normality. 'They told us we should have expected something like this and taken steps to protect ourselves and Taxi long ago. I blame myself. I swallowed that Frenchman as father because it was easy.'

'Don't blame yourself, Mama,' Mac said. 'We were all naïve.'

'Have you talked to a lawyer yet?'

'Herb Morrison. You've met him, Mama. He's Pinky and Wiz's father, and I gather he's pretty tough.'

Olivia sighed. 'I didn't want you to take Taxi, you know that, but now—'

Mac lifted his fork, put it back down. 'I guess I thought if nobody spoke up in the first few months, nobody would. And the idea that a legal adoption might be a protection never occurred to me. We've been living in our own little cocoon, stupid beyond belief. It's time we left here.' His voice was harsh.

'Peace, Mac,' his mother said.

'We were stupid. I don't understand how we could have been so stupid.'

"Dr. Rowan, I don't understand," Raffi said blankly, slumped in the small enclosure of the dormitory phone booth.

"Raffi, dear, I'm on my way to the airport. I've got to go to San Francisco to give a paper. I'll be back in a few days."

"I need you now."

"Do you want me to refer you to someone else?" Dr. Rowan asked.

"No, dammit! I want you."

"Sunday."

"You don't have office hours on Sunday."

"I get back from San Francisco Saturday night. Come in Sunday morning."

"You do care."

"Of course I care, Raffi. Too much. I'll see you Sunday."

Raffi left the phone booth and walked slowly past the living room to the stairs. "Hey, Raffi, you look sad."

Raffi shrugged. "Oh, PMS. It always makes me gloomy."

"Hey, Raf," one of her friends called out, "did you see your dad's show today?"

"It conflicts with my biology class." She had made sure that she had to be in class during the time of Taxi's show.

"He was terrific, truly, the way he handled that terrible lawyer."

"Thanks, Dorry."

Someone else asked, "When he walks down the street, do people recognize him?"

She made a face. "All the time."

"Like who?"

"People like you, policemen, pimps, politicians."

"How does he take it?"

"Oh, he's gracious, he's really nice to them."

Dorry, the adoring fan, said, "Of course."

"And your mom?" someone asked. "Does she get recognized?"

Raffi scowled, tried to turn it into a smile. "One day someone stopped my mom on the street to speak to her. We all looked surprised. Mom, Dad, and I. But this old gent remembered Mom from when she was dancing, and it was obvious he knew nothing about TV. Dad thought it was hilarious, Mom being recognized instead of him." She stopped abruptly. She had been talking to cover up her feelings. Had her father really been amused? He had been at his most charming, but had he just been acting for the benefit of the passersby on the street? That night he had been in a down mood, snapping at her mother for putting too much salt in the salad ...

One of the girls who majored in economics said, "I suppose soap-opera actors get well paid?"

"Very," Raffi replied.

"Do you want to act, too?"

Raffi shrugged.

"Are you going to try out for the spring play? They're doing a new play one of the seniors wrote, about the Brontës. Emily's the role you ought to try for. She's the most interesting one in the family."

Raffi kept her voice casual. "When are the tryouts?"

"They're having preliminary ones in a few weeks."

"Well, maybe," Raffi said.

"If you're in it, do you think maybe your dad might come up to see it?"

"Who knows. It would depend on his schedule."

"Or if he could even come to a rehearsal—it would be a terrific help."

"God, he's gorgeous."

"You're so lucky."

•

'Do you believe in luck?' Noelle asked when she called. 'I know this is awful timing, and I'm sorry, but Andrew has to come to Atlanta for a conference at Grady, so the timing seems meant. I want him to come by and see you all.'

'But, Noelle—' —Are you crazy? This is one piece of un-reason I can't cope with—

'Hey, I'm not crazy.' (Had Noelle read her thoughts?) 'Or unfeeling or any of those things. We've heard what that Harriet has up her sleeve, about taking Taxi, she's a fiend, and if Andrew sees you and the kids, and how good everything is, that will give him some clout when he speaks to Dad, and Dad does listen to him sometimes.'

'Let me speak to her.' Olivia held out her hand for the phone. Camilla gave it to her. They were in the kitchen, cooking hamburgers for the children's lunch, at Taxi's request. The children were in the yard. Frankie had Quantum in her doll carriage, a baby hat tied askew on the cat's head.

'Calm down, Noelle, and speak coherently. Tell me what you have in mind.' Olivia listened, and Camilla occasionally heard a few words as Noelle raised her voice. 'Mom is . . . as though Dad needs more kids . . . Harriet is a grasping, rich . . .' Finally Olivia said, 'It does make sense, Noelle. Tell Andrew we'll be glad to see him. Have him come to dinner, that's the best way for him to see what the family is like ... Thanks, Noelle ... Take care of yourself. Let us know when the twins arrive.' She put the phone down, turned to Camilla. 'It can't hurt. It may help.'

•

Andrew came, on a rainy spring evening. The children had a picture puzzle spread out on the living-room rug. Good smells came from the kitchen. Olivia was making one of her Greek dishes, which she could mostly prepare ahead of time. They sat in the living room, and Mac poured them a glass of wine.

Taxi, deep in the puzzle, said, 'You give me all the blue pieces, Frankie. That's the sky, okay?'

'I want to do the green. The grass.'

'Okay, but let's get the sky in first, then the rest of it will be easier.'

Andrew said, 'That looks like a fairly complicated puzzle for those little ones.'

'It's not as hard as it looks,' Mac said. 'They've done it half a dozen times before. It does serve to keep them moderately quiet.'

Andrew pulled a small camera out of his jacket pocket. 'Okay if I take a few pictures? This d-doesn't need a flash.'

'Sure,' Mac said. 'The kids are used to having their pictures taken by parents and grandparents and assorted friends.'

Olivia rose, and Camilla stood up, too. 'No,' Olivia said, 'you stay where you are. Everything's done. I just have to bring in the main dish and the salad.' She looked at Andrew. 'The children help set the table, and since they knew we were having a guest tonight, it may be a little unusual. Taxi wanted to have a lizard in a jar at your place, but we persuaded him that wasn't a great idea.'

Andrew snapped a few pictures, then followed Olivia to the kitchen, returned bearing a heavy earthenware dish with steam rising fragrantly. Olivia carried the salad.

Taxi looked up. 'C'n I light the candles?'

Mac said, 'You're not quite old enough yet, Taxi. You and Frankie can each blow one out after dinner. Pick up your puzzle.'

'C'n we finish it after dinner?'

Mac paused. Then, 'Why not? But don't forget it later on.'

'I won't, Daddy. Promise.'

After they were seated and had sung the blessing, Taxi said, 'The TV and radio keep playing sad music.'

Camilla murmured, 'Beethoven's funeral march. Every time we turn the radio on, that's what we hear.'

Taxi looked at Andrew. 'We're very unhappy because the President died.'

Frankie said, 'Mommy says the whole world is sad.'

Taxi continued. 'He was killed. It was very bad.'

'Yes, Taxi. It was a terrible thing.'

'Pictures,' Taxi said. 'On the TV and in the papers. Why does the camera see upside down? Mommy says it does.'

Camilla replied, 'Because our eyes see upside down, and then our brains turn everything right side up again.'

Taxi asked, 'It's an upside-down thing, isn't it, for people to kill other people.'

Andrew replied, 'V-very.'

Taxi looked at him. 'You took some pictures of us.'

Andrew smiled at him. 'And I hope they'll be right side up.'

Frankie held up her hand to get attention. 'Can everything be made right side up again?'

Andrew said, 'That isn't always possible.'

Frankie slid down from her youth chair and went to Andrew, climbing up on his lap. 'I want it to be.'

Mac's voice was gentle. 'Frankie, go back to your chair. You can sit in Andrew's lap after dinner—after you help Taxi pick up the puzzle.'

'Okay.' She slid down and went obediently back to her place.

Taxi said, 'Pinky—she baby-sits for us—says we're too young to understand.'

Andrew answered, 'There are lots of things grownups don't understand, either, Taxi.'

Taxi looked at him. 'Daddy says if we understood everything we'd be God. And we aren't.'

'Your daddy's right.'

With a small gesture Mac indicated to the children it was time for some grownup talk. He asked Andrew about Grady, about his practice in New York.

'And we'll be in New York soon,' Camilla said. 'I can't tell you how much I'm looking forward to it. It's home for me.'

'I'm liking it more than I thought I would. Liz drags me to p-plays and I take her to the opera, so we're both happy. And our practice is already as full as we can m-manage.'

When they had finished eating, Olivia suggested putting the children to bed, but Mac said, 'Let them stay up fifteen more minutes. They need to put their puzzle away.'

The puzzle was quickly tidied up. Frankie went to one of the lower bookshelves and pulled out a book, which she took over to Andrew, looking up at him questioningly, then climbed back up into his lap. Taxi came and sat on the edge of the chair.

'That's a long one,' Camilla warned.

'One chapter,' Andrew said.

'Fine,' Olivia agreed. 'Then I'll take them up and finish it.'

'All of it?' Taxi demanded.

'Until my voice gives out.'

When Olivia had gone upstairs with the children, Andrew said, 'I thought this idea of Noelle's was c-crazy, but having been with you for an evening, I can see what she had in m-mind. It would be criminal to disrupt this little family. Taxi is obviously content and healthy. Both children are delights. But Taxi doesn't l-look l-like R-r-r-ose.' Suddenly his stutter interfered.

'No,' Camilla said. 'He looks like me.'

'But you look like your f-father.'

'Two of my mother's sisters were dark, and there's a picture of one of them when she was young that could be a picture of me. Genetic patterns can be surprising.'

Andrew nodded. 'I w-will do whatever I can. Noelle credits me with more influence on our father than I have, but I will t-try. It's too bad H-harriet can't have children of her own, but this is surely not the s-solution.'

Mac said, tiredly, 'She told us she believes this comes from God.'

Andrew made an irritated gesture.

•

Luisa called. 'My God, Cam, what's going on? Andrew's office is just around the corner from mine and I bumped into him at his bus stop.'

'He told you.' Camilla's voice was flat, with no timbre.

'Why didn't you call me?'

Camilla spoke through a long sigh. 'Oh, Lu, it's all been so sudden. I was going to call. I'm glad you saw Andrew.'

'Maybe he can help, maybe not,' Luisa said. 'I'll certainly testify. I may not be a child psychiatrist, but I still may have some clout. No judge in his right mind would take Taxi away from you.'

N O ?

Andrew's words didn't help, nor those of his child-psychiatrist friend. Nor Luisa's. Nor Herb Morrison, Pinky's father, the toughest lawyer they knew. Nothing helped.

The story was all over the papers. With pictures. Columns and columns of words. More pictures. Taxi being torn out of Camilla's arms as Harriet plucked him away. Passionate opinions, pro and con. Grange was the child's biological father. But Mac was the one Taxi knew as father. Camilla was the one he called Mommy.

Camilla took Frankie to Florida, to the beach house. Mac moved to New York, to the seminary. The farewell parties the parish had planned dwindled away.

•

Luisa flew down to Jacksonville, rented a car, and drove to the beach. Olivia and Frankie were walking along the water's edge, occasionally picking up a shell, or scurrying away from an aggressive wavelet. Quantum was walking along slightly behind them, lifting his feet fastidiously from the sand, but keeping his amber eyes on Frankie.

Camilla was on the porch, rocking, as dazed as though Red Grange and his lawyers had literally beaten her over the head. Camilla looked at Luisa with dull eyes which seemed a muddy grey. 'I thought no judge would take a baby away from his mother.'

'But you aren't—'

'I am! I am Taxi's mother. Not his sister. Half sister. It was my milk that helped him over the worst of his allergies, my arms that held him when he had fever. Mac is his father. Mac picked Taxi up with one arm, Frankie with the other. Of course nobody would separate us. It wasn't human.'

'It isn't compassion that matters in litigation,' Luisa said dryly. 'Or even truth. And this was a tangled truth, and the lawyers tangled it even further.'

'Harriet's expensive lawyers.'

'Very expensive. Very clever. And Harriet got her child. Grange got his son.'

'He's not,' Camilla said. 'He can't be.'

'Legally, biologically, it seems that he is. Psychologically and spiritually of course he isn't. Mac is. I never knew Grange well, Camilla, but this isn't love for Taxi.' Luisa plunked herself down on the porch steps, her elbows on her knees, her chin in her hands, looking out to sea.

Camilla asked the ocean, the sky, 'Did anybody ask what this is doing to Frankie? She has nightmares every night. She screams for Taxi the minute she opens her eyes.'

'Can she see him? They wouldn't stop that, would they?'

'They've gone on a world tour, Harriet and Grange and— And we've spent all the money we have, and more. Mama and Papa have helped. Bishops aren't rich, contrary to what people think. We're all bled white.'

'I've come to help you pack, to get you moved,' Luisa said. 'Maybe it's best for Frankie to start over again in a new house, a new city, make new friends. Maybe Harriet is right that the break should be complete. Maybe this way the kids will heal.'

'Will they heal?'

'I don't know,' Luisa said bluntly. 'It's a hell of a trauma for them, but kids can be extraordinarily resilient. And don't forget you and Mac believe in God.'

'Some of the time,' Camilla said. 'Not right now.'

•

Nevertheless, the move to New York helped. There were no memories of Taxi in the spacious seminary apartment. But Frankie insisted that the two youth beds be in her bedroom. Every night she prayed for Taxi to return.

But there were other children at the seminary to play with, older ones for baby-sitters, not as much like family as the youth group, at least not yet. There were new things to do. Luisa brought Frankie an easel of drawing paper, and a set of large-sized crayons. 'She's a little young for this,' Luisa said, 'but it may help her get some things out instead of burying them inside where they'll fester.'

Camilla watched, awed, as Frankie took the crayons and scrawled, angrily, black, red, purple. No attempt at representation. In any case, she was far too young for anything more than holding a crayon in her small hand and making it move in a wavy line across the page, or occasionally banging the paper with heavy dots.

'Actually,' one of the women in Camilla's building said, 'she's really extraordinary for such a little one. This is a talent that can stand watching.'

Almost imperceptibly Camilla began to feel healing from the city where she had grown up. Through Dr. Edison's influence and, perhaps, Professor Grange's guilt, she quickly found a position at New York University, replacing a middle-aged man who had a heart attack and had to request a long leave of absence. After she had settled Frankie in a small play group, she walked daily from the seminary to Washington Square and NYU, feeling somehow younger as she revisited old haunts.

Luisa was living on the Upper East Side and had an office nearby.

'If I had all the time in the world,' Luisa said, 'I'd take the bus. Or even a taxi. Meanwhile, I'll have to ride the subway. How's Mac?'

'Working hard. He has too much to do, and that's probably good for him right now.'

New York was a world in which there had never been a Taxi. Camilla could not pray with Frankie for Taxi's return, because she did not think it was possible.

Occasionally Luisa would call. 'Hey, I can't use my opera tickets (or ballet tickets, or symphony tickets) tonight, so why don't you and Mac go?'

Camilla suspected that Luisa had no intention of using the tickets herself, that she knew that Camilla and Mac could not afford such luxuries, but she accepted them gratefully. It was a time not only to rejoice in the opera but for her and Mac to have a chance to be alone together. Sometimes it seemed that they did not know what to say.

'Hey,' Luisa said, 'don't worry. When people have been through hell it usually makes them mute for a while.'

.

When Camilla had been with Mac and Frankie in New York for several months, Noelle called. 'Andrew didn't think I ought to phone you,' she said, 'but he and Liz don't have children yet, and I thought maybe ...'

Camilla almost slammed down the phone. What could Noelle say that would not add hurt to hurt? Instead, she asked, trying to sound interested, 'How are the twins?'

'The most gorgeous creatures in the world, if they don't kill me first. Dad called Mom. I know it's weird, but then, so's everything else about all this. Harriet's getting on Dad's nerves, since he called Mom. They're not having an easy time with Taxi.'

'Did they expect to?' Camilla tried to keep anger out of her voice.

'Dad told Mom that Taxi needs constant attention. Mom asked, "Like his mother?" Sorry, Cam, but she does have a point. Listen, I know that sounded awful, I could bite my tongue off, but it's all so . . . I'm really, really sorry. But I know you want to know what's going on. I would, in your place. If my twins—'

'Yes. Thanks.'

'Actually, I don't think much is going on, except it isn't all like a movie, the way Dad expected, with Taxi happy and good as gold. I just want you to know that if I hear anything I will tell you. If you want me to.'

'Yes.' Camilla's voice was suddenly hoarse. 'Please.'

'What I mean is—maybe if it isn't as much fun as they thought it would be, maybe they won't want to keep him . . . well, who knows?'

'Don't,' Camilla said. 'Don't give us false hope, Noelle.'

'I'm sorry. Oh, Camilla, it's only because I care. You've been so good to me, and I want to do something to help, and I'm afraid I've only made it worse.'

•

"No wonder he's screwed up," Raffi said. "But does that give him a right to punish the rest of the universe?"

"My darling"—Camilla held out her hands to the applewood fire—"I'm not very objective where your father is concerned."

"He really was adorable as a little boy? Like in that picture over your bed?"

"Yes. Just as." Camilla smiled. "I gather quite a few of your friends find him adorable right now."

"Not my dad. That silly idiot he's playing."

"Raffi," Camilla said, "I hoped to make you understand a little."

"Give me time, Grandmother. Let it soak in. So how long did this Red Grange and his Harriet have my dad?"

"Three years. They were driving along the Riviera and they went over the edge on one of those hairpin turns, with a large bus coming toward them. Taxi was asleep in the back seat. He wasn't even hurt. But Grange and Harriet were killed. It seems they had been drinking." She kept her voice level, emotionless.

"So what happened?"

"Noelle and Andrew called us."

"Noelle? Andrew?"

"Grange's children by his first wife. Good people. Noelle and her banker husband are living in Berlin. Andrew's a physician."

"Oh, yeah," Raffi said. "Sure. I remember him. He was my doctor's husband, the doctor I had when I was a kid. Dr. Liz. I liked them both. But I was a healthy kid, so I didn't see much of them. So go on, Grandmother. What happened after Andrew and Noelle called?"

"Mac and I flew to France. At first Taxi didn't even recognize us. Then he was hysterical. I managed to get my arms around him, to hold him, with Mac's help, to quieten his kicking and screaming."

"Where was Frankie?"

"Mama—my mother-in-law—came to stay with her while we were away."

"So that was some kind of continuity for Frankie."

"Yes. Mama and Papa were always stable elements in their lives. Fixed stars." Camilla rose and put another log on the fire. Her hands were shaking. "Frankie simply took for granted that God had answered her prayers and Taxi was back."

"But he wasn't the same Taxi, was he?"

"Nothing was the same for Taxi. For any of us. We weren't in the familiar rectory in Corinth. The seminary was an alien place. Our apartment was strange. Everything on one floor. There was no Dr. Edith, no Pinky and the other kids in the youth group. Only Quantum, the cat, was familiar. No, he wasn't the same Taxi. He was three years older. He knew how to read. He spoke as much French as English. He wanted to go back to Corinth, to the way things were."

•

Night after night Camilla rocked Taxi, holding him as though he were a baby, rocking and crooning until he relaxed enough to go to sleep.

'Don't neglect Frankie,' Mac warned.

Camilla looked at him painfully. 'He needs so much, so much. What am I to do?'

'Take him to the beach, to Florida,' Luisa advised. 'That will at least be something familiar.'

'Yes, Mama and Papa have suggested that. But Mac can't get away. His schedule is particularly heavy right now.'

'I'll come with you. He needs to be in a familiar setting for at least a few weeks.'

'You, Lu? How can you?'

'I can manage for about ten days. It will be difficult, but I think I can do it.'

'Then please, please do.'

'I gather Grange and Harriet did the best they could with him, within their limitations, but he has the look of an abused child.'

'Oh, God.' They were in Camilla's little study, Camilla sitting behind her desk as though for protection. Luisa was lounging in an ancient but comfortable chair that Camilla had rescued from being put out for the Salvation Army. The children were at a neighbor's apartment where there were other children, and where they had been invited to watch a home movie. Taxi was not happy about leaving Camilla, even for a few hours, but the movie had been a sufficient lure.

'What about abuse?' Luisa demanded.

'I was putting him to bed. He wouldn't let me help dry him, but I saw a funny little round scar on the back of his shoulder and asked him about it. It was a cigarette burn.'

'What!'

'It wasn't done on purpose. From what Taxi told me, Harriet had evidently been drinking, and was waving her cigarette around one day at the beach when all Taxi had on was bathing trunks.'

'Were there any more scars?'

'Only that one.'

'Only that physical one. So Harriet was an alcoholic.'

'Evidently the crowd she and Grange went around with drank a lot.'

Luisa's voice was outraged. 'The beautiful people, with nothing to do but drink and smoke and gamble and wander from one playground to another, looking for God knows what. Did they stay abroad the whole time?'

'Yes. According to Noelle they kept talking about coming home, but they never did.'

'Where did they live?'

'The French Riviera mostly. Also Monte Carlo and places like Morocco.'

'So Harriet was loaded.'

'Yes.'

'Will Taxi get her money?'

'No.' Camilla stood up and went to the window, which, like most city windows, bore traces of rain and grime. It looked across the seminary close and she saw students hurrying up and down the paths, some with coat collars turned up against the wind. The brick buildings, over a century old, looked shabbily weathered. In the apartment there was a feeling of cold and damp seeping around the window frame. 'No,' she repeated, 'and I'm just as glad.'

'Why not, if Harriet regarded Taxi as her son?'

'She didn't have a will.'

Luisa groaned. 'Good God, it's amazing how many people put off making wills because it reminds them of their mortality.'

'Harriet lived lavishly. They stayed at expensive hotels and Harriet gambled. She lost enormous sums of money at the casino in Monte Carlo, so much she'd have been in serious trouble if she'd lived. What little she had left went to her brother, and he very generously offered to divide it with us. We told him to keep it and let us get on with our lives. We asked him to promise not to interfere with Taxi in any way, and he agreed. He has children of his own to educate.'

Luisa pressed, 'What about Grange?'

Camilla turned back to her desk. 'He wasn't a wealthy man. Most academics aren't. They lived on Harriet's money. He did have a will, an old one. What he had—it wasn't much, he gambled, too—went to Andrew and Noelle. Andrew wanted it all to go to Taxi.'

'Andrew's a good guy,' Luisa said. 'We frequently bump into each other over coffee at our local greasy spoon, and talk shop. He's referred some adolescent patients to me. You and Mac doing okay—I mean, financially?'

'Sure. We're finally out of debt. We're not rolling, but we manage, like most of the people at the seminary. And I have a salary, too. We're fine.'

'What about your father?'

'What about him?'

'He'd help, wouldn't he?'

'He would, if we needed him to. But we don't. Listen, Lu, your offer to go to Florida—'

'When were you planning to go?'

'This weekend.'

'Got your tickets yet?'

'No. I seem to be dragging my feet about everything.'

'Don't fret. I'll call my travel agent. I need a break, too. It'll be good for me.'

They heard the children come in, banging the door, and then they appeared in the study doorway. Taxi had found Quantum and was carrying him, nearly upside down.

'How was the movie?'

'Terrific,' Frankie said.

'Shitty. I want milk and cookies,' Taxi announced.

Camilla made no comment on his language. 'Help your-selves. One glass of milk, and one cookie each, understood?'

'Sure.'

Quantum slithered out of Taxi's grip, and the children followed him out, heading for the kitchen.

Luisa demanded, 'Are you taking Taxi to a shrink?'

'I will, as soon as we get back from the beach. Will you take him on?'

'No way. I'm your oldest friend. I'm much too close. I can give you a couple of referrals, and I'll check with Andrew. I'll be in the wings, always. You know that.'

•

"Oh, God, Grandmother, how did you manage?"

"The beach house helped, because it was familiar, because Mama and Papa were there, because Lu was there, because the ocean rolling in to shore always calms me, because there were lots of shells for the children to collect."

"But you couldn't stay there forever."

"The ten days Luisa promised. I had to get back to Mac, and we had to bring Taxi to the apartment in the seminary and teach him that it was home. And we had to let him start school."

"How was it?"

"For the first few days he was terrified, but then he began to realize that he could read more easily than the other chil-dren, and the teacher had him show off a little, not too much, just enough to give him some self-confidence."

"And Aunt Frankie?"

"She was ecstatic to have him home. But it wasn't the same."

•

"Mom," Frankie said, "you sound terrible."

"Oh, darling, sorry, I'm just tired, and I'm so glad you phoned. You do have the most marvelous way of calling when my morale needs a boost."

"What's up?"

"Nothing. I've been—I've been thinking about how hard it was for you when Taxi came back to us after Grange and Harriet died."

"Hard on all of us."

"The first few days you painted in brilliant colors, but then you splashed purple and black onto the paper, painting out your confusion. We got Taxi an easel and paints, too, but once he had them, he wasn't interested."

"No," Frankie said. "He didn't want his own paints. He wanted mine."

"And you didn't understand. How could you? He was rough with you. You were bigger than he was and defended yourself, but it broke your heart."

"Aunt Luisa helped, more than the shrink."

"Even the best shrink can't undo the past."

Frankie laughed. "Taxi called Aunt Luisa all kinds of horrible names. He picked up quite a vocabulary while he was away from us. As I look back on it, Mom, you were really good about that. You paid no attention to it, you didn't get uptight, and finally he quit."

"Finally."

"When he wanted to, he could be so terrific, making me feel I was the only person in the world who was saving him."

"In some ways you were."

"What charm, Mom, and it's real. That's why he's so popular on his soap. But it isn't all there is."

"Does that surprise you?"

"No, of course not. I remember when he first came back his nose always ran."

"He got his feet wet and caught a cold, and, yes, his nose ran, and he had a funny little cough."

"Mom, don't brood on it. What's been done has been done. We have to live with it and let it go."

•

'We need to find a pediatrician,' Camilla said to Mac, holding a tissue to Taxi's nose and helping him blow.

'How?' Mac asked vaguely. 'Frankie had all her shots and everything in Corinth and Jacksonville.'

Mac was retreating. Not physically. Not running away. But retreating inside himself, which was almost as painful as literal absence. Camilla asked her neighbor across the hall about a recommendation for a pediatrician.

'Dr. Wickoff' was the immediate reply. 'My kids adore her. But don't you have a doctor for Frankie?'

'Frankie's wonderfully healthy. Since we've been at the seminary she's had her shots and checkups in Jacksonville, where Mac's parents live. It's so much simpler there. Here in New York she hasn't had anything worse than a cold, so we've never needed to look for a doctor.'

'You'll like Dr. Wickoff. She's calm and reassuring, and I can see that that little boy needs a lot of reassurance. You're very brave to take him on.'

The seminary was as close a community as Corinth had been. Camilla wondered how much her neighbor knew of Taxi's history, and how much of what she knew was garbled gossip. 'He's our son,' she said.

'Would you like me to make an appointment for you? I have to call the office about Jesse's allergies anyhow.'

'Thanks. That would be very kind.'

'Would you like an appointment for your little girl, too? It's just as well for her to have a pediatrician here in the city.'

'Thanks. Thanks very much.'

Camilla tried to talk to Mac about taking the children to the doctor, but his eyes barely focused. 'I have to grade exams,' he said. 'You take care of it, Cam.'

At least he was still at home. At least he still turned to her with passion, both tender and strong in his lovemaking. That affirmation was all that kept her anxiety under control.

Her neighbor made appointments for the children, and Camilla took them uptown on the bus. She was glad that Frankie was included; it would be easier for Taxi if Frankie was along.

When they came to the office door Camilla stopped in shock. There were three names on brass plaques.

JAMES ANSLEY WICKOFF, M.D.
ELIZABETH WICKOFF, M.D.
ANDREW GRANGE, M.D.

How could she have forgotten that Andrew's wife was Wickoff, and that they were both pediatricians? The names on the door exploded at her. She had been so wrapped up in hurt over Mac's withdrawal, apprehension about Taxi, about Frankie, that she had not been thinking coherently. She wanted to turn tail and run, but the door opened and a woman came out carrying a baby, and a nurse in a white uniform saw Camilla and the children and beckoned them in. What would it do to Taxi and Frankie if she fled? Taxi needed a doctor.

She looked at him. He could read. He read aloud every sign they passed on the street, showing off. He must have seen the names on the door. They seemed to have made no impression on him, one way or the other. Grange and Harriet had kept him abroad, and he had had little or no contact with Noelle or Andrew, who were a threat to Harriet. And now Red Grange and Harriet were dead. Andrew and his wife had no part in the damage they had done.

Camilla looked at Taxi, who was clutching Frankie's hand.

He was nervous enough. She did not want to add to it further by what would seem irrational behavior. The nurse gave her forms to fill out for each child, and led the children to a large box of toys and a bookcase filled with books and games. Taxi started to put a puzzle together, and Frankie was absorbed in one of the picture books.

When the nurse called Camilla, she said, 'Let me go in alone for a moment, please.'

Dr. Wickoff's office was large and pleasant, with bright walls and flowered curtains, and stuffed animals in several chairs, the kind of office designed to set a frightened child at ease.

'Dr. Wickoff,' Camilla said, 'I ought to have recognized your name when you were recommended to me, but I didn't—'

Dr. Wickoff picked up the chart the nurse had placed on her desk. She sat back comfortably, her white coat open over a plaid skirt and red turtleneck. Her hair was brown and curly, and her brown eyes were smiling and inquisitive. For a moment her fingers tightened on the chart. 'Mrs. Xanthakos! Oh!'

The two women looked at each other.

'I didn't want to upset Taxi by rushing away, but if you think it's inappropriate for him—'

'No,' Dr. Wickoff said. 'If it's all right with you, I'd like to see him, and then we can make a decision.'

'Okay. Good.'

'Poor tyke, he's been through more than any kid should have to endure. Perhaps the fact that I know what has happened to him will help me to treat him in the most effective way possible.'

'Yes,' Camilla agreed. 'And I want the best for him.'

Dr. Wickoff spoke into the intercom. 'Bring the Xanthakos children in, please.'

She was easy with them, showing them the stuffed animals. 'See that giraffe, with no fur on its neck? That was mine when I was a little girl. And that elephant, with its trunk

stitched up? That was my very favorite, and my brother tried
to tease me by skating on it.' As she chatted, Taxi visibly
relaxed. 'Now, Frankie,' Dr. Wickoff said, 'will you help me
unbutton your blouse so I can listen to your heartbeat? You
can listen, too, Taxi, it's fascinating.' Whatever had to be done,
she did to Frankie first, and Taxi did not even murmur as she
drew blood from one of his fingers.

There was no question that she was a good doctor and that
Taxi liked her. When she was through with her examination of
the children she asked the nurse to take them back to the
waiting room, then turned to Camilla, her face tight and
strained.

'Was that a cigarette burn on Taxi's back?'

Camilla nodded. 'Accidental, I think.'

Dr. Wickoff sighed. 'He's underweight. Do you have a
good psychiatrist for him?'

'Luisa Rowan has recommended a Dr. Hayes.'

'Yes, he's good. If it's all right with you, I think I can help
Taxi and that feisty little girl of yours.'

'Thank you,' Camilla said. 'Taxi trusts you, and his sense
of trust has been pretty well battered.'

As Camilla was leaving with Taxi and Frankie, she saw
Andrew come out of a door at the back of the waiting room,
tall, slightly stooped, as though from bending down to his
small patients. His red hair was muted by streaks of silver. His
white coat flapped about his legs. He squatted down before a
little girl, who pressed her face against his chest.

This was not the time to speak to him.

•

That night, after the children were in bed, Camilla called
Luisa and told her what had happened. 'Was I nuts to walk
into that office once I saw Andrew's name on the door?'

'Both children were with you?'

'Yes.'

'What would be the least upsetting for them?'

'To act naturally. If I'd fled—'

'Yes?'

'They'd have known I was fleeing, but they wouldn't have known from what. And Taxi needed to see a doctor. Dr. Wickoff's the pediatrician everybody at the seminary uses. I didn't know anybody else. I called you a couple of days ago, but you were at some conference in Philadelphia—'

'Who are you trying to convince, Camilla? Me? Or you?'

'Not you. What I want to know is if I should look for somebody else now. Taxi really liked Dr. Wickoff, and he doesn't trust easily.'

'What does Mac say?'

'What?'

'What did Mac have to say?'

Of course it would have been the normal thing for her to have talked with Mac. But Mac had come home to take a shower and change his clothes, and told her he had a meeting with the dean. He took only a cursory look at Frankie's new painting, and didn't even see the hurt on his child's face. 'He had a meeting tonight. We haven't had a chance to talk.'

Luisa swore. 'He's walked out again, hasn't he?'

'No, Lu, he's here, he's just gone to a meeting.'

'He's walked out on you psychologically.'

'At least he's here. He'll come back when he's got it all absorbed. He always does.'

'Have you got it absorbed?'

'No, of course not. I'm taking it day by day, minute by minute. What I wanted to ask you about was Dr. Wickoff. I liked her. She gave me suggestions for a diet to help Taxi's allergies, and a couple of prescriptions. I thought she had an intuitive understanding of him. Of both of them. When she had to do anything that might be at all scary, she went to Frankie first, so Taxi would be less frightened.'

'Did it frighten Frankie?'

'No. Dr. Wickoff was completely reassuring.'

'She has a fine reputation, Camilla. She is, as far as I can see, not the problem. Did Taxi see Andrew?'

'He was in the waiting room when we left. I don't think Taxi knows him at all. I mean, Grange and Harriet had Taxi in Europe all the time, I don't think he's even met Noelle or Andrew. I'm not sure he even knows they exist.'

'What about you?'

'I certainly don't blame either Andrew or Noelle for their father. You know they did everything they could to help us—'

'Red Grange's kids are better than he deserved.'

'About Dr. Wickoff—'

'I think what you want me to say is what I'm going to say. Stick with Elizabeth Wickoff. If she's established a good rapport with Taxi, that's enough to keep you from looking for anybody else. And the fact that she knows Taxi's story will help her in understanding his problems. Your kids won't see much of Andrew when they go to the office, if they see him at all. He has a full patient load of his own, and he's a tactful guy and won't want to give you any more pain.'

'Thanks, Lu. I feel better.'

'Just don't expect Liz Wickoff to do miracles. You have a wounded little boy and it's going to be hard.'

•

Raffi said, "I'm glad Dad had Liz and Andrew as his doctors."

"Mostly Dr. Liz," Camilla said. "He'd have seen Andy only if Liz was away."

"I adore Dr. Andy," Raffi said.

Camilla looked at her in surprise. "I thought Dr. Liz was your doctor."

"Oh, she was, and like I said, I was a healthy kid and didn't see much of her other than to get my shots. But one day when I was maybe nine I was skating in the park and I fell and broke my wrist. Mom took me right to the office. I mean, she knew I'd broken it, the bone was actually sticking out, it was horrible."

Camilla shuddered. "I remember."

"Mom was wonderful, promising me it was going to be all right, and not all falling to pieces herself, which some mothers might have done."

"Yes, your mother's a wonder."

"It was my right wrist, and of course I'm righthanded."

"You learned to write with your left hand."

"I still can, when I want to. Anyhow, Dr. Liz was away, and Dr. Andy was there and he took care of me. He was so gentle, so calm, he even got me laughing. I was scared, really scared, to see my actual bone. And he was so matter-of-fact, and his hands seemed to take away the pain. I remember burrowing my face in his white coat, and having him put his arms around me, and at the same time he was so quick. And Mom, despite her calm—I think she was as scared as I was—and he was wonderful with her, too, making her know everything was going to be all right. I suppose he makes everybody feel special, one of my friends had a terrific crush on him, but he really did make me feel special. As though he really cared."

Camilla replied slowly. "I think that's part of his job, what makes him such a good doctor."

"Yeah, but it seemed to me more than that. He went to the hospital with us, and stayed with me." She held up her wrist. "See? There's still a tiny scar. I suppose Dr. Liz would have been just as good, but it happened to be Dr. Andy. And then when I went home what I remember is being read to. Dad read to me from a book of funny poems and there was something about an elephant who tried to use a telephant. Anyhow, he had me laughing my head off. And later, when I couldn't sleep, you read to me, one of Aunt Frankie's books, and then *Jack and Jill,* and a sledding accident, and Jill was really hurt, and it made me feel better and I went to sleep. So it really isn't a bad memory. It's more good than bad."

"I'm glad. I'll certainly never forget it."

"And Aunt Frankie called me from Seattle, just me, personally. I wish she didn't live all the way across the country in Seattle."

"So do I." Camilla's mouth tightened briefly. As she had lost Rafferty as a father when Taxi came, so, in a sense, had she lost Frankie. Frankie, who had had the wisdom to get out of the way. Not to run away. Not to walk out. Just to get out of the way so that she could have her own life.

Raffi was sprawled out on one of the sofas in front of the fire, which she had built up. "Last week, after your award bash, which was so terrific, Dad laughed at some of Aunt Frankie's marvelous kids' books."

"Lots of people think kids' books don't count, and Taxi seems to be in a putting-down mode right now."

"Did you do psychiatrists for my dad and all that stuff?"

"Yes, Luisa was very helpful, recommending good doctors. But a psychic wound isn't like an inflamed appendix. You can't open the body and cut it out."

"Surgery on the soul. Why didn't you send him to Dr. Rowan?"

"She's much too close, Raffi, like a member of the family."

"Yeah, I had to talk her into it. Seeing me." She looked warily at her grandmother. "Do you mind?"

"Anything but. I'm delighted. Has she helped?"

"Has helped. Is helping. I guess she's pretty important, isn't she? She keeps being called away on consultations and meetings and stuff."

"Lu's a good doctor."

"Grandmother, does my mom know all this, what you've told me about Taxi being taken away from you for three years and all?"

"Yes. She knows. Your mom and I've talked a good deal. Thessaly's a very compassionate person."

"Maybe that says something about why she hasn't left my dad, long ago. But why didn't they tell me?"

"Your father was very deeply hurt. He made it clear he didn't want to talk about it. I think that was probably a mistake. Your Aunt Frankie thinks it was. I don't know, Raffi. We do wrong, with all the best will in the world. And sometimes we do right without even knowing it."

"How much do you think my mom can take?"

"We don't know anybody's breaking point. But I don't think she's going to leave. She loves your father."

Raffi rolled onto her back. "So do I. I wish all this made me feel better."

"Give it time, Raffi."

•

When Raffi had gone Camilla called Frankie. Frankie was secure enough now so that Camilla felt freer with her than she had when Frankie had first married and moved to Seattle.

"I've been talking with Raffi again. Telling her."

"Good. You know how I've felt about all this secrecy."

"I know. It's so complex. Red and Harriet tried to change his name. They called him Tommy. Tommy Grange. He had forgotten he was Taxi."

"I'd forgotten that."

"You were only a child."

"I remember it now. I wonder why I blanked it out?"

"When he referred to himself as Tommy you shouted, 'Taxi! Taxi! You're my Taxi!' And that was that. More or less. His doctor advised us to call him Taxi, that it would help bring him back into the family."

"Did it, Mom?"

"When Taxi was taken away it was like—it was like an amputation. Something of the original Taxi was amputated."

"So," Frankie asked, "we had to settle for a prosthesis?"

"Yes."

"I remember you took us to the beach, with Aunt Luisa, and later just us."

"For spring vacation. Yes."

"Dad wasn't with us. Where was he?"

•

Away. He had been asked to give a series of talks in California, and he went.

'I hate to leave,' he said, 'but these talks are important enough to be published. I've had only a couple of articles accepted recently, and you know all the publish-or-perish stuff. I'll be gone only a couple of weeks. You can manage for that long, can't you? Things seem pretty stable.'

'Sure.' Everything Mac said was reasonable, comprehensible. But she didn't want him to go.

The seminary community was as curious and gossipy as a small parish in Georgia. People stared at Taxi. Whispered. Stole covert looks whenever Camilla appeared with the children.

Art was retired, and he and Olivia were living at the beach. While Mac was away the children were better off in Florida with their grandparents than at the seminary.

'It's all right.' Camilla sat with Olivia and Art on the veranda, resting her eyes on the ocean. The children were asleep upstairs, in beds that were familiar, in a room that was their own, in a beach house they loved. 'We all have a breaking point, and when Mac leaves, it's not forever. He always comes back.'

'Not everyone would be as forgiving as you are,' Olivia said.

Camilla mouthed back everything Mac had said to her. Then, 'Oh, Mama.' A slow shiver moved through her body. 'I get angry. I feel betrayed. If you and Papa weren't always here to put my pieces back together, I don't know what I'd do.'

'And yet'—Art rubbed his hands slowly across his face— 'it was I who caused Mac's breaking point. For an eight-year-old to walk into church and see his father and—'

'Stop,' Olivia commanded. 'This does no good.'

Camilla said, 'You've taught me, you two and Mac, that I can't blame my own fears and problems on my parents. I have some say in how I behave. By and large, Mac's done pretty well. He's a brilliant teacher. His students adore him. He's written a couple of wonderful articles, and he's right, he does need to do a book. What he emphasizes most is mercy, the kind you talked about, Mama, William Langland's. We have to be merciful to ourselves before we can be merciful to anybody else.' Then she laughed, harshly, like a seagull. 'I still do not feel very merciful toward Grange or Harriet.'

'Or Grange's ex-wife, for not having given him your mother's letter?'

Camilla leapt up as she heard Taxi scream. She ran into the house, letting the screened door slam behind her, and went up the stairs two at a time. Taxi was sitting up in bed, his eyes closed, screaming. Frankie was struggling out of sleep. Camilla sat down by Taxi and held him tight, pressing his thin body against hers, and the screams stopped.

Frankie said calmly, 'Taxi had a nightmare.'

'I know, darling,' Camilla said. 'He's over it now. Go back to sleep.' Her body moved rhythmically, rocking Taxi.

'Where you bin, Mommy?' he asked.

'Sitting on the porch with Mama and Papa.'

'Are you coming to bed soon?'

'Very soon.' She gently put Taxi down in the bed, covering him with the sheet and a light cotton blanket. If she got to him in time he did not fully wake up, and he would not remember the nightmare in the morning. She did not know whether or not this oblivion was the best thing for him. What good would it do him to remember whatever horror his sleeping brain was showing him? Grange and Harriet had not actively abused him. The nurse they had for him had told Camilla and Mac that the boy was thin because they had a hard time finding food he would or could eat. They lavished attention on him when they were with him. And presents. Toys, expensive toys. They did not discipline him, the nurse said. That was left to her, and it was apparent that the Granges wanted as little as possible. Mrs. Grange had talked about letting children express themselves, not repressing them. The nurse, herself, did not like a whiny child.

'I'm the fourth to have this job,' she said. 'I learned quickly that if I wanted to keep it I had to be softer with Tommy than I thought was good for him.'

Frankie said, 'Mommy—'

'Yes, darling?'

'Sometimes Taxi doesn't hear when I call him. Then if I say Tommy he hears, but he gets mad at me.'

'It's difficult to have your name changed.' Camilla kept her voice level.

'Why did they call him Tommy?'

'Perhaps they thought Tommy was an easier name.'

'Taxi's easy.'

'For us, because that's how we've always known him.'

'Mommy, he gets so mad, so mad. He hurts me.'

Camilla moved from Taxi's bed to Frankie's, took the little girl in her arms. 'I know. It's hard to understand. But when he feels secure again, he won't lose control of himself.'

.

When would he feel secure? Mac returned, and Camilla and the children flew back to New York.

Mac put his arms around her as they were undressing, getting ready for bed. 'I'm sorry.'

For a moment she stiffened in his arms. He had never apologized before.

'Darling, darling, I'm so sorry. I left you. I walked out on it all and left you. I'm not strong. I don't know how I'm going to manage.'

Now her arms were around him, too. 'We have to take it day by day.'

'He's so changed. He's not our son.'

'Yes. He is. No matter what happens.'

'He's your brother.'

'I'm his mother.'

'You're blood relations. I can't stand what he's doing to us, to Frankie.'

'I can't stand it either. But we have to.'

'Oh, God,' Mac moaned, 'why do I think it ought to be easy? Why do I think everything ought to be all right?'

'Because that's what we all want.'

'But that isn't how life is. I know that. I preach that. No promises of rewards if we're good, or punishments if we're bad. No promises, except that it matters. Cosmically.'

They sat on the side of the bed, still holding each other. 'Cosmically,' Camilla agreed, 'to the stars in their courses.'

'The stars aren't very communicative about it,' Mac said, and pulled her down onto the bed.

'The one time I would like a cigarette,' he said later, 'is now.'

'I didn't know you ever smoked.'

'For a while. Long ago. Did you?'

'Smoke? No. I didn't like it.'

'Darling, you're incredible, the way you just keep going and don't let it get you down.'

It got her down.

One day she came home from NYU and went out to the playground to collect the children. They were on the seesaw, and a slightly older child said, 'My turn next.'

'Okay,' Frankie said.

'So what's your name?'

'I'm Frankie. Frankie Xanthakos. He's Taxi.'

'Taxi Grange?' the older child asked.

Taxi brought his end of the seesaw down to the ground with a bang, and jumped off, so that Frankie's end, in turn, hit the ground. He rushed at the other child. 'I'm Taxi Xanthakos! Never call me Grange or I'll kill you!'

The older child backed away. 'I'm sorry, my dad told me your name was Grange—'

Frankie, trying to smooth things over, said, 'It was, for a while, when he was with his other father.'

'No, no!' Taxi shrieked. 'Daddy is my father. I'm Taxi Xanthakos! You shut up! Don't you ever say that again!' He jumped on Frankie and threw her to the ground. Grabbed her by the hair and began to hit her head on the hard-packed earth.

Several older people came running to Frankie's rescue, as Camilla, too, raced toward the children.

Frankie screamed. Screamed.

A young man, one of the seminarians, pulled Taxi off her. 'Cut that out, young man.'

Camilla came rushing up, panting. 'I'll take care of it. Thanks.'

A young woman had her arms around Frankie, who was sobbing. 'Her brother was—' Her voice was indignant.

'I know. I'm sorry. I'll take care of it.'

The children had long been too big for her to tuck one under each arm as she had been able to do before Grange and Harriet took Taxi away. She put a firm arm about Taxi, reached for Frankie's hand. 'Thank you all, very much. Thank you. Taxi. Frankie. Come. Right now.'

But she would never again be able to let them play alone in the playground.

•

Luisa said, 'Best send them to separate schools, a boys' school for Taxi and a girls' school for Frankie. That way there won't be too many questions asked. People need to let them be ordinary brother and sister for a while.'

Taxi's therapist agreed, although he was adamant about their not letting Taxi deny his paternity. 'We never do,' Camilla said, 'but Taxi does, and we're trying to let him heal so that he will be able to accept what happened.'

Luisa said, 'If they're in separate schools the problem won't come up.'

Camilla discussed it with Olivia and Art.

'Separate schools? It's a good idea,' Olivia said. 'For many reasons. Taxi and Frankie are older now. They need to be separated.'

The bishop made an affirmative grunt, then said, 'It was a delight to watch them play together like puppies, but the time for that is over, anyhow. They need to go their separate ways. Taxi has to do some healing on his own.'

Olivia asked, 'Is Frankie painting?'

'Colored pencils,' Camilla said. 'The kind you dip into water, so they're half pencil, half paint. Dr. Edith sent them to her and she adores them. She's painting tapestries, with small figures caught in ivy, or branches of trees, and frightened animals fleeing into the underbrush.'

'She'll work a lot out that way,' Olivia said.

'That's what the therapist says. Frankie gets it out in pictures, but Taxi acts it out. If my father weren't still alive I might do everything differently. I don't know. I can't keep on hurting him if I don't have to. I thought he was going to die when everything got splashed all over the news, with everybody eagerly lapping up our private tragedy. His voice on the phone changed completely. Despite everything, it used to be strong. But now he sounds like a very old man.'

The bishop said, 'He had three years of respite, as it were, when Taxi was away.'

'But he knows Taxi's back, and that things aren't easy. I still write him every week—I've never stopped—and so I've told him what's going on, lightening it as much as possible.'

The bishop said, 'I think this is one of the situations where there is no right choice. We have to pray that we make the choice that is the least wrong.'

Camilla sighed. 'Dr. Edith said that wrong breeds wrong. When one wrong is done, then other wrong things are going to happen.'

But where had this wrong begun? On the day when Grange came to claim his son? When Camilla and Mac agreed to take Taxi? When Rose got pregnant? When Rose was first unfaithful to Rafferty? How far back should it be taken?

Back to Art? Or Art's father? Or his father's father's father?

'Cepheids,' Art said. 'Taxi reminds me of a Cepheid.'

'What?' Camilla asked blankly.

'If I remember correctly,' Art said, 'I believe I read it in something you wrote, Camilla—Cepheids are stars which undergo a period of instability when they run low on hydrogen fuel and begin burning helium.'

'Yes,' Camilla agreed dubiously.

Art said, 'Taxi burned up all his hydrogen when he was with Grange and Harriet. And now, like a Cepheid, he's going through cycles of variation in brightness. He glows with incredible luminosity, whether with anger or pleasure, and then the flare is over and it drops back to its ordinary magnitude.'

Camilla laughed. 'Oh, Papa, I'm not sure what my colleagues would make of that image, but I get what you mean.'

TWELVE

WITH TAXI, nothing ever seemed to be enough. But new and quieter patterns were formed. Life did not return to normal, whatever normal once had been. But at least there was shape to their days.

Rafferty Dickinson died, which was not surprising. His arthritis had worsened. He who had never smoked had an odd form of emphysema. He begged Camilla not to come to him, and she honored his reiterated request, both with reluctance and with relief. After his death she and Mac went to New Mexico to bury him, to hold a service in a small nearby church. Camilla stayed on for a few days to tend to business, which was minimal, since her father had taken care of everything possible. She was surprised at the intensity of her grief for a father she had not seen for so many years.

What was also a surprise (though why should it have been?) was the amount of money she inherited. Rafferty had always been generous, though he had withdrawn from Taxi and his problems; the discovery that Grantley Grange was the child's father had, it seemed, wiped away from him any sense of responsibility.

But the money he left Camilla ensured that now she would

not have to worry about bills for continuing therapy for Taxi. Through the man who was not his father, Taxi would be able to have whatever he needed.

Then, having assured herself that Taxi would be taken care of as much as was humanly possible, Camilla breathed a small 'Thank you' to her father, and bought a new box spring and mattress for the big brass bed, and a new winter coat for herself.

Life at the seminary settled into a reasonable pattern. Taxi's moods, his unpredictability, were part of the pattern. When he withdrew from Frankie she shrugged and went to the dining table with crayons or paints. She had a small circle of girlfriends from school, and they were often over at the seminary. She was making her own life, her own way, freeing herself from Taxi.

One day, having walked home from the university to the seminary, Camilla dropped into the chapel for evening prayer and communion. She was a few minutes late, and Mac was already in the pulpit, partway through his homily.

'... and what are we promised?' he was asking. 'None of the ease the media offers us daily. Promises nobody can keep. Promises rejected by Jesus two thousand years ago.

'What happened to Jesus after John baptized him, after the Holy Spirit in the form of a gentle dove came and hovered over him, after God shouted from the heavens that Jesus was the beloved? Did Jesus have a chance, then, to go home and relax? To have a glass of wine and a meal with his friends? No. The Holy Spirit, that gentle dove, took him up the mountain and offered him to Satan. "Here, Satan. Here is the Messiah. Tempt him." And Satan tried, using all his psychic powers to tempt Jesus into refusing to be human, into refusing the very thing he had been born to be. "Jesus, you're hungry. You've been fasting. You're God as well as mortal, you know. Turn these stones into bread and feed yourself, and while you're at it, feed the rest of the world, too. Bread and circuses, that's what they want, and if you give it to them, they'll love you. No? Well, how about jumping from the highest pinnacle of the temple? You know the angels will protect you and not let you be hurt. Listen, Jesus, if you insist on being human, it's going to be awful. Being human means being mortal, being hurt, dying. Making wrong choices. You're going to choose all the wrong disciples, not the ones God would choose, and they're going to betray you; they'll leave you when you need them most. You're going to be hungry and thirsty, oh, how thirsty, and you're going to die horribly, killed by the very institution you love, and what is that going to do to your Godship, if you die like a mortal? You don't have to do it. Worship me, and I'll take care of you, I promise you."

'The false promises of Satan, and Jesus knew they were false, and he rejected them. And everything that Satan had predicted came to pass. His disciples did not understand him and they left him. He endured all the agonies that Satan forecast, yes. But Satan forgot all the rest, the unswerving closeness to the Source, the joy of eating with friends, of laughter; the wonder of healing, of making the unloved know they were loved. Yes, he took on our mortality and died like a mortal, and in doing so he gave us his immortality, and with him we shall live forever, forgiven, redeemed, and loved into and throughout eternity. Amen.'

After the service Camilla waited on the steps just outside the chapel until Mac came out. Her voice was diffident. 'Were you thinking of Taxi, and everything?'

He looked at her. Nodded.

'I don't know how to pray.'

'Neither do I,' he said. 'I just ask God to do whatever is best for Taxi.'

•

Luisa sat at Camilla's kitchen table, drinking tea. 'Your girl's an artist. That should see her through a lot.'

Frankie was in the dining room, painting. Taxi was still

at school, at choir practice. Camilla said, 'She spends as much time as she's allowed at school in painting and drawing. I think her pictures are becoming a little less violent. She lets a little more sun in.'

'How's she doing?'

'Her schoolwork is good. Her teacher says she's quiet, and tends to daydream into her pictures. But the other girls like her.'

'And Taxi?'

'He's a star in choir, and that's good for him. He's one of the youngest to get solos. His teacher says he's sometimes disruptive, but he gets good grades. If he finishes his work he sits at his desk and writes his name, TAXI XANTHAKOS, TAXI XANTHAKOS, over and over again. The other day I tried to explain to the teacher why it was so important to him, and he had a tantrum, flinging himself about on the floor and screaming.'

•

"Why now?" Raffi asked Luisa. "Why does he want it to come out now after keeping it secret all these years?"

"It was never meant to be a secret," Luisa said. "Your grandparents never meant to perpetuate a lie. If Grantley Grange, your grandfather, had left well enough alone, which he would have done if he really loved his son, your grandparents would have let Taxi know, gently, slowly, who he was. But whenever they tried to bring it up, after Grange and Harriet were killed, Taxi would get hysterical. His fever would flare up alarmingly. He believed, and he truly believed this, Raffi, that if they let anyone know he was not their child, Frankie's brother, it would mean that they did not love him."

•

He searched for constant affirmation. If Camilla or Mac praised Frankie, they immediately had to praise Taxi. Camilla was grateful for Luisa's suggestion of separate schools, where comparisons of the children could not be made. On the other hand, Taxi was often teased. His lovely child's soprano voice made him petted by the choirmaster and the older students but resented by his peers, who sometimes picked on him.

'If they were at the same school, Frankie would defend him,' Camilla said.

Mac asked, 'Wouldn't that be putting a heavy load on Frankie? I think it's best that they're apart.'

Camilla sighed. 'You're right, I know.'

'We too often do put too much on our girl,' Mac continued. 'It's hard to realize she's younger than Taxi. Chronologically.'

'Oh, Mac, once upon a time we used to be so happy.'

'That time is gone, my darling. We have to live where we are now, somehow trying to clean up the mess.'

—Don't leave me, Camilla wanted to beg. —Don't go away.

But she could not ask.

And Mac stayed.

•

That did not mean that they were not tested.

One day Taxi came home from school with his nose all puffy, and blood still on his upper lip, from where a couple of bigger boys had roughed him up. He was thin and not muscular and he was easy to tease because he responded with an immediate flare of rage.

When he told Camilla and Mac what had happened, he was angry. He wanted Mac to go to the school and punish the boys.

'What do you mean by punishment?' Mac asked.

'Hurt. I want them hurt for what they did.'

'That's not punishment, Taxi. That's retribution, and it only hurts you.'

Taxi's eyes filled with tears, and he flung himself at his father. 'Love me, Daddy! Love me!'

Did they love enough? What's enough love?

•

"He still wants love and more love, Dr. Rowan. Not just Mom and me. All his fans. All that adoring. He'd never have made it as a banker. People don't adore bankers."

Luisa said, "His acting was one way of coping with all that happened. A very successful way."

"So why now? Why did he pull out that idiot record and keep singing that idiot song? Why would he want to get at Mom and make me ask questions now?"

Luisa asked, "Has anything happened to upset him?"

Raffi pondered, then said, "He thought he was going to get a Tony for sure last year. He feels he's owed it. And he didn't get it. He's sort of sulked ever since."

Luisa asked, "Anything else?"

"Well—I mean, I think this should have thrilled him, but I don't think it did. It's weird. But you were at that bash for Grandmother, for her Maria Mitchell Medal. Mom evidently had to push Dad into being there."

"Did this disturb you?"

"It confused me. The medal was announced in the *Times* the same day Dad got a lousy review for a play he'd really counted on. And he was good in it, he's a good actor."

"An excellent actor, a real star," Luisa agreed. "But stardom—that kind—has never interested your grandmother."

Raffi laughed. "Her interest in stars is in another direction, eh?" Then she sobered. "I don't think I want to be a star. Just an actor, because it's the one thing I know I'm good at. What happens to people when they become stars scares me."

Luisa nodded. "Did your grandmother get down to New York to see your dad's show?"

"Of course. She always does. She was as upset by the bad reviews as he was."

"However, if your father wanted to hurt your grandmother, this would be a most effective way, wouldn't it?"

"You mean"— Raffi drew out the words slowly—"he's angry, so she's not his mother?"

"It's pretty classic, isn't it? How many kids get mad at their parents and decide they're changelings, switched in the hospital?"

"That's little kids."

"Is it?"

"So he still wants to punish everybody for the lousy deal the universe gave him?"

"What do you think?"

"Lots of people get lousy deals without getting all mucked up."

"And lots of people get mucked up, Raffi. Your father isn't an isolated example."

"Dr. Rowan, I love my grandmother."

"I know you do."

"Hurting her isn't going to do anything to make my dad feel any better about himself."

"What you have to worry about right now is what it's doing to you. Is it going to affect the way you love your grandmother?"

"No."

"What about your mother?"

"She's had a lousy deal, too, but she doesn't go around taking potshots at people. Sometimes I think she's crazy to stick with Dad, but she loves the bastard. That's what he is, isn't he? A bastard. Born out of wedlock to a woman who was a classy whore."

"Hold it, Raffi. I knew the lady. It's not as easy as that."

"No? From all I can gather, she was so beautiful she thought it gave her an excuse to do anything she wanted to do, and what she wanted was sex."

"Surely your grandmother did not give you this impression."

Raffi said reluctantly, "No."

"Who, then?"

"Oh, you can guess."

"We're all a marvelous mix, you know that, Raffi. Perhaps your father has a need to believe what he believes. But how about a little mercy?"

"Mercy? You mean, no matter what anybody does, we have to have mercy?"

"Mercy and permissiveness are not the same thing."

Raffi got up and walked restlessly about the office. "This woman who was my grandmother's mother was also my father's mother ..."

"Yes."

"Weird."

"You might call it that."

"You knew her?"

"When I was young, yes. She had great charm."

"Like my dad. Did she take potshots at people?"

"No."

"This Red Grange. Did you know him, too?"

"Slightly. I didn't take any of his classes. But your grandmother did."

"God, the generations are all mixed up, aren't they?"

"Yes. It used to be less uncommon when people had large families, ten or twelve children."

"Why didn't Grandmother have any more children of her own?"

•

When Camilla suspected that she was pregnant again she said nothing, not even to Mac, not until she had been to the doctor to have the pregnancy confirmed, not until she was past the first trimester.

Mac was ecstatic. Asked, "Shall we tell the children?"

"We'll have to, sooner or later. Let's wait till I begin to show."

Taxi and Frankie were nearly thirteen. Life had settled into a reasonable routine. Mac's book had been published and well received in the academic world, and he was working on another. Camilla continued to teach, wrote a book on astronomy for children, which Frankie illustrated in a charming, childish way, and which was a surprise success. Taxi was still restless, but took some of his energy out in running, was on the junior track team at school, and continued to be the lead soloist in the choir. He still demanded what, in another child, would have been inordinate displays of affection, of reassurance.

When they told the children about the new baby they were met with even more than the expected delight. Both Frankie and Taxi leapt from the dinner table, flung their arms about each other, and danced wildly around the dining room, leaping and squealing with joy, until finally Mac told them to sit back down and finish their dinner.

But at bedtime Taxi asked, 'Mom, do we really need a baby? Aren't Frankie and I enough?'

'Of course you're enough, darling. That isn't what it's about. We thought you and Frankie would enjoy a little brother or sister.'

'I s'pose. It'll be like a doll for Frankie. Girls like dolls.'

'And boys? I'll be counting on you to protect the baby.'

'Well, of course. I guess you want this baby, Mom?'

'Yes, Taxi, we all do.'

When she went to Frankie's room to say good night, Frankie had her sketchbook out and was making pencil drawings of babies. 'I suppose Taxi and I looked like that once upon a time?'

'And not so long ago,' Camilla said.

'Will Taxi and I get to see it born?'

'Not the actual birth, but certainly right after.'

'I thought families used to be all around when babies were born, and now it's coming back again.'

'Even in the olden days,' Camilla said, 'the mother needed to be alone with the midwife during the birth, and then the family came in after.'

'And everybody boiled water,' Frankie said. 'What was the water for?'

Camilla laughed. 'Probably to keep people busy and out of the way.'

•

She called Luisa.

'That's terrific. You're still plenty young enough.'

'Plenty.'

'Just don't overdo, especially in the first months.'

'Lu, I'm already into my fifth month. I didn't want to say anything until I was sure this babe was settled in.'

'You feel okay?'

'I'm fine.'

'Just don't lug heavy loads.'

'Lu, stop hovering. I'm not going to carry anything heavier than laundry.'

The laundry machines were in the basement of their building, and the easiest way to get to them from their apartment was out the front door, down a short flight of stone steps, and then into the basement. She said goodbye to Luisa and picked up a load of sheets, stepped on one of Taxi's roller skates, and fell down the stairs.

•

Olivia flew up from Florida, arriving shortly after Mac brought Camilla home from the hospital. Taxi was white and silent. Frankie took her watercolors and painted a dark, stormy landscape with small, fleeing figures. It was a long time since she had painted that way.

'Why was Taxi's skate there?' Mac asked angrily.

Olivia sat beside them on the bed. 'It was an accident.

Careless and stupid, but then, most teenagers are careless and stupid.'

•

Noelle called, one of her chatty reachings-out to Camilla. She had not heard of the miscarriage. Her mind was on little Ferris, one of the twins, and his jealousy of his baby sister. 'Amy seems fine about it. She'd play dolly with the baby all day if I let her. Little Ferris asked me what would happen if I stopped nursing the baby,' Noelle said, 'and I told him she'd get hungry and start crying and I'd have to nurse her again. Then he asked me what would happen if I stopped nursing her entirely, if she just didn't get fed. I told him she'd cry and be hungry and starve. Starve to death? he asked. And I said, Probably. And he said, Mom, stop nursing her. I suppose it's a classic case of sibling rivalry, but it turned my blood cold.'

•

"You didn't have any siblings either, did you, Grandmother?" Raffi asked. "You were an only, like me, weren't you?"

"Yes," Camilla said, without realizing that this was not entirely true until the word was out of her mouth.

"When Dad and Aunt Frankie were little, did they get along?"

Camilla replied, "They were like puppies. Enchanting. Later, when they were moving into puberty, your father was busy with choir. In the spring he was on the track team. And Frankie had a bevy of little girlfriends, when she wasn't drawing or painting. She and Taxi got along well together, but they weren't inseparable as they were when they were little, and that was as it should be, each of them finding separate ways. Then, when they were thirteen, Papa died. He had pancreatic cancer and it was mercifully quick. Less than a month before he died, we went down to the beach to spend a week with them, and it was beautiful."

"Beautiful? When Papa was dying of pancreatic cancer? It's one of the worst." Raffi looked and sounded disbelieving.

"Beautiful," Camilla repeated. "Papa was beautiful and loving in saying goodbye. We never knew how much pain he hid from us, but I saw nothing but serenity in his face and eyes. He and Mac had long, quiet times together. Taxi and Frankie each had their time alone with him. When it was my turn I simply sat by the bed and held his hand and told him how much I loved and honored him, and he called me his beloved daughter, and told me that death could not take away our love, and that he would be with me always." For a moment her voice trembled. "Then we went back to New York and he and Mama had their last weeks together."

"Beautiful—" Raffi's voice still questioned.

"Yes, it was beautiful, Raffi. Terrible, but beautiful. Papa had lived a long, full life, and he had come to terms with more than most people can begin to imagine. He was able to be merciful to himself, and to teach us to be merciful, too. He believed that God's redeeming love can come into the most terrible things, and while I do not have the kind of radiant faith that Papa had, I believed him."

•

They were all in the Cathedral in Jacksonville for the funeral. The great space was crowded. Extra chairs were brought in. People stood outside on the steps. Love and grief filled the air. Camilla might have been able to hold back her tears had it not been for the people around her, wiping their eyes, blowing their noses. She felt the sobs rolling through her body like the waves on the beach, sobs of grief, and of gratitude for all that Art had given her.

Taxi was clinging to Camilla's hand. Frankie stood solemnly beside Olivia, the two of them stiff, dry-eyed, containing their anguish deep inside them.

After the service and the interment they would go to the

beach house, where Art and Olivia had been living year round.

Camilla looked at Mac in his vestments, his face disciplined, unreadable, his voice calm. She was thinking, pleading: —Mac don't go now, don't retreat from this, don't flee. It would be too much for the children. For Taxi. Stay with us. Stay. Mama isn't strong enough to hold you right now. She needs you.

The words continued, as close to prayer as she could get in her grief and fear.

•

Mac wanted Olivia to come back to New York with them.

'No, my darling. I do not wish to be a guest in anybody's house.'

'Mama! You wouldn't be a guest!'

'I need my own home, Mac, and I couldn't take the cold weather. I'll come visit you. You will come visit me. But I need to be here, where Art and I have been deeply happy.'

•

The night after they returned to the seminary Taxi confronted Camilla and Mac in their bedroom after he knew Frankie was asleep. 'You are my parents. I don't want you to mention anything else to anybody else. Ever.'

Mac said, 'Taxi, there's nothing to be ashamed of.'

'I'm not ashamed,' Taxi shouted. 'Somebody told Frankie she was going to miss her grandfather. Then he said to me, You'll miss him, too, as though I didn't belong. Frankie said, We'll both miss our grandfather, and the man just gave us a silly sort of smile.'

'He didn't mean to be unkind,' Mac started.

Taxi broke in. 'I'm named after Papa. After my grandfather. I'm Artaxias Xanthakos, that's who I am. I'm Taxi Xanthakos. Aren't I?'

Camilla assured, 'Of course you are.'

'And you're my mom.'

'I am.'

'Not that Harriet, who made me call her Mommy.'

'Taxi, she wanted you to love her.'

'But she didn't love me. She wasn't my mother. And neither was that old woman I never knew.'

Camilla said, 'Taxi, if your mother hadn't died—'

'Not my mother! Not my mother!'

Camilla continued, her voice steady, gentle. 'If she hadn't died, she would have loved you with all her heart.'

'But she didn't. She died, and she didn't.'

(Luisa had said, 'To a child, death is a terrible betrayal.')

'And suppose—suppose—'

'What, Taxi?'

'If she hadn't died, what about Red? That's what he wanted me to call him. Red. Not Daddy. Red. He wasn't my father. He was only Red. If she—that old woman—that Rose—if she hadn't died, would he ever have known?'

Mac said, 'Probably not.'

'But she did die!' Taxi said. 'Don't talk about her! Don't ever talk about her again!'

'Taxi, darling,' Camilla said. 'She was our mother.'

Taxi's voice rose in a high wail. 'No, Mommy, no! You are my mother, my own mommy mother!'

Mac said, 'Calm down, Taxi, it's all right.'

What's all right?

•

Luisa asked, "Are you all right, Raffi?"

Raffi blew her nose, tossed the tissue into the basket. "I'm not sure about all right, but I think I know why Dad's in such a tiz and hitting out at everybody."

Luisa waited while Raffi blew her nose again.

"One of the women in Dad's show called Mom. It seems there's a rumor that Dad's contract is not going to be renewed."

"Surely that's no more than a rumor! He's immensely popular."

"Too popular, maybe? It seems that the producer's girl-friend, or maybe his boyfriend, I forget which, is in a bit part and is jealous of Taxi, and has the producer's ear."

"Sounds like nasty gossip to me."

"In the theatre, nasty gossip is often true."

"Has your father said anything about this?"

"No. He just looks like a thundercloud and nothing any-body does pleases him. It makes sense, Dr. Rowan. He's used to being a star and making pots of money, and if that should evaporate—"

"He has a good agent, doesn't he?"

"Yeah, but I don't think an agent can get his contract re-newed if the producer doesn't want to renew it. Dad's used to living high. Our apartment's expensive. Mom certainly couldn't go back to dancing at this point."

"Don't borrow trouble, Raffi."

"Okay, maybe to some extent I'm doing that. But it would explain a lot, wouldn't it? Why he played that silly record, why he's hurting the people he loves most, even if he hurts himself at the same time."

"Yes." Luisa rolled a pencil slowly between her fingers. "It would explain a lot. Let's hope the rumor is unfounded."

"On the other hand," Raffi said, reaching for another tis-sue, "I'm learning things I think I should have known about long ago."

•

"Mom."

Camilla was upstairs, in bed, reading, when the phone rang. She let the book drop, open, on the blanket beside her, realizing that she was half asleep and had no idea what she'd read for the last few pages.

It was Thessaly. Voice tight.

"Thess, what's up?"

"Oh, Mom, Taxi's made enemies on his show, and that isn't

like him. No matter how uncontrolled he sometimes gets at home, he's always professional in his work."

"What's happened?"

"Nothing, yet. But I had a call from one of the writers, who asked me if I knew why Taxi's being dropped from the show."

"Oh, Thessaly, surely not." She picked up the book with her free hand, put it back down.

"The woman's a gossipy bitch and I don't know how seriously to take her, but Taxi's been very up and down lately, and the downs have been very down."

"Taxi's downs always are. He's a good actor, Thessaly, and, as you said, he's always been completely professional."

"I know there's usually nasty gossip around the studio, but somehow Taxi's stayed clear."

"Let's hope it's no more than gossip."

"Oh, Mom, I didn't want to upset you, but I needed to have you tell me it isn't true."

Camilla leaned against the pillows. "It probably isn't true, though I can't promise you. The best thing I can say is that it's never good to pay attention to gossip. It's usually malicious and distorted even if it's partly true. When is Taxi's contract up for renewal?"

"Next month."

"I try to catch his show at least a couple of times a week," Camilla said. "He seems to me to have been particularly good lately, and done well with some difficult lines."

"Yes," Thessaly agreed. "I thought so, too. But it would explain some things, wouldn't it? His upsetting Raffi with that horrid record—"

•

When Taxi and Frankie were fourteen, Frank Rowan came for one of his periodic home leaves. His wife and children stayed with her parents, who had returned to the States, and

Frank came to the seminary for a visit with Mac and Camilla.

One day Camilla, checking the children's rooms to see what degree of untidiness they had reached, heard Taxi's voice from the kitchen, where Mac was having a cup of coffee.

'When is Uncle Frank going away?'

'He's here for another week.'

'Will he take Mommy with him?' Taxi's voice was anxious.

'Why would he do that, Taxi?'

'Well, I don't know, Daddy, I just get worried. He and Mommy spend a lot of time together while you're teaching.'

'Uncle Frank's our guest. It's perfectly natural.'

'Well, Dad, I was just afraid maybe it was more than that.'

'Taxi, what on earth are you talking about?'

'One of the kids in my class asked me who was the big handsome guy Mom was with. He saw them walking down the street together. He thought they were holding hands. So I was just afraid.'

Camilla came into the kitchen. 'What are you saying, Taxi?'

'Oh, nothing, Mommy.'

'It doesn't sound like nothing.' She looked at the boy, who was leaning against the fridge, slender in his school uniform, grey trousers, white shirt, navy blazer. He shifted uncomfortably from foot to foot.

Mac said, 'I think you'd better forget about all this, Taxi. Mom and Uncle Frank and I have always been especially good friends, and we're very grateful for all that Uncle Frank has done for us.'

Camilla kept her voice steady. 'Taxi, I was looking for you to tell you your room is a total mess. Please go and tidy it. Okay?' She left the kitchen and went into her study and stood leaning against her desk as though to support her weight, which had become intolerable. Mac followed, coffee cup in hand. Shut the door.

Camilla asked, 'What was that all about?'

'Taxi was asking some very ugly questions.'

'Why? Why is he so destructive?'

Mac's voice was tight. 'I think he was genuinely troubled, Camilla. Is there anything to it?'

'Mac! My God, Mac, no! How could you?'

'Taxi can be very plausible.'

'Frank's a good friend. Your best friend.'

'But once you and he—'

'When we were teenagers. Frank is happily married. I am happily married. Mac, you can't let Taxi do this to us.'

Then his arms were around her.

.

She phoned Olivia, who said, 'I don't know why he's striking out at you and Mac. But, classically, you're the ones he has to punish. In his poor, battered psyche, you are to blame for letting him go to Grange and Harriet.'

'Oh, Mama, the thing is, Taxi might have seen and misinterpreted—'

'What?'

'I was in the kitchen this morning, making Frank a cup of tea, and we were talking, sharing, the good things and the bad in our lives. And when I put the tea in front of Frank, I bent down and kissed the top of his head, and he reached up and took my hand and pressed it against his cheek. It was affection, Mama, nothing else. Our history goes a long way back. But if Taxi had seen—'

'Yes, he could easily have misunderstood. But you'll never know, my love. Can you let it go? Can Mac?'

'I think so. Mac knows I love him, utterly.'

'And he's learned staying power; that's something I wasn't sure was ever going to happen.'

.

After Art's death Camilla called Olivia daily, usually in the morning, before she roused the children. Not children anymore. Teenagers. She had talked with Olivia about the great unfilled hole of love in Rose. Had Taxi simply inherited that from his mother, a dose doubled by Grange and Harriet, so that his need for love was insatiable? Would he have remained a happy, secure child if Rose had never written that letter to Grange? If Grange had heeded Rose's request? If Grange and Harriet had not had clever lawyers? If they had not been killed?

'Where have we failed?' Camilla asked Olivia.

'My darling, you have not failed. You have loved, with strength, not sentimentality. Just as there are some wounds the greatest physicians cannot heal, so there are wounds of the soul that no human being can heal.'

'Oh, Mama,' Camilla said. 'How would I manage without you?'

Olivia gave a small laugh. 'One day you will have to. That is the nature of things.'

And one day when Camilla called Olivia in the morning there was no answer. Fighting down panic, she called a neighbor, who also checked daily on the old woman.

Olivia had died quietly in her sleep.

•

Camilla's grief was contained only by her need to help Taxi and Frankie with theirs. Frankie, who seldom cried, wept silently through the funeral. Taxi held Camilla's arm so tight that it was bruised. Mac, his voice low but steady, was the officiant, looking and sounding heartrendingly like his father as he spoke the ancient, affirmative words of the funeral service.

Afterwards there was a reception in the large meeting room in Diocesan House, above which were the offices of bishops and canons, and below which were archives. Camilla and Mac tried to smile, to be courteous. Frankie held her father's hand, still unable to control her tears.

'Where's Taxi?' she asked.

Camilla looked around. There was no sign of Taxi. Where had he gone, and why? She tried to control her anxiety. They stayed longer than they had expected to, until finally Taxi came into the hall.

'Where were you?' Frankie demanded.

'I needed to be alone. Let's go.'

One of the canons drove them to the airport, and they flew back to New York.

•

The next day when Camilla got home from her class at NYU she went into her study to leave her books and papers, and noticed a manila folder on her desk. In it was a document from the diocesan office in Jacksonville, an order of inhibition. In the document Artaxias Xanthakos was relieved of his priestly functions for six months because of an accusation of sodomy which had been neither proved nor disproved. Because of his fine record in his diocese and his Cathedral, the inhibition would last for only six months.

Camilla felt a wave of nausea sweep through her, and put a hand to her mouth as though holding in her rage. She knew about the document. Olivia had called her. 'It's outrageous. It's vicious, lying gossip. There's no truth in it. The Presiding Bishop has assured Art that he has absolute confidence in him. It comes from the diocese where the—' There was a choking pause.

'The organist?' Camilla asked.

'Yes. His hatred of Art is a sickness, but I feel no mercy toward him, only rage. I am far angrier than Art is.'

'Oh, Mama, Mama, I'm so sorry.'

'I still fail to understand this kind of sickness that wants to destroy.'

'It won't.'

'No. It won't destroy Art, because it is not true, but truth has not always kept lies from destroying. The church is a small

world, but tentacles reach out—and in. I was afraid you and
Mac might hear something.'

They had not. A few days later Olivia called to say that
the accusation had been withdrawn, and Art reinstated. Few
people knew that anything had happened. Why was the document still in existence for someone to find and—

She looked at the damaging, damning folder.

Who had put it on her desk?

Taxi. She shuddered. Why had she immediately thought
of Taxi?

Where had he disappeared after Olivia's funeral? Into the
diocesan offices above the reception hall, or below it, to the
archives?

There was a small fireplace in Camilla's study which she
used occasionally. She put the folder in it with some crushed
newspaper and burned it.

Then she went to Taxi's room.

Frankie's accusation was just: Camilla hated confrontation. But she could not refuse to confront Taxi about this.

'Yes, I took it.' He looked up from his desk, where he was
doing homework. 'I didn't want it there. I wanted to get rid
of it.'

'I have burned it,' Camilla said. 'It is a vicious lie. The
accusation was withdrawn.'

'Of course it's a lie,' Taxi said. 'That's why I took it. For
Mama's and Papa's sake. To get rid of it.'

'But, Taxi, you had no right to be wherever you were
when you found this.'

'I was looking for the bathroom,' Taxi said, 'and I opened
this door and there were a lot of file cabinets and I pulled one
drawer to see if it would open. I don't know why, I just pulled,
but it was locked. Most of them were, but this one drawer pulled
out. I think it had a weak lock. Mom, I'm glad I found this. I
don't want anybody else to see it.' Suddenly there were tears in
his eyes. 'Why would anybody accuse my Papa this way?'

Camilla sat on the side of his bed. 'Papa was very much loved. Where there is great love, there is often jealousy and hate.'

'Did Mama know about this?' his voice quavered.

'Yes. Mama and Papa did not keep things from each other. They bore their hurts together.'

'This hurt them?'

'Of course it hurt, Taxi, it hurt terribly.'

'I don't want them to be dead!' Taxi shouted.

'Neither do I, Taxi, neither do I.' She put her arm about him. 'But, Taxi, you must not go snooping into private places. This document was not meant to be seen. I had no right to burn it.'

'Yes, you did!' Taxi burst into sobs. 'It was the right thing to do. It was, it was! They can't say that about Papa! Not Papa!'

•

'You're right,' Mac said, 'you shouldn't have burned it. On the other hand, since Taxi lifted it, burning was probably the best thing to do. You couldn't very well return it to the diocese.'

'Mac, Taxi was totally shaken. He was in tears. It must have seemed to him just another betrayal.'

'By whom?' Mac's voice was sharp. 'Papa?'

'No, no, not Papa! By whoever made the accusation, whoever filed that document.'

Mac said, slowly, 'Darling, that document didn't just pop into Taxi's hand. He had to have been prying. What was he after?'

She shook her head. 'I don't know. With Taxi I'm never sure.'

•

In a strange and dark way Taxi solved the problem for them. Camilla, late one afternoon, took some folded laundry into Taxi's room, where she assumed he was doing homework. He was not there. She walked along to Frankie's room, and there they were on Frankie's bed, Taxi on top of Frankie.

It wasn't as bad as it had seemed. Nothing had happened. Nothing had, according to Frankie, preceded it. Taxi had laughed. 'Come on, Mom, don't make such a big thing of it.'

Luisa said, 'It's time you sent Taxi to boarding school.' She had come to them after work, after Taxi and Frankie were in bed, and normally Camilla and Mac would have retired, too. They sat in Camilla's study, which was the room farthest from the sleeping quarters. Mac had used some of their precious hoard of wood to light a fire.

He turned to Luisa. 'Will he see that as rejection?'

Luisa said calmly, 'I know you believe what they tell you, that nothing happened. But what about next time?'

Camilla asked, 'Would there be a next time?'

Luisa said, 'No telling. Taxi's unpredictable as well as damaged.'

Mac sat in the battered brown leather chair that had come with them from Corinth. 'Sending him away—it seems like failure.'

Luisa said, 'It's an honorable thing to fail, Mac. This seems the right time for many reasons. Isn't Taxi's therapist moving to San Francisco?'

'Yes.'

Another betrayal. Another loss.

'Talk to Liz Wickoff. She seems to have a better rapport with Taxi than anybody else.'

·

Dr. Wickoff said, 'Taxi clings to past wounds. God knows he has plenty. What we will never understand is why one child can survive incredible trauma and manage to get along fairly normally, and another has wounds which never heal. Taxi's variable. Sometimes he seems like an extremely bright lad with all the ordinary problems that go along with brightness. Sometimes, and I can see no predictable pattern, his light flickers and dims.'

—Like the Cepheids, Camilla thought. —Papa's analogy.

Dr. Wickoff continued, 'I know a good boarding school in Massachusetts where he will be challenged, and where there is an excellent psychiatrist in the next town, which may be better for Taxi than having to go to someone new here.'

Camilla spoke in a dull voice. 'It will be a relief to have him out of the house.'

Andrew came into his wife's office, squatted down in front of Camilla. 'Do not b-blame yourself for your feelings.'

'Or lack of them,' Camilla said.

'Whatever. Do not get hung up on the hook of false guilt.'

Camilla tried to smile. 'I come close to falling into Taxi's trap of wanting to blame someone, of wanting someone punished.'

'You'll get over that,' Dr. Wickoff said. 'It's a perfectly normal reaction.'

•

Noelle called. 'I spoke to Andrew. He says you're sending Taxi to boarding school. He thinks it's a good idea.'

'Yes,' Camilla said. 'It's probably time.' Andrew would not have told Noelle the reason.

'I wanted to talk to you,' Noelle said, 'because we're thinking about boarding school for young Ferris. He's my problem kid. He's been really disruptive lately. How do you feel about it, Camilla? Sending Taxi away?'

'Boarding schools still exist,' Camilla said, 'because some kids need the discipline, and a little separation from the parents can be a good thing.'

'Some people send their kids away to get rid of them.'

'Maybe. But not all parents, and the school Liz and Andrew suggested is known to be one where parents truly want the best for their kids.'

'Let me know how Taxi does. That's the school we're considering for Ferris.'

In a way Noelle's call was comforting. Other parents had disruptive children, too.

Noelle continued, 'I'm going back to school to get a master's. My brain has turned to mush with all this domesticity. I need a challenge. You're marvelous, the way you've managed to get on with your own work and yet not neglect your kids.'

'I hope I didn't. But I do know things worked better when I was teaching and doing research than when I had only the family on my mind.'

'That was true of Mom, too,' Noelle said. 'Andrew and I never felt neglected or unloved. Mom was pretty consistent with us. Dad tended to be erratic. Anyhow, when he married Harriet, we lost him. Harriet didn't want any living reminders that he'd ever had another life with another woman who'd had the kids she couldn't have. As far as I'm concerned, Harriet killed my father.'

•

"Everybody seems to have made Harriet the scapegoat," Raffi said. "Was she as bad as all that?"

Dr. Rowan said, "She was rich and selfish. I didn't care for her, but nobody's as bad as all that. She was desperate to have the child she couldn't have, and was used to getting her own way. You're right when you say she was the scapegoat. Everybody else's mistakes were conveniently put onto Harriet. Even Grange's. If he hadn't married Harriet, none of the horrors would have happened. However, he did marry Harriet, and that gives him a certain responsibility. He liked Harriet's money. He liked not having to work within the inevitable stresses of the academic world."

"Did he like my dad? His son? Did he love him?"

"Grange and Rose both loved being loved."

"But did they love?"

"Maybe they loved the idea of love, of being in love," Dr. Rowan suggested. "I don't know how to put limits on love, Raffi. People love differently. Some ways of love we recognize because they're at least reasonably close to the way we, ourselves, love. Some of it is quite different. When it stops being love I am not sure."

"We've been reading *Anna Karenina* in class. Seems to me Tolstoy saw most families as being unhappy. His certainly was."

"What's happy, Raffi? Speaking of which, any news about your father and his contract?"

"I haven't been home. I don't think there's any news, or Mom would have told me. Why did Tolstoy write about unhappy families rather than happy ones?"

"Isn't the new term dysfunctional vs. functional?"

"That's the present jargon."

"What strikes me, Raffi, is that your grandparents, despite everything, managed to have an amazingly functional family."

"But they're not my grandparents."

"Oh, yes, they are. Emotionally they are your grandparents, and that's been a blessing to you, hasn't it?"

"Well, yes. Grandmother. I never knew Grandfather, remember? Aunt Frankie seems to have done pretty well."

"Frankie's an amazing combination of love and forbearance and self-protection."

"She got away, didn't she? Far, far away, by marrying someone from Seattle."

"And also through her work. She's an excellent illustrator. Not a great artist, perhaps, but her work in the children's book world is highly regarded, and she has more jobs than she can accept. Frankie was born strong and loving, and somehow she's managed to hang on to that."

"Good genes?"

"Good genes help, but we do have to live our own lives and make our own decisions and abide by the consequences. Some pretty horrendous characters started out with good genes, and others, who had bad starts, have managed to do splendid things with their lives. Consider your father, Raffi. According to the world's standards, he's amazingly successful."

"Yeah, I guess that's true." Suddenly she stopped, almost shouted, "Hey, Dr. Rowan, I just remembered something!"

"What?"

"About Dad."

"Yes?"

"I don't have the faintest idea why I remembered it now. It was long ago, when I was a little kid, and Grandmother was still in New York."

"Go on," Luisa urged.

"Dad used to drink. He wasn't an alcoholic. It never interfered with his work, but he used to come back home from the studio and have a couple of drinks. Martinis, I think. And then he'd go into a gripe session, where nothing pleased him. One night he began shouting about how much he hated his father, and how his father had ruined his life."

"Which father?" Luisa asked.

"That's just it," Raffi said. "I'd never heard of this Red Grange character, so of course I thought he was talking about Grandfather. It was really weird, because usually he talked about how much he loved Grandfather and how sorry he was I never had a chance to know him. But that night he kept on talking about how selfish his father was, how he wanted only his own pleasure, and how he'd deprived Dad of his identity. Mom just took me up to bed and said Dad didn't know what he was talking about, gin breeds aggression, and I should forget it. Forget it, she said. How could I?"

"Go on." Luisa's voice was gentle.

"But I did forget it, after all, didn't I? I mean, I haven't thought about it all these years till this very minute. I remember Mom gave Dad an ultimatum. No more booze, no more drugs."

"Drugs?"

"Pot, I suppose. Maybe cocaine, that's what a lot of people were doing. Anyhow, Dad quit. Cold turkey."

"With the help of AA?"

"Dad? My dad didn't need AA. He could do it himself." Her voice was heavy with scorn.

Luisa asked mildly, "But he did do it himself, didn't he?"

"I guess he did. I never saw him drink any liquor after that. But, Dr. Rowan, don't you see? When Dad was going on about how he hated his father, he wasn't talking about Grandfather, was he? He was talking about this Red Grange who was his biological father. No wonder he hated somebody who took him away from where he was happy, from Aunt Frankie and Grandmother and Grandfather."

"Does it help you understand?"

"A little. Thank God Dad doesn't have any of Harriet's genes. If he has the same genes as Grandmother, and I guess he has to, half of them, if they have the same mother, well, he must have started out with a good chance. In the world's eyes, in my friends' eyes, Dad is terrific."

"Isn't he, at least some of the time?"

"Maybe."

"And you, Raffi? Are you terrific?"

"I've come to see that I'm not a total blot on anybody's escutcheon, and that I don't have to let all this screw up my life completely. I'd have to do that myself."

"This is a real breakthrough, Raffi."

"Is it?"

"You know it is. You've made remarkable progress. How's college?"

"I like it. I like having Grandmother nearby. I've made some good friends."

"How are your grades?"

"Good. I'll be on the dean's list, so that means I can try out for the next play, and I'm going to."

"Good," Luisa applauded.

"I'm beginning to realize I don't have to have Dad's approval. I've got the grades, so I can go ahead and do what I want. I may be stunted in some ways, but not academically."

•

Taxi did moderately well academically at his boarding school. His mandatory weekly letters home were brief and uninformative, and referred to the school as the prison to which he had been unfairly committed.

From the school's point of view, he had adapted reasonably well, got his work in mostly on time, and was the star both of the chorus and of the drama club.

He came home for spring vacation looking pale, then flushed. Camilla took his temperature and called Dr. Wickoff's office.

'You'd better bring him right in,' the nurse said. 'Dr. Liz isn't in, but Dr. Andy will see him.'

There seemed no reason to refuse. Taxi had met Dr. Andy, as everybody called him and, as far as Camilla could see, associated him with nothing unpleasant.

Andrew's office was, like Liz's, cluttered with things which might appeal to children. One wall was hung with photographs, some of young patients, some of family. Andrew and Elizabeth now had two little boys, who were prominently displayed. There were several snapshots of Noelle's twins and her younger little girl. Camilla's eyes were drawn to a large color photograph of Andrew and Noelle, Andrew an early adolescent, Noelle a charming child. Andrew's hair blazed, and Noelle's was a rather lank brown; no wonder she played with it.

Andrew examined Taxi methodically. 'I'll s-send this culture to the lab, but I'm betting it's strep, so I'm going to start you right away on medication—' He was looking carefully at the chart. 'Something you're not allergic to. You're to take all of it, Taxi, even if you s-start to feel better. Lie low for a couple of days. Read. Watch TV. Rest. You've grown a lot since I last saw you, and you're underweight.'

'I've no intention of becoming an obese slob.'

'No anorexia allowed in this office. Go home and let your family pet and pamper you.'

'Oh, yes, and then they'll send me back to that prison.'

'It's not a prison, it's an excellent school. The head's a friend of mine, and the report is that you are d-doing very well indeed, and that the other boys like and admire you.'

Taxi shrugged. 'Peasants.'

'Okay, T-Taxi. Strep does tend to bring out the negative. When your fever is gone and you're feeling better, the rest of the world will be brighter.'

•

Camilla and Mac went up to the school to see Taxi in *Amahl and the Night Visitors*. He was still small enough to play a younger boy, his voice on the verge of deepening but still pure and sweet. Camilla and Mac held hands and watched him transcend himself. He brought a quality to the opera seldom seen in an amateur production.

'I wish Frankie had come,' Camilla said.

Frankie was keeping her distance from Taxi, and the day of the production conflicted with one of her art classes. 'Give Taxi my love,' she said. 'He'll understand I can't skip class.'

Of course he didn't.

•

A few weeks later they had a troubled call from the headmaster. Taxi had been found in the stacks of the library on the floor with one of the girl students. Both of them were being suspended for a week. Then they would be allowed to return to school, on probation, under strict supervision.

Taxi came home, delighted to see everybody, not regarding the suspension in any way as a punishment. At dinner he said, 'There are quite a few shows I want to see in these few days, so I'm going to Times Square and stand in line.'

'Sorry, Taxi,' Mac said. 'This is not a vacation. No theatre for you.'

'I have my own money.'

'Nevertheless,' Mac said, 'you are to stay home at the seminary. I gather you have quite a bit of schoolwork to catch up on.'

Taxi shrugged. 'Okay.'

When Camilla finished the dishes—Mac had an evening seminar—and went to check on Taxi, he was not in the apartment. She left the building, crossed the close, and went to the main entrance. The student at the reception desk said he'd seen Taxi go out with the teenage daughter of one of the professors.

Camilla would not have called Luisa, but Luisa happened to call her.

'I'm sorry,' Luisa said. 'But this is not atypical behavior for Taxi. Don't make too big a deal of it.'

'I agree. I won't call him on it. Do I overreact?'

'Understandably, occasionally. Do you still love Taxi?'

'You don't turn love on and off like water in a faucet,' Camilla said.

'But do you?'

'I don't know. Sometimes I feel nothing but scar tissue, and scar tissue doesn't feel.'

'And you blame yourself for not feeling?'

'Of course.'

'Don't. You're not responsible for how you feel. You're responsible for what you do, and considering everything, you and Mac have done pretty well.'

'But—here I am talking about my scar tissue, and Taxi's the one who's been so terribly wounded.'

Luisa gave an impatient grunt. 'A lot of people get terribly wounded. The media saturates us with false images of happiness and security, but it's a lie. That's why I and the rest of my ilk stay in business.'

•

Taxi made it halfway through his senior year and was expelled. When Camilla and Mac drove up to the school to bring him home, he was not there. Finally, cutting through the subdued panic, one of the girl students went to the headmaster's office and said that Taxi had gone to join a small theatrical company in Boston.

'Let him be,' they were advised. 'If he can make it on his own, perhaps that's what he needs.'

'Who knows what Taxi needs?' Luisa asked rhetorically. 'Even Taxi doesn't know. Perhaps Taxi most of all.'

But Taxi did well in the theatre. Frankie was happy in art school, bringing friends home for the weekend, building a good portfolio of her work. She seldom talked about Taxi. After she completed her degree she moved out of the seminary apartment and into a loft with three other aspiring artists. She got a job with a prestigious gallery. She called her parents regularly. Everything she was doing was right and proper, but Camilla and Mac missed her.

'I think I'm having empty-nest syndrome,' Camilla said, as she and Mac sat in her study before dinner.

'That's natural,' Mac said. 'I am, too, even though I'm enjoying the peace and quiet.'

'Frankie wasn't exactly noisy.'

'No.'

And Taxi hadn't been around to make noise.

Mac added, 'But you know what I mean.'

Yes.

When Frankie married it was just a continuation of normal patterns. The wedding was in the seminary chapel, with Mac officiating, and Camilla was torn between a joyful sense of completion for her daughter and loss for herself and Mac. Frankie and Ben moved to Seattle, where Ben became a partner in his father's small publishing house, dealing mostly with technical books for a small but steady market. Frankie called at least weekly. Camilla and Mac made occasional trips to Seattle. They would probably have gone more often if there had been grandchildren to visit.

•

"Aunt Frankie sent me her new book," Raffi said. "It's terrific. Stuff you taught her about astronomy, and wonderful stuff of her own about Orion and hunting stars."

She had come across campus to have dinner with Camilla.

Camilla, looking at Raffi, whose cheeks were flushed with cold, her nose pink, drew her into the warm living room.

Raffi laughed. "It's winter, Grandmother. More snow tonight." She pulled off her woolen cap, shrugged out of her pea coat, and tossed it and her backpack onto one of the chairs.

"Dinner's nearly ready," Camilla said. "Let's go into the kitchen. I've made that pasta you like, with artichokes and cherry tomatoes and black and green olives and other goodies."

"Whoopee, I'm starved." Raffi followed Camilla into the kitchen. A large pot on the stove was steaming, and Camilla put in a small package of fettuccini. "This is the kind that cooks quickly. Three minutes." She set the timer. Started to ask, "What's on your mind?" but stopped. Raffi would tell her whatever it was when she was ready.

Raffi took a long wooden spoon and stirred the pasta. "Good news, Grandmother."

"Wonderful. I'm ready for good news. What?"

"Mom called. Dad's contract's been renewed for three more years. He was given some kind of a scolding, which made him livid, but if he was as stinky at the studio as he was at home, he deserved it."

"But he has the contract."

"Yes. Mom says she'll call you tonight. So now maybe we can relax."

Camilla nodded slightly and stirred her sauce, redolent of onion and garlic, cilantro and other herbs. She glanced briefly at Raffi, who said nothing more until the timer pinged. Then the girl took mitts and drained the pasta into the waiting colander, raising a cloud of steam.

"We're doing a section on poetry in Freshman English."

"Are you enjoying it?"

"Sure." They heaped their plates, then moved into the dining alcove. Raffi spooned Parmesan cheese onto her pasta. "I keep digging at you, Grandmother, trying to get at the truth, why Dad wanted to pull the rug out from under me."

"He—" Camilla started.

Raffi rode over her. "I know he was frantic about his contract, but what I'm coming to see is that truth is complicated, and the same thing can have a different truth for different people." She got up from the table, went into the living room, and dug a bulky textbook out of her backpack. She brought it to the table and opened it to a marked page. "Listen to this. We had it today. It's by Emily Dickinson.

Tell all the Truth but tell it slant—

That's my dad, isn't it? Maybe he can't help telling it slant. Maybe he got slanted and can't straighten up?" Without waiting for an answer, she returned to the text.

> *Success in Circuit lies*
> *Too bright for our infirm Delight*
> *The Truth's superb surprise*

> As Lightning to the Children eased
> With explanation kind—

Is the explanation kind, Grandmother, or is it cruel? I'm not sure I get this. Well, there are two more lines:

> The Truth must dazzle gradually
> Or every man be blind—

Is Emily Dickinson saying that if we know too much too soon we can't take it?"

"Perhaps." Camilla offered Raffi salad. "That's one of her poems I don't think I've heard before."

"Packs a wallop, doesn't it?" Raffi helped herself to salad. It was as though the ordinary acts of cooking, of eating, eased the truth, made it kinder than it would be if not slanted. She put down her fork. Then she said, "My dad's a very successful actor."

"Very."

"So on one level that's a truth, isn't it?"

"Yes."

"He's got what he wanted. His contract's been renewed. But he's still not happy a lot of the time. He's not manic depressive or anything, but he does swing up and down."

—Like the Cepheids, Camilla thought. "The down times don't last forever."

"The last time I was home, he got out an album of pictures of himself and Aunt Frankie when they were little kids. He showed them to Mom and me, and then he stuffed the album in the garbage. After he went to bed Mom got it out and cleaned it off and put it away. Now I guess I know why there aren't more pictures of Dad and Aunt Frankie after they were about four."

"Harriet and Grange must have taken pictures," Camilla said, "but we never saw any."

"What about after? After they were killed and my dad came back to you?"

"We took pictures. There are several albums."

"Where?"

"I gave a couple to your mother. And there are a few over there" —she indicated the living room and the wall of books— "on the shelf with all the scrapbooks of Taxi's clippings, playbills, reviews, articles from TV magazines, and so forth."

"May I see them?"

"Of course. The scrapbooks are pretty much duplicates of what your mother has."

"The photo albums?"

"They're there, on the bottom shelf. There aren't that many after your dad and Aunt Frankie got into high school."

"Did Aunt Frankie go to college?"

"She went to art school. She has a B.F.A. She dated an editor for a while—is that the right word? Do people still date? Or are they an item?"

Raffi laughed. "It doesn't matter. What about the editor?"

"He was the one who got her illustrating books for children, and doing book jackets. The year she broke up with her editor friend, she wrote her own first book—you know it."

"Yeah, the one about the twins who were separated..."

"And then she won the Caldecott Medal with her third book."

"Oh, yes, the beautiful one about the white wolf."

"Then she and Ben married and moved to Seattle, where Ben came from."

"So she and Dad were sort of like the twins in the first book ... Except the twins got back together."

"Except," Camilla said.

"Oh, Grandmother, it's sad. I hardly know my Aunt Frankie at all. She sends me really nice presents for my birthday and Christmas, and sometimes she writes me wonderful letters, but I don't know her. I hate that."

"I hate it, too," Camilla said.

"Was Aunt Frankie at—at any of Dad's weddings?"

"Yes. She came East when he married your mother. They liked each other. If it weren't for geography, I think they would have been good friends."

"What about the others? The first two? I know about them because sometimes when Dad's being ugly he slaps my mom by making comparisons."

"Sharilee didn't last long. Frankie did meet her, but we never got to know her."

.

When Taxi married Sharilee Swann ('Who thought up that name?' Frankie demanded), Camilla and Mac had not yet met her. The wedding was at city hall in Chicago, where Taxi and Sharilee were playing in a musical together. Taxi's pure boy-soprano voice was long gone, but he was now a passable tenor, and he knew how to put over a song. The charm with which he sang made up for any lack in his voice.

The night of the marriage he had called, sounding very young and excited. 'Mom! Dad!'

They were, of course, asleep.

'Sorry to wake you but I had to tell you! Sharilee and I are married! Her parents are the pits, so we had to do it this way. I'm really sorry, Dad, you know what I really wanted was for you to marry us.'

Mac had answered the phone, which was on his side of the bed. Camilla slid out and went to the extension in the kitchen, hearing Taxi say, '. . . you'll adore Sharilee. She really understands me, all my moods, my needs. She's so gentle and sweet. She's only nineteen, but she's had a tough life, and she's learned a lot.' Holding the phone between shoulder and ear, Camilla filled the kettle and turned on the gas. She and Mac would need something warm to relax them before going back to sleep. She reached for the two worn mugs, reminders of the days in the Church House.

She murmured, 'Of course we're longing to meet her, Tax.

When the show comes to New York—' There was no point in saying, No, Taxi! You're too young, much too young...

'I hope it gets to New York, Mom. We got mixed reviews here.'

At least he had called them.

They had honored his right to break away, separate himself, to find out who he was outside the warm nest of his parents who were not his parents. Ever since he had left school, he had made his own way financially, asking them for nothing. They had, he had told them, no rights. Love conferred no rights, and anyhow they did not love him or they would never have let Red and Harriet...

'Mom?'

'Yes, Taxi?'

'Wish us luck?'

'Of course, darling. More than luck. Many blessings.'

'I'll call you again.'

'Thanks, love.' She closed her mouth and kept from saying, 'Soon.'

They did not hear from him again until three months later, when the show came to New York and died quickly from the faint praise of the critics. They went, with Frankie, to opening night, applauding Taxi's songs and looking at Sharilee with doubt and concern. She was certainly not the nineteen years she claimed to be. Under the heavy makeup, the lines between nose and mouth were deeply graven. Her voice, too, was harsh, and did not, as the critics pointed out, blend with Taxi's warmer one.

Sharilee was outraged at the reviews, at being compared unfavorably with Taxi, whose youthful freshness and wistfulness pleased both audience and critics.

Camilla and Frankie went to the theatre for closing night, and then went back to Taxi's dressing room to help him pack up his belongings.

'She's a marvelous actress,' Taxi defended, carefully putting his makeup in a green metal box. 'The role wasn't a good vehicle for her.'

'You were terrific, Tax,' Frankie said. 'I'm glad I was able to get away to see it again.'

'Me, too,' Taxi said, though he did not ask Frankie how her art classes were going. 'I do want you to know my Sharilee. She reminds me a little of you. That's what first drew me to her.'

Camilla thought two women could not be less alike. She wondered when the scales would drop from Taxi's eyes.

But it was Sharilee who soon ended the marriage, moving in with an older actor who, at that time, had more prestige than Taxi, was making more money.

Frankie was contemptuous. 'She's a crass idiot. If she had an iota of sense she'd know Taxi's on the way up, and that guy's going to start on the way down.'

A few nights later Taxi went to the seminary, found Camilla in her study, knelt at her feet, and put his head in her lap. 'Mom, I'm such a failure.'

'No, darling, you're not. You're a rising young star. You work hard. You learn more with each role.'

'No, Mom, no. Not my acting. I know I'm good, or on my way to being good. My life. It's a mess. I couldn't keep Sharilee. I'm a failure.'

Camilla stroked his dark hair, not speaking.

'Mom?'

'You're not a failure, my darling. Everybody makes mistakes. That's not failure.'

'You don't understand. You've never failed at anything.' 'Taxi!'

He started to weep. 'You don't understand, Mom. Nobody does. I thought Sharilee understood me. But nobody does.'

He was, or seemed to be, happy with Beth. Beth was indeed only nineteen. She had waited outside the stage door to see Taxi, one of his most fervent admirers. Waited every night, just to stare, to admire, in awed silence, while others shoved programs at him for autographs. Finally he noticed her, curious and pleased at her fidelity, and asked her out for a sandwich.

They were married two months later at a church in Rye, a large, fashionable wedding in her parents' Presbyterian church. Camilla and Mac were there, looking hopefully at Beth's adoring face. Frankie was in Florence, studying, and though Beth's parents had offered to pay her airfare, some pride or instinct made Frankie refuse.

Beth already had an apartment on the East Side, into which they moved, though Taxi said it was inconvenient for the theatre. However, just as he was insisting that they find another place, he was cast in a soap which was filmed from a studio near the East River, just a short walk from Beth's apartment.

Camilla and Mac relaxed. Briefly.

Then Beth waited for Camilla outside her classroom at NYU, in much the same way she had waited for Taxi outside the theatre.

They walked together toward the seminary and had not gone more than half a block before tears began dripping down the young woman's cheeks.

'Beth, what is it? What's wrong?'

'Taxi—'

'What about Taxi?'

'He's having an affair with this—this creature who's on the show with him. I know she's older and more sophisticated—'

Beth wept all the way to the seminary and into the cup of tea that Camilla provided. Camilla washed the girl's face with cool water, talked with her until Beth was calm enough to call Taxi, who came rushing across town to her, full of love, of apologies, promising that the affair was only a stupid mistake, that it meant nothing, nothing compared to his love for Beth, which was his only reality.

After the third affair Beth refused to accept the excuses, the charm, the promises. Beth was Beth, not Rafferty Dickinson, and Taxi was Taxi, not Rose. Beth made Taxi a settlement that was more than generous, and divorced him.

'Oh, God, Mom,' Taxi groaned. 'I'm like that man whose bastard I am. Mom, who am I? I don't know who I am.'

'You do have some choice as to what you do, and what you do not do,' Camilla said.

'Mom, Beth is so bland, so—so nothing. I want to be a good husband, I want to be faithful, but I have so many needs she was too young and untouched to fulfill. Mom, I don't want to be like Red. I just want to be happy like other people. That's all. I just want to be happy.'

.

If Thessaly did not always make him happy, at least she was the only one who understood Taxi well enough to stay married to him. He was ecstatic when she became pregnant. Thessaly turned to Camilla for support, rather than to her distant parents. She had phoned her mother, who had taken the news calmly, as the natural thing, rather than giving the whoop of joy with which Camilla had responded.

The first weeks of pregnancy were not easy. Thessaly had terrible morning sickness, and was exhausted. A couple of times a week Camilla cooked a double portion of dinner and took a dish over. Taxi was a disaster in the kitchen, despite his concern about his wife.

One evening he called. 'Mom, could you come over? Thess feels really low, and if you could make some chicken soup, maybe she could keep it down. The doctor says all this throwing up will stop in a week or so. I mean, he doesn't think she's in any danger of losing the baby or anything, but she does need to eat something.'

'Of course.' Camilla heard the front door slam. 'Mac's just coming in, so let me see if he needs anything, and then I'll take some soup out of the freezer and come on over.' She put the phone down and turned to Mac, looking at him, appalled. 'Mac! What's the matter?'

He sank down into the old brown chair. 'I have a ghastly headache.'

She was on her knees beside him, putting her fingers gently to his forehead. 'When did this start?'

'About half an hour ago.'

'Darling, can you go lie down? Taxi just called and wants me to bring some soup for Thessaly . . .'

'Go, of course, go, especially if Taxi actually called you himself.' His face looked grey with pain. 'I'm just going to stay here, in our old chair.'

She looked at him anxiously. 'This is much worse than your usual headache . . .'

'It will go. I just need to sit here.'

'I won't stay long. Could you drink some tea?'

He shuddered. 'Nothing. Go, darling, and I'll feel better when you get back.'

When she got back he was dead, sitting there in the old chair, his face serene, all the lines of pain smoothed out.

•

"Grandmother," Raffi said, "I don't want to lose you or Grandfather."

"You can't."

"But I'm not even related to Grandfather!"

Camilla laughed. "In all the ways that count, you are. He had a way of making people feel loved, and I can see you doing that with your friends, making them feel that they matter."

Raffi grunted. "If they don't matter, then I don't matter, either."

"True. But not everybody realizes that."

"I think Dr. Rowan does."

"Yes, I think she does, too."

"She loves you a lot."

"I love her, too."

"Sometimes she almost makes me believe that life isn't just a pile of shit."

"I'm glad she got that across."

"But, Grandmother, you've had an awful life."

Camilla looked at her in surprise. "Oh, no! I've had a marvelous life!"

"How can you say that?"

"Oh, Raffi, I had a husband I loved all my life. His parents taught me about mercy and love. I've been able to spend my life teaching the subjects I most enjoy. I may not see much of Frankie, but she's a wonderful daughter. She has a happy and fulfilled life, and that's all any parent can ask."

"And my dad? Taxi?"

"He's taught me about mercy and love, too."

•

"Mercy and love, she said." Raffi looked at Dr. Rowan. "When I said she'd had an awful life, she looked totally surprised."

For once, Luisa appeared not to be listening. She reached across her desk and handed Raffi a framed color photograph of a pubescent child with flaming red hair, standing by a small brown-haired girl in a pink smocked dress. The background was a playground with swings. "Do you recognize them?" Luisa asked.

Raffi scowled. "The red-haired one in jeans is me. I don't know who the little kid is."

Luisa said, "Oh, God."

"What's the matter, Dr. Rowan?"

"Raffi, I want you to do something for me."

"Sure. What?"

"You remember Andrew Grange?"

"Dr. Andy? Sure."

"When did you last see him?"

"I don't remember. I sometimes saw him when I went to Dr. Liz for shots, but that was a long time ago."

"This picture belongs to him. Will you take it to his office and return it? It's just around the corner—"

•

Camilla left her office, where she had been seeing her honors students, and walked slowly across campus to her house. Her knees felt stiff, reminding her of her age. The evening was cold, with a biting wind rising from the lake. The sky still held color, a pale lemon at the horizon, slowly staining up into rose and mauve and then a deep, darkening blue as night came closer.

She let herself into her house and heard the phone ringing, and hurried to answer it. —Why are we so compulsive about phones? she asked herself. —Is there any news I really want to hear?

She picked up the phone and heard Luisa's exasperated voice. "Where on earth have you been? I almost hung up."

She replied calmly, "I've been having office hours. I just got in. What's up?"

There was a moment's hesitation. "I haven't seen you as much as I'd like since you left New York."

"No."

"Remember what an interfering little bitch I used to be?"

Camilla laughed. "I don't think you would have called it that."

"One thing I learned in medical school and after is non-interference. I really learned it. Some shrinks are very directive. That's not my policy."

Camilla frowned. Something was wrong. "What's on your mind, Lu?"

"Did you know that for the past few years I've been seeing your Raffi on a fairly regular basis?"

"She told me. I'm glad. Things are not easy for Raffi."

"To state it with your famous moderation."

Camilla felt the familiar feeling of anxiety. What had Taxi done now? "What's happened?"

"I've intervened. I don't know whether it's the worst thing I've ever done, or the best. I just wanted to let you know in case Raffi needs you. You're the one person she really trusts."

"Where's Raffi?"

"In New York at the moment. She's coming back to college tonight. At least that was the plan. Excuse me, Camilla, I have a patient coming in. I'll talk with you tomorrow." Without giving Camilla a chance to speak, she hung up.

•

When Raffi went into the doctors' office the nurse gave her a startled look. "Can I help you?"

"Dr. Luisa Rowan asked me to return this picture to Dr. Andy. I'm Raffi Xanthakos. I was Dr. Liz's patient when I was a kid."

"Of course. Just a moment. I'll see if Dr. Andy's busy." She picked up the phone, spoke into it, then said, "He has a patient with him right now, but he won't be more than a few minutes. If you'll just have a seat and wait, he'll see you."

Raffi was too restless to have a seat. This was about something, but she didn't know what, except that it frightened her, and she didn't know why. She wandered to the shelves of books and games. Looked in the big toy box and pulled out a stuffed pink piglet which had been one of her favorites. It no longer had any eyes, and one ear was gone, but she was sure it was still the piglet she had cuddled when she went into Dr. Liz's office for a shot.

One of the doors at the back of the room opened and Andrew came out. He glanced at Raffi, then stopped, looking at her intently.

She looked back at him, white-haired, stooped, his stethoscope dangling out of the pocket of his long, white coat. "Hello, Dr. Andy, remember me? I'm Raffi Xanthakos." Unthinkingly, she held out the picture.

"What have you got there?" Smiling, he took it from her.

"Dr. Rowan asked me to return it to you. Why do you have a picture of me?"

"Oh, Raffi. Raffi. C-come w-wi—" He shook his head, unable to continue.

The other office door opened and Elizabeth Wickoff came toward them, listened to Andrew's stuttering with alarm, and followed him and Raffi into his office.

Andrew thrust the picture into his wife's hands. "L-look at th-this."

She glanced at the photograph, looked at it probingly, then turned her gaze on Raffi.

Raffi said, "Dr. Rowan asked me to return this to Dr. Andy. It is me, isn't it, with the little girl?"

"No, Raffi," Elizabeth said in her calmest voice. "It's of Dr. Andy when he was eleven or twelve. The little girl is his sister, Noelle."

"The one in jeans—it's a boy? It's not me?"

"No, Raffi. It's Andrew."

"I thought it was me."

"It does look like you," Liz said, "far more than when you were a little girl."

"But why do I look like—" She looked at Andrew, frowning, then went and stood in front of a long mirror where some of Andrew's young patients liked to preen. Then she turned to face Andrew. "I look like you, don't I? Enough like you to be your—" Her voice rose, frightened, excited. "Dr. Rowan gave me this picture to bring to you because—because you're—oh, Christ! You're my grandfather, aren't you? You're my father's father, not—not—"

Tears slid down Andrew's cheeks, but his voice was back in control. "Yes, Raffi. Yes."

"But why didn't you tell?"

Elizabeth looked the same question at her husband.

Andrew said, "By the time I knew, too much had happened. Too much pain. I didn't want to add to it." He looked at Elizabeth. "Didn't you—"

"I guessed." She sighed. "But I kept quiet for the same reasons you did." She sat down abruptly opposite Andrew. Raffi sat in a small wicker rocking chair sized for Andrew's young patients, but into which her slender body fitted comfortably. Liz probed, "But, Andrew—"

Andrew said, "A long time ago I had a brief fling with Rose Dickinson."

"In Chicago?"

"Yes. She was so beautiful. And needy."

"And you were young and vulnerable."

"I don't excuse myself," Andrew said.

"Hey," Raffi interrupted. "How did you find out? Because I look like you?"

Elizabeth said, "As a small child you didn't, and I haven't seen that much of you since you were older, but something—something—made me wonder. Made me guess."

Raffi asked, "Dr. Andy?"

"Not guesswork," he said. "Proof."

Elizabeth asked. "DNA?"

He nodded.

Raffi had been rocking back and forth in the little chair. Now she said, "But you knew, now, before I brought you the picture?"

"Yes, Raffi. I've known since Taxi came home from boarding school with a strep throat. Liz was away, so he came to me."

"And?" Elizabeth rested her clasped hands on his desk.

"I never thought about that one time with Rose seriously, but every once in a while the question would flick across my mind: My dad? or me? And then Camilla brought Taxi to my office ... He was a sick kid and I took care of him. And then

I thought I'd put my mind at rest, once for all, so I gave him some antibiotics and then I drew his blood to test his D-d-d-d—" For the moment his stutter was back.

"DNA?" Elizabeth prompted.

He nodded. Swallowed. Pushed his fingers through his hair. Finally he said, "When the tests came back—and DNA does not lie—I was appalled. Unbelieving."

"But you had to believe it."

"Yes."

Elizabeth put her hands back in her lap. "Why didn't you tell me?"

"It was too late. Taxi's world was insecure enough. Camilla and Mac were his parents. The fewer people who knew, the better—even you, dearest Liz."

"Oh, God," Raffi moaned.

Elizabeth asked, "How did Luisa Rowan get this picture?"

Andrew said, "I referred a patient to her and she came to my office to meet the girl yesterday. She stood looking at all the pictures. Took this one down from the wall. When she was ready to leave, she asked—asked—"

"She asked to borrow this picture?"

He nodded.

"Did she tell you why?"

"No."

Raffi exclaimed, "She must have guessed. About you and my dad. And me. You already knew when I broke my arm, didn't you?"

He nodded.

"You knew you were my grandfather."

"Yes, Raffi. I knew."

"So I *was* special to you—" Raffi's arms were around him. She was hugging him, crying, calling aloud, "I'm so glad! So glad!"

He put his hands on her shoulders, holding her off so that he could look at her, a dazzled joy in his eyes. She pressed her

face against his starched white coat. "You're my grandfather!
I haven't had a grandfather, ever! You're Taxi's father! You're
my dad's father! Oh, don't you see? He hated his father, the one
he thought was his father. Don't you see what a difference this
can make to him?"

•

"So you expected miracles?" Dr. Rowan demanded.

Raffi's voice was hoarse from crying. "He was angry with
me! He screamed at me! He said I was an interfering little
bitch!" Again she sobbed.

"Wait," Dr. Rowan said. "I was the interfering bitch. Wait,
Raffi, let him absorb what you told him."

"I thought it would make him so happy."

Luisa looked across the desk at her. "Has your father ever
been predictable?"

"I hate him!"

"Do you?"

"Dr. Rowan, I want Andrew Grange to be my grandfather."

"He is."

"And I want my dad to be glad."

"Wait, Raffi."

"That's what Mom said."

•

Camilla was in bed asleep when the phone rang. "Mom.
It's Taxi. Did I wake you?"

She leaned up on one elbow in alarm. "What's wrong?"

"Mom. I don't think anything's wrong. I think—oh, Mom,
I think maybe I can be who I am."

She said, softly, "You're my son, Taxi."

"I will always be that. It'll be easier, now, now that I know
who my father is."

He told her, told her what Raffi had told him with such

joy. "I slapped her down, Mom, I don't know why. But we've made up. She understands. She's a terrific girl. She's on her way back to college now. She'll need you."

"I'll be here."

"I'm going to meet with Andrew in the morning. Meet with my father. Mom, you don't know what this has done for me, what a weight's gone from my shoulders. It changes everything. I know who I am. Finally I know who I am. It'll be all right, Mom. You'll see."

•

Would it be all right? Terrible damage had been done. But Andrew's revelation was a mercy, a live coal that did not need to be dropped into the sea, but could flame quietly, and by which they could warm themselves. She hoped it was a mercy for Andrew, too.

•

It was midnight when Raffi rang the doorbell. Camilla put on a warm robe and went down to let her in, holding out her arms in greeting.

"Grandmother," Raffi said. "Here I am."